# *The Brave Daughters*

## Mary Wood

PAN BOOKS

First published 2020 by Pan Books
an imprint of Pan Macmillan
The Smithson, 6 Briset Street, London EC1M 5NR
Associated companies throughout the world
www.panmacmillan.com

ISBN 978-1-5098-9261-7

1 3 5 7 9 8 6 4 2

A CIP catalogue record for this book is available from the British Library.

Typeset in ITC Galliard Std by Palimpsest Book Production Ltd, Falkirk, Stirlingshire
Printed and bound by CPI Group (UK) Ltd, Croydon, CR0 4YY

Visit **www.panmacmillan.com** to read more about all our books
and to buy them. You will also find features, author interviews and
news of any author events, and you can sign up for e-newsletters
so that you're always first to hear about our new releases.

*For my late, much-loved eldest brother, Charlie, who showed me that in life you have to strive for what you want to achieve. Love and miss you always, and I know that you would have been so proud of me.*

FLORS m. CYRUS

ALICE  FREDDY  RANDIE  MARJIE  MONTY
*(deceased)*

ELLA
**Married three times**

PAULO  SHAMUS  ARNIE
*(deceased)*  *(deceased)*
No offspring

MAGS
**Married twice**

HAROLD  JEROME
*(Flors's brother, deceased)*
No offspring

Love child with
MONTEL
*(deceased)*

CHRISTOPHE  PAULO  LONIA
*(deceased)*

BELINDA  BETH

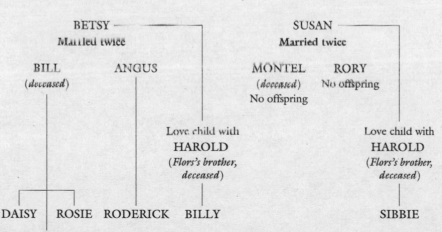

BETSY
**Married twice**

BILL  ANGUS
*(deceased)*

SUSAN
**Married twice**

MONTEL  RORY
*(deceased)*  No offspring
No offspring

Love child with
HAROLD
*(Flors's brother, deceased)*

Love child with
HAROLD
*(Flors's brother, deceased)*

DAISY  ROSIE  RODERICK  BILLY

SIBBIE

FLORRIE

# PART ONE

# Britain and France, 1939

~

## *The Families*

# CHAPTER ONE

# *Blackburn*

## Sibbie and Marjie

As the car that had fetched her from the station travelled the long drive towards Feniscowles Manor, Sibbie felt the usual excitement grip her, on seeing the lovely house with its many windows gleaming and reflecting the sunlight. The ivy covering its walls seemed to shimmer a welcome in the August heat, and its backdrop of the beautiful hills of Bowland provided the perfect setting for this, her second home.

On arriving outside the house, her anticipation rose so much that she was out of the car and running up the steps before her Aunt Mags's driver had time to alight and assist her. As she reached the door, it opened.

'Sibbie! How lovely to see you, darling. Come on in. Marjella, Beth and Belinda are in the garden, taking advantage of this lovely day. They're all excited to be seeing you again.'

'Hello, Aunt Mags, how are you? I've missed you. It seems ages since I left for the summer holidays. Oh, and Aunt Betsy and Mum said I'm to give you their love.'

Sibbie found herself enclosed in her aunt's arms, having

3

seen in her lovely, big brown eyes the same underlying concern that marred everyone's lives right now – an overwhelming fear of what might happen in the near future. This was disconcerting to Sibbie, as Aunt Mags, a close family friend – whom Sibbie loved dearly and had called 'Aunt' all her life – was a strong and capable businesswoman who headed the board of the largest mill in the area and rarely indicated that anything unnerved her.

Tall and slender, Mags was the epitome of the lady of the manor. She always wore her light-brown hair, now peppered with grey strands, in a bun at the nape of her neck, which added to her elegant appearance.

Holding Sibbie at arm's length, Aunt Mags kept her voice light. 'Dear Betsy and Susan, I'll ring them later to let them know you've arrived safely. Now, let me look at you. Being back in Portpatrick for the summer has done you good. You were looking peaky when you left. Those long hours in the classroom had taken their toll.'

'I had a lovely time, being spoilt by everyone, but I'm ready to get back to studying.'

'That's good. Well, everyone's fine here, if a little worried about all that's happening in the world. That aside, the girls are looking forward to their new term at school, and Marjella has arrived safely. She's very excited to be joining you in your language studies this term.'

'I can't wait to see her – it's going to be wonderful having her here. I just wish this cloud wasn't hanging over us all. Mum and Aunt Betsy are very nervous.'

'I can understand that, as we older ones have vivid memories that heighten our fears.' Aunt Mags sighed. 'It's unbelievable to think we're on the brink of war breaking out again. But let's not spoil your first day back with what a horrid little man in Germany is doing to the world. I've made lemonade for you all, and Cook has baked those shortbread biscuits you love.'

'Mmm, lovely.' Although she said this, Sibbie groaned inside. She was full to the brim with shortbread and, much as she liked it, she wouldn't care if she never saw another biscuit in her life. It seemed everyone wanted to serve them to her: at home in Scotland, her mum and Aunt Betsy thought she would have missed their shortbread biscuits more than anything; and here in Blackburn with Aunt Mags, Cook seemed to think she couldn't live without them! Sibbie smiled to herself at these thoughts, as they brought home to her how she was surrounded by the love of so many people.

And now her lovely cousin Marjie, as she called Marjella, was here from France to join her on the language course she was taking, which meant they were going to spend a lot of time together. Life couldn't be better, and she prayed that all the fears of war would come to nothing.

As Sibbie followed her Aunt Mags through the wide hall of Feniscowles Manor she turned towards the kitchen. Opening the door, she called out, 'Hello, Cook. Aunt Betsy sends her love.'

'Sybil! You've arrived then, lass. I'd give you a hug, but I'm covered in flour. How is Betsy?'

'Ha, that's as it should be – I like to see that nothing has changed. Oh, Betsy is fine; they all are. I'll give you their news later.'

A lovely rounded lady, Cook had been part of this house for as long as Sibbie could remember, and she loved the way Cook always used her proper name. She was the only one who did. Not that it mattered, because being called

'Sibbie' reminded her of Montel, who had first shortened her name.

An ever-present ache nudged Sibbie at this thought. Montel had been her proper daddy, if not her real one. What she knew from her mum about how Harold Roford, her blood father, had led his life, she didn't like, and she had never felt any kinship to him. She would have liked to have met Harold, though. Just so that she could have kicked him in the shins.

As they walked through the withdrawing room towards the French windows that led to the garden, Sibbie took in the graceful furniture and the calming colours of pale blue and cream that adorned this room. The familiarity of it reinforced the fact that she was very much a part of this house, as Aunt Mags was like a second mother to her, so 'home' was wherever she was.

Marjie coming into view drew Sibbie's attention away from her lovely surroundings. 'Marjie! Oh, Marjie!'

Marjie jumped up and ran towards her. When they collided, they hugged and twirled around together, as if they would never part again.

Mags laughed out loud at them. 'You two – you would think you were sisters, not cousins. I'll leave you to it, and go and organize Cook to bring tea and biscuits.'

Although Sibbie and Marjie had been brought up in different countries – Marjie in France, and Sibbie in Scotland – they had bonded the moment they met, when Mags first took Sibbie to France at the age of eight to meet her Aunt Flors, Marjie's mum and the sister of Harold Roford.

Sibbie had loved France and being part of the Domaine de Florella, the vineyard that her Aunt Flors and Uncle Cyrus owned, along with Aunt Ella and her husband, Arnie.

When they came to a standstill, Sibbie linked arms with Marjie. 'I can't believe you're here. And what do you think of England, and more especially Blackburn?'

'I know, I can't believe this time has come at last. It's so good to see you, Sibbie. I haven't seen much of England, or Blackburn – only through the windows of trains and cars – but I know I am going to love it here.'

'You will – I do. This village, the beauty that surrounds it all, the town of Blackburn and Aunt Mags's mill, and Uncle Jerome's veterinary practice: it's all so lovely. And you'll love the language school. Professor Hillson is adorable – eccentric, but a marvellous teacher. So, how was your journey?'

'Long, and very boring, but at times rather frightening, as the stations were crowded with soldiers, especially in France. It made me appreciate the reality of what my parents and brothers are talking about all the time.'

'I saw a lot of soldiers today, too; even women are being recruited here. I'm just too young to be called, although I really feel like offering my services.'

'But what would you do? And what about your studies?'

'I don't know, but the fact that I speak French and am studying German might be of use in some field or other. Anyway, there may not be a war. We are just speculating.'

Beth and Belinda had run across the lawn and were now demanding attention. For half-sisters, they had a lot of similarities, although Beth, at fifteen years old, was looking more like a young woman than a girl. Her shining black hair and beautiful, huge dark-brown eyes reminded Sibbie so much of Beth's late father, the beloved Montel.

As Sibbie pulled the girls in close, she told them, 'Look how beautiful and grown-up you are.' Belinda giggled, but

Beth smiled up at her, bringing Montel to mind once more. Although Sibbie had only been four when Montel died, she'd never forget him.

'I've grown an inch taller than I was before you left at Easter, Sibbie, and I've turned thirteen now, you know.'

'You have, Belinda. Oh, it's good to see you both, and I hadn't forgotten it was your birthday last week – I have brought you something from Scotland. It's from Aunt Betsy's and my mum's shop. Well, actually you have two presents, as I brought something for everyone.'

'Ooh, I'm glad it's not from Uncle Angus's fishing business – I'm not keen on fish.'

They all burst out laughing. Belinda took after her father, Uncle Jerome; she was witty like him and always made everyone laugh, and she could come out with the funniest lines.

'Beth, Belinda, come and help with the trays, please.'

As the girls ran to obey their mother, Sibbie felt Marjie grip her hand. 'Sibbie, if it does come to war and you volunteer, then I will too. My dual nationality will allow me to, and besides, I will be useful as well. I speak English, French and Polish – and now I am going to be learning German too.'

'You speak Polish? I didn't know that.'

'Yes, Aunt Ella has taught us over the years, as she wished to speak her native language from time to time. Even Uncle Arnie speaks Polish with her when they are at home. It seems that once you have mastered two languages, it gets easier to learn more.'

'Maybe we can do something together. Oh, what fun that would be! We can win the war and then continue our studies. I'm not that keen on being a teacher yet, anyway.'

'Nor me. Paulo is the one who wants to take up that profession, and Aunt Ella is seriously considering sending him over here to study. She is afraid for him because of her Jewish ancestry, which makes him half-Jewish.'

Sibbie felt both elation and fear: to have Paulo here would be a dream come true. She'd fallen for him the moment she'd met him as a little girl, but he looked upon her as a cousin, even though they weren't related at all. But then Flors, Ella and Mags had brought up their families to be one unit, and she was part of that unit, being the daughter of Flors's brother.

The news reports on the treatment of the Jews in Germany made her shudder, and she couldn't bear to think of such things happening to her beloved Paulo. 'Oh dear, Marjie, I felt so happy to be coming to see you, and at the prospect of us studying together, but now I feel really downhearted. Suddenly it seems everyone, and everything we love, is in danger.'

'Yes, it does feel like that, but it is also a wonderful time for us. Let's not talk of war; instead let's have a magical time for the next two weeks until we start our lessons. We can picnic at weekends, if this weather holds – I can drive now and—'

'Me too! We can go into the Bowland Hills and into Clitheroe. I can show you Pendle Hill, where it is said they burned witches long ago.'

'Ooh, will we see ghosts?'

'They say you can at Halloween, and that's only a couple of months away.'

'Where have I been sent? I thought I would be safe here, but now it seems I am to be near ghouls.'

Sibbie made a face, growled and put her hands up, in a

mock attempt to scratch Marjie. 'Now you know the truth: we are all witches.'

They fell about laughing at this, their cares forgotten.

Marjie's laughter was a lovely light sound, which lit up her face and made her even more beautiful.

The family resemblance between the two girls was evident in their looks, height and colouring. Both had dark-brown hair and very dark eyes. Sibbie's face was more rounded than Marjella's clear-cut features, making her pretty rather than beautiful, whereas Marjella's beauty and French chic made everyone look twice.

A warm feeling overcame Sibbie. It was so good to be together, despite the ominous reasons that had prompted Aunt Flors and Uncle Cyrus to let Marjie come and study in England. But Sibbie did wonder how their lives were going to pan out over the next couple of years or so, and silently prayed that war wouldn't happen.

# CHAPTER TWO

# *Laurens, Hérault, France*

## Ella and Flors

Flors smiled bravely as she stood on her doorstep and waved and waved until her husband Cyrus's car, carrying their sons, Freddy and Randolph, was out of sight. The agony that she and Cyrus had been through, since the conscription papers had arrived, had almost defeated her. Now the pain set in, as the reality of what Freddy and Randie would face if war broke out took root.

Ella stood by her side. 'Come on, Flors, let's do as the British do and put the kettle on.'

'Oh, Ella, to think of them having gone is unbearable.'

Ella clutched Flors's hand even tighter and whispered, 'Hug?'

Painful memories of the past and fears for the uncertain future vied for prominence in Flors's heart as they hugged tightly. She knew that dear Ella would be feeling these same emotions, too.

As they emerged from the hug, they linked arms and went into the kitchen. A snore made them both jump, and nervous giggles consumed them. Rowena could sleep through anything when she was in her favourite rocking chair by the side of the stove. Even on a hot day like today, she professed that she felt the cold in her old bones. Rowena had known Flors since her childhood in Stepney, and now lived with her.

Flors felt glad of the light-hearted moment. She'd been on the brink of crying, but hadn't wanted to; she'd save her tears for her own bed at night, when she was snuggled into the arms of her beloved Cyrus. Sighing, she told Ella, 'It's as if my nest is emptying all at once.'

'I know. My darling Arnie is even saying that he will volunteer, if Britain ever comes under threat. And Paulo talks of going too, if necessary. It doesn't bear thinking about.'

'Oh no. Oh, Ella, everything we know and have built up, since the terrible things we went through in the last war, is under threat.'

'They say we should be safe here in the South of France, and it's the north-east that will bear the brunt, if an invasion does happen. But Hitler is threatening Poland at the moment, and I'm so worried about my sister, Calek.'

'I don't know what to say, Ella. We can only pray that the Germans don't succeed in their quest to invade Poland, or that a miracle happens and they heed Chamberlain's ultimatum.'

'They *have* to. Oh, Flors, it's Calek's and Abram's only chance; I fear they are in grave danger. Look at how Germany is treating its Jewish community, if the rumours of their cruel treatment are to be believed . . . Oh God, I can't think about it. My dear nephew Zabrim is only fourteen.'

'And there's no answer to your last letter yet? Surely they will take up your offer to come here?'

'I am praying for that, but I haven't heard from them.

At least if they sent Zabrim to me, that would ease my mind a little. I'm thinking of going to Poland to find out how they are. I checked and all the trains are still running. Maybe if I do, I can persuade them to come back with me.'

'No, Ella, no! It's too dangerous. Please think again, Ella, please. What does Arnie say about it?'

'I haven't discussed it with him.'

'You haven't discussed what, darling?'

'Oh, Arnie, I didn't see you. I – I . . . well, nothing – nothing really. I'll tell you later.'

'There's no time like now. If you can share whatever it is with Flors, then you can share it with your husband, can't you? Come on, old thing, what is it?'

As Ella poured out her thoughts, Arnie surprised Flors with his response. 'I think that unless you do this, you will have an agonizing few years ahead of you, Ella – and I don't want that. But I also think that you should wait to see if Hitler decides to take heed of Britain and France's ultimatum – which I don't think he will. If he doesn't and invades Poland, it will be too dangerous for you to even think of going.'

Flors couldn't believe the enormity of what Ella had proposed, and even less so that Arnie was partially agreeing that she should go to Poland. After all, she had the feeling that Hitler would find a way of doing as he had in Czechoslovakia and fully invade Poland. And what if that happened when Ella was there?

'I know what you're thinking, Flors, but I understand Ella better than she does herself. Now that she has her family back in her life, it will kill her to think of the unspeakable things that might happen to them under a German regime.

That applies to all of Poland, but for the Jewish community there – well, it doesn't bear thinking about. I have to support her in this or I will be letting her down.'

They were all silent for a moment, unable to comprehend how quickly their ideal world had changed, and what the future might bring.

Their vineyard, Domaine de Florella, was one of the finest in the Languedoc region – not that this was Flors's major concern. That she reserved for the safety of her dear friends Ella and Arnie and their children, but most of all for her own family – her dear husband, Cyrus, had been a prisoner in the last war. Surely he wouldn't have to fight again? And Freddy and Randie were facing God-knows-what. Then there was her problem child, Monty. At seventeen, he was becoming more troublesome, showing traits of his despicable late uncle, Harold.

*Oh, why am I thinking like this? Monty is just going through a phase, I'm sure.*

Flors's thoughts turned to her beloved and beautiful daughter, Marjella. Her heart cried out with the pain of missing her, but knowing that she, at least, was safe, staying with Mags in the countryside of Blackburn, helped her to accept the separation. Surely nothing could befall Marjella? If war did come, England would be safe from the fallout, wouldn't it? It would join with France and beat Hitler back to the borders here, she imagined.

The door to Flors's chateau was flung open as the kettle boiled.

'Mama, am I too late? Have Freddy and Randie left?' Ella and Arnie's six-year-old daughter Lonia stood in the doorway, a distraught look on her face. She was spoilt by everyone, and everyone loved her, but none of the attention they

14

lavished on her had any effect, for she remained a sweet child, caring and always concerned for everyone.

'Yes, Lonia, they left a few moments ago.'

'Oh, Mama, why didn't they wait to see me? Papa has just brought me from school.'

'They couldn't chance missing their train, darling. Once they are in the army, they are under its discipline. An order is an order, and they cannot risk breaking one for the sake of little you.'

'Oh, Mama, I'm going to miss them. But I'm not going to be sad, because Freddy said that I must be very grown-up and think of others – especially you, Aunt Flors: you're much sadder than me, and that must hurt a lot.'

'It does, darling. As does missing Marjella. But we must carry on. Look, I have some nice grape juice cooling on the cold slab in the pantry. I'll pour you some and we can all sit out under the shade and look after each other.'

The high-pitched whistle of the kettle boiling seemed to seal this as a good idea. True to form, Rowena woke – the one thing that never failed to stir her was the thought of a cup of tea. She sat up and her lips smacked together in her podgy face. 'Is that there the kettle, honey-child?'

'Ha, it is, Rowena. Are you coming outside for some fresh air?'

'There's nothing good in the fresh air for my old bones. It's no fun being ninety-one, Missie Flors.'

'Don't be silly, you're just getting lazy – Ella and I will help you outside. The sunshine is good for your bones, and what's all this "Missie" business? I'm your honey-child, nothing can change that. I hate the term "Missie"; it makes me feel that you think you're a servant.'

'No, honey-child, it an old Jamaican way of speaking. I've

15

been dreaming I was back on the white sand, gazing out at the sea, and the woman I worked for was going to take a branch to beat me with, for being lazy.'

'Oh, Rowena; and then I go and say you are lazy. I'm sorry, my darling. But I know what you mean and how you feel. We're all displaced from where our beginnings were. You must long for home.'

'No, not old Rowena. I know where me bread is buttered, and it ain't in Jamaica, or in the cold and damp of the East End, where we met, honey-child. It's right here with you, in sunny France. Or any place you choose to go.'

Touched by this and by the love she felt for Rowena, Flors hugged her. 'I love you, Rowena darling. But I'm still going to insist that you come outside with us. None of your flattery will change my mind.'

Rowena grinned, showing her one tooth and lighting up her face. A tear plopped onto her withered cheek. It shone against the blackness of her skin.

'I love you too, Rowena.' Saying this, Lonia, who had been named after Ella's late and much-loved nanny, climbed onto Rowena's knee and put her arms around the old lady's neck.

Although the gesture was lovely to see, Flors could tell it was causing pain to Rowena and was glad that Ella saw, too, as she gently steered her daughter away. 'Lonia, go and tell Paulo and Monty to come for their break, there's a good girl. They should be in the bottom vineyard. Tell them you aren't bringing their tea to them, as Aunt Flors needs us all around her.'

'Yes, Mama.'

As the inner fly-door closed with a bang, Flors turned to Rowena. 'Let us help you, darling. We'll take you to the

16

bathroom and get you nice and comfortable. You can put that yellow frock on that we all love. You might feel more like sitting in the garden then.'

'I'll make the tea while you're busy, ladies.'

'Thanks, Arnie. Come on, Rowena.'

'Huh, men these days. Not like in my day. Them's never turned their hands to women's work, and we wouldn't let them. Get under your feet, they does.'

They all laughed at this, but there were no further objections from Rowena as Flors and Ella lifted her, washed her down and freshened her up. Flors did worry, though, about the weariness Rowena displayed.

With Rowena now settled in her rocking chair outside in the shade, Flors whipped off the blanket that had covered Rowena's chair and wrinkled her nose.

'I'll wash the chair down, Flors. Have you a clean blanket to put over it?'

Once they'd finished, Flors had to smile. 'That was like old times, Ella. We turned into nurses again.'

Ella smiled, although it wasn't without pain, and Flors realized that what she'd said must have jarred. Nursing didn't hold good memories for Ella. In the past she'd had to nurse loved ones as well as having terrifying memories of nursing in the Somme and then in Belgium.

The horror of it all returned to Flors at that moment, but she straightened her back and, as if there hadn't been a pause, announced, 'Anyway, a nice cup of tea is waiting for us.'

Ella still didn't speak as they washed their hands together in the huge pot sink. But she did hold on to Flors as they went outside with the laden tray.

The shade that Cyrus and Arnie had built provided a cool

respite for them all from the rays of the blistering afternoon sun. This was a time Flors loved normally, when their cares were few; a time when as many of their families as possible met to drink tea or lemonade, and have a break until the sun cooled enough for them to continue their day's work.

Paulo, Ella's son, tall for his eighteen years, stood with the sunlight on his back. He reminded Flors of his father, also called Paulo, the lovely French officer Ella had met towards the end of the war and had married soon after it finished. Badly wounded, to the extent that he couldn't walk, Paulo had eventually succumbed to the agonizing lung condition that was a consequence of the gas attacks in which he had been caught up. But he lived on in his son: that same clean-cut handsomeness, the rakish hair that flopped over his face and the piercing blue eyes. But for all his French looks, Paulo junior had the features of his mother's Polish Jewish ancestry, too. And this was of grave concern to them all.

'Don't do that, Monty.' Lonia's voice broke into the silence. 'You are so annoying.'

Monty pulled Lonia's ribbon from her hair, leaving her ringlets to cascade over her face – a normal teasing gesture for his age, but one that seemed to cement Flors's feelings about how Monty was turning out. He never took life seriously: not his studies or his work in the vineyard. He seemed to have no purpose, and his 'I want, and I will have' trait reminded Flors of the worst times from her life with her brother, Harold.

The secret that she and Cyrus held from their children reverberated through her. They had never found the courage to tell them they were half-brother and sister. Even now as the thought shook her, Flors felt the familiar fear of anyone finding out. Rowena knew, and of course Ella and Arnie did, and Mags and her husband Jerome. But all others who had known were no longer on this earth.

After marrying and having children, she and Cyrus had found out that they shared the same father, when it came to light that Flors's father bore Cyrus with his long-term mistress, whom Flors never knew existed. But despite the sin of their love, that love was too strong for them ever to make the break, so they had carried on together as a loving husband and wife, only they had to do so far from the shores of England – their home.

It was this connection between her and Cyrus that made Flors worry about Monty; well, about all of her children really, but so far none of them but Monty had turned out to be a Roford in character.

Cyrus had told her over and over again not to worry about Monty, that it was a passing phase, but Flors couldn't help herself. She'd witnessed at first hand the horrors that her brother was capable of. She'd spoken to Mags about it when she had visited, and Mags had told her that the child that Betsy – Mags's oldest friend – had birthed to Harold was just the same. Billy, his name was. Mags had said that over the years the attention Billy had received from his stepfather, Angus, had helped to temper the trait a bit, but Billy also held a cruel streak from which his half-sister, Sibbie, often suffered. Flors had never met this nephew of hers, as Billy hadn't wanted to come to France to meet them all, but she didn't like the sound of him. Her niece, Sibbie, was different, taking more after her mother, Susan, who had worked in Flors's family home as a maid and whom Flors had always liked. Sibbie had Susan's gentle nature. Thinking this, she hoped that Sibbie would never be used by a domineering man in the way that Harold had used Susan.

'Monty, you've done it again! I've only just fixed it.'

'Monty, leave her alone. It's too hot to be teasing her.'

Monty obeyed Paulo and sauntered away. He always hung on Paulo's every word. This wasn't the case with his older brothers, or even with Cyrus. Just as often he gave back-chat to them, which resulted in arguments breaking out.

Although cross with her son, Flors hated to see him left out. 'Monty, come back and finish your juice, darling.'

'Leave him, Aunt Flors, he's feeling down, with his brothers having left. I had to stay in the field with him, as he wouldn't come down to see them off. We said our good-byes earlier this morning.'

Flors smiled at Paulo, but felt at a loss. Lonia was now in tears. It was obvious that the second yank Monty had given the ribbon had pulled her hair and caused her pain, and yet she was distressed at having upset him. This all reminded Flors so much of how she'd been with Harold. Trying to please him, almost begging for a small amount of kind attention, and feeling cast out and very lonely when nothing was forthcoming.

Arnie held his sobbing daughter close to him. 'Don't worry, Flors. Boys will be boys, and Lonia has to learn that. Far better if you had moved away, Lonia, and then Monty wouldn't have been able to do the same again.'

Flors saw red. Lonia wasn't to blame. It was a silly thing, but it meant a lot that Monty was made to apologize. 'Paulo, please go after Monty and ask him to apologize to your sister.'

It was a relief when Monty returned and said he was sorry and that he'd only been teasing. The day was saved, except for Rowena, who slapped her lips once more and nodded knowingly at Flors. For all the world, Flors wanted to defend her son, but knew that she couldn't. All the same, she praised Monty for doing as she'd asked, and was rewarded with a smile so like her brother's that the hair stood up on her arms and she felt as if ants were crawling all over her. History couldn't repeat itself, could it?

Cyrus, returning at that moment, changed the atmosphere. Even though Flors could see that he had shed a tear, on saying goodbye to their sons, Cyrus soon had them all laughing at how the boys had got onto the wrong train, and at the antics they'd all been through to get them settled on the right train.

A week later Flors received a letter from Marjella that further lightened her cares and lifted her fears. Marjella was happy. Her cousin Sibbie and she were enjoying their time together and had made many plans. Marjella didn't specify what plans, but Flors was sure these would be silly girlie things.

Cyrus and Arnie had taken Paulo and Monty under their wing since the day the older boys had left and had decided to teach them more about making wine, instead of leaving them to do field work. Paulo still spent hours sitting under a tree with his head in a book studying, but accepted that his dreams of becoming a teacher had to be put on hold.

Monty was taking to this side of the business and his mood lifted. Teatime talk was of the graded grapes, of the presses and how they worked, as well as the lovely wine he'd been involved in making and how he thought it would be the best they had ever produced. His enthusiasm was just like his father's, and this had pleased Cyrus beyond words.

All in all, the bleakness was lifting a little. There was still hope that Hitler wouldn't invade Poland and that the war they all feared might not happen at all. Flors prayed that it wouldn't and that soon her boys would be home, and so would Marjella. Then life could get back to normal – her happy, carefree world put back together again. Oh, how she hoped so. *Please, God, let it happen.*

## CHAPTER THREE

# *Portpatrick, Scotland*

## Betsy and Susan

'Betsy, stop your fussing, hen. It is what it is.'

'Aye, I knaws that, Angus, but it feels as though me world's tumbling around me and I can't stop it. All the young 'uns will be in danger – me girls and our Billy. And Roderick's coming on fourteen – what if it goes on a long time and he has to go? I can't bear it, I can't.'

'I ken what you're saying, me lassie, but we canna influence the goings-on of the wider world. Och, nothing may happen anyways, and then you'll have fretted for nothing.'

'And besides that, Ma, we want to do this.'

'Eeh, Daisy. It were bad enough for me as each one of you went off to Dumfries to do your training, but I got used to that, and you weren't in danger or owt. I miss you every day you're not here, but this is different, lass.'

'Och, I knaw, Ma. But times change. We all decided together, didn't we?' Daisy looked at her two sisters, Florrie and Rosie. They both nodded.

Betsy's heart felt as though it would break, but even so, she never ceased to find it funny to hear how her daughters spoke a mixture of their native Blackburn dialect inflected with a smattering of how the Scottish folk expressed them-selves. But then it wasn't surprising, as Daisy had only been seven, Florrie six and Rosie four when she'd moved up here with Mags after her Bill, their da, had died. Sighing, she dispelled the memory. Visiting it was just too painful.

'Was that a resigned sigh, Ma?'

'Naw, it wasn't, our Florrie. I'll never be resigned to you three going off to the army. It's like cutting me heart out.'

Angus coughed. Looking over towards him, Betsy saw him raise his eyebrows and knew that he was willing her to give her daughters her blessing. *Oh God, how can I? How can I let them go?* But then she had to admit that they would go anyway, and better they did so with her acceptance. They'd have enough to contend with, as it was.

'Eeh, me girls. I knaw as you have to do this, and I want you to knaw as I'm proud of you all. When you each took up nursing as your chosen career, I were like a peacock fluffing me feathers and told anyone who'd listen what me girls were doing. And nursing the wounded is sommat as will be needed, if there is a war. But don't forget: that's what your Aunt Mags and her mates did in the last war, and from what she told me, there's a lot for you to contend with out there and it ain't the glamorous life I knaw you're all anticipating. It's blood and gore, and dodging randy men who haven't their wives to keep them happy.'

All three girls, and Angus, burst out laughing at this. 'Aw, Ma, you're a one.'

'It's the truth, our Rosie. You mind me words. Aunt Mags has a terrible tale to tell of her time nursing the wounded. But then she made friendships that sustained her and have lasted her lifetime. Still, one thing pleases me – at least you'll have each other.'

'It's not set in stone that we'll stay together, Ma. Yes, we've all been accepted into the Queen Alexandra's Nursing Corps, but they could send us anywhere.'

This shook Betsy. The thought of them watching out for one another had given her a little comfort. She looked at each of her girls, all beautiful to gaze at; well, Rosie was more pretty than beautiful, with her hair falling in ringlets and her features a little softer that those of the other two. Betsy felt pride in noting that her daughters had all taken after her, with their curly chestnut hair and slim but voluptuous figures. But it was this last aspect that worried her. *Eeh, I had to fend off the men who leered at me for one thing, and one thing only. I were strong, and I thought I would allus be a faithful wife . . . Aye, well, there's no good raking over the past. Not now, not ever. What's done is done.* But even as she tried not to think of it, she knew she could never forget the affair that had led to Billy being born. *Oh, why am I thinking like this, and at a time when I should be giving me girls a good send-off.* With this, it occurred to Betsy that that was exactly what she would do – throw a party to give her girls a good memory to take with them.

'Reet, if this is the way of things, then we'd best do it good and proper. We'll have a do, to see you all on your way and be sommat good for you to remember. By . . . nurses, me three lasses. I'll never get over that. I thought you'd all end up in factories, or married with a brood of young 'uns, but you've made good of yourselves. Eeh, I'm sorry as it's led to this, though, and I'm going to miss you and worry over you. Come here.'

They were in a giggling huddle when Billy came through the door, followed closely, as always, by Roderick, Betsy's youngest, and the only child she'd had with Angus.

'What's going on, Ma? Why the big hug?'

Florrie answered Billy. 'We've all joined the Royal Army Nursing Corps, Billy.'

'All of ye? Ye're lucky beggars. I'd give a wee penny to go. Not to be a nurse, but to do army training to prepare for war.'

Betsy nodded at Billy. 'Aye, well, thank God you're too young by a year, our Billy, and it could all be over when your time comes. Anyroad, we're going to have a party to give our lasses a good send-off, so let everyone in the village knaw, as you go about. It'll be on Saturday night as seven, in the back room of the inn.'

'Hold on, hen, ye've nay asked the landlord yet.'

'Aw, they'll be naw problem, Angus. It isn't as if they'll have any other do on or we would have known of it.'

'Aye, that's so, but it is high season and the visitors are many – the landlord may ne'er cope, lassie.'

'He doesn't have to. We'll do owt as needs doing. He just needs to sell his ale. It'll be grand. I'll start baking this afternoon.'

Betsy saw the look exchanged between Angus and her brood and smiled to herself. They knew when to stop objecting to any of her ideas. She'd won that one, and felt the excitement of all the organizing she would have to do. Grabbing her cardigan, she made for the door.

'Where is it you're off to, lassie? Ye change as quick as the tide; I ne'er know where I am wi' thee.'

'To see Susan. She opened the shop by herself this morning. I'm to see if she can cope for a couple of days without me.'

'I could help her out, Ma, unless you need me, that is.'

'Oh? Have ye no work to go to, Rosie?'

'Naw, Da. We all finished yesterday. We . . . well, we didn't want to worry you by telling you too soon.'

'Och, I ne'er realized it'd all happen that quick, me lasses. A wee hasty for me liking, but still, there's no undoing what's done.'

Betsy sighed, as it all became real to her. How was it that the country was preparing to the extent of taking her girls into the army, when war wasn't yet declared? *Eeh, I thought it would be a while yet, but it's happened – it's really happened!* But this frightening thought didn't dispel the nice feeling she got, on hearing her girls call Angus 'Da'. And she knew it pleased him, too. It was something they'd only started to do recently. They'd all been having a laugh with Angus, when he'd chastised them for the way they left their rooms so untidy when they were home, and Rosie had said, 'You knaw, ever since you married our mam, you've been like a da to us, and from now on I'm going to call you that.' Then Florrie and Daisy chipped in that they had always wanted to, but were waiting for Rosie to be sure she wished to. This had led to a group hug, and Betsy had looked at her brood and her fine husband – and had felt the love for them all surge through her. Now it was possible that she was going to face seeing her family torn apart by a force she couldn't stop. How was she going to bear it?

The shop looked lovely, with all the crafts that she and Susan sold on display: knitted items, like the Fair Isle jumpers that were very popular with the sailing crowd who brought their boats into the harbour; and the cable knit pullovers that the fishermen liked. Then there were the tartan items: tammy hats and scarves, and household items in tartan – cushions and lampshades.

Montel's wonderful paintings of local scenes adorned the walls. Dear Montel, he'd made the shop's fortune in the beginning, with his portraits. People used to flock to the shop to have a painting done of themselves or their children, or even their pets. But none of his work was for sale now; the paintings all belonged to Mags, and she'd thought their rightful place was here, where she and Montel had been so happy. Betsy had thought that Mags would never be happy again after she lost Montel, but it pleased her that she was – and with the lovely Jerome, whom Betsy adored.

As she looked towards the shop front, Betsy felt pride in the pottery items displayed on the shelves there, as they were made by her and Susan – vases, plant pots and all manner of gaily painted bowls and ornaments took pride of place. The counter was positioned amongst them and Susan was sitting behind it. When she spotted Betsy and Rosie, her face lit up. 'Betsy – thank goodness, I've been rushed off me feet and have had a job to cope.'

'Aye, well, I'm not stopping, lass. Rosie is, though. She's going to do the next two days with you, if that's all right.'

Telling Susan about the party didn't get the reaction Betsy thought it would, though why she expected Susan to see the fun in having a do, when she'd been full of doom and gloom since the first rumblings of war began, she didn't know. 'We've to make the best of things, Susan. Half of what we worry over may not happen, anyroad.'

'I know, but I feel bereft even when Sibbie goes to Mags's home, so I can't imagine how you're feeling, Betsy. All three of your girls going, and to God knows what. What if war does come, and your lads and my Sibbie have to go?'

'Let's not meet trouble that might not be travelling our road, Susan. One thing at a time. Me girls are going, and I want to give them a send-off to remember. We'll deal with owt else as it comes along.'

'You're right, of course. I'll try to lift meself. It's just that everything seems spoilt, or on the brink of being so.'

Betsy couldn't deny this. But seeing Susan's distress nudged her own pain, which she'd tried to suppress. 'Come here, lass. I reckon as you could do with a hug.' With this, she took Susan into her arms and held her. She and Susan had built a strong bond over the years, which had grown from having both been duped by the evil Harold Roford, who had fathered both her Billy and Susan's Sibbie.

Her thoughts turned to Mags, who'd suffered most at Harold's hands during her marriage to him, when he'd taken all that she had. And how, after her own shameful encounter with Harold, and Susan's hurt on thinking he loved her, the lovely Mags had helped them both, by making them see that they weren't to blame but, like herself, were victims of Harold's evil ways.

Her worry about Billy's character being similar to his father's surfaced then, but Betsy wouldn't let this settle in her as, shaking herself mentally, she thought that any lad was bound to take sommat from his da; but then Billy had many traits that he'd picked up from her Angus, and it was more than likely these that would shape him. Already Billy was showing signs of this good influence in his life, displaying bravery in wanting to go to war and do his bit, while Harold Roford had pulled every trick in the book not to have to fight in the last one.

Feeling comforted, Betsy patted Susan and told her, 'No matter what happens, we're in this together, lass. Me and you, like we've allus been. And we have two good men to care for us, and a lovely friend in Mags. So, chin up for the younger ones, eh?'

Susan came out of the hug and gave her lovely smile, and

Betsy felt that she would cope. She'd find the mettle she'd shown in the past when she'd needed to, and this made Betsy feel confident that, together, they'd get through whatever was thrown at them.

All the same, her heart was in her belly as she walked down the hill to the inn to book the room for her girls' party. *How did we come to this? God in heaven, didn't we go through enough in the last war?* But something told her this one was going to be far worse, as they were saying it was likely it would be fought on the home front, and not just abroad. A deep sigh came from her. *Eeh, it's all doom and gloom, and me heart's in me boots. But, as always, we've to get on with it.*

# PART TWO

# Britain and France, 1941

~

*Taking Up the Challenge*

# CHAPTER FOUR

# Digby RAF Station, Lincolnshire

## Sibbie and Marjie

Sibbie's heart leapt. 'Paulo has written to me!'

'Yes. Here it was, in with my letter from Mama. Aunt Mags had it delivered by courier. But oh, Sibbie, things are not good.'

Sibbie held her breath.

The past two years at the RAF station had flown by. Both Sibbie and Marjie had graduated with a first-class degree in languages and often practised, having a whole day when they spoke only in German or Polish, and at other times in French, so that Sibbie could keep up her excellent accent and Marjie could enjoy speaking her native tongue.

As soon as they could, after leaving school, they had joined the Women's Auxiliary Air Force – WAAF for short – as by then Marjie was unable to return home and war was raging around the world. Marjie's dual nationality had meant that she was readily accepted.

And now, after a short training period, they were working as plotters, attached to RAF Digby, a small station in Lincolnshire. Sibbie enjoyed the work. She threw her heart into deciphering the plots that came through to them, and knew the exhilaration of getting the expected raids spot-on, as early warning to the nearest airfields was invaluable. But even though she knew the importance of her work, she didn't feel challenged.

They were on their break, and Marjie had taken a detour to the postroom before joining Sibbie on the flat roof above the stuffy Ops room – a favourite place of all the staff, no matter the weather, and on this late September day it was showery and the air held a chill.

The general idea, during the ten minutes they took as a break, was for staff to skip or do some rigorous exercise, to relieve the tension of bending over the large plotting table for hours on end, but most simply walked up and down, enjoying the views over the countryside – and a cigarette, if they were smokers. The roof was littered with discarded butt-ends.

Two Canadian squadrons of Hurricanes were stationed on the base, and Sibbie found it exciting to see them taking off and landing. Even the noise they made sent a zing of exhilaration through her. She wanted to be part of that action. Not flying, but actually *doing* something – taking an active role in fighting this bloody war. Not showing others where that action was likely to be.

'Oh, Marjie, it's not terrible news, is it?'

'It – it's Randie. He's missing.'

'Oh no! Oh, Marjie.' The silence that fell held all their fears, because in that moment the reality of war hit them. Wanting to comfort Marjie, and needing comfort herself, Sibbie reached out. Marjie almost fell into her arms.

'It's unbearable to think about. It's the not knowing. Is – is he dead? Captured? Oh, Sibbie . . .'

Sibbie couldn't answer. A picture of Randie, a quiet young man just a few months younger than herself, came to her. To imagine him fighting – wielding a gun and charging –

was difficult. He was more at home with his head in a book, sitting under a shady tree once his work was done. She couldn't bear the thought of never seeing him again.

'I'm sure he's been captured, Marjie. Oh, I know that's bad, but at least he would still be alive, and might escape or outlive the war and come home. There's always hope – we must never lose that.'

Marjie didn't answer. Sibbie felt her body trembling. Hardly daring to, but needing to know, she asked, 'And Freddy? Is there any news of Freddy?'

Like Marjie, both of her brothers, Freddy and Randolph, had dual nationality and had been conscripted into the Allied forces under the command of the British, following the German occupation of France and the dissolving of the French army.

'Freddy was by Randie's side when they were ordered forward. Mama says he wrote that there was heavy fire between the German line and theirs, when their officer ordered them to move forward. They had adequate cover from field guns, but despite that, many fell. Some he knew were taken prisoner, and a hundred or more were killed. Mama received an official letter saying that Randie was "missing in action". She says, like you, that we must hold on to hope, as the night Freddy volunteered to go on burial duty, he and his fellow soldiers searched the bodies, but Randie wasn't amongst them. Freddy then made enquiries about all the injured, and Randie wasn't listed there. He told Mama that he was certain, after that, Randie must have been taken prisoner.'

'There, you see. He's alive, I'm sure of it.'

They fell into silence again, clinging onto each other. All the while their other, as-yet-unopened letters lay between them . . . It was almost too painful to open them, even though

35

they seemed to live from letter to letter at times, hungry for news of their loved ones.

The news Sibbie had, when she eventually opened one of her letters, was a further blow to her. Her brother Billy had been conscripted, much to his delight, and was soon to be deployed – heaven knew where. The whole world seemed to be on fire, and soldiers could find themselves sent to France, Africa or the Middle East. But Billy, more than any of them, was ready. And this worried Sibbie. His last letter was full of bravado, as if he was going to win this war single-handed.

Aunt Betsy's girls, Daisy, Florrie and Rosie, whom Sibbie looked on as her sisters, were safe, though. Much to their chagrin, they hadn't been dispatched to foreign places, but were nursing in various hospitals in and around London and Kent. They loved their work and spoke of the value of taking care of the wounded who were shipped to them day after day, but all secretly harboured a desire to work in field hospitals right at the heart of the action. Sibbie longed to be with them.

Marjie broke into her thoughts. 'Mama says that they didn't know where Paulo was until his letter came. Aunt Ella had been going half-mad. It appears that he received a notice that he was to be conscripted into the *Service du Travail Obligatoire*.'

'What? Isn't that the service that is forced to work in Germany?'

'Yes, Mama says it is terrible, and that young men are never heard of after they go. I am ashamed that my people in the South of France are collaborating with Hitler.'

'I know, but tell me, where did Paulo go?' Even as she asked, Sibbie's desire to read the letter he'd sent her burned into her heart, but she suppressed the longing, wanting to hear out Marjie and to comfort her.

'He just disappeared into the night, but they now know that he joined the Maquis, a Resistance movement.'

'Oh, Marjie, no! And Aunt Flors dares to put this in a letter to you?'

'No. Well, not in so many words. Before I left for England, Mama told me that if war did break out, she would communicate in code. It's complicated, and something she learned during her war. It involves misspelling, so that you are alerted to a sentence being in code. Here, look.'

Taking the letter, Sibbie read: *The eldest of Ella's pigons has flowen the nest.*

'See: it is the bad spelling of "pigeon" and "flown" that tells me this is code. Ella's eldest is Paulo – he has gone.'

Next, Sibbie read: *He did not like the confines of the enclosure and would not work alongside the other birds. We heard that he has gone to Monsiuer Marqs's coop. But our youngest bird will do whatever is asked of him and is ready to fly our coop when asked.*

'Code again, and this time it tells me that Paulo has joined the Maquis, the underground movement. See: "would not work" and "gone to Monsieur" – which she spelt wrongly – "Marqs's coop", which tells me it's the Maquis group. And then "our youngeot", meaning my brother Monty, "will do whatever is asked of him" – means that he is willing to go to Germany, if called. Oh God, Sibbie, it just gets worse and worse. Poor Mama cannot express how she feels, but I know that her own heart, and Papa's, must be breaking. Look, here she has written: "We are well, but often sit with the river flowing from the heart of the villag." Code again, shown by the misspelling of "village". So I decipher, this doesn't mean they sit next to the river, but that through their hearts flows a river of tears.'

'I'm so sorry, Marjie. It is all so awful for you – and for me, as I love them all dearly. Oh God, Paulo is in such danger!'

They fell silent again and held hands. In the distance they could hear a plane take off, followed by another, and then the sky above them darkened as they were encased in the roaring sound of the engines. Their eyes followed the craft travelling south, indicating that even more bombing was expected in the London and Kent regions. Had she thought her dear Rosie, Daisy and Florrie were safe? *Please, God, don't let any of the hospitals they are working in take a hit. And please take care of all of our families.*

When the bombers had passed over, Sibbie realized that she and Marjie were clinging to each other as if their life depended on it.

'Marjie, I know that letter brought sad news, but the coded messages are so clever. Look what she wrote, before her talk of birds: *Life here goes on as normal. The grapes were good this year, though our hobby of keeping pigeons isn't helping, as when they fly around, they peck the grapes, which annoys your papa.* They don't have pigeons, do they?'

'No. And that is something that also alerted me there was a coded message to come. But now I fear that Mama will have to be even more careful, because with Paulo not answering the call to work in Germany, they will be looking for him, unless Aunt Ella has a reason for his whereabouts. And I'm thinking that part of their looking might be to intercept any mail.'

'Yes, I can see that, but the code itself is brilliant. Your mama has even typed it, which makes it more authentic, as the misspelling could be typing mistakes. I think we should practise it. Write notes to each other. It will be fun to see if

38

we always get the message. Then, if ever we need it, we can use it to communicate in secret.'

'Do you think such a time will come? I can only think we will want to ask each other if we are going to the village "hop". Ha, I still find that so funny – as if we are going to hop around the village, like this . . .'

Marjie let go of Sibbie's hand and did a hop, skip and dance around the roof. She looked so funny that Sibbie burst out laughing. 'One way to keep warm,' Sibbie said and then joined in; and before they knew it, they were bent double, their laughter soaring into the now-still air.

A flock of birds took off in squawking protest. Marjie stopped laughing and looked heavenwards. 'They too have flown the nest.' With this, her tears spilled over.

Sibbie walked over and held her. Her own heart was heavy with unshed tears. She just clung onto Marjie, both giving and taking comfort.

It was hours later that Sibbie got the chance to open her letter. When she did, she was filled with joy and sadness at the same time.

She and Marjie were back in their billeted home, with Mrs Parkinson, a bright little widowed lady of around sixty who, not having any children of her own, was like a granny to all the village and was always busy knitting, or organizing fund-raising events and making sure the village children had all they needed.

Sitting on her bed, placed next to Marjie's, Sibbie lay back. Marjie had her eyes closed and didn't open them as Sibbie opened Paulo's letter, wondering as she did so how it had ever reached her. Her imagination showed her Paulo hiding out in the forests of Hérault, or even in the hills and mountains that surrounded it. Did he have shelter and food?

Her heart ached at the notion that he might not have. The envelope containing the letter seemed to resist being opened, but she knew this was caused by her impatience and not wanting to spoil anything about this precious gift, by tearing it.

*Sibbie, this is written very quickly and with a deep hope in my heart that you are well and safe, as I am.*

*In these terrible times that have disrupted all our lives, I have to speak out and say how I feel about you. I want you to know that I have loved you ever since I met you. At first as a kind of cousin but, as I grew older, my feelings deepened with every visit you made, until now there is an ache in my heart that compels me to tell you.*

*On your last visit we had no time alone, but I felt that you had feelings for me. Is it possible that you do? It is important for me to know, as the knowledge will sustain me and help me through all that we face.*

*Please keep safe, my darling, and don't take up any occupation that will put you in danger. Then I will know that one day we will be together.*

*I love you, my darling Sibbie. It is the thought of you that keeps me going. Write back soon.*

*Paulo x*

As Sibbie clutched the letter to her breast, she felt the racing of her heart as it pumped a feeling of great happiness through her veins. *Paulo, oh Paulo. Paulo loves me!*

Without opening her eyes, Marjie asked, 'Good news or bad?'

40

'Good. Oh Marjie, Paulo is in love with me! I can't believe it, and yet I can, as I knew it was destined to be. But I am so afraid for him.'

Lifting herself onto her elbow, Marjie looked keenly at Sibbie. 'I'm happy for you, Sibbie; and for Paulo, that at last he has spoken out, as we were all sure of how he felt, but he would never confirm it. But forgive me if, at this moment, I cannot help but ask if he says whether he is safe, or if he mentions Monty or gives any indication of what life is like for them?'

'No, nothing. Just his declaration of love for me. But it wouldn't be easy for him to say anything.'

A deep sigh from Marjie spoke of the anguish they both felt for their family.

'I thought they would all be safe. I thought Marshal Pétain would stand firm against Hitler's regime and mobilize the French army and swell its numbers to fight back, but he is a traitor!'

Sibbie knew of what Marjie was speaking. At first, when the invasion of France happened, they had both taken comfort from knowing that Hérault was part of Vichy, the declared Free Zone in the South of France. And Marjie had been really happy to know that its government was under the leadership of Marshal Pétain. But now, with Pétain hanging on Hitler's every word, the Nazi regime was really in charge. Life for their family was unsafe, as they would be looked upon as the enemy. British citizens, and especially Jews, were in a very dangerous position.

'How can Pétain behave as he is doing? He was a hero in the last war. He fought the Germans! It doesn't make sense. There is no Free France, because of Pétain and his wretched appeasement and bowing down to Hitler.'

41

'I know; he's imposing some very harsh regimes on his own people. It's frightening.'

'Sibbie, I haven't liked to say, but I'm so worried about Aunt Ella and Paulo and Lonia. I know they aren't practising Jews, but . . . Oh, Sibbie, what if Aunt Ella's background is found out? What will happen to her, and to Paulo and Lonia? They say that all Jews are being deported to camps. But no one knows what is happening to them after they have gone.'

The joy that had filled Sibbie turned to ice-cold fear. Yes, she'd pondered this before, but it had never struck her as it did now. 'It's terrifying. Oh, Marjie, why didn't Aunt Ella and Uncle Arnie get Paulo over here? They were thinking of doing so. They should all have come before this happened, as we all knew it was on the cards.'

Marjie left her own bed and climbed onto Sibbie's. Tears were flowing down her face, and her body trembled. 'I'm so afraid, Sibbie. Somehow it has dawned on me how dangerous the situation is for our family. Aunt Ella's because they are British Jews; and Mama and Papa because they are British and it's possible that they will be looked upon as sheltering Jews, which is against the law. Oh God, we have to do something! I know what we are doing now is vital work, but there must be something more that we can do?'

Putting her arm around Marjie, Sibbie felt a dread in her heart that she'd never felt before, and it forced her to voice what she'd been thinking for a while now. 'We could apply to be considered for a more active role. We could be doing all sorts of things with our languages. Perhaps undercover work? Surely the government has secret agents working in France. We would be especially useful working in the Vichy area, as we know it so well.'

'Yes, you're right, there must be agents gathering intelligence and helping the Resistance. But how do we apply, and to whom? They must know all about us, because when we applied to join the WAAF we filled in forms that gave our backgrounds. And at the time the interviewing officer was really interested in the fact that I had dual nationality and could speak four languages.'

'I had a similar reaction, too, when I said yes to the question about speaking any foreign languages. So why weren't we offered something where those skills would be useful?'

'Maybe they didn't see the right kind of person in us. I mean, perhaps we didn't show our true spirit?'

Sibbie thought about this and knew Marjie was right. They must have come across as two young women who were merely capable of working in the background. 'We need to show them our mettle, Marjie.'

'But how?'

'Why don't we ask permission to volunteer for the local home-defence unit in our time off? Or ask for further training in combat – anything that will show that we are ready to do more.'

Filled with enthusiasm as their ideas began to develop, they chatted long into the night about the possibilities of future roles for them.

By the time they settled down, Sibbie knew that a change had occurred. She and Marjie were no longer just two WAAFs doing an important but mundane job; they were two strong young women ready to take on the world and to right the wrongs. Part of her yearned for it to happen, but another part recognized the danger that their intentions would place them in. *But I'm ready. I'm truly ready. I need to do more. I need to be out there.* She'd always known this, and now it was time to make it happen.

# CHAPTER FIVE

# The South of France

## Ella and Flors

'What's that?'

'It's me, Mama. Paulo. Don't be afraid. I had to see you, but besides that, I have a message for Papa.'

'What? Oh, darling. Where are you, I can't see you,' Ella cried.

Light flooded the room as Arnie sat bolt upright and pulled the cord above their bed.

Paulo stood in the doorway, a finger on his lips. 'Shush, don't wake Lonia. She will be afraid.'

'Go downstairs, Paulo – we'll be there in a moment.'

Paulo nodded and crept out of the bedroom, at this from Arnie.

'Oh, Arnie, what do you think the message is? And how did Paulo get a message for you, and from whom?'

'All our questions will be answered, darling. Get your dressing gown on. Come on, old thing, Paulo can't hang around – it's too dangerous for him. We don't know if the house is being watched.'

Paulo was anxiously pacing the kitchen when they got downstairs. This room had always been the hub of the family.

Ella had painted the roughly plastered walls, between the huge oak beams that criss-crossed them, a pale yellow. Onions and garlic hung in bunches above the grand brick fireplace and iron stove, where the beams met. Next to them, copper pans of all sizes gleamed in the light of the oil lamp, which Paulo must have lit. There was no danger in doing so, as the heavy wooden shutters on the windows of the chateau blacked out any light from being seen outside.

The scrubbed stone floor felt cold to Ella's slipper-clad feet as she walked over to the scrubbed table, which took up most of the middle-floor space. Her whole body felt chilled, even though a fire still glowed in the hearth. She looked around her. Why didn't anything feel or look familiar to her? *But then I know why. Nothing about my world is familiar any more. I am cocooned in constant fear.* Glancing over at the clock, she heard the tick-tock filling the space, as if telling of doom. She felt none of the pleasure she would normally feel at the sight of the dresser adorned with all her china, standing next to the grandfather clock.

Her surroundings didn't reflect the love she'd poured into them over the years. It had all drained away, as if in slow drips, since she'd been unable to go to her sister Calek to try to save her. War breaking out sooner than they expected had prevented her efforts. For two whole years she'd heard nothing of Calek and Abram's fate. During that time she'd had to contend with Paulo disappearing into the forests, and a cloud of anxiety descending further around them till it almost choked her.

Hurrying across the kitchen to Paulo, Ella took her dear son into her arms. He held her tightly. She could feel his heart beating wildly in his chest. At that moment she knew that all her fears had become a truth.

'Mama, I have to tell you quickly. First, you, Lonia, Aunt Flors, Uncle Cyrus and Monty must leave now, tonight. Not by car, as there are roadblocks – I will guide you through the forest. I have people waiting on the other side, and they will take you cross-country to the border, to Geneva and into Switzerland. Some of that will be by tractor across fields, but mostly you will walk, so you need to dress accordingly and carry little with you. There are safe houses along the way, where you will be fed and given a night's rest; they will ask nothing of you, and you must tell them nothing. These people are trusted, but without information they cannot have it tortured out of them. On the last leg of your journey you will be given the details of a contact who will help you further.'

'What? How . . . ? Why?' Ella looked from Paulo to Arnie. 'Arnie, what . . ? Oh God!'

'Mama, the government has been rounding up British citizens for a while now. With you living so deep in the country, you haven't yet come to their attention, but I know that you are now on a list. They will be here any day. And, Mama, if they pick you up, they will soon find out that you are . . . Oh, Mama, please go now and pack a bag. Get everything ready, compose yourself and convince Lonia that she is going on an adventure. Please, Mama.'

If Ella had thought herself afraid before, she now felt sheer terror tear through her. 'What of Arnie? You – you said you had a message for Arnie. And, Paulo, Monty has already gone. He went days ago. He had his call-up to join the workforce going to Germany.'

For a moment a look of shock crossed Paulo's face, then anger quickly replaced it. 'How could he? He should have joined us. I told him how badly he will be treated by the Germans, but . . . Well, never mind, we have no time to discuss it. Papa, I have this letter for you: it is from the War Office in Britain, with orders for you. The letters were brought in with the last drop. The pilot specifically asked for me. At the time I didn't realize that British Intelligence knew about me. The pilot told me that I am looked upon as the leader of the Maquis de Laurens, and that I will receive orders from them through you.'

Ella still hadn't moved; she felt suspended between the life she knew and the horror of what lay ahead. She saw the official seal on the brown envelope that Paulo handed to Arnie. As Arnie took it, he seemed to become a different man. Always upright and strong, he straightened his back even more and looked, to Ella, more like an officer in service than her beloved husband.

The sound of the envelope being torn open grated on her nerves, because something told her that the contents would take her beloved away from her.

After a few moments, Arnie spoke. 'I have been given the rank of officer once more and am conscripted into the army, as a senior agent. It is judged that I will not need intensive training, as I was highly trained in the last war, and in any case it would be difficult to get me out and then return me. And so the next time a plane comes, a training officer will be on board and will stay for a week, to bring me up to date with the latest equipment and clandestine knowledge. I am to take up a post as coordinator of the various factions of the Maquis Resistance in this area. I am to be briefed by you, Paulo, on them, and where they camp. And then I will receive specific orders from London about our missions, and I will be the one to organize us in the execution of them.'

A silence enveloped Ella. She stood staring in horror at Arnie.

'Darling, I have no choice. I have my orders. I have never spoken of what I did in the last war, but I worked with the War Office gathering intelligence. I have always had to keep them informed of my whereabouts. I'm only surprised they haven't called on me before now.'

'Papa, Mama, I cannot stress how important it is that you prepare to leave immediately. I will go and alert Aunt Flors and Uncle Cyrus. But hurry, please hurry.'

Once back in their bedroom, Arnie took charge, and this helped Ella. 'Right, get dressed, my darling, quickly. Grab what you can, by way of clothes for you and Lonia, but be selective, darling, or it will be too heavy for you to carry. Once we are ready, get Lonia up . . . Oh, my darling, how am I to live without you both?'

What sounded like a sob came from Arnie. In some strange way, it put strength into Ella. 'We will get through this, Arnie, my darling husband – we will. We'll do everything we are told. I'll find safety in Switzerland and then, as soon as it is possible, I will find my way to England. You are an amazing person: you will be strong, and your strength and wits will keep you safe.'

As if they had willed it, they found themselves in each other's arms, clinging to each other, wanting never to let go.

Earlier Arnie had made love to Ella, taking her to a wondrous place where she had called out in abandonment and her world had felt safe. 'Arnie, my darling, every night at this time I will think of your lovemaking tonight. We didn't know it would be the last time for a long time, but it was very special. You do the same, and that will link us. Wherever we are, we will be joined in our minds and hearts at that moment.'

Arnie snuggled his head into her neck. 'My Ella, my darling Ella.'

A noise shot them apart. They listened, the air between them tangible with their fear. A cat squealed, and Ella let out a nervous giggle.

'Right, my darling, let's do this. We can; we did it before. We rose up, when asked to do so, and we can do so again.'

Taking her cue from Arnie, who was now in control of his emotions, Ella felt the spirit of yesteryear enter her. She was up to this challenge. She wouldn't let anyone down.

It seemed like no time before the little group of shocked, loving friends and family trudged in silence into the darkness. At the edge of the forest that surrounded their land, Cyrus, Ella and Arnie, who was carrying a sleepy but excited Lonia on his back, paused and looked back. As they did so, Flors's whisper seemed to echo in the darkness. 'Will we ever see our home or our family again?'

Cyrus pulled her to him. 'We will, my darling. We will.'

'Cyrus, at this moment, as never before, I'm glad that dear Rowena has gone to heaven, where she is safe. She couldn't have trudged miles in the dark, and if we are caught, she would have had to face so much, because of being Jamaican. From what I have read and heard about this Nazi regime, only Aryans are really acceptable to them.'

'Yes, Rowena's happy and safe, darling. I know it has been difficult for you, these last months since she died, but now you can be happy for her.'

By the time they met up with a man and woman, whom Paulo introduced to them to as Mona and Philippe, dawn was breaking. The sky looked beautiful, streaked with vivid reds and dark shadowy blues, watched over by a pale moon that was being hidden by the tops of the mountains. Outlined against the last brightness that the moon gave, the trees stood, black and majestic. Ella's thoughts were that such stunning beauty had no right to be the backdrop to her misery, and yet the scene was full of hope of a new day dawning, and she prayed that such a day would bring hope to her once more.

'We have to leave you here.' Paulo's voice shook with emotion. He had long since taken Lonia from Arnie and was holding onto his little sister as if for the last time. Ella felt her world shatter. To say goodbye to her beloved husband and son was tearing her to shreds.

Memories assailed her, as Paulo – her beloved late-husband – came to mind. How proud he would be of their wonderful son, his namesake, who was showing the same bravery fighting this war as his father had shown, when he'd fought his war. Paulo would be saying, 'Be brave, *mon amour*. Give your husband and our son a smile as you send them off to their destiny.'

And that's what she would do, for Lonia's sake and theirs. 'Well, my darlings, though my heart is breaking, let us part with a smile for each other, and for Lonia to remember. Think of us when you carry out all that you have to, and let our memory – and our need for you to return to us and take care of us – make you take greater care of yourselves in your actions and decisions. We will pray for you every day.'

How she said all this without breaking down, Ella didn't know. A lot of the courage that she had gained, when nursing just behind the front lines of the Somme and Ypres, had seeped back into her now. She'd experienced so much. She never thought to see it again and had managed to tuck it away, and get on with her life. Now that wonderful, beautiful life they had made lay in tatters and she knew not what the future held. But she had this moment, didn't she? This one moment in time with her loved ones.

'My darling, I . . . Oh, Ella.'

Arnie's arms were around her. Every fibre of her was alive to his touch and the feel of his strong body. Ella was etching it into her memory, so that she could at any time close her eyes and relive this moment. His lips, when they touched hers, felt like warm velvet. She could taste the sweetness of him and clung onto him. When he gently removed himself from her, the soft glow of the early sun, peeping over the mountain top, lit up the tears in his eyes.

'Smile, my darling. Let me leave you seeing your lovely smile.'

His face creased into a smile of his own, the beauty of which stunned her for a moment. His cheeks dimpled. A tear that clung to his lashes spilled over. Ella watched it trace a path down his beloved cheek, then wiped it with her thumb. 'I love you beyond my heart and my life. I will be by your side in all you do, my darling. Stay safe for me.'

'Oh, Ella. Thank you for this send-off. Our parting is breaking me, but your courage gives me strength. It lets me know that you will be all right, and so will our beloved Lonia, in your care.'

Ella wanted to scream out that she wouldn't be, but she held on to her composure. 'I will protect our daughter with my life.'

'And I will do the same for our son.'

This warmed Ella's heart, as it always pleased her that Arnie had accepted Paulo as his own. 'Then he will be safe, as I know that Paulo, his father, is looking down on him, too – on you both. I know he will watch over you.'

'That's a wonderful thought, darling. As I have said many times, I wish I could have met Paulo.'

'You have.' As she said this, Ella turned and gazed over

at her son, Paulo. 'He doesn't only have his father's name; he is his father personified.'

Paulo smiled back at her. Yes, he had tears glistening in his eyes, but she could see his love and courage shining through. Passing Lonia to Arnie, he embraced Ella.

In the arms of her beloved son, Ella could feel the heart of his father pulsing inside him. As Paulo pulled from her, he looked into her eyes. 'Mama, I love you. We will get France back. We will all return to our home one day.'

'I know, my darling.'

'Mama, if you get to England, will you tell Sibbie how much I love her?'

'You do? Oh, Paulo, that's perfect. When . . . I mean, how long have you known this? And does Sibbie know? Because she loves you, my son. She has loved you for a long time. I have often wanted to awaken you to her love.'

'Really? Did she say so?'

'She did to me, Paulo.' Flors stepped forward and put her arm on Paulo's shoulder. His face was now shining with the biggest grin Ella had ever seen him give. His happiness shone from him.

'Really? Sibbie loves me? That's wonderful. I could skip and dance.'

A little tinkling laugh from Lonia filled Ella with both the sadness and joy of the moment.

'Paulo, though we are pleased for you, we must hurry you all. It is important that we get across the open fields before the sun is fully up and the *gendarme* patrols begin to monitor the road.'

The moment was spoilt at these words from Cyrus – necessary words, and from another very brave man, who now faced knowing that one of his sons, the beloved and gentle Randolph, was probably in a prisoner-of-war camp, just as Cyrus himself had been in the last war.

Ella sighed; she had captured the moment and put it with her other memories, and she knew that was all she would have for a long time – memories of how life used to be.

'Come on, little one. It's time for us all to go on the next leg of our adventure. Kiss Papa and Paulo goodbye. And give them your very best smile,' she said, taking Lonia's little hand. Turning away was the hardest thing Ella had ever done. But when she looked back and saw that her beloved husband and son had gone, her heart split in two.

An arm came round her, and she looked into Flors's lovely face, where she saw once more the courage of yesteryear. 'We did it once, and we can do it again, Ella. We're together in this, as we were back then in Brussels.'

'Let me take Lonia. I can give her a piggyback.' Cyrus's voice shook with contained emotion as he said these simple words.

'Oh, say yes, Mama.'

Helping Lonia climb onto Cyrus's back lightened the moment. But when he galloped away with her, pretending to be a horse by neighing, and the air filled with Lonia's laughter, Ella broke down.

As always, Flors caught her and held her. Clinging onto Flors, Ella bent double with the weight of her sorrow. Sobs rasped her throat. Tears seemed to be draining from every part of her. 'I can't go on – I can't.'

'You can. And you will, my dear friend. I will be by your side, as will Cyrus; and as you will be by our side in our grief, too.'

'Oh, Flors, it can't be happening again. It can't. We – we've lost everything . . . everything.'

'No, we haven't. Ella, listen. Everything is on hold, that's all. You have to go forward with the spirit you showed back there, when you said your goodbyes. Lonia, and Cyrus and I, need that of you. You did so much for me as I watched your courage. Don't crumble now, Ella; don't, please.'

These words from Flors got through to Ella. She straightened and calmed her wails of distress.

'That's better, my darling friend. I know you needed that moment, but it has passed now. You will cope. It's what we do, remember? We cope with whatever this bloody world throws at us.'

'Ooh, Flors, you swore!'

Flors giggled. It was a giggle that turned to a laugh, which Ella couldn't help let into herself. She smiled at the warmth and comfort it gave her.

'You have to admit, Ella, there's never been a generation that's gone through the hell of two world wars.'

Ella linked arms with Flors. 'And we beat them last time, and we can do it again. Just let them try to destroy us altogether, and they'll have a fight on their hands like nothing they are experiencing now.'

'It's Flors and Ella against the world once more.'

'And when we get to England, it will be Mags, Flors and Ella against the world.'

'Yes, watch out, you Germans: we're on our way.'

They both laughed at this, which prompted a loud 'Shush!' from Philippe. This made them giggle even more and, as if they were children, stuff their fists into their mouths to try to quieten the noise.

\* \* \*

It was fully light by the time Ella, Flors and Cyrus got to speak again, and the late-September sun was warming them enough for them to remove their coats.

Ella didn't know how far they'd walked, only that she was beginning to feel the ache of their trek in her calves, and that hunger was knotting her stomach. Lonia had walked quite a lot of the time, and had been carried by them all at others. She had taken to Mona and was now holding her hands and Philippe's and was chatting away.

Ella, Flors and Cyrus also held hands, gaining comfort from doing so. They'd been told they would reach the first safe house by eleven, and now they could see it in the distance. They'd walked for the most part in silence, each with their own thoughts, but Ella now felt compelled to voice hers.

'Flors, I've been thinking. I think I will return to nursing.'

'I thought you would. I was wondering how you were going to cope, and it occurred to me that you might consider taking up nursing again. I agree, it would be a good way for you to get through however long it takes for you to be reunited with Arnie and Paulo. I'll help with Lonia all I can.'

Ella smiled. 'You know me so well. And yes, I feel that I have to do something. I can't live out however long this takes waiting, day after day, for news. I'll contact the Red Cross once we're settled back in England.'

Cyrus interrupted them then. 'Did you bring any money, Ella?'

'Yes, I did, Cyrus. Quite a bit.' She told him how, during the initial part of their journey when Arnie and Paulo had still been with them, Arnie had told her that he'd put the cash he kept in the safe, to pay the casual workers, in the bottom of her case and it amounted to quite a bit, to see her on her journey. 'He also said he would transfer money to the bank account that I still hold in London, so that I can afford to find a place to live for me and Lonia and will be able to cope financially.' Saying this prompted a thought and she asked, 'What do you think will happen to the casual workers, Cyrus?'

'Being Gypsies, they will disappear, once they see that we are gone. I hope so, as they are not safe. As well as the British and Jews, all Gypsies and homosexuals – and those who are physically and mentally disabled – are being rounded up. It is a tragedy . . . But you'll be safe, Ella, I promise. We'll get you and Lonia home.'

'I know, Cyrus. But it is all so unbearable. Why? How can people be so inhumane? How can one man influence so many with his warped views?'

They were quiet for a moment as each absorbed the enormity of what Cyrus had said.

After a while, he changed the subject. 'You have no need to find a home, Ella. The last communication I had from our estate agent in England was that our house has escaped the bombing, but the people renting it have moved. They have gone to live in the North, with the husband's family. So you and Lonia are very welcome to live with us. There is plenty of room.'

'Thank you, Cyrus. That sounds wonderful.'

What Cyrus said next lifted Flors's heart. 'And maybe Marjella can get transferred to a nearby station and live at home, too, Flors – that would be something, wouldn't it?'

'Yes, that would be a dream come true, Cyrus! I have felt bereft since all our children have left.'

'You are so brave, Flors.' Ella tugged Flors nearer to her, so that she could feel more of her close up.

'I don't feel brave. We cry at night together, when no one sees us.'

'Hush, darling.' Cyrus's hand brushed Ella's shoulder as he put his arm around Flors. 'We have to keep positive. Yes, we weep at night for our young, but during the day we must keep going.'

'We will, Cyrus. You don't have to worry about me and Flors – we've weathered bigger storms. And thank you again for your offer. I would love to live with you, and it would really help me.'

'And us, especially Flors. Anyway, Ella, I asked about your finances because I'm thinking that we will never make it, walking across the Alps. Not with little Lonia, and none of us are really physically fit enough to do so. The high altitude would kill us. For the right money, there must be someone willing to fly us over.' In French he shouted to Philippe, 'What do you think, Philippe? Is it possible to find someone to fly us into Switzerland?'

'We will talk over breakfast. Right, here we are at the safe house.'

Inwardly, Ella gave a deep sigh of relief. The house – a farmhouse in the middle of nowhere – looked as though it was falling down. She couldn't imagine anyone living there, let alone feeling 'safe' within its crumbling walls.

'Come, the entrance is round the back. The Brebecks live in the basement. The house is in a dangerous condition, but they are safe down there. Passing Germans think it's a ruin. They have been known to stop there and piss on the walls, and yet not realize there is a home below. The people who live here are refugees from Poland.'

Ella's heart lifted at this. *My fellow countrymen. At last I might get some news of what is happening in Poland.*

Philippe was now saying, 'They found this wreck and squatted in it. Monsieur Brebeck is an engineer and has adapted the underground rooms, leaving the main building looking as it does – an old wreck. It is hard to detect that it is occupied, unless you know.'

As they descended into the basement, Ella's elation left her, as it felt as if they were taking steps down into the bowels of the earth, and she wondered if that's what their life would be like once more . . .

# CHAPTER SIX

# Maidstone, Kent, and Portpatrick

## Daisy, Florrie and Rosie

'Eeh, it's grand to be together.' Rosie huddled in between her sisters as they walked along the promenade, against the might of the strong wind lashing the south-east coast of Herne Bay.

'Aye, it is. But, by, it's cold. Is there a tea shop nearby, Rosie?'

'That's where I'm taking you, our Florrie.'

A gang of POWs were working on the sea wall and, as the girls passed, one called out, '*Guten Morgen*, Rosie.'

Daisy gasped. 'You knaw a German, Rosie!'

'Aye, lots of them. They're all right, nice lads – naw different from our own.'

'You're blushing, Rosie. You're not . . . Eeh, Ma would scalp you. Tell me you're not fraternizing.'

'By, Daisy – "fraternizing"? That's a strong word for being friendly, ain't it? British, Polish, German: we treat them all the same. That bloke I spoke to is called Albie – well, Albrecht is his real name. His plane came down in the sea.'

'Eeh, I've never heard the like. Treating him's one thing, but being friendly with him is quite another.'

'Aw, don't be so stuffy, our Daisy. He's just another human being I nursed. That's all.'

The girls were quiet for a few steps, then Daisy, the eldest, asked, 'You ain't falling for him, are you, Rosie? Ma would have a blue fit – she calls the Germans sommat rotten.'

Rosie didn't answer.

'Rosie?'

'Aw, Daisy, let's drop it, shall we? This is meant to be the first day of a grand week together. God knaws we get very little time together.'

'Oh, Rosie. Come here.' Rosie found herself encased in Florrie's arms. 'Whoever you fall for, it's all right by me. We can't help who we fall in love with.'

'Naw, that's true. I suppose as Florrie's right. I hope you don't fall for a German, though, Rosie; it would be awkward and would change things. But then I'd still be envious of you. It'd be good to meet a man I could fall for, but I don't see it happening somehow.'

'You will, Daisy. You're only twenty-six and a beauty. You've the best figure of us all – you're not so busty as me and Rosie. I don't knaw about you, Rosie, but I get leered at more than admired.'

'Aye, I knaw what you mean.'

'Look, Rosie, I didn't mean owt. I'm just worried about you. You allus fell head over heels for anyone as showed you some attention.'

'That's not true, our Daisy. Aw, come on, don't let's fight. I wanted this time together to be the best ever.'

'Me too. Let her go, Florrie, and give me a turn. I want a hug an' all, Rosie.'

'Eeh, Daisy, I've missed you.'

'Missed sparring with me, no doubt.'

They both laughed at this, though Rosie knew there was some truth in it. Coming out of the hug, she told them, 'Let's hurry – the tea shop is one street back, so we'll cut off the promenade here.'

Turning off the promenade was like going into a wind tunnel, as the strong gusts found an outlet. Bending double, the girls had almost to fight their way forward. When at last they heard the clanging of the doorbell announcing their arrival at the tea shop, they all giggled with relief. 'By, I thought Scotland were the place for autumn winds, but that nearly cut me in two.'

'I knaw, we get some easterly winds here at times, Florrie, and though it's only September, they can really chill you.'

'Shut the door quickly, girls, and keep the heat in. What can I get you?'

'Three teas and three of them scones, if you've got three, please, Kath.'

'Right-o, Rosie. Are these your sisters, then? Not that I need to ask. They all look like you. I've a nice fire going in the other room, so take yourselves in there. It's early in the year to light it, but I thought today warranted it.'

'Thanks, Kath. Come on, you two, follow me through. You're in for a treat.'

'Eeh, Rosie, this is cosy.'

'Aye, it is, ain't it, Florrie? We can kill time here until our train's due – the station's only just up the road. Eeh, I can't wait to see Ma, and all of them.'

Rosie had waited for this day with both eagerness and trepidation. Eagerness because not only was she seeing Florrie and Daisy, but they were all to travel to Scotland together to stay with Ma for a week; trepidation because it would mark the last time, for who knew how long, that they would all be together.

Florrie made straight for the roaring fire. A small side room carpeted in red, this part of the tea shop was Rosie's favourite. Low-ceilinged with beams hung with shiny brasses, the room had four tables set against bench seating fixed to the wall, each table covered with pristine white tablecloths.

Joining Florrie, who was warming herself by the roaring fire, Rosie snuggled into her sister.

'You'll get red blotches on your legs, the pair of you. Get away and let the warmth circulate.'

Pulling a face at Daisy, but not retaliating, Rosie sat down at the table that Daisy had chosen.

'You can look like that, Rosie, but I have to watch out for you.'

They smiled at each other, and Rosie felt a deep love for her elder sister. Never mind that they were often at logger-heads, they were really very close, and it was their similar natures that caused friction.

With tea served, their chatter quietened, as each knew it was time to talk of their future. Rosie started the conversation by asking, 'So, do you knaw where it is that you're going?'

'We do.' Daisy's voice was muffled as she juggled the mouthful of scone she'd bitten off. 'Singapore. We've been told to be at St Pancras station at ten in the morning, ten days from today. Anyroad, we'll tell you all about it when we're on the train. You're sure that the one we're catching will get us into London in time to catch the overnight to Glasgow, aren't you, Rosie?'

'Aye, I am. By, it's going to be grand to spend this time with you. Though sad, as it will be goodbye when it's over.'

'I'm hoping not. Can you get some time off, to see us on our way? Only we've written to Sibbie, and she telephoned me at the hospital and said that she and Marjella have a few days' leave then and can make it to London to meet up with us and wave us goodbye. It'd be grand if you could come too, Rosie.'

'I don't see a problem. You see, I swap my regular rest days with the local girls, as I ain't got much to do down here. Then they do me the same favour, so that I can take a few days together and can travel to see Ma. I'm still owed plenty, so I'll sort it as soon as I get back. Eeh, I envy you both. I sometimes think I'll be stuck here for the duration. Not that it's a bad posting, I'm happy enough, but it'd be good to see a bit of the world.'

'Aye, it will. I'm that excited.'

'Me too, Florrie. I can't wait. I joined the Queen Alexandra's to get a bit of excitement, and now it seems we are going to. And it'll be good to be together an' all.'

Rosie experienced a feeling of being left out of something. Her mood fell, but it lifted again as she watched the POWs being marched past and saw Albrecht look through the window of the cafe. He winked at Rosie, sending a tingling sensation through her. *No, I can't feel this way – I can't.*

At this thought, Rosie tried to dispel Albie from her mind. *Oh God, don't let this happen. Our Daisy's right – me ma would skin me alive. I can't fall in love with an enemy of our country, I can't.* But Rosie didn't know if she could stop herself, even though she knew it was a forbidden love.

'Look at you, me lasses. Eeh, I'm that proud of you.' Betsy felt worry enter her as she welcomed Daisy, Florrie and Rosie home. 'Now, come on, what's your news? Oh, aye, I knaws

63

as you have some – I can see it in your face, our Florrie.'

'Ma, there's naw easy way to tell you, but me and Florrie have been posted.'

Betsy's gasp rasped in her throat. The moment she'd been dreading was upon her.

'Now, don't worry, Ma. It's a good posting – not to a trouble-spot, but to a military base. We may not even see any wounded.'

Despite this reassurance from Daisy, Betsy didn't feel at ease, though she began to as she listened to their excited chatter about their expectations of Singapore.

'So how's things here, Ma? Have you heard from Billy?'

'Naw, and I'm worried for him. The last we heard he was going to the Far East an' all. Malaya, aye, that were it. It's all too much, at times. I have four of you all over the place, and Roderick, well, he's only three years off call-up age, what if—'

'Oh, Ma. Come here.'

At this from Florrie, Betsy found herself in the arms of her girls. Her heart was breaking.

'Oh? And what's this all about? You all look like doom and gloom's hitting home.'

'Aunt Sue!'

'Whoops, careful, Florrie, me darling, you nearly knocked me off me pins. It's good to see you all – you're a sight to cheer us.'

'I'll put the kettle on.' Betsy could think of nothing else to do or say. Things were as they were, as Angus was always telling her. But although her usual way would be simply to get on with it, she just couldn't. What ma could, in such circumstances? She was going to be left with none of her brood safe – none of them.

This thought had hardly left her when the dreaded hooter sounded, signalling that the lifeboat needed to be launched. It was a sound they were hearing a lot lately, as stricken boats hit a mine or were shelled by enemy aircraft. 'Eeh, that'll mean Angus and Rory have to go out. I tell you, it's all driving me mad.'

'Ma, why don't you do sommat that'll help the war effort? It'll make you feel better, I'm sure.'

'Like what, Daisy? What can I do, stuck up here?'

Betsy felt excitement as she listened to Daisy's suggestions. She hadn't imagined that she could help by getting her workers to knit socks and suchlike for the soldiers, or by collecting tinned food for them in London. The prospect cheered her.

The door flying open caught their attention. 'Ma – Da's gone out to sea. There was an SOS from a sinking ship that had hit a mine. But in the control room we picked up a report of a German U-boat torpedoing another ship.'

'Eeh, naw, lad – naw.' This was too much to bear. Her Angus was in danger.

'What about your Uncle Rory? Did he go as well, Roderick?'

'Aye, he did, Aunt Sue. They'd gone after the smaller ship, before the distress signal concerning the U-boat came in. There was nothing to be done to stop them.'

Betsy looked from one to the other. Her whole world was crumbling as she did so. A gasp from Susan brought her out of the anguish that clothed her. 'They'll be fine, Sue. Our men are indestructible; they knaw every wave of that sea, and that'll give them an advantage. Afore we knaw it, they'll be coming through that door whistling, as if nowt's happened. Now, let's get that tea.'

Betsy's hand shook as she pushed the hot plate holding

the kettle over the flames of the fire, but preparing the teapot and getting the mugs out helped her. She was better when she was busy; and aye, she thought, it was time she showed the mettle she'd always had within her. Moping about the injustice of everything wasn't helping anyone.

With this new-found courage, Betsy moved through from her kitchen to where the others were gathered in the front room. She still loved this old house, which belonged to Mags; well, her half of the house did, as Mags had divided it up to make a home for herself, too, and still used her half on visits. But even so, Betsy had ample space, with three bedrooms, a bathroom, a living kitchen and this posh room, which she hardly ever used these days.

'Right, cure-all: a lovely pot of tea, or a Rosy Lee, as you sometimes call it, Sue. Eeh, you London lot, you talk funny at times.'

Susan laughed out loud at this. 'Me? I like that. What with you calling ears "lugs", and women "lasses" and a mug of tea "a pot"! I think you're the funny talker, out of us two.'

They all joined in the laughter. It wasn't a real belly-laugh, like those they used to share, but it was a start, and it showed Betsy how much she could influence the mood of so many people. No matter that her young 'uns had grown up and left, they still relied on her, and she hadn't been the strongest for them since this war broke out. Well, that was going to change.

'Does you miss your old life in London, Sue? In all these years, I've never asked you.'

'Sometimes, Betsy, but not often. I've felt bad lately, with how my city has taken a hammering, but I love it up here.'

They were standing on the quayside, as were most of the townsfolk. The lifeboat hadn't returned, and they hadn't heard any news about how it was faring. Wives and children huddled, hardly talking, their eyes pinned on the distant horizon and the glow over Ireland that lit up the night sky. 'Them lot's lucky not being involved in this war.'

'The Irish, you mean?'

'Aye, well, the southern Irish.'

Susan didn't answer. Betsy knew that she was as knotted with fear as she herself was. For all her bravado, she was worried to the bones of her, now that it had been so many hours since the lifeboat had left the shore.

'Ma, I've brought you a hot drink of cocoa; and you, Aunt Sue.'

'Ta, Daisy lass. Are Florrie and Rosie asleep?'

'They are. I didn't wake them once they'd gone off. We had a long journey and hardly any rest on it. I've used Aunt Mags's telephone and rung for an ambulance to be here on standby. Where's Roderick?'

'He went out on the second boat. There's been a few that have left the harbour. Since he turned fifteen, and with the shortage of men, he's been a junior lifeguard. Oh, lass, I hope they find the menfolk.'

'They will, Ma. Keep strong. You were a different person this afternoon, keeping us all going.'

'It's me job, lass. I knaw as I shirked it for this past year, but I want you to knaw as I'm here for you all. You can write me owt that's happening. I want to knaw. You've naw need to be guarded with me any more.'

Betsy felt Daisy's arm come round her shoulders. 'Good to hear, Ma. You knaw, I reckon as our Rosie has sommat to share, but is afraid to.'

'Oh, what? What's our Rosie up to that she can't share, eh?'

'That's all I'm saying, Ma. For one thing, I might be wrong. I think you should talk to her as you did to me just then; let her knaw as she can be open with you, naw matter what's on her mind, and without upsetting you, but getting your counselling.'

'Eeh, our Daisy, have I been that bad? I feel ashamed of meself. I've only looked inwards. And there you all were, going out into the world without me. I'll find me moment to talk to Rosie, if it presents itself to me.'

Daisy held her tighter. 'Ta, Ma. We all need you, you knaw. Forget how it's been. I promise you that I'll write only the truth to you from now on. Well, that is, as much as I can, as we have to be careful what we say.'

Betsy sighed. Turning into the hug that Daisy gave her, she snuggled into her eldest daughter, and had the strange feeling that her own ma was holding her.

An engine noise in the distance got her pulling away. A hush descended over the huddle of folk. Far outside the harbour, a light could be seen coming closer. And then another. Neither of them told her that these boats included the lifeboat, but at least she knew there could be news.

When the news finally came, it was grim. The lifeboat had been lost – blown sky-high by a torpedo. Betsy felt her legs start to give way, but a moan from Susan filled her with strength. 'Come on, lass. And you, our Daisy. We might be needed. Let's get nearer to the landing station.'

With a heavy heart, Betsy pushed her way through, consoling and encouraging the gathered lasses as she did so. 'Let us through – Daisy here's a nurse, she might be needed.'

When they reached the landing station, both boats pulled in and someone called out, 'Help us unload these men –

they're injured, but we left a life-raft out at sea, so we have to go back to it. There's ten men in it.'

The sea was surprisingly calm now, lit by streaks of bright moonlight, and Betsy would have said it was beautiful to behold, if the circumstances had been different. She scanned the faces of the injured, but there was no Angus or Rory. Her heart dropped, but she was determined to hold on to her emotions.

Someone else shouted, 'The inn's open, take them there.'

'Right, that's where we're going an' all.' Turning Susan round, Betsy held her hand. 'We can do this, lass. We can help them as have made it back, whilst praying that our men are on the raft.'

Once inside the inn, Betsy was surprised and pleased to see Daisy take charge. 'Ma, go and get our Florrie and Rosie. Tell them it's urgent.'

Betsy didn't hesitate. As she left the inn, she saw injured men, but didn't know any of them, and assumed they were from the lifeboat that had been blown up, as all of them were badly hurt and many of them had burn injuries. The rescuers would have brought them in first, which indicated that those left in the raft were less in need of urgent care. Just as she got to the door, she saw Roderick. And thanked God that he was back safely.

'Ma, we'll need an ambulance – it should have been on standby.'

'It's on its way, lad, don't worry. And your sisters will do all they can. Now, go up to the house and get Florrie and Rosie here, and get yourself into some dry clothes. Eeh, my lad, I'm right proud of you, but they shouldn't take one so young with them.'

* * *

Betsy marvelled at the skill of her girls. In the hour it took for the ambulance to arrive, they had administered to all seven injured men, bandaging wounds with ripped-up sheets, setting broken limbs with splints made from pieces of wood that the landlord provided, and stemming blood-flow with tourniquets. But it was when she witnessed Daisy removing shrapnel from a man's stomach that she felt the most admiration she'd ever felt in her life.

Orders shouted by Daisy were obeyed without question. Needles were brought to her and sterilized by Betsy and Susan, in the pots of boiling water that the landlord kept going on his stove; as was fine fish-gut, which was used to stitch the wound and gashes sustained by other patients.

As the last man was put into a van that was to follow the ambulance, everyone cheered. The landlord came over to Daisy and Florrie and held up their hands in the air. 'Well, me lassies, I ken ye did a great job there. Ye deserve a medal. Lives have been saved this neet, so they have. I'd offer everyone a drink, but our own lads aren't back in yet. We need to keep a vigil going.'

'Thanks, Willum, but can you get everyone to set to and scrub this room, and can you sterilize everything again? Rosie and Florrie, come with me, we'll get cleaned up. I ordered the ambulance to come back. We need to be ready for when the next boat comes in.'

It was two hours later that they brought in the men from the raft. To Betsy's great relief, Angus and Rory were on it, and neither was hurt, just shocked at what they'd seen.

'Me bonny wee lassie, I've visited hell.'

Betsy looked up into Angus's weather-beaten face and felt

her love for him swell inside her. 'Eeh, Angus, thank God you're home.'

Within the circle of his arms Betsy felt a lifting of all her troubles, but she couldn't enjoy it for long, as her help was required. 'Take yourself home, love. I'll be there as soon as the girls are done here.'

'I'll have meself a wee dram first, lassie. I'll be in the bar, as I see Willum has opened it up, now that we're back.'

'Go on with you. Any excuse.'

'Are ye not for thinking that I have the best excuse ever, then, me lassie?'

Betsy laughed, and it was a relief to do so. There were times tonight when she had thought she was visiting hell, too. But it was a hell made better by the skill of her girls. She'd never again raise any objections to anything they wanted to do. They were no longer her young 'uns, but good, strong young women who could make their own mark on the world.

As they walked back to their home, after the last of those brought in injured were on their way to hospital, Betsy linked arms with her girls. Rory had long ago taken Susan to their home, and Angus and Roderick had gone home fifteen minutes or so earlier.

The four of them walked along to the sound of the sea gently lapping the shore, and a backdrop of light still shining across and reflected in the water, creating a magical sight.

'Eeh, you'd never think as there were any bad in the world when you gaze at that, would you? But we've witnessed the result of evil tonight.'

'We have, Ma.'

'Aye, but you, me lasses, are doing nowt but good. You have the skill to right some of the wrongs and make folk live, who would have died without your help. I'm ready to let you go.'

'That's a funny thing to say, Ma.'

'Naw, Rosie. It's what I'm doing. I'm letting go, and yet I'm standing in your corner. It's naw longer me place to berate you for owt – you're your own women, and I'll support you in owt an' all, no matter what me views are.'

'Eeh, Ma, have our Florrie and Daisy been telling tales?'

'Naw, it's just that I've realized that I've to open a path to you all to travel along towards me, if you need to, and aye, without fearing the consequences.'

'Aw, Ma. You're the best ma in all the world, and we all love you an' all, with all our hearts; and it's going to be grand having you there to talk our problems over with. Not that we couldn't always, but well . . . some things you weren't good at hearing.'

'By, me little lasses, I'll change, I promise. And I love you an' all. And with all me heart and soul. Come back safely to me, once this war is done. I'll be waiting.'

A strange feeling overcame Betsy as she said this, but she shook it off. Such feelings were natural, with all that was happening. 'Anyroad, me little lasses, you've nowt to worry over now. Your ma's safe and here for you. And everything'll pan out. It allus does.' Saying this didn't stop Betsy looking heavenwards and praying to God to make it so.

# PART THREE

# Britain, France and Singapore, 1941

~

*Fear a Constant Companion*

# CHAPTER SEVEN

# Blackburn and London

## Sibbie and Marjie

Sibbie clung to her Aunt Mags.

'Oh, my darling girls, I'm so glad you are here. We have missed you.'

As Sibbie came out of her aunt's hug, her Uncle Jerome took her into his arms. 'So happy to see you, dear Sibbie; and you, Marjella. Now, don't keep us in suspense – you said you had news?'

'Yes. We have had orders to report to London. And that's it really, except that we were given two weeks' leave, with immediate effect, and told to visit all of our family. They indicated that we will be working near London, but that our work will be so intense and top-secret that we won't be granted much – if any time off that will be of a duration long enough to make visits.'

'Oh? I wonder what they have in mind for you. Code-breakers? Interpreters? Translators? Anyway, whatever it is, I imagine you will be kept very safe, as your work will be of the gravest importance. So it is worth the sacrifice of not being able to see you often.'

Sibbie hoped it was none of these things. When the order

to go to London had come through, it had come via their senior officer, and he had said they were going to be tested for their suitability to carry out special operations, but that they were to say nothing of this to their family; only that the work they would be doing would severely limit their visits home, if not curtail them altogether until the end of the war.

'Yes, sounds boring, though. Still, if that is what they call us to do, ours is not to reason why. I'm just so glad that the date we have our initial interview is two days after Daisy and Florrie leave, so that we can see them off and spend a little time with Rosie, who will need our support.'

'But have they not given you any indication of what you will be doing? And you are sure it will be in this country?'

'Mags, darling, you know better than to question them.'

Sibbie smiled at her uncle. Jerome, a reluctant doctor-turned-vet – due to his love of working with animals, and of the land – was a lovely man. She'd always loved him, and he had accepted her in the same light that Mags looked upon her and had been like a father to her. Always ready with advice, without interfering in her decisions.

Sibbie thought how lucky she was to be surrounded by so many who cared for her. Rory, her stepfather, a shy man, was also a stable father-figure for her to look up to.

'Sorry, I should know better. Anyway, let's make a pact – no talk of war whatsoever. You're only here overnight and I want to enjoy every moment of that time with you. Did you hear of what happened at Portpatrick? Daisy, Rosie and Florrie were quite the heroines. And Aunt Betsy has had a profound change of heart, thank goodness. It was getting difficult trying to lift her spirits when I can only talk to her over the telephone.'

'No. Is everyone all right?'

Listening to Mags relay the tale of the loss of the lifeboat, and how Daisy, Rosie and Florrie had treated the injured men, brought home to Sibbie how much the war was hitting everyone, whether they were actively involved or just going about their daily business, but in particular those whose jobs put them in danger – fishermen and lifeboat crew especially so.

'Oh, Aunt Mags, thank God they are all safe. I can't wait to see Mum and all of them.'

It was much later when Sibbie and Marjie retired, after a lovely evening catching up on how busy Aunt Mags was, as the mill was thriving. And although they had said no war talk, that was one of the good things that could happen at times like they were experiencing – an abundance of employment for local folk, as the mill had won the contract to supply all manner of clothing for the forces, as well as parachute material. Uncle Jerome was experiencing a busy time, too, as farms had to produce double quantities of everything and had more livestock than they'd had previously.

As they got into bed that night, Marjie expressed something that had struck Sibbie, too. 'How uncomplicated life is here, Sibbie. Business as usual, with added bonuses. I wish our lives were so. I'm anxious about what lies in store for us. The not knowing is awful.'

'I know. I keep wishing, and hoping, that we are to be sent on a secret mission abroad somewhere, and yet it terrifies me, as I don't know whether I am up to it or not.'

'It sounds like we will know if we are, before they send us, as they are going to test our ability and suitability.'

'What on earth will that entail? I hope it isn't fitness, as

I've never been a physical animal. I always preferred a book to the rough-and-tumble of the boys in our family.'

'If it is what you hope for, then it is bound to be along those lines, Sibbie. Any work abroad isn't going to be done behind a desk. Perhaps we can start to do exercises this fortnight? Go for long walks, do those push-up things where you lie on the floor and push yourself up on your arms – that sort of thing.'

'That's a good idea, and perhaps we can go to the swimming baths. I'm a good swimmer, and I always swam in the sea, even in winter. We could do that every day when we are in Scotland, though it'll be cold; not like your sea in the South of France.'

'Mmm, I might pass on that one. I don't like the cold.'

'You're a softie, so we need to toughen you up. But oh, it will be good to see my mum and Aunt Betsy – and all of them – before we report for duty.'

'We're travelling the length and breadth, at this rate. London tomorrow to see your Daisy and Florrie off, then to Scotland and back down to London. Not that any of that worries me. It will be lovely to meet the girls, and your mum and Betsy, and all their families. I'm just sorry we weren't able to catch Beth and Belinda before they went back to school.'

'I know. I can't believe this is Beth's last term before she goes to college, I only hope this war is over before she gets to the end of her education as, knowing her, she will want to do something wildly dangerous to help fight it.'

'Oh, I wish it would all just go away.'

'What's really bothering you, Marjie?'

'Well, my family; they are constantly on my mind. I know I had that letter, but it was dated a couple of months ago.

I was hoping against hope there would be another waiting for me here.'

Sibbie felt so much for Marjie and didn't know how to make her feel better. There was nothing she could say that would console her. After all, their family and Aunt Ella's were in grave danger, as the news coming out of Vichy France wasn't good; many expatriates were fleeing their homes to avoid being detained by the regime.

Her own thoughts were with her Aunt Flors and Uncle Cyrus and her cousins, and with Aunt Ella's family, especially – and even more so – her beloved Paulo. She hoped against hope that the work she and Marjie were being assessed for involved them going to France. That would help Marjie, too. She'd know first-hand what was happening there.

It was the one subject she'd wanted Aunt Mags and Uncle Jerome to approach, hoping they would have some reassurances for them. But once they had said no more talk of war, only the way domestic affairs were being affected was discussed.

Yawning, Sibbie changed the subject. 'It was nice to see Cook looking so well. Bless her. I worried about her, when Aunt Mags wrote that she was poorly. But whatever was ailing her seems to have passed. It will be good to tell Aunt Betsy that.'

'Go to sleep, Sibbie. You're such a darling, worrying about everyone and trying to make everyone's world right – you're like a whirlwind that I have to keep up with!' Marjie's laughter sounded good, as sleep overcame Sibbie.

The train pulled into London's Kings Cross station a little later than expected the next morning. Excited to see the girls whom she looked upon as her sisters, Sibbie jumped onto the platform. 'Come on, Marjie. Hurry! Oh, look, there they are – under the clock at the entrance.'

'They look exactly like you said. Just look at their lovely golden hair. I can't wait to meet them.'

'It does look golden in that light, but it's more chestnut. Daisy! Florrie! Rosie . . . we're here!'

Before she could take a breath, Sibbie found herself being hugged and asked a dozen questions: how was she? How was Aunt Mags? Was her journey all right?

'Let her breathe, girls. Eeh, poor lass, she'll be sorry she came, at this rate.'

Sibbie laughed. 'It's all right, Daisy. Oh, it's so good to see you all. It must be two years since our paths crossed. I can't wait to hear all your news. Oh, this is my cousin, Marjella – only we call her Marjie.'

Marjella looked bemused as each of the girls gave her a hug.

Linking arms, they left the station. The sight that met them outside shocked Sibbie. For a moment she halted the group's progress. 'Oh God, look at the destruction!' All around her, buildings were broken. The air had a tinge of burning debris and the street was littered with blackened bricks, chunks of smouldering wood and shards of glass. 'I never dreamed my first visit to London would mean seeing it in such a sad state.'

'This is nowt compared to what it was like during the Blitz. A couple of bombs dropped last night and caused this, but imagine thousands of bombs dropping in one night. It were a living nightmare, with everyone facing their possible death every day.'

'Oh, Daisy, I knew of course – it's part of my job to know; and the news was full of it, but until you see what damage a bomb causes, it doesn't hit home. Even newspaper pictures don't give you the true feeling of it all. Poor Londoners, how did they come through it all?'

'Many didn't. It's a grieving city, but a city with spirit. The folk here have a good outlook on life. Allus laughing and seeing the funny side. Anyroad, let's forget it all for one day, and hope that Hitler does an' all. I'm going to show you as much as I can. Not that it will be a lot, as it's nearly lunchtime now and we've to be at St Pancras station by four.'

'Don't worry about the tour. All I want is to be with you all. And I feel as though we have been travelling for days. Let's go and eat, and just talk and well . . . be together.'

They all agreed to this.

It was as if Marjie had known the girls all her life, the way she chatted easily with them. They sat in the Old King's Head pub on Euston Road, listening to the excited chatter from Daisy and Florrie about their forthcoming trip to Singapore and how they were being assigned to work in the Alexandra Military Hospital and would be caring for all military personnel and their wives and families. 'And Malaya isn't far. That's where our Billy is. Maybe we'll be able to see him an' all.'

'That'd be grand, Daisy. If you do, give him me love, and tell him to write an' all – to me and to Ma. Tell him how much we worry about him; and, aye, how much we love him.'

'Aye, Rosie, we will. Well, Florrie will, no doubt. She and Billy have allus got on well, as you knaw, so it'd come better from her. Me and him are like a red rag to a bull. Mind, I am worried about him, and I do love him.'

'He knaws that. But, you knaw, it's strange how you two and Billy have all been sent there. There's nowt much going on to do with the war out there, is there, Daisy?'

'Aye, we thought that, but nowt's done that's not warranted these days, so maybe there's sommat afoot. Anyroad they told us, didn't they, Florrie, that Singapore is an important port of call for troops and merchant seamen an' all, and that keeping them healthy is vital work. And even if there is or isn't much action, we're going to enjoy it. It sounds such an exotic island.'

'Aye, it does; and I suppose, being British, it has to be protected, and there'll be ships coming into its ports with troops on. I reckon as you'll be kept busy, whether it's with war casualties or not.'

'I think you're right, Rosie.' As Sibbie said this, she felt that now was the time to change the subject. 'We have news, too.'

'Eeh, you kept that quiet. Don't say as you're being posted? I thought you were safely tucked away in Lincolnshire for the duration.'

'So did we, Rosie, but we didn't want to be, so we both applied for transfers. It's all right working in the observation field, but not challenging, and we didn't think it used all of our skills to best advantage.'

'Oh? I hope you're not going to be doing owt that's dangerous?'

'Everything's dangerous these days, Florrie. Even us sitting here in the heart of London, enjoying pie and peas. But we're not fully sure what we'll be doing, so we can't tell you much.'

'That sounds ominous. I thought, with us going to an island that hadn't seen any trouble, Rosie safe in Herne Bay and you two tucked away in Lincolnshire, we'd all make it through this nightmare.'

'Well, like you, we want to help the nightmare end. We

don't know yet what we are going to be asked to do, only that our language skills will be useful.'

They all fell quiet, each with their own thoughts, wondering about the uncertain future. A sigh from Marjie broke the silence. 'It is a terrible nightmare. The uncertainty is the worst thing.'

The sisters all looked at each other. Sibbie could see they were a little shamefaced. Yes, they were doing their bit, and so were their half-brothers – Billy, who was away from home, and Roderick, who'd stepped up and was working tirelessly with the lifeboat crew, going out with them whenever he could, not to mention fishing on a daily basis, a very dangerous occupation. – But they knew their mum and stepfather were safe up in Scotland, just as she did. None of them had to face what Marjie had to contend with.

'Oh, I'm sorry. Look, this is meant to be a happy occasion that we can all remember – especially you sisters – and I've dampened it.'

'Naw, lass. It's good to share our worries. And you have more than most,' Rosie said as she gave Marjie a hug. 'Eeh, I'm glad I've met you, Marjie. We've heard so much about you that I feel I knaw you. Anyroad, we're all rooting for your family. And whatever it is you are assigned to, don't forget that if it's near London, I'm only at Herne Bay. I can come and meet the pair of you any time. I can be in London in half an hour.'

'That would be lovely, Rosie.' Marjie gave her a smile.

Holding Marjie's hand, Sibbie decided to change the subject. 'Anyway, there must be good news on the horizon. Has any of you any love-life to report?'

'That means you have, Sibbie. By, I can see it on your face. Who is he? One of them Canadian pilots?'

'No, Florrie. Not nearly warm. What about you, Rosie – you're blushing. You have, haven't you? You've fallen in love; come on, tell.'

'Er, well . . . Naw, I ain't. There's naw time for that; it's work, work, work. But I can see, as Florrie says, that you've been up to sommat.'

'Paulo! Paulo loves me.'

All three clapped their hands together. 'Oh, Sibbie, I'm right pleased for you, lass. You've carried a torch for Paulo for a long time.'

'You've all teased me about him, you mean. But yes, you're right, Daisy. I have carried a torch for Paulo since I were knee-high to a donkey, as they say. Right from my first visit to France. And it seems that he has for me. I had a letter. I'm so happy.'

Happiness wasn't the entire truth of how she felt; more a sad longing, and a deep hope for Paulo's safety. But she was glad this turn in the conversation had done what she intended and lifted the mood.

'Well, we'd better make a move.'

'Oh, naw, Florrie, is that the time? I don't want you to go.'

Sibbie suddenly realized how upset Rosie was going to be, not to have her sisters in the same country, as she jumped up and clung to Florrie.

'Don't make it any harder for us, Rosie lass.'

As Daisy wiped a tear away, Sibbie felt a surge of emotion as the reality of the situation hit her. The four of them had been together most of their lives, or at least within a distance where they could reach one another, but now two of them were going thousands of miles away. Fear came to her, as she let her mind visit what she'd refused to think about.

Florrie and Daisy would be on a ship voyage for weeks and weeks, and the seas were so dangerous. *Oh God!*

She'd envied them, but now she was afraid for them.

At the station they all hugged and hugged, as if for the very last time. Marjie looked lost as she tried to comfort them all.

It was Daisy who, as usual, settled everything down. 'Eeh, this won't do; me make-up's run all down me face, and me a sister an' all. Let's all start to laugh instead of cry. Let's have a happy send-off, eh?'

It took an extreme effort, but Sibbie did make them all laugh. 'You look like a panda, Daisy – how much mascara did you use? I bet Rimmel's got none left.'

The giggles were watery, nervous ones, but they were giggles, and they lightened the mood.

'Ech, help me . . . Naw, don't spit on your hanky, our Rosie. That's what Ma used to do when we were kids. I hated it when she rubbed me face with her wet hanky.'

This made them laugh even more, as memories came from one girl and then another.

'I have some toilet water. I'll put that on my handkerchief, and you can tidy up your eyes with that.'

'Ta, Marjella. Somebody with a sensible suggestion at last.'

With Daisy and Florrie looking more presentable, they all bravely walked them towards the group of nurses wearing the same grey-and-maroon nurse's uniform. Then as they disappeared, only to reappear with their heads hanging out of a window, they all waved and waved, until the smoke puffing from the engine took them from view. Silence fell for a moment. Sibbie felt lost. It was as if a large part of her had left on that train.

## CHAPTER EIGHT

# London and Portpatrick

## Sibbie and Marjie

The vast buildings of London that still stood seemed to engulf Sibbie, as she and Marjie alighted from their taxi in Baker Street. As Sibbie looked up, she had the feeling they were proudly proclaiming to the world that they had survived the Blitz with honours.

Finding Druce & Co. furniture store on the corner, as instructed, the girls didn't speak as they entered the hallway of the doorway next to the shop. Sibbie's first impression was of entering someone's home, as the thick golden-brown carpet silenced their tread.

They were shown into a large waiting room with leather chairs placed around the walls. A table in the centre held newspapers and magazines. Neither Sibbie nor Marjie bothered with these, and both of them, attacked by nerves, sat together and waited quietly.

Sibbie was called first by a young army officer, who didn't introduce herself. 'Would you come this way, Miss Roford? You are to see CD. We don't use names or ranks here, just code letters. M will also be present.'

This added to Sibbie's nerves, but she marched behind

86

the officer, feeling as if she were on a charge for some misdemeanour.

Sitting in a cafe an hour later, Sibbie could tell that although they hadn't yet talked about their experience, Marjie was as excited as she was. The briefing had been just that: very brief and to the point. 'You will be told nothing about the expectations of you, or what your role will be, until you have passed out from several training courses. The first one will be an assessment process – a preliminary training course. If you get through that, you will be told what is next. In the meantime, say absolutely nothing about your experience today, or what you know so far. Enjoy the rest of your leave, as if it is your last, and report back here one week from today, at ten a.m. precisely.' And that was that.

'What did you think, Marjie?'

'I'm not sure, but somehow, I don't think we should discuss it here. Let's talk when we're back at our boarding house, as we pack for Scotland. We only have two hours before we catch our overnight train, and I'm hungry. I think I'll order a pie and peas – I really enjoyed that yesterday.'

With this, Sibbie felt she had learned her first lesson, and that Marjie was more prepared than she was for what might lie in store for them. Feeling a little ashamed of herself, she left the subject alone. 'That would be lovely.'

As Marjie got up to order, Sibbie had the strange feeling that a change had already taken place in her cousin and her best friend in the world. It was as if she was saying, 'I'm ready.' Sibbie wondered if she should feel like that, instead of having this excited feeling of a great adventure opening up to her. But then it was an adventure, and surely that was a better way of looking at what might lie ahead for them, as it would mean they accepted whatever they were getting into.

Shrugging her shoulders, she decided that however Marjie wanted to deal with whatever lay in store for them, she would respect it. One thing she did know: both of them wanted – no, longed – for this to lead to them working in France. How, and as what, she didn't know; her imagination would only show her the terrifying world of an undercover agent. *Am I up to that?* Something told Sibbie that she would soon find out.

On the overnight train to Scotland, they found themselves in a carriage on their own and were at last able to chat, as there had been no time once they arrived at the boarding house, having had to wait longer for their meal than they had anticipated.

'My impression was that we are to be tested to our limits, Sibbie. And if we get through, I think it is certain that we will be working undercover. Why else would such secrecy surround our future?'

'Yes, I've come to that conclusion, and it frightens me.'

'I think that to be frightened is good. It gives you an edge and keeps you on your toes. I'm desperate to succeed. Even if we don't go to France, I will stand a good chance of getting information as part of an undercover movement.'

'I am desperate, too, for the same reason and the possibility of being able to contact Paulo.'

'Oh dear, do you think our motives are the wrong ones?'

Sibbie thought about this for a moment. 'Marjie, I think they may be, but strong motivation is a good thing.'

'Yes, I can see that.'

'Then I can't see us failing. Let's try to get some sleep, eh? It's been a long day.' With this, Sibbie put her rucksack on the bench seat opposite, to use as a pillow, and unfolded the blanket that had been left for her use. Marjie did the same.

The gentle sway of the train, and the rhythm of its wheels on the track, soon lulled Sibbie to sleep. A sleep in which she dreamed she was running across a field and Paulo was running towards her. Happiness filled her, until they reached each other and Paulo suddenly disappeared. Anguish got her waking for a moment, only to fall back to sleep almost immediately and for the dream to resume. Now they were together in a beautiful, peaceful light, holding hands, and Paulo was looking into her eyes. 'We'll never be apart again, my darling Sibbie.'

The next time she woke, Sibbie checked her watch and found it was five in the morning. She could see nothing through the windows, as it was still dark. Sitting up, she couldn't understand the unsettled feeling that haunted her from her dream. Shaking it off, she decided to go to the bathroom a few carriages down and freshen up, before Marjie woke.

By the time this was done, Sibbie had rationalized her feelings and laughed at herself. If the dream could come true, she'd be the happiest person alive, though she hoped the part where Paulo disappeared never, ever happened.

'Ech, lass, it's good to see you. Your ma's going to be over the moon. And this here is Marjella. My, you're a pretty lass, just like that photo Mags showed me of your ma. Now, let me give you a cuddle, Sibbie lass. Eeh, I've missed you.'

Aunt Betsy's cuddles were always comforting. Her huge,

soft bosom was like a cushion of love to Sibbie and had, on many an occasion, eased her distress if something had upset her. Just to be snuggled into Aunt Betsy was a good feeling.

'Now, Sibbie lass, your ma's in the shop. We have a different set-up in there. We're using the storeroom at the back as a workroom where we make warm clothing to send to the Red Cross. By, it's grand work. We make socks and woolly vests, and scarves and hats. Our outworkers help, and some of the youngsters of the village an' all. They knit squares, which we sew together to make blankets.'

'Well, you have been busy. Daisy told us you were both going to make an effort for the war. I think what you are doing is wonderful. And I'm glad you're busy, and coping.'

'It helps, let's put it that way, but an aching heart for you all is my constant companion.'

Sibbie took Betsy into her arms this time and held her close. 'We have it to do, Aunt Betsy. And remember, you prepared your children – and Mum prepared me – for whatever we came up against in life, so we're all well equipped to cope.'

'I hope so, lass, I hope so.'

Coming out of the cuddle, Sibbie saw Betsy wipe away a tear. This brought home how much she was suffering. 'At least you still have Rod at home. Oh, I know as he is in danger out at sea all the time, but Angus will keep him safe.'

'Aye, he is, lass. A very brave lad, and I'm proud of him. Like you say, he is in danger, and that adds to me worries. But you knaw, no matter how long this war goes on, they won't take him to fight. He's had a lot of pain in the arches of his feet and the doctor told him that he has flat feet, and he should be glad of them as they'd save him from going to war. That put him in the doldrums as he's been counting the days off, hoping he'd make the age limit before it was all over, but for me it were the best news going.'

Sibbie nearly did a jig, she felt that happy. 'That's good news, Aunt Betsy. He'll never have to go to war now. Have you written to the girls about this? I know they will be so happy to hear their brother will always be here with you.'

'Aye, though when Daisy and Florrie will get their letters, I don't knaw. My only hope now is that Rosie isn't sent abroad an' all, then I'll have peace of mind about two of me brood.'

Sibbie didn't answer this, but told Betsy, 'Daisy and Florrie got off all right. We were at the station with Rosie to see them board the train.'

'Eeh, I'm glad. That's made me day. I thought they'd have no one to wave them off, as Rosie wasn't certain she'd get leave. Ta, Sibbie. Now, we're leaving poor Marjella to twiddle her thumbs. Come on, lass, let me greet you the northern way, with a hug.'

Marjie just giggled and accepted the hug. Sibbie could see that she was getting used to the way of how things were done up in the North.

'You should have visited us afore now, but then you had your studying, and that was important. Let me get me coat and bonnet and we'll go down to the shop. I daren't even offer you a hot cuppa, as your ma will be mad at me for not bringing you down sooner. But she couldn't take today off, as we have a collection tomorrow. She's the knitter and, as you knaw, the one who is wonderful with her sewing – you can't even see where she's joined them squares together. I'm all right at them crafts, but not as good as Sue. I'm better at the pottery, and at painting and varnishing the pottery items for the shop.'

The girls were out of the door before all this was told to them and following Aunt Betsy down the slope.

Marjie gasped at the beauty that met them. 'It is like a painting. So different from my home by the sea. We have blue sea and sky and forests and a mountain backdrop, and here is rugged, wild and, well, stunning.'

Sibbie glowed at this praise of her home town. 'As you know, Mum's a Londoner, and did consider taking us back to London when Montel died; she loved him dearly, he was such a good friend to her, and like a father to me.'

'Yes, I have heard a lot about him from Aunt Mags – she and Montel were very much in love, weren't they? And the story of his life is fascinating, with his escape from France and then his eventual recognition by the French as a hero. I would so love to have known him.'

'Montel was an amazing man, and being here I feel so close to him, even though it was the scene of his terrible death. I feel he rests easy on these shores. And I think that's what helped Mum make her mind up to stay. Though she kept some of her heritage – always insisting that I call her "Mum" and never letting me pick up the local Scottish accent, or the Blackburn one that Betsy and the girls have. Not that there is anything wrong with either. I just think she wanted to hold on to a bit of herself.'

Marjie linked arms with Sibbie and then did the same with Betsy, who smiled warmly. Sibbie thought it a lovely gesture and squeezed Marjie's hand in appreciation.

'I'm glad you like our little neck of the woods, Marjella. I love it, but by, I miss Blackburn at times. Folk here are lovely, but it ain't like them back in me home town. I knew them all as lived around. I expect it were the same for your ma, Sibbie, though she never says so. What you just said shows it, though – there's nowt can substitute for your beginnings. Now, here we are.'

Betsy opened the huge wooden doors at the back of the shop building, which were about the only reminder that this had once been a boathouse.

'Mum! Oh, Mum!' For some reason, Sibbie felt all her pent-up emotion gush from her at the sight of her mother. Tears streamed down her face.

'Sibbie, my Sibbie. Oh, it's so good to hold you. I've missed you so much,' Susan said.

Hearing this and the sob in her mum's voice, Sibbie controlled her feelings. The last thing she wanted was to worry her mother. 'We're a daft pair. I didn't mean to blab. I'm just so happy to see you.'

'And me, you. How long can you stay?'

'A few days. We have to report to London in a week . . . Oh, I mean— Well, I do have news, Mum, but I'll tell you when you're not working. Now, let me introduce Marjie.'

'Well, Marjie, it's lovely to meet you at last. I can see you are a Roford, like . . . I mean, I – I . . .'

'It's all right, honestly. I am like my mother, though everyone says I am like my father as well.'

The moment was awkward for Sibbie, as it brought her history into focus – the long-running affair that her mum had had with Marjie's late uncle, Harold Roford, her genetic father. But there seemed to be something more. As if her mum had nearly blurted something out. What it was, Sibbie couldn't imagine. Only now, Mum was all of a fluster.

Sibbie took the best action she thought possible. 'We'll go for a walk, Mum, and let you finish your work. We'll climb the steps to the Portpatrick Hotel. Do they still have afternoon teas? I'm famished.'

'Eeh, we can put the kettle on here, lass – can't we, Susan?'

'But we need to eat, Aunt Betsy. We snatched a sandwich on the station at Glasgow, between running to catch the connection to Stranraer. And then we had the bus journey here. We'll be fine – a walk will do us good.'

'Are you sure, Sibbie? I didn't embarrass you, did I, girl?'

'No, Mum, why should you? We'll see you later, when you get in. Is the key in the usual place or is Rory home?'

'No, he's out on his deliveries. Not that he has much meat to deliver these days, but he comes by a bit from the poachers. Though he spends most of his time on the boats, with Angus and Roderick. We're planning to all eat at ours together tonight. I've everything ready to put on, and Angus will bring the fish to fry – he'll gut it ready for me.'

'That sounds wonderful, Mum. I love fresh fish. See you later then.' Sibbie linked arms with Marjie and turned her round as she called her goodbyes.

'Sorry about that, Marjie. Poor Mum got herself tongue-tied.'

Marjie was quiet for a moment. When she spoke, she shocked Sibbie with what she said. 'Sibbie, I've always thought there is a lot about the past that we don't know. And I got the feeling then that your mum knows what it is. I felt there was more than her just having an affair with my mama's brother, Harold. I won't call him "Uncle", as from what I have heard about him, he doesn't deserve the title . . . Oh, I'm sorry, I know he was your father, but . . .'

'Don't be. It has given me a lovely cousin in you, and a lovely aunt in Aunt Flors, not to mention how my relationship with Aunt Mags became so close. That said, I hate to even mention his name. I do get the feeling, though, that

94

my mother once loved Harold very much. I don't suppose we will ever know the truth about what went on.'

'No, nor why my mama and papa ended up in France, almost exiles, and had nothing more to do with Mama's family.'

'Let's forget it all for now. Come on, it's quite a climb to the hotel – that's it up there. I hope they have something nice to serve us.'

The hotel manager remembered Sibbie and fussed over them, bringing them delicious baked ham sandwiches and even a slice of fruitcake. 'Chef has found some ingenious ways of adapting his recipes to the shortages, and I bet you can't tell the difference, Sibbie. Tuck in and enjoy; we're very proud of you and all our young people, for all they are doing in the war effort. Though we miss you all, and your giggles.'

Sibbie laughed. 'I bet it's really peaceful now without us. Thanks, Mr Duffy, this looks lovely and is very welcome.'

Mr Duffy beamed before leaving them alone. Sibbie glanced out of the window. Below her lay the whole of the bay of Portpatrick – her home. A wistful feeling entered her, one she hadn't felt since this adventure began, but one that tugged at her heart now, as she wondered if she would ever see it again after she left to take up her new challenge in life.

Sibbie ached in places she didn't know she had, and neither sitting nor standing helped to relieve them. Marjie had fared better, sailing through the initial rigorous training with ease. Her encouragement had been all that had got Sibbie through it.

They had arrived in Arisag House, somewhere in the

Inverness area, a week after they had left Portpatrick, and after a wonderful few days of fun and laughter, which ended in floods of tears as they said their goodbyes. Now, five weeks later, after intensive training over the unwelcoming terrain of Inverness, they were packing, ready to take the next step of their training.

Already equipped with skills in unarmed combat, taught by two ex-Shanghai municipal police officers, Sibbie was amazed and a little frightened to realize that she could kill a person with techniques that wouldn't alert anyone in the vicinity. The chilling methods went under the sinister name of 'silent killing' and involved using a knife or quick strangulation, and the even tougher breaking of someone's neck.

Just the thought of having to kill someone – silently or not – had shown her the reality of her own and Marjie's situation and had terrified Sibbie. But she'd got over this and had enjoyed, and really excelled at, the next method of killing they'd learned: how to 'shoot from the hip', a technique where they had to hold their gun close to their hips rather than taking aim; she had been surprised by how quickly she learned to hit the life-sized figure that was fixed to a winch and came at her with great speed.

In this she'd fared better than Marjie, and it had been Sibbie's turn to help and encourage. They would practise together, with Sibbie hiding and jumping out in front of Marjie, who would have to get her pretend gun into position and shout, 'Bang!' just at the right moment. Always they ended up laughing and messing around as if they were youngsters again. These moments helped them both keep everything in perspective.

The demolition and explosives training was something they both enjoyed and were good at. Using dummy explosives, they practised real-life scenarios that got their adrenaline pumping, as the training for this was carried out on a stretch of train line, with a real train coming at them. Laying the charges in darkness, and timing yourself so that you could be in hiding before the train hit them, gave them a feeling for what sabotage meant and how dangerous it was. They both took this part of the training very seriously and soon became experts.

They had become stronger, not only physically, but mentally and emotionally. And Sibbie felt at last that she was ready – well, at least to take the next step: further training, which they had been informed would be in the New Forest. For Sibbie, it couldn't come soon enough, as she felt eager now to get to the next stage, and knew that Marjie was, too.

Still there was no news from family in France, and this worried Sibbie, though she marvelled at how Marjie was coping – in the daytime, that was. Sometimes at night she heard sniffles, but she left Marjie her privacy and pretended to be asleep. She prayed fervently that they would hear from them soon and that it would be good news.

CHAPTER NINE

# Eastern France

## Ella and Flors

Flors sat with Cyrus on one side of her, and Ella holding a fretful Lonia on her knee on the other. They were all tired, cold and afraid. The stone floor they sat on, staring at the whitewashed, concrete walls, added to their discomfort. Part of the wall opposite jutted out, forming a cubicle, which housed a stinking lavatory, of the kind you had to stand over with one leg on each side.

'Shush, Lonia. Don't make any noise. We don't want the men outside to know we are here.'

The men were German soldiers. Their presence struck terror into Flors's heart. She clung to Cyrus and prayed that Ella would be successful in quietening Lonia. They had travelled more than three hundred miles, on foot and in trucks driven by sympathetic 'safe-house' owners, and for a short duration by train.

Flors had felt elated when they had boarded the train, thinking their long, arduous journey would soon be over, but three stations in they'd encountered a checkpoint. They got through by both Flors and Ella feigning sleep, while mercifully Lonia was truly asleep. Cyrus talked for them, telling the soldiers that he was travelling with his wife and his sister and her child to visit his parents, who lived in eastern France. He used a mixture of French and German, as those living in the east, near the border of Germany, spoke both languages. He showed them the false papers they had been given at the first safe house they'd stayed in.

Whether these soldiers were fed up or at the end of their duty time, they didn't know, but they were surprised by how readily they accepted what they were told and shown. But they dared not take the risk of being challenged again, so they had got off the train at the next station, near Valence.

It had taken them three days to reach Voiron. The bitter October winds and mostly rough terrain, through forests and over hilly country, had left them exhausted. For most of the journey they took turns to carry Lonia on their backs, but she did make noble efforts to walk a lot of the way. In the relative safety of the trees Lonia was happiest, but when they had to walk through a built-up area she picked up on the nerves of the adults and became fretful.

Their last safe house had been an apartment near the church of Saint-Bruno in Voiron, within a hundred miles of Geneva. They'd eaten hungrily, devouring the local cheese and home-made bread offered to them, and had been glad of a bath and beds to sleep in. The food packed up for them was a godsend and had sustained them as they'd travelled, heading for a farm near Aix-les-Bains, where they would be picked up and taken to a makeshift airfield used by the RAF to drop supplies to the Resistance army. From there they would be flown to Switzerland in a plane owned by a wealthy businessman, who now used his plane, which had once been an indulgent toy, to help the Resistance. His missions took people to safety or fetched supplies from Switzerland for them. He always flew very low, and they were told that sometimes he had to make his passengers parachute, if the weather was too bad for him to land. He would only take their money in order to help the Resistance, as he did with all that he was paid by those fleeing France. Their arrival in Aix-les-Bains would be radioed through, so that the pilot could make the necessary checks for his next scheduled flight. They all prayed these would prove that a landing was possible.

Now, just a few miles out of Voiron, they had come across a convoy of German soldiers taking a break. Dashing back to this building, which they had passed by, they had taken shelter. Cyrus had thought it the ruin of an old farmhouse, as there was no other explanation for it having a toilet. But it hadn't looked like a wreck of a home. A square building, it had only one door. The floor was concreted, the walls ran with green water and a thick mildew had formed around the one window, which lay to the right of them.

'I'll take a look and see what the soldiers are doing.'

Flors watched Cyrus creep over to the window. He took one look and shot backwards, his face white, beads of sweat forming on his head. Before he had time to speak, the door opened and two soldiers, laughing together, entered. Without looking into the corner where the family were huddled – or at the window by which Cyrus now stood, like a statue pressed up against the wall – and just inches from Flors, the soldiers threw down their cigarette butts and went towards the toilet.

Terror held Flors stiff; she was unable to release the deep breath she'd taken in, as she turned her head to the left and looked at Ella, who had her hand over Lonia's mouth. This must be a regular stopping point for the soldiers as, still laughing, they made straight for the cubicle. The sound of them both urinating, and giggling while they did so, told Flors they must somehow have stood on each side of the hole. Although she could only pick up a smattering of what they said, they were acting the fool and peeing on each other's shoes, as any young men might do. In a strange way, she felt sadness at this thought. No matter what side they were on, at the end of the day they were just youngsters like Freddy and Randie.

Then anger seeped into her. No, these were not just any youngsters, but the sons of a country that was tearing Europe apart, as it had done twenty years ago, and she wanted to go over and beat them with her fists.

When the soldiers appeared again, they were still doing up the buttons of their flies. This was holding their attention as they made for the door.

They were only a second from leaving, when one of them dropped something. As he turned to pick it up, he caught sight of Cyrus. Shock registered on the soldier's face and time was suspended.

'*Wer bist du?*' *Who are you?* His question brought the world alive again, and Flors felt it tumble around her.

Answering in German, Cyrus told him the same story he'd told the soldiers on the train, then he added, 'We were out for a walk and came in here to rest.'

'*Nein! Sie verstecken sich!*'

With this, the soldier pulled out his gun and pointed it at Cyrus. His fellow soldier ran outside, shouting.

Ella whimpered. She'd dropped her hand from Lonia's mouth and was now holding the crying child to her.

In French, Flors asked, 'What did he say, Cyrus?'

'He said he thinks we are hiding.'

'*Halt die schnauze!*'

Flors's heart, already heavy, beat strongly against the side of her chest. These words she did understand – the soldier had told them not to talk. But if she had felt terror before, it was nothing compared to what she felt as Cyrus suddenly lurched at the soldier. A gunshot rang out, deafening her and making Ella scream out, 'No . . . No!'

Cyrus stood over the soldier's slumped body. Without stopping to explain, he bent and grabbed the man's rifle. His own gun came flying through the air towards Flors. 'Quick, Flors – the window. Shoot any approaching soldier!'

Not knowing whether or not she could do this, she stood up slowly.

'Please, Flors, we cannot let them take Ella and Lonia.'

The sudden realization of their plight – and especially that of Ella – urged Flors's body forward.

'You have three bullets left: make every one count. There seem to be about eight soldiers. I should have six shots. It's our only chance.'

Looking through the window, Flors saw the soldiers creeping forward on their bellies; the sound of the shot must have made them take up this position. Glancing at Cyrus, she saw him riffling the body at his feet. When he stood up, he held a hand-grenade. Hope seeped into Flors, but then she realized that the other soldiers must have these weapons too, and her hope died.

'As soon as they get near, fire.'

She couldn't answer. Peering towards where the Germans were, she saw a hand come up. 'He has a grenade!'

Another shot almost deafened her as the sound ricocheted off the walls. A crack shot, Cyrus had hit the arm of the soldier wielding the grenade and had stopped him from throwing it. Within seconds an explosion saw the bodies of four soldiers – those surrounding the one who'd dropped the hand-grenade – do a hideous dance in the air, before coming to rest, never to move again.

Cyrus pulled the pin of his grenade and threw it among the remaining soldiers. Another deafening explosion, and then nothing – no sound, no movement, nothing. Not even a bird tweeting broke the silence.

'Stay where you are, Flors. Keep watching.'

Cyrus's voice sounded muffled and a long way away, but she did as he bade her and kept her eyes peeled.

A gun being cocked and pointed through the window and into her face shocked Flors. *'Lassen sie ihre Waffe fallen!'*

Flors dropped her gun and raised her hands. Sheer terror shook her body as the soldier ordered more of his men to come round to the front of the building. The realization hit her that the Germans must have split up and surrounded the building. Her own death stared her in the face.

Her life flashed through her head and she saw her happy family laughing and joking on a balmy evening at the beginning of summer. Part of her wanted to smile as she remembered the antics of Freddy and Randie, as they shook a bottle of the new fizzy wine that their vineyard had produced and sprayed each other. Mayhem had broken out, but happy, funny mayhem. The thought faded as more commands came from the German: 'All of you, drop your weapons and stand back from the window and the door. NOW!'

Flors jumped back. She beckoned to Ella to run into the toilet area, but Ella didn't move; she stood, as if frozen, against the wall. Lonia's eyes were as wide as saucers and her mouth dropped open, spit dribbling from her mouth.

'It's all right, Lonia. We'll take care of you.'

Looking from them to Cyrus as he said this, Flors saw

that he hadn't dropped his weapon. She went to shout at him to do as the Germans instructed, but at that moment Cyrus dashed outside, shooting as he did so.

Flors screamed at him to come back, falling onto her knees. 'Cyrus, no! Oh God!'

Frantic orders shouted by the Germans saw one lone soldier come through the door. With his gun, he indicated that she should move over to where Ella was. Crawling on her hands and knees, Flors listened to the panic outside and knew, by the way the voices faded, that Cyrus had run into the forest and the rest of the soldiers were chasing him.

Finding Ella's hand, she held it in her own, trying to find some courage to give her. But Ella's eyes held despair and fear, which Flors didn't know how to combat. Their situation was desperate and their lives were in grave danger. But with the courageous action that her darling Cyrus had taken, he was in even greater danger than they were, and she feared she'd never see him again. *Oh, Cyrus, my love, I cannot bear to lose you. Please, God, let him get to safety.*

His action, Flors knew, had been a last-ditch attempt to save them all. He had the dead soldier's ammunition belt and a powerful gun, and every chance of winning this last stand, given his training in warfare. Putting her arm around Ella, Flors pulled her close. The soldier demanded that they let go of each other and stand apart. Flors could see that he was only very young and that his nerves were on edge, just as theirs were. She and Ella were probably similar in age to his mother, and he might have a younger sister like Lonia. This gave her courage because, if her thoughts were true, that might make them safer. She imagined her own sons in a similar position and knew they wouldn't shoot their prisoners. They wouldn't be able to.

The sound of shooting in the distance filled her with fear. Flors held her breath. It stopped and then started again. *They've caught up with my darling. Please, please, God, let him be the victor.*

She watched the soldier, saw a nerve jumping under his eye. His hands shook. He backed to the door, keeping his gun trained on her. She knew that he wanted to know what was happening, as she saw him bend backwards and peer towards the trees. Then her heart dropped as he gave a smile of relief and renewed his stance.

Two soldiers came through the door. One was bleeding from a wound on his arm, and both were agitated. Straining to understand what was being said, Flors could only make out a few words, but realized that the rest of his comrades were dead, and that the infidel was still out there and, if they didn't leave, they would all die, too.

Turning to her and Ella, the young soldier demanded that they follow him and hurry. When they didn't move, one of the soldiers who had just arrived fired a shot in the air. Lonia screamed. Ella gasped.

'*Schneller. Schneller!*'

At this command for them to move faster, the German came forward and pointed his gun at Lonia's forehead.

'*Non! Non!*' And then, in broken German mixed with French, Ella told him that they would do everything he asked.

Flors nodded. It wasn't what her instincts told her to do, but what choice did they have? The evil in this soldier's eyes spoke of him having no compunction about shooting Lonia.

Bundled into the first truck of four in the convoy, they lay with the barrel of this evil man's gun trained on them. The other two soldiers had got into the cab. As the truck set off over the rough terrain, their bodies were rolled from side to side. Dampness soaked Flors's trousers. Lonia was between them, sobbing her distress, and Flors realized the poor child had wet herself. Her heart went out to her and Ella. To fear for your own safety was terrifying, but to fear for your child's safety was beyond words.

The reality of what was happening hit Flors. *Will they realize I am British and, worse than that, that Ella is a Jew?*

A tear seeped out of the corner of her eye. She looked over at Ella and saw that her heart was breaking. Flors tried to give a smile of reassurance, but a sob from deep within her stopped her. Silently they wept tears of despair.

They had only been travelling for about an hour – their progress slow as the terrain became even rougher – when, without warning, the soldier banged on the window of the cab and called for it to halt. When the driver came round and opened the truck, Flors saw that outside there was no sign of any buildings; just trees and more trees on each side of the road.

The driver asked what was wrong. The answer sent a streak of horror through Flors and, by Ella's gasp, she knew that she too had grasped the meaning.

'I am ready to have some fun.' The soldier grabbed his crotch and laughed, indicating that watching Flors's and Ella's bodies roll from side to side had made him feel randy.

The younger man jumped down from the cab and laughed. 'No, they are like my mother.'

The other soldiers were amused at this and told him that he could keep guard and watch them enjoying themselves.

'*Non – nein! Bitte nicht.*' Ella beseeching them was dealt with by her being pulled by her ankles to the edge of the truck.

Without thinking, Flors screamed: 'No – don't! Stop!'

'*Engländerin? Raus hier!*'

In the moment of terror, she'd given away their nationality. With fear gripping her even deeper now, Flors did as he instructed and got out of the truck. What was said next she didn't understand, but it was stated with extreme anger and hatred.

The butt of the evil soldier's gun dug into her ribs. She doubled over in pain, but then called out in agony when her hair felt as though it was coming out at the roots, as he grabbed her by it and excruciating pain seized her.

Rendered helpless, Flors felt herself being dragged into the trees and then flung to the floor in the first clearing. Fearing she was going to be shot, she closed her eyes and prayed fervently. But another blow to the side of her face, and being commanded to remove her trousers and knickers, brought the realization of what was going to happen.

With a gun held at her forehead, she did as she was told. The sound of Ella's cries, and the grunting noises coming from the direction of the truck, filled her with despair, as she knew that poor Ella was being raped. Feeling consumed with rage, Flors kicked out at the German who held her captive. She missed hitting him in his groin, but landed a heavy kick to his stomach.

She scrambled away as he gasped for breath, but he recovered quickly and caught up with her, cracking her head with the butt of his gun. Her eyes clouded, her head spun and the sounds of the world faded to a muffled pitch, where she couldn't make out Ella's cries from the annoyed squawks of the birds and the squeals of forest animals disturbed from their rest.

Though she knew her body was being manoeuvred, she couldn't stop it happening. She felt the German enter her and tasted his panting breath, which reeked of the many cigarettes he'd smoked on the journey; she felt the despair of her rape, and the violation made her want to vomit. But she couldn't protest.

On and on it went, until at last he became still. His head was near hers, and his moans and grunts sickened her as she felt him pulsating inside her.

No sooner had he rolled off, and the thought came to Flors that it was over, than she felt the weight of a different kind. This soldier wasn't so heavy. His movements weren't so hurried and brutal. He lay a moment, stroking her hair.

Flors tried to fight through the layers of what felt like spider's webs clogging her head, but she couldn't. She thought a sound came from her as she tried to say, 'No, please don't.' But whether it had or not, the quickening of the German's breath and his fumbling told her that she was to be raped for the second time, and this was surely the young man who had said that she was like his mother.

Somehow this disgusted her more than the older man doing what he'd done. This was like her sons carrying out this despicable act. Finding her voice, she shouted, '*Non – nein!*' and twisted her body. But other hands came and held her, and a hateful voice in the background urged on her rapist. Once more she knew she was being violated, and the feel of this hurried, inexperienced German was even more repulsive to her, if that was possible.

His thrust was hard, and his feelings came out in more than the grunts the other one had used, as he loudly groaned his pleasure and called out something she didn't understand. Nor did he last as long, for soon he was hollering and pressing down on her, and once more Flors felt the soldier pulsating his seed into her. With this, he slumped down on her, making it difficult for her to breathe. His senior pulled him off, laughing as he did so. The laugh mocked her, but congratulated him.

Flors didn't move. Still in a half-conscious state, humiliated but unable to influence anything that happened around her, she tried to focus on listening out for Ella. But Ella's cries had stopped. The sound of the back of the truck being banged shut made her jump. Peering through the haziness, she saw the Germans still standing over her, even though the engine of the truck roared into life. *Why aren't they taking me back to the truck?* A gun was cocked. Flors froze. *They're going to kill me!* Terror gripped her, making it impossible to breathe.

A shot rang out, and then another in quick succession. And yet – nothing. She hadn't been hit! Confused, she forced her eyes open. No one was there. She heard the truck roar away. And then a sound to the side of her. Looking in that direction, she saw the bodies of the Germans slumped in a heap next to her.

Arms came around her, lifting her. 'My darling – my Flors, my love.' Tears that hadn't come from her own eyes wet her face . . . *Cyrus?* 'I'm here, my darling . . . I'm so sorry.' His voice held his anguish. 'I criss-crossed the forest, sometimes having you in my sight, sometimes losing you, but always finding a shorter route than the road takes until I caught up with you. I – I didn't make it in time to save you . . . from . . . Oh, my darling, my love.'

Tormented that he knew by the state of her what the soldiers had done, but comforted by his voice, she tried to tell him it wasn't his fault, but the fog in her brain thickened and she felt darkness descend upon her, taking her into the blessed peace his presence gave her.

# CHAPTER TEN

# France and Switzerland

## Ella and Flors

Ella ached all over. Her hand felt cold and stiff as she held onto a silent Lonia. They stood looking at the huge gates. She knew they were still in France, somewhere south of Reims, as she had seen signs for that city on the journey, but exactly where they were, she had no idea.

After the soldier had raped her, he'd bundled her into the back of the truck. She'd waited, praying that Flors would be brought back, but at the sound of gunshots, the soldier had slammed the tailgate and driven off at a roaring speed. He'd driven all night without stopping. Ella had slept some of the time, but most of the journey she'd fretted about being separated from Flors, and with worry about what had happened to her dear friend. She felt certain Cyrus was dead, and she feared that Flors was, too. The thought was unbearable to her, and yet she couldn't cry out against it. Her soul had been drained.

When they'd reached a checkpoint she'd heard the soldier shout out what had happened to the convoy, and demand that they radio HQ and report the incident. Leaving her lying in the back of the truck, he'd disappeared. Ella was glad of this, as she never wanted to look into his hateful face again or smell him anywhere near her. He'd conjured up terrible memories from her past that she'd tried to suppress – of her time with Shamus – but at this moment she thought of the soldier as the viler of the two.

But now she had knowledge of even greater evil. Having been picked up from the checkpoint, she'd been taken to Paris, a long, arduous journey crouching in the back of another truck, clinging onto poor Lonia. Having been separated from Lonia, she'd been shoved into a cell in Gestapo headquarters and interrogated for hours.

'Who helped you? And who were the others you were travelling with? Where is your husband?'

'No one helped me. My friends are dead. They, too, were British, but your soldiers killed them – they raped us. RAPED ME AND MY FRIEND!' This scream had earned her another slap, which calmed her. 'My husband is dead also.'

'LIAR! Your child says that he left you to go back to your home. Where is he?'

The realization that they were questioning Lonia terrified her. 'I don't know. I – I had to leave him and take my child. I had to try to get her to safety.'

'But not your other child – your son?'

*Oh God, Lonia has mentioned Paulo. My son, my darling son, is in danger!*

'Where is your son? Paulo Rennaise? Oh yes, your child told us that he has a different name from her. And do you know what else she told us? She told us all about her family. That she has an aunt and uncle and a cousin living in Poland, and that you are sad because you cannot get any news of them. Aunt Calek and Uncle Abram. And she told me that

111

she thinks their surname is Wronski. Ha! I have news of them. I wired my comrade who is on the occupying force in Poland, and they are dead. Dead, like you will be! You are a Wronski. YOU ARE A FILTHY JEW!'

Ella had wanted to scream out the pain of hearing this news, which she'd prayed so hard not to be true, though the fate of her darling Calek had been preying on her mind.

'Answer me!'

'No! No, we are British . . . I have a British passport. Calek and Abram . . . they are friends. I – I went to Poland as a girl. I made friends with Calek. I – I have always said to Lonia that Calek is like the sister I never had.'

'LIAR!'

This time the blow to her head was more severe, making her ear smart and jarring her neck on her shoulders.

'We will make further enquiries. Your child will tell us so much more, if we start to slap her.'

'No-o-o . . . No, please don't hurt her.' Between rasping sobs, with tears running from her eyes, Ella had gasped out, 'I – I am of Jewish descent. I'm not a practising Jew. I . . . was brought up in Britain and never knew my family in Poland. Then, I – I discovered my father had married again. He had a daughter, Calek. I visited her. But not with my daughter, she has never been. She is British. Sh – she has a British father.'

'Ah – so, Jew, you talk when you know your child may be hurt; well, we can hurt her to get to the truth, especially now that we know she is a Jew, like her mother.'

'No . . . Please, please . . .' *Oh God, help me – help me!* 'I will tell you everything you want to know.'

'Lies, you mean.'

'No . . . If you promise not to hurt my child, I will tell

you the truth. Please . . . Oh God, please don't hurt my child.'

The questions and the torture had gone on for hours, until finally they took Ella back to her cell. Lying on the stone floor next to Lonia, she had taken comfort in seeing a glass that had once contained milk lying empty on the floor. But no comfort alleviated the hatred that she felt for herself. She had sacrificed one of her children to save the other.

She had betrayed her husband and her son. She'd admitted that they had stayed behind to fight. Telling the soldiers who Flors and Cyrus were hadn't felt so bad, as Ella was certain they were dead. *Oh God . . . That's if there is a God! If there is, how can He let such things happen? And what about me? Isn't He meant to love me? I have suffered so much in the past, and now I'm going to die. My daughter is going to die . . . And all because my father was a Jew!*

After this, the days had come and gone, marked only by the occasional bowl of slop being shoved through the door, and a trickle of light coming through the bars on the window. Ella had no idea how long she was kept there. Her fears for Lonia got her crying out in a pitiful voice for help, but no one came, and Lonia's health deteriorated.

When the door had been finally, and very suddenly, kicked open, the soldier who entered almost vomited. The smell in the cell was repugnant, as the bucket left for them to use had long overflowed. To Ella, it had become the normal smell on waking up, and was nothing worse than she'd experienced in her past life as a nurse.

'Go! Get out!'

For one wonderful moment, Ella had thought they were releasing her. She had stepped outside the cell, only to gasp

113

as a bucket of freezing water was thrown over her. Trying to protect Lonia, she grabbed her child, but the woman in front of her forced her to let go.

'The child comes with me.'

'No, no – please.'

'What kind of mother are you? The child is ill. We will look after her.'

Ella's misery had deepened when Lonia made no protest, and for the first time she realized the true state of her darling baby. Lonia's eyes were like saucers, in a face that had no flesh on it. Her teeth protruded, because her cheeks had sunk inwards.

Before Ella could say or do anything, she had been pushed back into the cell. 'Take it! Go on, take that bucket.'

Lifting the bucket caused more of its stinking contents to spill over.

'Hurry!'

The soldier's words were hard to discern from behind the handkerchief he held over his mouth and nose.

Dragging the bucket out of the cell, Ella moved towards the door that the soldier indicated. The door was opened and she found herself in a yard. 'Empty! There!'

Ella did as she was told and emptied the bucket down the uncovered hole.

'Put it back. That lid – put it back.'

The English, interspersed with German, was easy for Ella to understand.

Dragging the manhole cover back into place proved too much for her. She had collapsed into a heap. The world around her spun and, as it did so, Ella had sunk into a deep, dark hole that welcomed her into its depths.

More time had passed – Ella had no notion of how long

it was – and she had found herself in a hospital bed, surrounded by doctors and nurses. Not daring to speak, she had waited. A nurse said, 'You have had pneumonia. Do you know what that is?'

'Yes . . . I – I am a nurse.'

'You are?'

'Where's Lonia, my child – where is she?'

'She will join you tomorrow. You are going to a camp for the British.'

Ella had felt gladness enter her, as she'd realized that perhaps her troubles were over.

On the journey, she'd sat in the back of a truck with two soldiers. She could feel their eyes on her. Pulling her coat around her, against the bitter cold coming in from the top half of the truck's door, she made sure the blanket they'd been given was tucked around Lonia.

Lonia hadn't spoken a word to her. She hadn't smiled, and neither had she cried; nor had she shown any emotion on seeing her mother, after Ella didn't know how long apart.

Now the huge gates swung open. The man attending them seemed too old for the German uniform he wore. Ella stepped inside and looked around her. In front of her was a building that looked like a hotel. To her left, she could see two ladies playing tennis on a court that appeared to have a green carpet covering it. Groups of women sat around chatting to each other, and children played nearby. Ella's heart lifted. She and Lonia were safe. Interned, but safe. *There is a God.*

A bitter wind cut through Flors as she stood with Cyrus on the landing strip prepared by the Resistance workers. Trying to get some warmth from the nearness of him, she followed his eyes heavenwards. They were hoping against hope that the pilot of the plane that had a drop for the Resistance would be able to fly them into Switzerland.

Cyrus had taken them back to the safe house, after the terrible incident. This one was also a farmhouse. The farmer had converted the roof space of his barn into a hiding place. It was accessed through a hatch that was so cleverly done. It lifted out, rather than being on a hinge, and was cut to precision, so that when the hatch was in place, it was difficult to see the joins and discern that there was anything different about the wooden-beamed ceiling, especially as the hatch was situated above a beam, which gave it even more camouflage. Access was by a ladder, which they climbed up into the loft, pulling the ladder up with them by the rope attached to it, before replacing the hatch.

Inside the loft the floor was covered by straw, to deaden the sound of movement, and contained a chair and two beds piled with blankets, as the only warmth came from the sun through a skylight that couldn't be seen from the ground. At night it was bitterly cold. A bucket was the only sanitary arrangement. This was lowered in the morning and emptied into the cesspit, then cleaned out, using the only access they had to water – a tap in the farmyard.

The farmer would whistle a certain tune when all was clear, and periodically he'd bring them some food and drink. There was another tune if danger was in the vicinity, but luckily that had never been whistled.

Flors, though happy that Cyrus was unharmed, and in awe of his bravery and the skills he'd shown, had suffered deeply from what had happened to her at the hands of the soldiers. All the heartache that had happened in her life took its toll and she had been taken ill. Weeks had passed, during which the emotional trauma had ripped them both apart, leaving a schism in their relationship.

It was one they both tried to ignore and pretend wasn't there, but Flors knew it was. She knew the look on Cyrus's face, which spoke of his feelings at coming across his wife being raped. They couldn't broach the subject, but it was there like an invisible cord holding them apart.

When Flors's health had recovered, Cyrus came to her as she lay in bed and told her that he'd been back to the bunker and had found that their cases and Ella's were still in the long grass where they'd thrown them. 'Everything is as it was – no dampness or anything. I've opened Ella's case and taken out the money that she told us Arnie had placed there, and I've put it into yours. We can pay it back, but it will greatly help our cause.'

With her heart breaking, Flors had asked, 'Was there anything personal in there – any mementoes?'

'Yes. A photo of Arnie and Ella with Paulo and Lonia – the one that stood on her sideboard; and another, an old one of her husband Paulo, with the baby they lost. And – and Lonia's blanket, the pink one that she was never without as a toddler. I've put those into your case, too.' Cyrus had lowered his head and she'd seen his body jerk, in a movement that told Flors that he was crying. Although she'd thought her body drained of emotion, her own tears flowed from her.

They'd held each other, in a way they hadn't been able to previously. Cyrus had got onto her bed and lain beside her. For the first time, Flors knew Cyrus wanted to make love to her, but she hadn't been able to bear the thought. She'd turned away.

But now she had a happier memory. Last night they had sat and talked excitedly about the prospect of today bringing them freedom, and Cyrus had joked with her, making her laugh till she'd ended up in his arms. Then he'd made love to her and she'd accepted him willingly. It was nothing like their usual passionate joining, but was nice and gentle – a beginning.

The sound of the plane came to them now, before they caught sight of it. Flors's heart lifted, though she prayed fervently that the pilot could take them, not taking it for granted that he would do so.

Cyrus held her closer, kissing her hair, before clinging to her. Flors's heart now beat a different rhythm. Something wasn't right.

'Cyrus?'

'Hush, darling. Don't ask me anything. Just hold me.'

Fear zinged through Flors as the realization came to her. Cyrus hadn't taken his rucksack out of the car that had driven them here. 'Cyrus, no. No, please don't leave me. I – I couldn't help what happened. I couldn't . . .'

'My darling, this has nothing to do with that. I wish we'd spoken of it, but I didn't want to cause you further pain.'

'I thought you blamed me.'

'No, my darling. It hurt me. It cut me in two, but I never blamed you. I just felt the terrible pain of not being able to protect you. I ran off to do that. I hoped the soldiers would follow me. I nearly won, but two escaped – the two that . . . Oh God, I'm sorry; I'm so sorry, Flors. Forgive me.'

'I have nothing to forgive, my darling. You did all you could. And to know that you don't blame me releases me from so much. Yes, we should have talked.' With her thumb, Flors wiped away the tear that had trickled down Cyrus's face. 'But don't leave me now, please don't.'

'I have to, my darling Flors. Oh, if only my mother and aunt were still alive and living in Switzerland, then you could have been with people who loved you and could have waited out the war till I came. But you have to go back to England, darling. It's too dangerous for you here. And I have to get back to Paulo and Arnie. I have to tell them what happened, and I have to fight with them. I cannot leave.'

'No . . . no!'

'Oh, Flors, help me. Help me to do this, for Ella. Arnie will have organized the Resistance by now and may have agents in from Britain. If he knows what has happened, he may be able to save Ella. Remember, darling, that dear Ella is a Jew. What if they find that out? Oh God, it doesn't bear thinking about. And little Lonia, she will perish, too. But who knows what she will tell the Germans, before she does so? Help me. Flors, help me to help them.'

Clinging to him as they both sobbed, Flors knew Cyrus was right. If he stayed and found Arnie, then Arnie could do something to save Ella. She had to make this sacrifice. For her dear friend, she had to.

'Go with my blessing, my darling Cyrus. I love you so much. And if it is possible, I love you even more for this courageous act.' Flors's heart was breaking as she said the words she least wanted to say.

'Thank you. Now, I can do this. And I will find Arnie and, together, we will save Ella and Lonia, I promise.'

His kiss was made with quivering lips, as his emotion almost spilled over. Leaning back, Cyrus looked intently at her. 'I have put most of the money we have into your haversack, because paying the pilot will take all of Ella's money, but I need a little, to help me to get back to Hérault. Now, you know how to access the money in our bank in

England. There is plenty there for your needs. Take care, my darling. Don't get involved in anything dangerous. Help the war effort by knitting, or something.'

'Knitting!' Flors felt a smile coming to her. 'Knitting, indeed. I'm more likely to be an ambulance driver, or something like that.'

'Oh, Flors, I know. But promise me it won't be anything more dangerous than that. Promise me.'

'I promise.'

The noise from the plane was now too great to talk over, as the pilot landed expertly on the landing strip.

'Go, my darling – and my love goes with you.'

'Oh, Cyrus. Cyrus!'

'Let go, my darling; let go and walk to the plane. I will wait to make sure the pilot will take you. Wave to me with a smile. I need that. I need your help, Flors.'

With acceptance from the pilot, Flors felt as though her heart had split in two, but she did as Cyrus bade her to. She boarded the plane and waved through the tiny window, with a smile on her face. She hoped he couldn't see the tears running down her face, as she could see them running down his. And then the plane was roaring down the runway and Cyrus was gone from view. When they were airborne, she could see the car going back along the road they had come along. In that car was her love. Her life. When she would see her Cyrus again she didn't know.

Letting herself into her old home in Brixton, Flors felt exhausted in every way. Memories flooded through her: of Rowena and her Nanny Pru. All she could do was collapse into a chair and stare around her. Everything looked shabby and grey, and she shivered with the cold. Even opening the curtains didn't help, as it was almost Christmas and the grey sky covered a grey-looking world. She wanted to rid the place of the staleness that had permeated every corner, but it made her shiver even more.

'Hello, love, I saw you get out of a taxi. My, it's good to see you. Though I can see, from your face, that all's not well. I brought some tea, but I've no milk or sugar – bloody Hitler! Not to worry, though, he'll go the same way that Kaiser did. We'll soon kick this one's arse for him.'

'Mrs Larch! Oh, Mrs Larch, it's so good to see you. And you look amazing.'

'For me age, you mean. Ha, at eighty, I can still beat all these youngsters: me step's scrubbed before they get out of bed.'

Flors laughed out loud. It was a good feeling – that she was back among friends. Back in Brixton, among those she'd come to think of as her own. 'Come here and let me give you a cuddle. I feel as though I walked out of the door only a few minutes ago, instead of twenty-odd years ago. Thank you, Mrs Larch, you've made me feel that I can cope.'

Coming out of the cuddle, Mrs Larch giggled. 'Nothing round 'ere's changed, luv. Well, a few have turned up their toes and I visit them in the graveyard, but there's still Mrs Harper – you remember, she used to read to us. And Mrs Randall, who lost her son Tommy in the last lot; she's a wiry little soul, nothing will see her off. Now, let's get that kettle boiling. I assume you have got one? There's nothing like a Rosy Lee to put you to rights. And shut those bleedin' windows – it's like the Arctic in here.'

Flors laughed again. It was as if all her troubles were leaving her. 'You'll need to turn the gas on, Mrs Larch, and I can't remember where the tap is.'

'I guessed that much, luv. I know where it is. It's in your cellar. I even brought a copper for the meter and some matches with me. We'll soon have the kettle whistling. But while it's coming to the boil, write out an order and I'll pop it to the shop. Put anything on it, you never know your luck. I'll tell Percy that you can pay – I assume you can?'

'Thank you, you're still the darling I remember.'

Mrs Larch grinned at her. The grin crinkled her already deeply lined face and showed gaps in her teeth, which hadn't been there before. Her kindly eyes lit up. And as she nodded, the few grey curls sticking out from her scarf – wrapped around her head and tied at the front – bobbed up and down.

Flors smiled back. 'And you don't have to worry. I'm all right financially, though he will have to take a cheque, as I only have francs on me.'

'That's good. That you can pay for extras, I mean. But you can forget the cheque – Percy wants cash, especially for stuff such as sugar and the like. Gets it on the black market and charges through the nose. Bleedin' swizzler. He forgets we're his bread-and-butter customers, war or no war. But you'll get no favours from him.'

'Well, just something to see me through will do. I'll write a list and you can tell me what I'm likely to get, and what he'll need cash for.'

Once Flors knew the gas was on, she borrowed a match and lit the gas fire that Cyrus had instructed their agent to put in, a couple of years ago. He'd thought it simpler for their tenants, and easier to get tenants, the more modern equipment they had. It was already proving a godsend, as its warming flames began to thaw out the chill of the place.

With the tea made, Mrs Larch settled down by the fire. 'Now, luv, I want to hear all the news. I'm guessing as old

Rowena turned her toes up, or you would have brought her with you. But how's your Cyrus, and what about your children?'

By the time Mrs Larch left, having been on the errand she had promised, the groceries were delivered, the bed was aired with hot-water bottles, the bedding was aired around a roaring fire they had lit in the front parlour, and all Flors had to do was make her bed and soak in the bath. Even her evening meal was taken care of, as Mrs Larch took herself off to the pie shop, which hadn't been there when Flors was last here. 'You'll love pie 'n' peas. There's nothing like it to compare. My treat. I'll see you in an hour.'

As Flors lay back in the bath, she realized that she'd not given a thought to how she was all alone, and how all those she loved were in danger. It all crowded in on her now and the floodgates opened, leaving her a sobbing wreck.

But she didn't mope for long. She had always been one to do something about her situation rather than dwell on it. Thinking everything through, she decided that the first thing she would do was write to Marjella. *Please, God, make it possible that I can see my beloved daughter again and hold her close to me.*

With this plan settled, Flors thought of her dear friend, Mags. *How is it that so much was asked of us all in the last war, and now here we are, all suffering again?*

Thinking about their friendship during such times and how it sustained her, Flors made her mind up that as soon as she'd heard from Marjella, she would visit Mags. It would be so nice to be with her. And maybe she could arrange a visit to Scotland, as she'd heard so much about Betsy and Susan.

Then came the thought she'd avoided: her need to visit her little Alice's and Nanny Pru's graves. Closing her eyes, she let her mind drift back. Beautiful memories came to her, but so did some very ugly ones. The past was buried and should remain so, but oh, how it still hurt at times. *Maybe I will visit my parents' grave. Perhaps take them some flowers.*

The thought cheered her a little, but the feeling soon died, to be replaced with a bitter one: *How could two people treat their only daughter as if she didn't exist?*

As the tears prickled her eyes once more, Flors sat up and prepared to get out of the bath. There was too much sadness to deal with today, without visiting that of the past. *Oh, Cyrus, my beloved, if only you were by my side, at least some of this would be bearable then.* Her thoughts turned to Ella, and she prayed that Cyrus, Paulo and Arnie would find Ella and Lonia and make them safe. Prayers tumbled from her – for her sons, especially Randie. *Where is he, dear Lord? Please let us find out soon. And look after Freddy. Keep him safe. And Marjella, and Monty. Oh God, how am I to bear it all?*

# CHAPTER ELEVEN

# The New Forest and London

## Sibbie and Marjie

'Wow, this is lovely.' Sibbie gazed out of the window of the military bus that had picked them up at the station and brought them to the New Forest. Trees, tall and majestic, allowed the low winter sun to filter through the branches in rays that caused hazy shadows and lacy patterns to splash across the green banks lining the road.

They were on the way to a part of Lord Montagu's estate that housed five different security departments. Their briefing had told them that each department would cover topics such as agent technique, clandestine life, personal security, communication in the field, how to maintain a cover story and how to act under police surveillance. All of which would have terrified Sibbie a few weeks back, but for which she now felt equipped.

'It reminds me so much of the forests at home.'

There was a wistful note in Marjie's voice. Many times, over the last few weeks, she had broken down, her worries for the safety of her parents and brothers almost consuming her, but Sibbie had learned that Marjie had an inner strength that she could call upon to get her through these times, and she knew that their tutors had all recognized this quality in her.

'Marjie, I've been thinking: why don't we ask permission to make a telephone call? Given the circumstances, I think it would be granted.'

'No! Sibbie, haven't you realized how fatal it would be to admit any form of weakness or need? We have to cope with whatever is thrown at us. It is only to you that I can unravel now and again. But you must never think to seek help for me.'

This shocked Sibbie and was another valuable lesson that she learned. Of course they had to forget everyday life and remain focused on their one objective. Right now, that was to fully equip themselves with all the skills they would need. 'I won't – sorry, Marjie. I didn't mean to add to your worries. I won't speak of it again. You've made me see that trying to help our family in any way, or even contact them, would be a mistake. But I am here for you. In our private moments with me, you can give in to your feelings. It helps me, too, as I am worried for Aunt Flors and for all of them.'

Marjie's hand came into hers, and Sibbie felt reassured that the moment had passed and that they had an understanding that would stand them in good stead. Yes, they would have times in the future when they simply wanted to give in and seek help, but she now realized they must never do that, but instead must carry on and find a way out of all they had to face.

Two week later, this lesson really hit home.

They had been taught things they'd never dreamed they would have to learn: how to pick a lock, although it was more manipulating a lock back, using a protractor, than what she thought burglars did – pick a lock with a hairpin or something. And how to communicate in code: ways that made the code that Aunt Flors had devised seem like child's play. And how to take an impression of a key: just a matter of carrying a matchbox full of plasticine.

Other skills had involved disguising themselves, and it wasn't by wearing a wig, but by simple methods of changing what people noticed most about you – whether you wore glasses or not, how you wore your hair, and even how you walked. And adding a scar to your face, using special make-up. Such changes made an amazing difference to you being instantly recognized.

The easiest bit for them both was learning their cover story, as this entailed many things they already knew about France. The only gaps in their knowledge were recent changes – wartime measures, such as how sugar rationing worked in France, and information on curfews that were in place.

And now they were both to be tested.

They were to work together under the warning that, despite all they had achieved, fail in this and they wouldn't be sent out 'in the field' – the expression used for an agent being given an assignment.

They were to be dropped off in London, with a map and very few clues. The person they were to make contact with was given the name of Ted Brown; other than that, they had his last-known address and his line of work – a butcher. His story was that he was running a branch of the underground and would be valuable to them.

'Let's treat it like a game, Sibbie. See who can unearth the most clues about our Mr Brown.'

When they tracked him down, they found that Mr Brown was being kept prisoner. The last time he'd been seen he was being taken into a flat above a shop. They decided they would wait until nightfall and then break into the shop and rescue him. They only had hours left to report that they had made contact.

All was going well. Sibbie had managed to 'pick the lock' and they were inside the shop. Using torches, they found their way to a door that looked likely to lead upstairs, when suddenly the ringing of bells, indicating that a police car was approaching, had them standing like statues, unsure whether to run or to continue their mission.

'What if these were Germans coming after us – what would we do?' Marjie's voice shook as she asked Sibbie.

'Run. Run as fast as we can and try to outwit them, and of course fire our guns at them, but we can hardly do that here.'

'Not unless we do it as we did when practising . . . Bang, bang!'

Sibbie muffled the laugh that wanted to burst out of her. That Marjie could make her laugh at such a time boded well. For at this moment they were in a sticky situation.

'We could call in. We have an emergency number, and HQ will explain to the police.'

'No, Marjie. I think this is part of the test. Come on, they're getting nearer.'

Both girls shot out of the door, almost tripping each other over. Running like the wind, they made it to the end of the street before the police pulled up outside the shop.

'The Germans won't warn us by ringing a bell, you know.'

'Yes, I heard they were mean like that.'

'Oh, Marjie, stop it. This is serious!' Despite Sibbie's mock reprimand, they giggled, as much from relief at not being caught as anything else.

'We still haven't made contact. Shall we hang around and

see if the police leave, when they see they haven't caught anyone red-handed?'

Before she had time to say yes or no, Marjie came up with a good plan. 'I know, let's walk along the street as if we are going about our normal business. We can say we know the man who lives there, and would the police see if he is all right?'

'Brilliant. Right, best foot forward, and charm to the ready.'

Sibbie couldn't believe how well it all went, and how easily they got to speak to Mr Brown. One of the policemen believed them and knocked heavily on the door that Sibbie and Marjie thought led to the flat upstairs. Without waiting for a reply, the policeman opened the door and shouted, 'Is there a Ted Brown there? Are you unharmed?'

A man came down the stairs. The girls looked at each other, as he didn't fit the scant description they'd had. But Marjie wasn't going to be put off. 'Where's Ted?' And then, with a stroke of genius, she used the code-words they had been given: 'fallen apples'. 'Ted, are you up there? My mum has told me to call in and tell you that she has some fallen apples for you.'

Sibbie felt like jumping for joy when a voice called out, 'Yes, I'll be down in a minute.'

They'd done it! The feeling she had, Sibbie knew Marjie had too, as her face beamed.

'Ted' came down the stairs, smiling. He nodded at them both, but didn't speak. The other man pulled out a card and showed it to the policeman as he ushered him towards the front door and went outside with him.

When he came back in, he was alone. 'I explained to the police what was going on and who you were, and that they had no need to look for anyone else in connection with a burglary. Well done, girls. You will do your country proud. I'm Captain David Howkins, by the way.'

Both girls stood to attention and saluted.

'Stand at ease. Now, what are your names?'

'I'm Sibilia Charvet, sir.' Sibbie had chosen to use Montel's surname as her cover name, and she'd been told to use a similar name to her forename, so that Marjie didn't get mixed up and could still call her 'Sibbie'. Marjie had chosen Margarita, for the same reason, and her surname because it rhymed with Hérault, where she was born, and would be easy for her to remember. 'And this is Margarita Barrault.'

'Excellent. I really hoped that you wouldn't break your cover and fail at the last hurdle. Look, I'll get clearance from your commanding officer – you can listen in, if you like, so that you are sure – but we would really love to take you to dinner. You can't have had any fun since being dumped here. Where have you been staying?'

Sibbie felt unsure, and she could see Marjie did, too.

'Ha! You two are tip-top. Come, let's talk to your commanding officer and then we'll report to Baker Street and let them know how you passed with flying colours. Then you can relax and not feel as though we are trying to trick you.'

Sibbie looked at Marjie and saw that she was blushing. Her eyes were fixed on Captain William Parsons, and his eyes on her. Sibbie looked from one to the other, before answering, 'I think that is a good idea, sir.'

Captain Howkins smiled and nodded knowingly. 'I think someone has been struck by lightning, don't you?'

'I do, sir.'

They both laughed, bringing William and Marjie out of their near-stupor, to join in with them.

Sibbie would have said that Captain Howkins was the handsome one of the pair, but then he had dark good looks and she'd always been drawn to them – look at her Paulo, the most handsome man in the world, and he had very black hair and eyes.

Fair-haired and blue-eyed, William's features were very precise, making him good-looking rather than handsome. He wasn't as tall as Captain Howkins, but somehow had an elegance about him.

After the phone call was made, all four jumped in a taxi to Baker Street. The congratulations there were wonderful – a real recognition of the way Sibbie and Marjie had both applied the skills they had learned. A short interview, during which they were spoken to in French and then in German, concluded the proceedings.

'Well, Captain Howkins, I think you can release these two to their parachute training, and then it will be back to London to await their assignment. Good luck, Officer Roford and Officer Harpinham. First-class work.'

Once outside, arrangements were made for them to be picked up at their hotel – a small, nondescript bed-and-breakfast off Shepherds Bush Road. 'Just send a taxi – we are known there as two French girls, who were at school here and are trapped in England. We aren't meant to know anyone, and speak mostly in broken English. They would think it funny if two British captains came to pick us up.'

'Good thinking, Harpinham. Look, may we become less formal? May I call you Marjella and Sybil?'

'No, you may not, William! I'm Marjie and Sybil is Sibbie.'

William laughed. 'In that case, I'm Wills. But David is David, I'm afraid. "Dave" just doesn't suit him.'

Marjie laughed as she looked up into Wills's eyes. Sibbie sighed, as she could see heartache ahead for them both.

\* \* \*

131

Sibbie and Marjie had been lucky to find a dress shop on Shepherds Bush Road, and each had found an outfit. Both chose warm woollen costumes, because the weather, now that Christmas was approaching, was icy cold. Sibbie's was charcoal-grey. It had a pencil skirt and a fitted jacket that fell just below her waist. The collar and lapels were edged with black braiding, and there was a thin leather belt to accentuate the waist. She teamed this with a pink silk blouse and a small black, beret-type hat.

Marjie chose a rust-brown costume that also had braiding around the collar and box jacket in a chocolate-brown. The skirt flared very slightly, her blouse was a rich cream colour and her hat was a jaunty affair, with a slanting brim decorated with a rose fashioned out of the same felt as the hat.

Their best find, though, was that the lady owner of the shop offered them some silk stockings – a rarity these days. The stockings didn't only look glamorous, with the lovely sheen they had, but were warming, too. When it came to their shoes, they had to compromise as there were very few available, but they did find some brogues that didn't look too schoolmarmish and settled for those.

'Well, that's us ready for the ball, Cinders.'

'You look lovely, Sibbie. But, well . . . I'm not sure about me—'

'You look beautiful, darling Marjie. Stunning. That colour really suits you; it brings out the lovely Mediterranean glow that your skin has – slightly tanned and creamy. I do envy you. And Wills is going to be bowled over.'

'Do you really think so? He's so handsome, Sibbie. I felt really funny when he looked at me, as if he was drawing me into his soul.'

'It's called falling in love, and anyone could see that it

was happening to him, too. I'm so happy for you, Marjie; but sad, too. I don't think it will be long before we are sent on a mission and you'll have so little time to woo your man.'

'I know, but if it is meant to be, it will stand the test of time. Nothing is going to stop me helping my country.'

'Well, let's forget all of that for one evening and have a good time. Though I wish it was Paulo taking me to dinner.'

'It will be, one day. And you're right. Let's paint the town red with two handsome men by our side. I'm so looking forward to this evening.'

'I'm looking forward to a decent meal, more than anything.'

Marjie laughed at this, and the sound warmed Sibbie. 'You and your food, and yet you don't put on an ounce of weight. I can gain weight easily, and I have to be careful. Now, just check the seams on my stockings are straight, Sibbie.'

'Yes, they're perfectly straight,' Sibbie said as she stood behind Marjie. 'And I envy you your legs – they're perfect.'

'And so are yours, Sibbie. Look at how slim your ankles are, and very elegant. Turn round and let me check your seams.' Marjie had to make a little adjustment to straighten Sibbie's stockings, but was very gentle, so as not to snag the delicate fabric. '*Voila!* We shall go to the ball.' Giggling like two girls let out of the school gate, they ran down the stairs to the waiting taxi.

Although most of the city was broken, Sibbie saw what Daisy had told her about – that the spirit of London was very much alive, and fun could be had behind blacked-out windows. The restaurant was one being run in a cellar. The owners had once owned a plush place on the edge of the West End, but had been bombed out. The way they'd turned this basement into the glamorous venue it had become was nothing short of a miracle, because getting hold of materials and labour was very difficult. Huge chandeliers reigned over plush gold-velvet furnishings and mahogany furniture. A thick ruby-red carpet covered all but a small dance floor. Music greeted them as a five-piece band sat on a raised area in front of the dance floor, playing popular songs. It was all wonderful, and Sibbie felt transported to another world.

The good food, fine wine, laughter and dancing were spoilt only by the absence of Paulo, although seeing Marjie so happy, dancing closely with Wills, made up a little for that.

David, too, was missing his fiancée. Sibbie got into a deep conversation with him and told him about Paulo, then listened as David related to her how his plans of marriage were on hold for the duration of the war. The whole evening was turning out to be a release from everything going on in the wide world outside.

They learned that David and Wills had been out in the field on missions and were 'resting' for a while. 'We enjoy helping in the training of others now. But we both want to go back out. Whether that will happen depends on whether they can get us safely undercover again. Our cover was blown by a traitor, and we had a hair-raising escape. Beware of everyone when you are in the field, Sibbie. Even those you most trust can be your enemy.'

'I'm sorry that happened to you. I suppose it isn't easy to decipher who is genuine and who isn't, at such times as we live in. But you have to trust some people, because you can't work alone.'

'If I go out again, I would keep vital information close to my chest until such time as it is needed. It can be done. If you get an order to derail a certain train, gather your team and tell them to be at a certain place at a certain time – but not the assignment place. Tell them what to bring, and that's it. Do all the planning for the mission yourself. Then instruct them only when you are all together, ready to go. Then none of them can send messages to anyone – it's something they should have taught us on the curriculum. Wills and I are working on various things that should be included, and there is to be a new set-up for the training very soon. A shorter version, as a lot of what they teach isn't needed. Anyway, no more talk of business.'

David seemed sad as he said this, and Sibbie gathered that whatever had happened to him and Wills still lived with him. She could imagine what the fear felt like: to have your mission known to the enemy and have them lying in wait for you. She so wanted to know how they escaped, but knew from his expression that he no longer wanted to talk about it.

What he'd said so far had brought home to her just how dangerous it was working amongst the enemy, trying to sabotage their work and maintaining your cover and secrecy. But she felt ready.

Marjie broke into her thoughts. 'Sibbie, I am going for a walk with Wills. I'll see you back at the hotel.'

Sibbie stood and hugged Marjie. In her ear she whispered, 'Stay out as long as you want – don't worry about me. We have so little time.'

Marjie pulled back and looked deeply into Sibbie's eyes. 'Oh, Sibbie, I'm on cloud nine, and I'm not going to let anything spoil that.'

'I'm glad.'

They hugged again and Marjie was gone. Sibbie hoped, with all her heart, that this was the start of something wonderful for Marjie, and that the war didn't change that.

'They certainly both seem to have found their soulmate. I've never known Wills to be like this with a girl before. He has girls forced upon him by over-eager mothers looking for a good match all the time, but he hates the whole business. Such things come with being the son of a lord, but Wills avoids debutantes like the plague. What's Marjie like?'

'A lord! Well, I can't say I am surprised. I think it shows. I knew, from first talking to him, that Wills was different in some way – just a sort of air that he has about him. Anyway, you have no need to worry, as Marjie is a beautiful person.'

'Good, I'm glad, as he deserves only the best. Now, you look tired. It's been a lovely night – a distraction. I'll see you back to your hotel. And, Sibbie, good luck for the future. I sincerely hope our lives cross again, but as long as I'm office-bound, I will be watching your progress.'

Marjie walked hand-in-hand with Wills. The pavements were icy and the air so cold it chilled them to the bone, but she didn't care. How this had happened to her so quickly she couldn't imagine, but it had, and her heart was heavy with the thought of them having so little time together.

'Marjie, I'm afraid for you. It isn't easy in the field. Please don't take any chances.'

'The nature of the work is all about chances, as I understand it, Wills. I have been trained. Try not to worry.'

He stopped walking and pulled her round to face him. 'I can't bear to lose you, Marjie. I know it was only today that we met, but I feel as though you are the completion of my life.'

She was looking up into Wills's eyes, and although the darkness prevented her from seeing him properly, the small amount of moonlight captured the lovely depth in his look.

'Oh, Marjie, I can't understand what is happening. I've never felt this way before.'

'Nor me. Not that I have had any boyfriends before . . . Oh, I – I didn't mean that. I . . . I mean—'

'I am your boyfriend. At least, I want to be. Will you have me as that, Marjie?'

'I will. Oh, Wills, I will.'

'And although it will be difficult, will you write to me occasionally?'

A deep sadness entered Marjie. Why – why did this happen now? She had been so ready. Ready to take on anything asked of her. Now she didn't ever want to leave London and Wills's side.

He didn't speak again, but took her chin in his hand and bent his head towards her. The moment she'd ached for all evening was upon her. When his lips touched hers, Marjie melted into his body. The kiss consumed her, taking her to a place where her body floated, and her heart filled her chest. Wills's muttered 'I love you', as he came out of the kiss, completed her world.

'I love you, Wills. I don't know how, or why, but I do.'

Wills chuckled as he pulled her into him and cuddled her in his arms. 'The *how* is out of our control, darling Marjie; and the *why* is something that I am mystified by. But I am so happy that it really doesn't matter.'

Marjie wanted never to come out of his arms.

'Will you spend Christmas with me, Marjie? I mean, really with me? You will have orders tomorrow, accompanied by train tickets to Manchester for your parachute training. But that should finish before Christmas. I can pick up you and Sibbie and take you to my father's apartment in Mayfair. I can arrange for it to be decorated before then, and for a

Christmas dinner to be ready for us – well, of sorts, depending upon what Cook can source, which is usually surprisingly good fare. Please say "yes", darling.'

'Yes. Yes, I will. I'll look forward to it, and it will get me through what is the most frightening training of all to me.'

'Don't be afraid – parachuting is easy, I promise. I am afraid of heights, and I got through it. I closed my eyes and jumped . . . Oh, my dear, you're shivering. You really are afraid.'

'Afraid, yes, but it won't stop me. I too will close my eyes and jump.' To demonstrate she jumped off the step. 'Just like that.'

Wills laughed out loud. A window opened above. 'Who's there? Clear off! First night's sleep in a long while, and I get a couple of idiots on me doorstep. Clear off or you'll get me piddle-pot all over yer.'

Marjie giggled. Wills caught hold of her hand and ran with her. By the time they reached her hotel they were out of breath, but still laughing – until Wills caught hold of her again and pulled her to him once more. His lips met hers and she was lost. Coming out of the kiss, Wills said, 'I've fallen in love – me, a confirmed bachelor! Ha! And it feels wonderful. Oh, Marjie, I can't believe that you feel the same way for me.'

Marjie laughed with him, a happy laughter that showed her joy. 'I do. I felt it the moment you looked into my eyes when we met. I can't explain it, but . . .'

'Don't even try, my darling. Just let it happen.'

*He called me his darling. Can this really be true? Can love happen to us as suddenly as this?*

Melting into his kiss, Marjie knew that it could, and had. She loved Wills with all that she was. Another thought entered her head. *Why now? Why did we find each other when we have to part and go on to face such danger that we may never see each other again? I can't bear it – I can't.*

'We have such a short time together, Marjie. I can't wait until Christmas. I want you by my side forever, from right now.'

Calling on all the strength she had, Marjie held him close. 'Our future is on hold, Wills, but I know our bond will get stronger, even when we are apart. Over Christmas we will make memories to sustain us, and then one day we will be together again. We must hang on to that.'

They clung together. Marjie never wanted Wills to let her go. But these days life was full of bittersweet partings, and their life was to be no different.

# CHAPTER TWELVE

## *Singapore*

### Daisy and Florrie

With Christmas just two days away, the hospital matron summoned Daisy to her office. When she arrived, she found that all the ward sisters were in attendance. The mood was sombre.

'There is danger in the air, Sisters. Some nurses, particularly our younger ones, are feeling very nervous. The Japanese are closing in; they are advancing down the Malaysia peninsula and it is likely they will soon attack us here. I want us to be ready if that happens. Evacuation procedures will be practised from now on, but with good humour, so as not to further dismay the lower ranks.'

Daisy understood the fears everyone had and the importance of the senior staff keeping everyone's spirits up. Every day news came in of atrocities, and fears surrounding the Japanese advancement grew as the wounded, who had been trying to hold them back, flooded the wards. She and Florrie had the added worry of Billy, too. Both dreaded him being brought in badly hurt. They'd hoped to visit him in Malaya, but now that was impossible and, as far as they knew, Billy had no idea they were even stationed so near him. But they reassured themselves with the knowledge that between Malaya and Singapore there were so many British forces stationed, and ready to defend them, that they felt confident they would beat the Japanese back and keep Singapore British.

When they had arrived in Singapore on 15 November there had been little talk of war. It all seemed to have been left behind. They'd been in awe of the beautiful island, and Daisy was glad they had explored as much as they could during that time.

She remembered feeling a strange sensation of belonging as she and Florrie, and the other fifteen nurses and one other nursing sister, were helped off the boat by laughing, very friendly coolies. They had then been transported up a shady, tree-lined road.

A snippet of conversation came back to her: 'Eeh, Florrie, I never knew such places existed. It's grand.'

'If our ma could see us now, she'd be astonished.'

The ride in an open-topped bus, which had seen better days and puffed out fumes as if in annoyance at still being in service, was a little hair-raising, as children ran alongside, calling out to them and greeting them, but also asking for a cent. One was really cheeky and shouted, 'British rich, British give me one dollar.' Daisy and Florrie had laughed their heads off.

The chatter on the bus was full of anticipation, interspersed with the waving of hand-held fans, as the true heat that they would experience came home to roost.

They were taken to the Royal Alexandra Military Hospital, a beautiful white building with many windows and balconies, surrounded by lush green grass and trees that provided a gentle breeze.

Matron greeted them as they entered the reception area, a place of cool calm – an oasis after stepping out of the midday heat. Here, white stone walls surrounded the tiled floor, which shone like glass. A desk took up most of one wall and several doors led off to places unknown at the time, although they later found that they were passageways to the wards, theatres and staff quarters.

Matron, a tall lady, whose only claim to beauty was her piercing blue eyes, which distracted the onlooker from her crooked nose and slightly buck-teeth, made up for what she didn't have in looks with her charm. Daisy had taken to her from the off and had listened intently as she made her welcome speech.

'I'm Matron Prinder and I'm very pleased to welcome you all. I have a list of your names, but at the moment you are just a sea of faces. We will rectify that tomorrow, but today you are free to do as you please. Tindrenshai, who is an orderly here, will take you to your quarters and, once you have unpacked, he will be waiting in the corridor to take you to lunch. Then I want you to explore, so dress in something cool and be at the front of the building by two p.m. The bus will be waiting and will take you on a trip. Oh, if you have packed your swimwear, take that with you, as you are in for a treat at the end of your tour. You will be taken to the European Swimming Pool, a place that we all frequent during our time off. Enjoy yourselves, then report to my office at nine a.m. tomorrow morning, dressed for duty.'

A warm feeling had overcome Daisy and she knew it had Florrie, too. 'By, I reckon as we've landed on our feet here, Daisy. Fancy having a matron like that! My last one bawled me out for sommat or other, the moment she set eyes on me.'

'Aye, they can be tyrants. I've had a few like that. But I suppose it's being in this wonderful place – I mean, how can you not feel in a constant good mood? Everyone's so happy.'

'They're a good lot that we're with an' all. That Phoebe, I thought she'd be stuck up as she speaks in such a posh voice, but she's a real giggle.'

'That's where you have the advantage on me, Florrie. Me being a sister, I have to keep meself a bit aloof or I'll never command any respect during working hours. But Bett, the other sister on this trip with us, is a nice girl. As you knaw, we're friends already. Oh, there she is. I'll leave you now, lass, as we'll be taken to different quarters. But we'll have a lovely afternoon together.'

They visited Raffles Place in the afternoon, a bustling, exciting area of white buildings of a similar style to the hospital, some with domed roofs and others with pointed ones, all different in a subtle way. The thing Daisy remembered, and that made the most impression, were the large number of windows, which glinted as if they were made of a thousand diamonds.

The streets were lined with shops and cafes and the traffic was heavy, with cars and military vehicles. The air smelt of fried food, as delicious-looking delicacies were being cooked in the open. They were told that Sir Stamford Raffles had taken the island of Singapore from the Dutch many years ago, and that many of the important places were named after him.

After a cooling iced tea in a pavement cafe, they'd been taken to the pool – a wonderful place that seemed to lie at the heart of British social life. Daisy and Florrie decided they could spend the rest of their lives enjoying the respite from the heat given by the huge ceiling fans, and watching the comings and goings in the square. Soft music played, and drinking and socializing seemed to be the main occupation, when the full dance band came into its own.

The pool had been a wonderful cooling experience, and Daisy and Florrie had both impressed others with their ability in the water and their diving skills – something they had learned off the jetty at the end of the old boathouse, which was now their ma's and Aunt Susan's shop. They now joined the swimming club for a fee of two dollars fifty a month, and would spend most of their days off and many exciting, glamorous evenings here.

It had been here that they had met Alex, a senior medic with whom they had only had brief dealings at the hospital, and Giles, an officer based at the military depot.

Daisy was head over heels in love with Alex; and Florrie and Giles, Daisy knew, were very attracted to each other. Giles was a little hesitant, though. He didn't believe in the kind of romance that could occur in such a place, and thought that the place to meet the love of his life must be England. However, Daisy suspected that his feelings for Florrie were breaking down this resistance, which she thought had its roots in snobbery. Florrie, with her northern accent and lovely open nature, which displayed no sophistication whatsoever, wasn't exactly officer-wife material. Despite this, Daisy liked Giles and felt sorry for him being trapped by convention.

As she listened to Matron now, Daisy's heart felt heavy. The rumours were terrifying and a whole different atmosphere permeated the hospital than had been their first experience. Bett nudged her. It was something she often did when she'd seen something to giggle at, so Daisy was shocked when she glanced at Bett's face and saw a look of terror.

Bett's lovely face, which dimpled when she smiled, distracted from the rest of her body, which showed that she liked to eat a lot. Normally a jolly person, taking everything in her stride, it was disconcerting to see that happiness desert her. Moving a little closer to her, Daisy found Bett's hand and squeezed it, trying to offer reassurance.

When Matron dismissed them, Bett's voice shook with fear. 'If the Japanese come, we'll all be killed. They slice your head off. Oh, Daisy, I'm so afraid.'

'I knaw, we all are, but we can't show it. Matron said there are plans to evacuate us all, if it looks like the defence of the island won't hold. Take every note of the procedures and you'll be fine. We all will. The army will protect us, and there'll be plenty of ships to take us away from here. Try to be strong for the younger ones, Bett. It's our duty.'

'I will, Daisy. I suppose, where you come from, you are born tough. But I've known nothing but a gentle life, being protected from harm, and I don't know how to do that for myself.'

'I were protected by the best ma that a girl could have, but not mollycoddled; we had to learn to stand on our own two feet. You've done that, too, Bett. You left the family home and trained to be a nurse; you cope in some dire situations, when we ain't got enough beds and men are screaming in agony around us. I've even seen you give your own blood for a soldier and carry on working to administer it, to save his life. You are brave and strong, Bett – you are. And it is now our turn to protect those in our charge. We can do it.'

Bett seemed to grow in stature in front of Daisy's eyes

as she listened, and Daisy saw her gain control as the terror left her. 'Yes, I can. I'm sorry, Daisy, I lost it there for a moment. Thank you for making me see that I am brave – I know it now. Just let any of those Japs try to touch one of my nurses and it'll be me that does the slicing.'

'That's the spirit, Bett. Now, I'm off-duty in an hour and meeting Alex, and I'm going to forget it all. But first I'm going to reassure my nurses that there is a procedure in place, that we will be practising it and they will be safe.'

They hugged as they parted, something they'd never done before. Daisy smiled at Bett. 'Nursing sisters to the rescue, eh?' With this, she charged down the corridor pretending to hold a gun, to the sound of Bett laughing as if she was fit to burst.

Alex was waiting outside in his car for her when she stepped outside the hospital an hour and a half later. She felt good in the calf-length frock she'd bought recently – made of cotton, it was a colour she'd put somewhere between cream and soft yellow. The fitted bodice had tiny sleeves that were gathered into a cuff that fell well above her elbows. The square neckline showed a hint of her bust. Gathered at the waist, the skirt fell in wide pleats that gave a smart appearance. She'd teamed this with white gloves, a white handbag and white-heeled shoes. Her hat – a woven floppy-brimmed affair – gave her shade and had a cream silk band around the base of the brim, which was finished in a huge bow at the back and flowed to her shoulders, keeping her neck cool as the breeze played with it, causing a fan effect.

'You look beautiful, darling. That colour really brings out the golden strands in your hair.'

Alex's light kiss thrilled her. A voice calling her name got her looking back. Florrie stood on the balcony of her ward, waving madly and blowing kisses. Daisy thought she'd like to keep that picture in her mind forever – her lovely sister, a kind, gentle person whom she loved dearly. Alex waved, too, then he pleased and surprised Daisy by saying, 'Florrie's lovely. I think I'm going to like having her as a sister-in-law.'

'Oh? So you're thinking of marrying one of the family then?'

Alex laughed. She loved his laugh. She loved everything about him, even when, like now, he was teasing her.

'Yes, I am thinking about it. You said you had a younger sister, didn't you? The prettiest of you all, with a petite figure, not a buxom one, like you.'

Daisy hit him with the gloves she'd removed from her hands. 'You told me you like your girls to be nicely padded in the right places.'

'I do, my darling. So you will have to be the one to marry me, if I am to have Florrie as my sister-in-law.'

Not sure if he meant this or was still joking with her, Daisy didn't reply. She giggled and was rewarded with a look that melted her heart.

Alex drove in silence for a while. He surprised her by not turning towards the town, but heading for the countryside instead. The road wound around, bend after bend. The roar of Alex's sports car made it difficult to carry on any further conversation, so Daisy enjoyed the time, just looking at him. Watching how his dark, curly hair flopped about in the wind; imagining his twinkling blue eyes looking into hers, and herself snuggling into his strong body.

But Alex's mention of Rosie had Daisy feeling unable to concentrate, as her sister kept dancing into her head. And so did the image of her German man, for she was certain that Rosie did carry a torch for him. Suddenly she wanted to tell Rosie that it was all right to love whoever she wanted to; that she understood the feeling of falling hopelessly in love, and how you didn't choose the person, he was chosen for you in some magical way – otherwise, why didn't it happen to her until she was thousands of miles away from home, in a land she'd never in her wildest dreams thought she would ever visit? And if Alex hadn't been British, but a German, or African, or Japanese for that matter, it wouldn't have mattered; she would love him and want to be with him. *I'll write to Rosie and tell her this. I can't bear the way I was with her. I need her to know that I approve of whoever she loves.*

Why she felt this compunction, Daisy didn't consider at this moment, as Alex had pulled off the road into a dirt track. A tingling excitement grabbed the muscles of her stomach as he switched off the engine and turned to her.

'I've brought a picnic with me. I had the kitchen staff make it up. I want you all to myself, Daisy. I don't want to share you with a roomful in a stuffy restaurant.'

Daisy couldn't speak. There was something in the way Alex was looking at her, and in the tone of his voice, that held her suspended.

As he got out of the car, she did the same, watching him shyly, as if this was their first meeting. Out of the boot he took a large blanket; he must have taken it off his bed, as she had one on hers exactly the same, a sort of cotton, woven fabric that kept you cool and yet warm, once the temperature dropped.

'Spread that out, darling, and I'll get out the box they packed for us. I have no idea what is in it.'

After lifting out the small box, Alex bent over his boot again, and this time he brought out a bottle of champagne and two glasses. Daisy wanted to make a joke and ask what they were celebrating, but the moment didn't call for triviality.

Once she'd laid out the blanket, she sat on it and looked around her. They were high up on a hill surrounded by other hills, all lush with greenery and trees. In the distance she could see the sea shimmering in the heat, a deep blue against the white sand. *I'd like heaven to be like this, please, God.* A shudder went through her at this thought.

'Are you all right, darling?'

The sentence had slipped off Alex's tongue as if he'd always spoken in this serious way, instead of his usual jokey manner.

'Yes, someone walked over my grave, as they say.'

'You're not going to be in a grave for a very long time.' He lowered himself down beside her. She could see that he was holding something clenched tightly in his hand. 'And I hope you will spend that time with me, my darling Daisy. Will you marry me?'

This second proposal of the day was heartfelt, his look so sincere and full of love for her that Daisy's spirits soared, and she realized she was truly in heaven now – this very minute.

'Yes, yes, I will. Oh, Alex, I love you.'

A tear glistened in his eye and his lips came down on hers, his body pressing her until she was lying beneath him, looking up into his beautiful face, with the sun forming a halo around it.

'I love you, Daisy. Will you do me the honour of wearing my mother's ring, to bind us together in the legacy of love that she left with it, and had with my father?'

Daisy could only nod as Alex took her hand and slipped a diamond ring on her left finger. Her own tears of joy matched his.

'Oh, Daisy, my Daisy. I love you.'

'Alex . . . Alex. I can't believe you're me fiancé. Ta, ta ever so much. I'll love you forever.'

His lips kissed the ring, then came down on hers. Her heart beat so loudly and swelled in her chest as she accepted his love. 'Daisy, I want to make love to you. I want to make you mine.'

'I want you to. Oh, Alex, me love, I do.'

With a sudden movement that took her by surprise, Alex sat up. 'I'm sorry. I shouldn't have asked. It was the heat of the moment. Forgive me. I love you too much to—'

'Shush.' Sitting up, Daisy put her finger on his lips. 'Who knaws how long we have, Alex. Make me your lass – truly yours. Let's make a memory that will last us forever, in case the unthinkable happens to either of us.'

There were no more protests, only a deep loving – a giving and a taking – as Alex gently made Daisy his. The pain she'd expected on him first entering her didn't happen. She didn't understand why, and Alex didn't question it, but only, to her intense pleasure, deepened his thrusts into her, once he knew she was ready, loving her with his hands, his mouth and his whole being until they were truly one, calling out in ecstasy their complete and utter joy.

Lying in his arms afterwards, she allowed her body to cry out its release and the pent-up anguish she was feeling about the world and her loved ones. Alex allowed her time, soothing her, telling her of his love and kissing her chestnut curls, which tumbled around her face.

Part of Daisy worried that he might be questioning whether he was the first man she'd made love to, but he showed no signs of worrying. She just wished she could get the nagging worry out of her head that he might think it at some time, for he had truly been her first. Suddenly she decided she had to broach the subject.

'I expected it to hurt me the first time. Ta, me love, for being so gentle.'

'Oh, darling, I thought you were worrying about something. Hasn't your training taught you that most women don't have an intact hymen by the time they are twenty-five? And not because they are not virgins, but because it has been broken by some activity or other – something as simple as riding a bike or a horse can do it. I never doubted you for a moment. In the short time I've known you, your honesty is only one of the many things 1 love about you. You say it as it is: take you or leave you. I know where I am with you, my darling.'

They laughed together at this. 'Well, I'm telling you this now: you are all 1 ever want in a man, and you made me feel the best I've ever felt in me life just now.'

They held each other in silence for a moment.

When Alex turned his head and whispered, 'We will better that, my darling, in a lifetime of making love,' Daisy snuggled into him and wanted to remember this moment forever.

Lifting her head, Alex looked into her eyes, then kissed her so passionately that soon she was lying beneath him once more, yielding to him, crying out with the sensations that were taking her to an even higher place than the first time, as wave after wave of pleasure vibrated through her. Alex's moans joined hers as he explored every part of her, taking her clothes off as he did so, until she was naked before him and the sun kissed every part of her.

They lay afterwards, spent but in a happy place they thought no one could ever touch. A place that blocked out the world and the war, and all they had to deal with as medics, and cocooned them till they felt safe.

Coming down to earth wasn't easy, for their senses and awareness of each other were heightened beyond anything Daisy had ever thought possible.

It was hunger that prompted them to become practical, but even as they sat and ate the delicious delicacies – squid, breaded and fried, vine leaves stuffed with olives and fish, and small naan-breads laced with a seaweed spread – there was a sensuousness about the atmosphere surrounding them.

It was Alex who brought some normality back between them, as he joked that he felt as if he would grow fins and start to open and close his mouth if he was here in Singapore much longer, as they served so much fish. 'You are what you eat, my father used to say, when he tried to make me eat Brussels sprouts. Have you ever met anyone who liked Brussels sprouts?'

'Yes – me. I think they're grand. Me ma cooks them all crunchy. But she won't buy them till there's been a frost, as she reckons as they're not ready till then.'

'I can't wait to meet your ma. She sounds such a wonderful person. And your little sister and your brothers. All the people you talk about with such love. I miss my mother so much.'

'I'm sorry, darling. By, it comes to sommat when God takes two lovely folk, like your ma and da were taken.'

'Yes, it was a massive blow to see mother dying slowly, and then for Father to have a heart attack at her funeral. Being an only child, that left me with one elderly great-aunt. She's very lively, though, and a joy to be around. She lives in my house and keeps everything running. You'll love her when you come to live there.'

'Aye, I knaw I will. She sounds like a posh version of me ma, the way you talk of her.'

'Yes, I think that's what she is, as I feel so close to your ma, when you talk about her. Well, my darling, we'd better sort ourselves out and get back. I'm on-duty this evening.'

'Oh? I was hoping we could make an evening of it – go dancing or sommat.'

'Sorry, I can't, but we have the rest of our lives in which to dance, so don't look downhearted. Hold my hand and let me help you up.'

When Alex lifted her, he took Daisy into his arms. His body began to sway to a tune he was humming. And there, deep in the hillside country of Singapore, they danced a waltz. She never wanted this moment to end – the afternoon would be etched in her memory. She was dizzy with love, and nothing could ever change or hurt that. Nothing.

Only the shiver that seized her body seemed to be saying otherwise. She dismissed it. Everyone felt these moments of anxiety. How could they not, with their lives in danger every moment of every day? And now the safe haven that she and Florrie thought they had found was in greater danger than most.

## CHAPTER THIRTEEN

# *London*

## Sibbie and Marjie

Feeling better after their bath, Sibbie and Marjie curled up on the sofa. They'd not been able to talk to each other about anything they either knew or speculated about, for fear of being overheard, but now at last they could.

'Well, here we are, Marjie, this is the last leg. We're in this flat now until they contact us and give us our orders. It's scary, isn't it?'

'It is, but I sometimes think there's many sides to us all, especially to women. And we can do a lot more than is normally expected of us. Look at how we have come through the same training as the men on our course. I try to hang on to that, as it tells me that although I am scared, I am up to whatever they throw at us, and that helps to give me confidence.'

'Yes, you're right. We did well, and for the most part, I enjoyed it. But that was training, and now there is the reality to deal with.'

'I don't seem able to. My main emotion is . . . well, it is going to tear me in two, seeing Wills again and then having to leave him. Do you think he will feel the same way about me as he did?'

'Of course he will. I have told you, Marjie: he couldn't contact you, it would be against the rules.'

'I know. And yet, knowing him for just one day, I am so nervous about it all.'

'You're bound to be. I bet you he'll be here any moment. Being one of our seniors, he knows exactly where we are at any given time.'

'What? No – I am in my dressing gown. He can't!'

'Ha, you daft ha'p'orth. If anyone knocks on the door, I'll go – curlers an' all.'

'You sound like your lovely Aunt Betsy.'

'I know a bit of northern lass comes out in me sometimes, when Mum isn't listening.'

They were quiet for a moment, each thinking of loved ones.

This flat they had been brought to was the kind of place young people rented: shabby and yet functional. The leather sofa, with its high rounded arms, had seen better days, and so had the rug in front of the gas fire. There was very little else in the room; just a small table under the window, with a wireless on it. Victor Sylvester's 'You're Dancing on My Heart' was playing, but, like the whole country, Sibbie and Marjie were waiting for the music to stop and for the news to broadcast. The BBC's bulletins had become the only link to know what was happening wherever loved ones were serving abroad.

Sibbie so wanted to hear that the nurses of the Alexandra Military Hospital in Singapore were safe. As it was, she was worried sick about Billy and knew Aunt Betsy must be, too, as the news coming out of Malaya wasn't good.

These thoughts spurred her on. 'You know, Marjie, although I am desperate to see Paulo and hope that we go to France, more than anything I want to help to bring this war to a successful end. I want to make this a safe world once more.'

'Will it ever be that, Sibbie? Our mothers and fathers fought such a war, and yet here we are, once again in a very unsafe world.'

'I don't know what my mum did, as she never talks about it, but my father didn't fight; he wormed his way out of it all. But your mum and Aunt Ella, and Aunt Mags, did all they could, as did Uncle Cyrus and Uncle Jerome, and the man I loved as a father – Montel. And yes, you're right, all it did was give twenty years of peace, and here we are again. Oh, I hope it isn't too long before we hear about our assignment. I'm eager, but the longer we have to wait, the more I'm frightened that the scared part of me will take over and I won't be able to do it.'

Marjie's voice had a tremor as she said, 'Me too. But we will, won't we, Sibbie?'

With her plate now empty, Sibbie leaned forward and put it on the small occasional table in front of them, then took Marjie's plate from her, before putting her arm around her, feeling sorry now that she'd unnerved her friend.

'We will, Marjie. Don't mind me and my doubts. Our training will kick in and we'll be fine.' She didn't feel as confident as she sounded, though. Her heart was beating wildly at the realization that this was it. No further distractions, as the training had been; and nothing more to undertake, to prove that they were able. Just the job ahead of them, which would take them into the unknown, and then so much would be expected of them.

Marjie's head came to rest on Sibbie's shoulder. 'I wish

we could wake up and it would all be a dream.' She'd hardly said this before a loud wailing got them both jumping off the sofa.

'Oh, Sibbie, an air raid!'

The sound of a distant droning noise shot terror through Sibbie. Marjie's eyes showed that her fears matched Sibbie's, and this spurred her to action. 'We have to dress very, very quickly and find shelter. Hurry, Marjie.'

It was the quickest either of them had ever dressed in their lives. Within minutes they were running down the stairs from their second-floor flat, with Sibbie shouting, 'The Underground. Let's make for there. We passed Charing Cross Road Underground station when we were being brought here, and it was only a little way down the road. I've read that Londoners make for stations in an air raid.'

As they ran along the road, the shadows of the aircraft darkened the pavement, and the noise filled Sibbie's head to the exclusion of everything else, leaving her with a desperation she'd never felt before.

'Come on, luv, get yourselves in 'ere.'

The woman standing at the entrance to the Underground sounded as calm as if they were running from a rainstorm, instead of for their lives, and this reassured Sibbie.

'That's right, run along down them steps there. There's a few of them, but you'll be safe down there. Besides, they haven't dropped their bombs yet, so we should miss this lot.'

'Thank you.' Her own voice sounded alien to Sibbie. Feeling Marjie's hand in hers gave her comfort as they skipped down the steps together.

When they reached the bottom, women in Salvation Army uniforms greeted them. 'We've some hot tea on the go,

157

girls. Find somewhere to sit; we don't reckon it'll be long before the all-clear.'

All the benches were taken, but they found an empty space next to a wall and sat down. With the cold of the concrete slabs filtering through their clothing, they both caught their breath and then giggled with the relief that the feeling of being safe gave them.

A child a little way away from them began to cry. Sibbie called her over. 'What's your name?'

The little girl tearfully told her that she was called Susan.

'Ha, that's my mum's name. And, you know, she told me that all Susans are very brave. So don't cry, love. It'll only upset your mum.'

Susan smiled and wiped away her tears with her grubby fists, making dirty marks under her eyes.

'How about we play hopscotch? Have you ever played it?'

Susan nodded. 'We need a stone, and there's not one 'ere.'

'We can use a penny. I have two in my coat pocket. The winner keeps the penny – how does that sound?'

'We ain't got no chalk.'

''Ere, Susan, stop being so bleedin' awkward. You can count, can't yer? Yer don't need the numbers written down to know where they are.'

Sibbie was shocked; she wanted to shake the woman, as she saw more tears brim in the child's eyes. An urge seized her to take Susan in her arms and hug her. This wasn't how a child should spend her time: frightened and hiding away from bombs, with dozens of other people, most total strangers to her.

'I know, we'll play toss the coin instead. I've got my

lipstick in my pocket. I'll place that on the ground, and we both have a penny each and take turns to toss it towards the lipstick. The one who gets the nearest to the lipstick is the winner.'

"'Ere, luv, I've heard of a woman never going anywhere without her lippie, but that's taking it a bit far, ain't it?'

Sibbie laughed. The lipstick had just happened to be in her coat pocket, but she didn't say this. 'A girl's got to look glamorous wherever she goes. I mean, you never know.'

At this, the women around her laughed and Sibbie felt that they were now on her side. She turned back to Susan and saw that her face was lit with smiles. This warmed her heart, as she knew she'd made this frightening moment a little better for the girl and, in doing so, she'd lost her own fear. The thought came to her that when the memory returned, as she knew it would, she would think of this child, and all these people who lived their lives in fear, and maybe that would give her the courage to carry on.

With the all-clear sounding two hours later, Sibbie and Marjie walked back to the flat. The air had a tinge of smoke in it, but they were relieved to find that nothing near them had been hit. When they reached the flat, Wills was standing outside, smoking a cigarette. Marjie gave a gasp of delight and ran towards him. 'Wills. Oh, Wills!'

He threw his cigarette down, put it out with his foot and met Marjie, lifting her and swinging her round. 'Marjie, at last! I've missed you so much.'

Sibbie smiled at them, but didn't hang around. She skipped up the steps, feeling happy for Marjie, but a little lonely at the same time.

When the two joined her a few moments later, Wills told them that he was on official business. 'I've come with news of your posting. You're scheduled to be dropped into France, but not until the fifth of January.'

'Where in France?'

'I'm not party to that yet, Sibbie. Some sensitive information is held back until the last moment; and sometimes, even then, the agent isn't told until they are in the air. But I have your reporting instructions here. You're to report to Baker Street for a final briefing on Monday the fourth at ten a.m. Take nothing with you but dress warmly – jumpers and that kind of thing. Some essential wear will be delivered to you: overall-type clothing, with lots of useful pockets. You'll be given secret weapons and items that you have been trained to use and assemble – such as the pen that is really a transmitting component for the wireless that you will take with you. The Resistance group you meet up with will put the wireless in a secret place and then, when you need to send a message, you only need to carry the pen on you. This means that if you are apprehended and searched, nothing will give your mission away. Without the component, the wireless is useless, so if it is found it cannot be used.'

Excitement vied with fear in Sibbie. 'Marjie, it's really happening, at last.' Marjie didn't respond, as she and Wills held each other's gaze. 'Look, I'll leave you two to it. I could do with an early night,' Sibbie went on.

'No, Sibbie; I have more to tell you and, well, Marjie may need you.' Wills shuffled in an uncomfortable way before moving closer to Marjie. 'Sit down, Marjie. I have some news for you.'

Marjie sat on the sofa, her movements zombie-like, her wide eyes staring up at Wills.

Sibbie felt the fear of the moment. She took a deep breath,

but what Wills said wasn't the terrible news she was expecting to hear. 'Marjie, your mother has been in touch. She is here in London.'

'Oh, Wills, that's wonderful news. Where is she? Is my father with her, and Aunt Ella . . . and . . . What is it, Wills? What's wrong?'

'Your mother wrote to the War Office asking to be put in touch with you. She said you were in Lincolnshire and wanted permission to visit you. Look, Marjie, what I'm going to tell you will be a great test for you. I want you to open your mind as to why what was done had to be done.'

Fear registered on Marjie's face. Sibbie wanted to go to her, but couldn't move. Her imagination was showing her the possibilities of what could have happened to dear Aunt Flors.

'We had to interrogate your mother.'

'No!'

'She's fine, and she wasn't hurt in any way, but it seemed very strange that she should suddenly turn up, telling the story that she had escaped from France. That the Resistance had organized her passage to Switzerland and told her about contacts there who would help her. These contacts arranged a passage for her, on a flight with a diplomat who was being transported to the South of England. A great deal of suspicion surrounded your mother's story, and questions were asked: Was she a collaborator? Did she know about your training? And then – when that was clearly not so – what could she tell us about operations in her area? To that effect, she has been very helpful.'

'Wills, you're talking about my mama! Not about a spy. How could you?'

Wills dropped onto one knee in front of Marjie. 'Try to

understand, darling. We had no choice. After your training, you should expect no less of us, and you know our ways. You will have to follow them yourself, no matter who the person is that comes under suspicion. The secrecy of our agents, and our organization, is paramount. You have to be prepared to shop even me, if you think I am acting suspiciously.'

Marjie was quiet for a moment. Then her expression changed. 'Of course. I'm sorry . . . I was just shocked. Am I to be allowed to see my mama, and where is she living? Is she in her house in London?'

'Marjie, we have to protect you and Sibbie at all costs. There is a lot invested in you. The job you are going to do will contribute greatly to the disruption of the Germans' plans.'

Although Sibbie, too, was shocked, she did understand, but she knew how difficult it would be for Marjie, if permission wasn't granted.

'Is the answer "No"? Can you not even tell me if she is alone, or what has happened to the rest of my family?'

'I can give you news, but whether you should have any contact is still being considered. I'm sorry, Marjie, so very sorry. Your mother knows you are well and, until a decision one way or the other is made, she has been told that your work involves you being on duty at all hours; that you are a spotter and plotter in Lincolnshire, whose leave is so short that you don't have enough time to travel. That she can write to you, and will receive letters on a regular basis; and she has been assured that you are safe.'

'But how will I be able to write to her, if I don't know what she is saying to me in her letters? I don't understand.'

'Before you go, you will write many letters – both of you

will. They will be censored, so make them general. No talk of the war, just about your health; make up little things that you do together when you snatch an hour's respite. Keep them reassuring, so that none of your families feel concerned about you. Your mother knows, Marjie, that she will only receive three or four letters a year at most, so write enough letters to cover two years and we will space them out accordingly, adding the date, and so on . . . Marjie, I am so very sorry, darling.'

'Don't call me that!'

'Marjie, please. Let me report back that you dealt with this professionally, and in a manner that spoke well of your future conduct, when faced with difficult situations.'

'Is that what this is: a final test?'

'Yes, and no. Of course it is important how you react, and to that degree it is a test, but I haven't been sent specifically to test you.'

'Marjie, I feel terrible that this has happened, but at least you have news of your mother.'

'But I don't, Sibbie. All I know is that Mama is here. I know nothing of my father and Aunt Ella, or my brothers.'

They were all quiet for a moment. Sibbie didn't know what to do or say, as this was something she could offer no comfort on; it had to be worked out by Marjie, and Marjie alone.

'I can give you news about all of your family, but none of it is good. Oh, Marjie, I feel that I am losing you, and I have longed for your parachute training to be over, just to spend some time with you before you leave. I should have let someone else come and tell you, but I couldn't bear that. I had to be the one, and now I want to support you.'

When Marjie was unbending in her reaction to Wills,

Sibbie felt so sorry for him. She listened as he told them that much of what he would say was classified information, and that they must remember they had signed the Official Secrets Act.

Then the horrific tale unfolded: of Randie going missing; of Freddy fighting with the Allied forces; of Monty's whereabouts being unknown; that Marjie's father, Cyrus, was assumed to be with the Resistance, while Arnie was acting as a coordinator over the different factions in the area; of how Paulo was leading the Hérault Resistance group; and then of the terrible plight of Ella and Lonia.

'We know that Ella is in a camp in northern France for British citizens. There has been an application by the Red Cross for aid for her – the British POWs receive a monthly allowance and regular Red Cross parcels, once they are registered. But the main worry is that she told the Red Cross that the Germans know she is of Jewish descent.'

Both Marjie and Sibbie gasped at this.

'The programme to deport the Jews from France is gaining strength, and we know that there are many Jews in this same camp; they are posing as British citizens and are refugees from Poland. They are moneyed folk, and of high standing in their communities. They could bribe and pay their way out of Poland, but if the Germans find out about them, we dread to think what will happen.'

'And my mama knows all this and has to bear it all on her own – away from Papa, and with no news of her sons, and only false news of her daughter? It's barbaric. My poor darling mama.'

At this, Marjie broke down. Sibbie slid into the seat next to her on the sofa. Her own heart was breaking for her aunt and uncle, and for all her cousins; and for Aunt Ella, Lonia,

Paulo and Arnie, who must know by now, from Cyrus, that Ella had been taken.

It was then that Marjie voiced what had just occurred to Sibbie, as she asked how it was that her mother and Ella got separated.

'I didn't want to tell you this part, but . . .'

What Wills told her next was worse than anything he'd told them before. Marjie broke down completely, sobbing on Sibbie's shoulder. Sibbie's own composure broke then and they cried together.

Wills didn't move from his crouching position in front of Marjie. When Sibbie looked up, tears were streaking his face. And it came to her that these two had found something so beautiful, so very suddenly, and it couldn't be snatched away from them like this. None of this was Wills's fault; he wouldn't have been the one to order Aunt Flors's interrogation. And yet, knowing all he knew, he'd volunteered to be the one to come and tell Marjie. At this thought, Sibbie knew that she had to say something.

'Marjie, you have lost so much. As your cousin and friend, I share that loss and understand in the way that only someone who loves you can. Wills loves you and knows your pain. Don't shut him out. He knew the cost to himself in coming to tell you everything, but his love for you drove him to do so. He isn't the perpetrator of the deeds done to our family – simply the one who chose to bear the burden of giving the terrible news to you, so that he could be here for you.'

Marjie didn't move for a moment. Her head remained on Sibbie's shoulder. Slowly she lifted it. When she was sitting up straight, she put her hands out to Wills. 'Hold me, Wills. Help me. Help me to bear it all in the way that I should.'

Wills lifted Marjie up off the sofa until she was standing, then held her to him. Sibbie got up and walked out of the room and went to the bedroom she shared with Marjie, thanking God that she'd been able to make Marjie see the situation as it really was.

She thanked God, too, that her immediate family were all right – at least her mum, her stepdad Rory and Aunt Betsy, Angus and Roderick and Rosie; and now Aunt Flors, too, was safe. But so many were in danger. Kneeling by her bed, she prayed harder than she'd ever prayed before in her life, for all those she loved, but as she did so, her head sank deeper and deeper into her chest with the realization that there was so much to face.

# CHAPTER FOURTEEN

# *London*

## Sibbie and Marjie

Christmas, in a day's time, was all planned, as Sibbie found out the next morning. Wills was taking them to his home, just as he had said he would.

'He'll be picking us up around eleven. I can't see him today, as he said he has an important assignment. And, Sibbie, I don't know how to say this, but . . . well, we are staying the night and I – I . . .'

'You don't have to explain anything to me, Marjie. I'm very happy for you. I saw that your bed hadn't been slept in, and I heard Wills leave about an hour ago.'

Marjie blushed, then giggled. 'I thought you would think I'd got up early and made my bed.'

Sibbie picked a cushion up and threw it at Marjie. 'You – make your bed? Ha, that'll be the day.'

Catching the cushion, Marjie burst out laughing. The sound was such a relief to Sibbie.

'Thanks, Sibbie. I have so much tugging at my heart that I don't know how I'm going to get through it all.'

'Well, we will be together. We'll help each other through this, Marjie, we will.'

Marjie nodded. 'And to have the memory of Wills – and of me truly being his – will help me, I know it will.'

'Marjie, really, you don't have to explain. You deserve Wills's love, and the happiness he gives you. You are so courageous. If I had the news about my mum that you had of yours, I would go to pieces. I nearly did anyway, as it was devastating to hear what poor Aunt Flors and Aunt Ella have been through. I know you went to pieces at first, but look at how you have dealt with it. You are truly amazing, and you inspire me. Let's have one of our hugs.'

As they hugged, Sibbie thought that having Marjie by her side would help her and drive her actions. *I will always think of her safety before my own – that's not what we have been taught, but it is what I'll do, and that will help to give me the courage I will need.*

When they arrived at Wills's apartment the next day, they were taken aback, when faced with the truth of his wealth. His home wasn't really an apartment, as they had thought, but a four-storey house in Kensington.

The basement, accessed separately, was where his main staff lived: his cook and her husband, who was Wills's driver and manservant. The ground floor housed the kitchens at the back, with the entrance from street level at the front of the house. This took you into a magnificent hall, from which a spiral staircase with golden, intricately designed spindles and a highly polished deep-mahogany handrail led up to Wills's living quarters – a sumptuous four-bedroom, four-bathroom two-storey apartment that was just beautiful. The first floor of the apartment was divided into three rooms: a study, with the usual mahogany desk, red leather chairs and book-lined walls; and a music-cum-leisure-room, with a grand piano, an assortment of deep-seated cream sofas and matching armchairs. Occasional mahogany tables were dotted about, some of which housed games – chess was laid out on one; backgammon on another; and a third table had a green baize top, with two packs of playing cards neatly stacked on it. Magazines were piled tidily on another. A drinks cabinet, which was almost a full bar, graced one corner of the room; and on the opposite wall, behind royal-blue curtains, was a French door, which led on to the walled flat roof of the floor below. This was immaculately laid out as a garden, complete with a small fountain.

But it was the lounge that really took their breath away. The cream and royal-blue scheme continued in here, but the furniture was huge. A sofa dominated the room. It was at least eight feet long, with very high back and arms. Its cushions were feather-filled and welcomed you as if cuddling you. Four matching chairs, which again were much bigger than ordinary armchairs, were placed so that wherever you sat, you were near to and facing the wonderful marble fireplace, which held a roaring log fire, flanked by a dazzling pine Christmas tree that gave off the wonderful smell of the forest it had come from.

Elegant marble statues of Roman women stood in each corner, and the occasional table that graced the centre of the room was also made of marble. Paintings that seemed authentic artworks by Old Masters graced the walls. At that moment Sibbie wished she knew something about art, in order to compliment Wills on them. But she didn't try to; she simply enjoyed the magnificence of their presence.

For all this, Wills was just Wills, and he welcomed them as if he was doing so into a terraced house in the East End, in a lovely 'make yourself at home' way. And Sibbie thought him more handsome than she had previously, as his casual dress – slacks topped with a checked shirt and a knitted sleeveless pullover – gave him a rakish look. She could see the admiration and love in Marjie's eyes as he greeted her with a hug.

After they had finished their lunch and were in the games room, and had each decided to challenge Wills to a game of chess, as he'd been boasting how good he was, Wills brought out the best surprise of the day so far. 'Before we play, Marjie, I have further news for you. I have managed to get M to agree to you seeing your mama.'

Marjie screamed with joy. 'Mama! Oh, Mama. How? When? Oh, Wills, why didn't you tell me as soon as I came?'

'I had to wait for privacy. With the staff taking your coats, then serving us drinks and our meal, it wasn't something I could broach. But, darling, I can tell you that we are working to fix up a meeting. It can't be at her home, as that might make someone suspicious.'

This alarmed Sibbie, and she could see how it shocked Marjie, but they said nothing, letting Wills continue.

'We know there are many spies among us, but we don't know who they are, or where they are. We feel it is possible that an alert will have been sent to these spies about your mother. Not that she is in any danger, as we feel confident, from what she told us, that it won't be thought she knows anything of interest. When we brought her in, we did so in such a way that any spies wouldn't know where she was going, and we made sure she wasn't followed. But just the same, as a precaution, we have warned her that she may be being watched. If these spies find out that she has a daughter here, they might look into what you are doing. We can't take any chances.'

'I understand, and I trust you to take care of her, darling. So is this what you were doing yesterday? How did you manage it, as you seemed so certain that I wouldn't be able to see Mama?'

'When you told me last night, darling, about your mother's heroics in the last war, I decided then to try to do something, using that information. I was granted an interview with M. He was very interested to hear about how your mother got herself and two other nurses out of Belgium. He intends to look into it further, once this war is over, when he may have recourse to interview people who were involved and prepare a case for the women to receive an award.'

'That's wonderful. They so deserve to be recognized. And this led to him relenting and letting me see Mama?'

'Yes. Your mother was brought in. She was there a long time, because before M would see her, I had to take her through the Official Secrets Act and get her to sign it. She was then questioned about you, and it was learned that she had told a neighbour you were stationed in Lincolnshire. She was told by M to tell this neighbour that her information was wrong, and that you had since transferred to the Medical Corps; that at home you had been a member of the Red Cross society, had trained in first aid and are now stationed in Africa.'

'How was Mama, and how did she take all of this?'

'Remarkably well. She showed the mettle that she must have had as a young woman, when she was in Belgium. M was very impressed.'

'He won't think of recruiting her, will he?'

'No, although he expressed regret at this. But it isn't policy to recruit members of the same family. Your father is a possible encumbrance, as it is. But we are working on a plan to have him informed of our intentions for him, if he will come home. If he agrees, he will be lifted out at some stage.'

'That would be wonderful. I would feel so much better knowing that he is safe.'

'Yes, and he could be very useful to us: his knowledge of the area will be used; he will be brought into the office, given the status of an officer and will work with us on what we are trying to achieve in the area. Not only that, but M has promised to do all he can to locate Randolph.'

'Really! And does Mama know this?'

'Yes, M told her everything. She was very professional and thanked him, even though it was clear that all she'd been told was tearing at her emotions. She really would make an excellent agent. You share her qualities. How you handled knowing that your mother was here, and that you were refused permission to contact her, has greatly impressed M. It demonstrates that you are the right calibre of person for the job.'

Marjie and Sibbie felt elated and began to really enjoy the rest of their day, even more so than they had until now. By suppertime they were a little merry, laughing at the silliest things as if they were children, as they ate delicious canapés from the silver platters on which they were presented.

When Wills wound up the gramophone, once the remains of the food had been cleared away, Sibbie decided it was time for her to retire. To her amusement, neither Marjie nor Wills protested. 'Would you like a hot drink bringing up to you, Sibbie?'

'No, just a jug of water, thanks, Wills.'

'You'll find that by your bedside already, and your bed

172

will be turned down for you. Have a good night's sleep, Sibbie, and thank you for a lovely day.'

Marjie stood up then and gave Sibbie a hug. As she did so, Sibbie felt a deep longing in her heart, for she so wished she could be with her Paulo. To know him as Marjie knew Wills. To be shown his love for her, in the way that Wills had shown his love for Marjie. The feeling was almost too painful to bear.

Always in tune to Sibbie's feelings, Marjie walked with her to the stairs. There she took her hands. 'It won't be long now, darling Sibbie. I feel certain, from what Wills said about my father and other things, that we are going to Hérault. It makes sense anyway, as the Resistance is active in that area, and we both know the area so well. Then you will be reunited with your Paulo and can express the love you feel for one another, but have only been able to speak of till now.'

'I know. I can't wait, and if they don't send us to that area, I will find a way to visit him, once we are in France. It feels so strange – having been in love with him for so long, and then to find out by letter that he felt the same, and not being able to tell him of my love.'

'Your time will come; I know it will.'

Realizing she was putting a dampener on Marjie's happiness, Sibbie made a huge effort to giggle and to make Marjie do so. Mimicking her Aunt Betsy, she said, 'Eeh, it'll be grand, and you won't see owt of me for a week!'

Marjie laughed out loud, her happiness shining from her once more.

As Sibbie went up the stairs, the thought came to her, as it had before, just how much courage Marjie had. Her happiness must be bittersweet, knowing that this short time she had with Wills would soon come to an end and they would be parted, for an unknown, but probably very long time.

The same thought was going through Marjie's mind, as part of her heart was heavy with all she had to bear, and for her dear friend; and at knowing that this time she had with Wills was so limited. But she was determined to fill whatever time they could spend together with happy memories, to sustain her when they were apart.

The beautiful song from Vera Lynn, 'A Nightingale Sang in Berkeley Square', filled the room as Marjie went back in. A welcome draught wafted through the French doors, billowing the curtains. 'I thought the room was getting a little stuffy, darling. It's quite a clear night, after all the fog we've had lately. If you are not too cold, I thought we would dance under the stars.'

A feeling of euphoria surged through Marjie. Going into Wills's open arms, she began to sway to the music with him. 'I would love to dance outside – I don't care how cold it is.'

Wills switched off the lights and the fire's glow lit the room in a flickering way. 'That won't be seen from outside, so we won't get into trouble with the air-raid wardens.'

Holding hands, they went through the curtains, careful to close them afterwards. Wills guided Marjie in the darkness.

'There's no moon visible tonight, as it is a new moon. When it does show from behind the clouds, it will only be a faint impression, so there's no danger of any bombing, and that means few air-raid wardens will be about.'

Marjie giggled, feeling like a naughty child. Then Wills took her in his arms and, to the now-muffled strains of Vera's beautiful voice, they danced.

Being short of clothes, other than her uniform and a couple of day-outfits, Marjie wore the same costume she'd worn on the first day she'd met Wills. She'd discarded her jacket, and the flared skirt lent itself well to the dance movements of the waltz.

The wind was keen and tried its best to freeze them, but Marjie felt strangely warm, as if it were a summer night. Nothing could daunt her happiness as Wills held her close. She could feel every part of his strong body, and thrilled at his kisses as he muzzled her neck. 'Marjie, oh, Marjie, I wish we could marry before you leave, but with the Christmas holidays, the offices are closed for a week and it isn't possible to get a quick licence. Would you marry me, if I could do so?'

'I'll marry you right now, darling. Right here. We can say our vows to each other. In France, the bride and groom can say their own words, after the formal vows.'

The music had come to an end and, in the silence, they clung to each other. 'Let's do that, Marjie. I know what I want to say to you. But are you warm enough?'

'I think, if we're not dancing, I will need my jacket; and my scarf can act as my veil.'

They giggled again at this, and it felt to Marjie as if she was on a wonderful adventure.

'You get your jacket, darling. Wilson will have put it on the coat stand on the landing. But hurry back.'

When Marjie returned, Wills had over his arm one of the net curtains that hung behind the room's drapes. 'Here you are, darling, you can use this as a veil. And this' – as she took the veil, Wills plucked one of the beautiful silk lilies from the display that stood on a marble pedestal next to the grand piano – 'can be your bouquet.'

'And the ring?'

'Oh, I hadn't thought of that. Look, it will be too big, but will you accept my father's ring? My parents went to America before the war. An elderly aunt on my mother's side, who emigrated there many years ago, was very ill, and Mother was fretting about her. It has been too dangerous for them to come back, and I am glad of that. I was already an officer, having passed out of Sandhurst, and of course there was a strong inkling that war might break out. My father didn't want to leave, but he wouldn't have been able to take part in active service, for he . . . well, he lost a leg in the last war.'

'Oh, I am sorry, Wills.'

'No, he is fine and he manages well; he can even walk for short periods of time using a false leg. Anyway, before he left, we had a talk and, at the end of it, he gave me his ring and asked me to wear it, then he would know that I had a part of him with me, wherever I was.'

'That's a beautiful story, Wills. I love your father already.'

'He is a special person, and so is my mother.'

'I'd be honoured to accept your father's ring.'

'It will just be for a couple of days, and then I will buy you your own ring. And we can go to a church and say the proper vows over it, when no one is about.'

'Oh, Wills, that will be lovely. One day this will be all over and we will be together, and I will meet your parents, and you my family.'

'Yes, and I will present you to them as my wife. As you will be that from tonight, in all but the official documents.' Taking her free hand, he led her outside once more.

Despite the wind, Marjie managed to fix her veil – she didn't think of it as a curtain – as she lifted a hairpin from each side of her head to clip the net into place.

'Leave your hair to tumble over your face, darling.'

She smiled up at Wills. With the veil secure, she whispered, 'I'm ready.'

Wills pulled the curtain back so that the light shone on her. 'You look beautiful. Oh, my Marjie.'

Dropping the curtain, he gave her the lily. His face was so close to hers, she could feel his breath on her cheek and, despite the darkness, see the tears glistening in his eyes. 'Marjella, I give to you all that I am. I will love and honour you till the day I die. I will cherish every moment I have with you. You are the completion of me, and I take you as my wife.'

Marjie's throat constricted and her heart swelled. 'William, you are my rose, my sunny day, my rippling, timeless river, my pine tree in the forest where I live – my world. I will love you forever. You are me. You are my beloved husband.'

His kiss was gentle. He held her as if she were a fragile, precious being. To her he gave his love, and she accepted it. As he slipped the ring onto her finger, it didn't matter that it was huge. It was the symbol of their love, and always would be.

Taking her hand, Wills led her inside. With no words passing between them, they climbed the stairs. Once in Wills's bedroom, he once again took her in his arms. His kiss this time was passionate. It held his longing and lit hers.

Slowly they undressed each other, until they lay on the bed naked. Wills gazed down at Marjie. 'You are so beautiful that I want to kiss every part of you.'

'And I want you to, my husband – I need you to.'

The sensations this gave her took her to a blissful world

that only she and Wills inhabited. When at last he entered her, she felt that world burst into a million stars of love, happiness and, most of all, hope.

Marjie's meeting with her mama, the next day, was a joyful reunion mixed with a tearful well of anguish. They clung to each other as they stood, like any other mother and daughter, saying goodbye on Victoria station. The platform was crowded with couples kissing goodbye, anxious parents seeing their sons off to war, and people who looked as though their own world was the most important one, as they strutted towards trains or exits carrying briefcases.

'My darling, I am so proud of you – if, as expected, so very afraid for you. I don't know which is worse: not seeing you and not knowing, or seeing you and knowing.'

'Oh, Mama, seeing you is so much better, and having you understand my position, too. I know you will worry, but at least you won't think that I don't care about you. I have missed you so much and have longed for information about you all.'

'I would never think that, darling Marjella. And I wish I had better news for you. But try not to worry. I know your father and Arnie will do all they can to get to Ella and Lonia and to rescue them. And no news from, or about, Freddy is good news. As for me, I'll go and stay with Aunt Mags for a while, and she will help me.'

'I'm proud of you too, Mama. You are so brave, and yet you have so much to contend with. I hope you soon hear news of Randolph. As for Monty, we'll just have to pray for him. I am more worried about him than any of them.'

'Me too. Why he held the views he did, I do not know.

He genuinely wanted to go to Germany to help in the war effort there . . . Well, maybe I do know why. He has always reminded me of your late uncle Harold.'

'Oh, Mama. Monty was so young and idealistic; he was misguided, that's all. All that Harold did to you is in the past and won't rise up again. Poor Monty.'

They clung together, and while she was in her mama's arms Marjie whispered, 'Can I tell you something wonderful?'

Mama held her at arm's length. 'You're in love. I could tell the moment I spotted you, and the man is William, isn't it? You were looking up into his face when you came into view.'

'I am, Mama, so very much in love, even though we haven't known each other long. Do you think love this deep can happen in an instant?'

'I know it can. As I came through the checkpoint at the Belgian border I had to report to your father. He looked up at me – and it happened. This complete stranger was the love of my life, my world. It happened for him, too.' Mama's eyes misted over.

'Mama, we married last night. Well, we pledged ourselves to each other, in our own service. To me, Wills is my husband.'

'That's wonderful, my darling. I am so happy for you, and yet so sad for you.'

'Don't be. I'm so happy, and I want that happiness to last for the rest of the time we have together, and beyond.'

'I understand. The memory of the time I had with your father, before our war took him away, has lasted with me to this very day.'

They were both quiet, and Marjie thought of the injustice

of it all. That her parents went through all they did, only to face it again now. It broke her heart.

'Don't cry, darling. Wipe your tears and smile. It's the only way. Let me remember your lovely smile till we meet again.'

They smiled at each other, both struggling to contain the tears that threatened, but they felt the other's heartache, despite their brave efforts.

'Goodbye, Mama. Keep strong.'

'Goodbye, my darling girl, until we meet again.'

With this, Marjie walked away. As she reached the steps she turned, but her mama had vanished into the swirling crowd. She understood. Sometimes the only way to deal with things was to walk away from them. She had to do that, too.

# PART FOUR
# Britain, France and Singapore, 1942

~

*The Thin Thread of Life*

# CHAPTER FIFTEEN

# *Maidstone*

## Rosie

With the news coming out of Malaya, and Hong Kong having fallen to the Japs, the talk was of the danger to Singapore. Rosie was beside herself with worry. The last letter from her ma told of how she'd heard nothing of Billy, but to keep strong, as they would surely hear if something terrible happened.

Poor Ma, she was coping well. How Rosie longed to go to her, but time off was at a premium and the hospital was busier than ever with all the returning wounded, and most rest periods were taken in the nurses' quarters, so as to be on hand if they were needed.

Rosie had long since given up badgering the powers-that-be to allow her to serve abroad. The last letter she had received from her superiors had told her that, with her sisters already abroad, they didn't think it prudent to send the last girl of the family into a danger zone.

Rosie now let out a long and anguished sigh.

'That was a deep one, Rosie. You fed up then?'

Rosie looked up at her friend, who had just come off-duty. 'Naw, Freda. I were having a to-do in me brain.'

Freda laughed. 'If I know you for a hundred years, Rosie, I'll never cease to find you funny. It's your sayings. A "to-do" in your brain? What's that, when it's at home?'

Rosie laughed, too. 'You knaw: when you're trying to solve a problem and you knaw you should do one thing, but you really want to do another.'

'Yes, I know. Is this over you wanting to serve abroad?'

'Aye.'

'Rosie, it isn't all that's bothering you, is it?'

'Don't ask, Freda. I'm trying me best to ignore that part of me.'

'It's Albie, isn't it? The German POW brought in with appendicitis. I know how you feel. I've known these last months, since he first came in when his plane ditched in the sea.'

'Did it show?'

'Not to anyone else, but since we have become closer, I could see what was happening, where Albie was concerned. Meeting him struck you like a bullet. Look, if it helps, he's being moved from surgical to medical, so you'll be caring for him. Though prepare yourself, as he isn't well.'

'What? Why?'

'His appendix burst and he has peritonitis. He'll probably be in your high-dependency beds when you get back from your break.'

'Eeh, naw.'

'Look, Rosie, take some advice from me, and try your hardest not to show how you feel.'

'I don't have to be told, Freda. I'm well aware of how folk look on fraternizing. I'll get back now, but I don't mind telling you, I hope I'm assigned to give Albrecht special care. I can't bear to think of anyone but me doing it. Not

184

that I don't trust them to give him the best of care, but things have changed a bit since the beginning, when the German pilots were first brought in. A lot of folk have lost brothers and sons, husbands and fiancés, and there was that bomb in the town. Attitudes towards the Germans around here are changing.'

'You're right, they are – and you can't blame people. Most of us knew the girl who was blown to smithereens a couple of weeks ago. And then there's that pilot who is terrifying everyone. He flew as low as three hundred feet the other day. Mrs Davis was hanging out her washing and she saw his face as clear as day. She thought he was going to shoot her, but he just stuck his tongue out at her. Pig!'

Rosie sighed. If someone as lovely and caring as her dear friend Freda could take such an attitude towards the Germans, then there was no hope for them. Not that she wanted there to be. She wanted to hate them herself, and in general she did. But Albie? No, she could never hate him. *I could love him, though.*

Shaking this thought away, she hurried back to the ward. Sister Jones met her, with the instruction she most wanted to hear. 'Nurse, come into my office.'

Closing the door behind her, Rosie waited until the sister sat down behind her desk. 'Is summat wrong, Sister?'

'No, nothing wrong. We have a German POW on our ward.' The sister went on to instruct Rosie that she was to do what she most wished to: be the nurse responsible for Albie's care.

Going through his notes with the sister put fear into Rosie. Albie truly was very ill, and it was touch and go for him. Trying to control her feelings, Rosie sent up a silent prayer: *Please, God, let Albie survive this.*

'Right, I want you to go and get some rest now, Rosie. As you know, we are very short-staffed, but the ward is quiet at the moment, and Nurse Blowen is coping. She has finished the bedpan round, and we have a young Red Cross student working as an orderly, so she is taking tea around. Nurse Rawlings is taking care of our POW, but I want you with him overnight, and I don't know when I will be able to relieve you.'

Rosie wanted to scream that the POW had a name; that he was a person, not a thing to be called by an acronym. And that she wanted to go to him now. What if Albie died this afternoon and she'd had no time with him? But she just took her leave politely and made her way to the nurses' quarters.

Once there, she couldn't sleep. Or even rest. She alternated between praying for her sisters and brothers – begging God to keep Daisy, Florrie and Billy safe – and almost screaming at Him to make Albie better and make it possible for them to be together one day. After a while she knew that trying to sleep was useless, and decided to take a long soak in the bath – a luxury not often afforded to her, as dozens of other girls needed their turn in the bathroom.

Lying back in the hot water, Rosie allowed her tears to flow. But they didn't bring her any release from the anguish that was her constant companion. She tried to think of something; anything rather than fear for her brother and sisters. The letter she'd had from Sibbie came to mind, but it didn't help. Oh, how she missed everyone.

Sibbie didn't give any details about the mysterious posting she and Marjella had talked about, when they'd all seen Daisy and Florrie off. She simply wrote:

*Me and Marjella are now settled in new posts and are
very happy about them. I won't be able to write much,
if at all, as my work will be intense, and I'll be based
deep in the countryside. But when I can, I will; and, as
everyone is saying these days, no news is good news, so
don't worry about me.*

Rosie pondered just what Sibbie and Marjie could possibly
be doing deep in the countryside that would mean they had
no time to write letters. But she couldn't come up with
anything other than deciphering intercepted messages that
were in German or French.

*How did life change so much?* They'd all been so happy,
as children.

Drying herself, Rosie checked her watch for the umpteenth
time. Still only four o'clock. Sister had said not to go on duty
until seven. Donning her dressing gown, she walked to the
window and looked out over the stark, late-January winter
scene. The trees in the hospital grounds were bare of leaves,
and their branches and the normally lush grassed areas were
clothed in last night's frost, which had not yet thawed. It was
a pretty scene that did nothing to lift Rosie's spirits. *This 'not
knowing' is awful. And although I know that for those actively
fighting this war there must be a lot of fear to contend with, for
those of us left holding the fort, there is both fear and deep anxiety.*

The door being flung open brought Rosie out of her
thoughts. 'Here you are! I went to your ward to see you,
but they said you were off-duty. How did that happen?'

Freda looked flushed, giving Rosie the feeling that something was amiss. She told her of Sister's plan.

'Well, why aren't you asleep? You'll be dead on your feet
before the night's done.'

'I knaw, but so much is going around me head.'

'Look, I'm off now, and Jeannie is, too. She's on her way, but you know Jeannie – she had to stop off at the canteen to see if there was anything she could snack on. Anyway, why don't the three of us go for a walk and have a cuppa in the tea shop. It might help you to forget your troubles for a while.'

Even when they wrapped up in their nursing capes, the freezing air bit into their bodies. The familiar sound of the clanging of the doorbell as they opened the tea-shop door was very welcome. They hurried inside and closed the door before Kath could shout at them, as she stood by her counter and turned round with that look on her face.

'Ha! We beat you to it, Kath. I tell you, if ever you close this place, you should get a job as a doorman – you'd enjoy that. Then you could open and close doors to your heart's content.'

'None of your cheek, Jeannie, or I won't be serving you any of the scones that are just about to come out of the oven; and you like them while they're still hot.'

Jeannie laughed. 'If you don't serve me, who are you going to serve? You're not exactly rushed off your feet, Kath.'

'Don't remind me. This weather's keeping everyone inside. I'm glad to see the three of you. Sit down and I'll bring your usual.'

'Phew, Jeannie, I thought for a mo that you'd cooked your goose with Kath. I've known her to throw people out who've riled her.'

'Not if they eat like me, she wouldn't. I'm her best customer.'

Rosie smiled at this. She loved the happy-go-lucky attitude of Jeannie. A plump girl, due to her eating habits, she had a pretty face that always seemed sunny, as she smiled all the time. She had lovely even, white teeth and full lips. Her hair, though, was her crowning glory: thick and very dark, it shone with many natural highlights – copper colours. She wore it wound into a bun while working, but when she released it and her hair fell around her face and hung down her back, it was beautiful.

Freda was the exact opposite. Tall and very slim, almost skinny really, she was fair-haired, and wore her hair cut short and curled under at the bottom – a style made popular by the lovely Queen Elizabeth.

'Right, we're here to get you out of the doldrums, Rosie. So start by telling us what's bothering you, eh?'

'Oh, Jeannie, you knaw it's me brother and me sisters. I told you they're stationed right where the Japs are closing in. I'm terrified sommat'll happen to any of them.'

Neither Jeannie nor Freda spoke for a minute, but then what comfort could they offer? Facts were facts, and what was being revealed about the Japanese methods of war, and their disregard for the conventions, was terrifying.

'All we can do is pray for them, Rosie, and I will, love.'

'Ta, Jeannie.'

'And I will, love. But although that's a terrible burden, you've other things on your mind, haven't you?'

'Aye, I have. But, well . . . it don't do to talk about it.'

'Look, we all know what it is; and you're right, it ain't a good idea to talk about it. But even so, I want you to know that I don't condemn you, but would warn you not to do anything about how you feel until the war's over and attitudes have changed a bit.'

'They'll only do that if we win, Jeannie.'

'And we're going to – we have to hang on to that, or we'll be without hope.'

'Jeannie's right. No matter how you feel, just keep a lid on it all. Albie's going nowhere; he'll be a prisoner till the end of the war, whatever the outcome. And if he feels the same about you, then what will be, will be.'

'We have to get him well first. I didn't like the look of the reports that came with him from surgical.'

Once again they all fell silent. Kath serving them her delicious scones helped. 'They smell grand, Kathy – remind me of home. Me ma does a lot of . . .'

'Come on, Rosie, cry it out. Holding it all in will cause you to have a breakdown, and you're with friends now.' An arm came round her. She looked up into Kath's face. 'I can't have this, crying in me cafe. Cheer up, girl, it may never happen.'

'She'll be all right, Kath. Things get on top of us now and then.'

'I don't wonder at it. And especially those of you who aren't from round here. I'll tell you what – I'll put the wireless on. They play some nice music in the early evening before the news comes on.'

'We can do a jig, Rosie; that'd cheer you up.'

As the music blasted out, Jeannie got up, scraping her chair loudly on the floor as she did so and, stuffing a mouthful of scone into her mouth, began to jig around in a hilarious fashion, holding up the skirt of her uniform.

'Oh, Jeannie, you are a clown.'

'Ha, I could dance you under the table, Freda.'

The music turned to a Scottish reel, and Freda stood. 'We'll see about that.'

'Now, girls, mind me furniture.'

Taking no notice, Freda linked arms with Jeannie and swung her round. Then she skipped away, before turning, and this time both girls met and linked arms again and did a twirl. The sight, and the sound of the music, lit something in Rosie. Having lived in Scotland since she was a little girl, she knew plenty about Scottish dancing. Getting up, she kicked off her heavy shoes and raised one arm above her head. Putting the other on her waist, and being light on her feet, she danced a proper, elegant Scottish jig, bringing the others to a standstill in amazement.

The feeling that she got as the music pulsated through her lifted Rosie and made her heart soar, making her feel as if she was in the inn at Portpatrick, dancing with the locals as Ma and Angus clapped along. The clapping and cheering were almost as loud from the three of them watching her, and they hooted as the dance came to an end.

'That was amazing, Rosie. Well done, you. And you look so much better now.'

'Aye, with the smell of the baking and the Scottish music, I felt as though I were at home, and it felt good.'

'You need some leave, Rosie. I'm going to tackle Sister about it. It's as Kath says: it ain't so bad for us as live around here, or in London, as I do. Freda can go home every night, and I can every time I have a day off. But you can't, and it ain't right. Leave has been cancelled for too long.'

As Rosie went on-duty, leave was the last thing on her mind. Albie had worsened, and now there was a fear for his life. Checking all of his vital signs further worried her. Putting her hand out, she stroked his blond hair from his burning forehead, leaving her hand resting there for a moment as she gazed down at him. Her love for him flowed from her.

Albie opened his eyes, his long eyelashes brushing his high cheekbones. 'N – Nurse Rosie?'

'Aye, it's me. I'm here, Albie, and I'll not leave you. Fight, Albie – get well. You can, you knaw. It sometimes only takes willpower, naw matter what we do. I'll not give up on you.'

'R – Rosie, I – I have the letter. For . . . my *Mutter*.'

'You'll not need that. You'll see your mother again, Albie, and you can tell her what you want to say. This war will end, and you'll go home, I promise.'

'*Nein*, Rosie. I – I'm . . . *fertig*.'

Rosie didn't fully understand, but thought Albie was telling her that he was finished. Usually an excellent English speaker, in his illness he was reverting to his native tongue.

'Naw, you're only done if you give up. Fight, Albie.'

His eyes closed. Rosie did her medical checks again, frantic for them to tell her that he wasn't entering the last phase of his life, and then sighed with relief as they showed a slight improvement. 'Sleep, Albie. Rest easy. You'll see your *Mutter* – you will.'

An hour later, after checking him a further time, Albie showed signs that his fever was deepening, as sweat stood out on his forehead. Fetching lukewarm water, Rosie began to wash him down, to try to cool him and make him more comfortable. Sister looked in at that point. 'How's he faring, Nurse?'

'His temperature is very high, Sister. I'm trying to cool him.'

'Open the window. I'd fetch a fan, but they are all in use.'

Rosie already knew this, as she'd sent an orderly in search

of one, but she had come back saying none were available; and yet Rosie knew that no one in the ward needed a fan more than Albie. It would be the senior nurses refusing. How they could do so, she did not know and she wanted to shout at Sister that – German or not – Albie deserved to have his life saved. But then she'd be doing Sister an injustice because no one cared more, even if in a cold detached way, than Sister did.

Opening the window blew a gale into the room and chilled Rosie.

'No, that's not acceptable. I'll be back in a moment.'

Rosie could have hugged Sister as she came back bearing a fan. 'There, I found one. Concentrate it on the patient. Nurse, I know we can't help how we feel, and I can see that this case has got to you, so I may think about swapping you with Nurse Potts, who is also on night-duty.'

Wanting to plead, but knowing that would mean that she would be taken off Albie's case for certain, Rosie kept her voice steady. 'Naw, I'll be fine, Sister. I feel no different about this patient than I do about any other. I just care deeply and want to save his life. I might be speaking out of turn, but some are not so caring of the German patients. I don't blame them, and I understand, but this man's life is hanging in the balance, and I want to make sure he gets the best attention we can give him.'

'No. You're not speaking out of turn, Nurse, and it's why I wanted you to do this. I can go to my bed resting easy, knowing that he is in your care, but please try to keep your emotions in check. Don't let your judgement be impaired by over-caring. Be professional in all you do, and he will have the best chance he can possibly have, in your hands.'

Sister was right, Rosie knew this, and nodded her head. 'I will, Sister. But can you instruct that if I need owt, I'm to have it, because not getting a fan was frustrating me. That's all my emotions were – anger and frustration.'

'Very well, I'll do that. Now, goodnight, Nurse, and good luck. If anyone can bring the young man through, you can with your excellent nursing skills.'

'Ta, Sister.'

With Albie now washed down, and a fresh sheet under him and another over him, Rosie concentrated the gently whirring fan on him. Albie gradually rested easier than he had, and Rosie was glad to see that after a little while his temperature lowered by a fraction. If that kept up, he would stand a chance.

Two hours later, Albie hadn't moved. His breathing was shallow, but steady. Checking his oxygen levels prompted Rosie to put an oxygen mask on him. As she tugged the heavy cylinder from the corner of the room to stand nearer to Albie, she prayed to God to make him better. Holding his hand, she whispered fervently what she'd told him earlier: 'Fight, Albie. Don't give in.' Then, without thinking, she added, 'Please don't give in, me darling.'

Albie stirred. His hand tightened on hers, his lovely blue eyes opened and seemed to contain a plea.

Rosie understood. 'Yes, Albie, I do love you. Get well for me.'

His weak hand let go of hers and she saw that he'd fallen asleep once more. But this time he seemed very much at peace.

Pulling her chair over to his bedside, Rosie sat down and took his hand in hers once more. Watching the rise and fall of his chest, she willed the movement to get stronger, and for Albie to breathe more deeply. But tiredness overtook her after half an hour, and the whirring of the fan lulled her to close her eyes.

'Nurse. Nurse!'

Rosie sat up, startled by the sudden intrusion into the dream she was having of running down the beach, holding Albie's hand, without a care in the world.

Looking up, she saw Nurse Potts staring down at her. Realization dawned on Rosie that Albie's hand had gone cold in hers. Slowly she looked back at him, not wanting to know the truth, but seeing what she feared had happened. Albie had gone.

'Naw . . . naw.'

What happened next was completely unexpected, because the cold-as-ice Nurse Potts grabbed Rosie and held onto her. 'Rosie, poor Rosie. I'm sorry. I know . . . well, I know how you feel. My fiancé was killed.' This came out on a sob.

'Oh, Elizabeth, I had naw idea, lass.'

Nurse Potts dried her eyes. 'I know. I've never spoken about it. Anyway, we must be professional at all times – it helps, you know. Forgive me for that breakdown. Now, we need the doctor. He will have to certify this young man's death. I'll send the night-porter; he's on the ward at the moment, bringing oxygen cylinders round, and wanted to know if we needed any. That's why I came in to check. In the meantime I'll inform the night-sister, and you take the oxygen off this young man, close his mouth, and so on. You know the drill.'

Taking no heed of the tears streaming down Rosie's face, Nurse Potts left the room.

'Oh, Albie, and I wasn't with you. How could I have fallen asleep?' But then the thought came to Rosie that she was with him, for his passing. She'd run along the beach with him in her dream. But it wasn't a dream. It was reality. And now she knew that any other dreams she'd harboured about Albie were never going to come true. Bending and kissing his lips, she said her goodbyes. 'I promise that one day I'll deliver your letter, Albie.'

Before she left, she took the letter from his personal effects and put it in her pocket. The address was on the envelope, but she wouldn't post it. All letters were heavily censored. Whatever Albie had said to his ma was personal to them both, and would stay intact.

Back in the nurses' dormitory, Rosie fell onto her bed. She couldn't cry any more tears. The loss of Albie was a strange feeling, as their love had never developed. It had just been there in his look, and in her own heart. Now it never would develop, but she'd treasure his memory forever.

# CHAPTER SIXTEEN

# *Narbonne, France*

## Sibbie and Marjie

Sibbie giggled every time she saw Marjie put her small, round glasses on. Fitted with plain glass, they really did disguise her, especially with the way she combed her hair, pulling it straight back into a bun at the nape of her neck.

Then there were the freckles, for which she had a template. Sibbie always did these for Marjie, and had to be sure to get the template in the same place across the bridge of Marjie's nose and over her cheeks; it was important, too, that she used the correct mixture of the facial make-up they'd been given. As so little was needed each day, the amount they possessed was stored inside the case of a pen.

Their drop into Languedoc-Roussillon, close to Hérault, had both thrilled them – as it was exactly where they wanted to be – and frightened them, as the parachute jump had to be from a much higher altitude than they had ever jumped before.

Lit torches had guided them to the right place on the ground, and both girls had made a perfect landing. Not that they had time to think about it, as they were immediately surrounded by Resistance fighters, who hurried them away. To Sibbie's disappointment, Paulo didn't appear and now, three weeks later, they still hadn't been contacted or given any instructions from HQ in Britain.

They were billeted with the mother of one of the Resistance men, Madame Bachelet, in Narbonne, a beautiful city, and worked in her grocery shop on the corner of rue Michelet, where it met rue Garibaldi – a central position, behind and dominated by Narbonne's magnificent cathedral, which was dedicated to Saints Justus and Pastor.

Their work was a good cover, as groceries had to be delivered on special bikes, with a huge basket built onto the front. No matter what messages they were asked to take where, they would simply look as though they were delivery girls.

They were passed off as nieces of a cousin of Madame Bachelet. They'd listened many times to Madame relay to customers how her cousin, who lived on the outskirts of Paris in the Saint-Denis area, had fled the country and left the girls to make their way down to her for help. 'My cousin brought them up, as both of her sisters – who were my cousins too, of course – died: Margarita's mama at her birth, and Sibilia's in a car accident when Sibilia was just one year old. Their fathers married again, and in the beginning rarely visited their daughters, until one day their visits ceased. My cousin was good to the girls, but dared not take them with her. She had an English husband and had to go with him. A whole family would have attracted too much attention. So she gave the girls my address and told them to come to me. It is a great burden, but what can I do? Still, they are making themselves useful.'

\* \* \*

'Sibbie, you're getting so good at this. It only takes you a few minutes to freckle me now, when it took almost half an hour the first time.'

'Keep still, Marjie. When you talk, you move your cheeks.'

'Of course I do!'

'Well, shut up then.'

The disguise was very important, as Marjie was not far from an area where she was well known. Not in Narbonne itself, which lay some thirty-six miles from Laurens, where her home was, although people Marjie knew did travel there, for whatever reason, and she must not be recognized.

They had kept their cover names from their training days – Margarita for Marjie and Sibilia for Sibbie – which made things very easy for them, as they could continue using the same nicknames they had for each other. All in all, they had settled into their roles well, but both of them so wanted to be sent on their first mission.

When the coded message arrived a week later, they were excited to realize it was from their Uncle Arnie, but fearful as to whether they were doing the right thing by obeying the order. 'Be at the cathedral for one p.m. Bring essentials. A.'

'Essentials' were their papers and what they'd come to look on as the tools of their trade: the component for activating a radio transmitter; a pen that was really a knife; a strangulation cord, which was threaded through a seam of their coat sleeve and could be quickly accessed; and their special boots, with the parts of a gun that could be speedily assembled concealed in the heels.

There was no cover story or any other information. 'I'm not sure about this, Marjie. I know Uncle Arnie is the coordinator, and that A is his code-name, but we were told to await a message from HQ and that it would be transmitted.'

'Should we check this out with them? I know our instructions are that we retain radio silence until the order is given, but what if this is a trap?'

After a moment Marjie came up with the plan to go to the assigned area, but to stay out of sight until they could see who arrived to pick them up. She knew most of the members of the Maquis.

'What if it's someone we don't know, but who is still genuine?'

'Then we don't go, Sibbie, as we have no way of knowing they are genuine. Like you, I have serious doubts. I mean, would Uncle Arnie put us in such a position? He must know what our orders are.'

'If this is fake, it means that our cover is blown. But how? No one has questioned our status. They've all accepted Madame Bachelet's story.'

'I did have one person question me – a man. I took a delivery to a house in rue Etienne Gaillard. A man opened the door and seemed genuine in his enquiry. He said, "You're new – where are you from?" I gave him our cover story and he just said, "You were lucky to get out of Paris, but I'm glad, as I don't like having to fetch my own grocery order from the shop. It has been a while since the delivery boys were taken for forced labour."'

'Oh, you never said. What did you reply?'

'I didn't. I told him the amount of his bill, took his money and left.'

'Well, it doesn't sound suspicious. I shouldn't worry, Marjie.'

'No – it could have been nothing. We'll go along with our plan and see what happens.'

Madame showed her surprise when they told her they

were to leave, and didn't know how long for. 'But what am I to say to people? I was told you would be working from here at all times. If that had changed, I would be informed and given another cover story.'

This further alarmed Marjie. 'Sibbie, I don't think we should go. If this is a trap, then we will have blown our cover. I think we should stay until we receive a transmission.'

Sibbie thought this over. Their radio transmitter was hidden in the store shed behind the shop. Every night at seven p.m. they went there, as instructed. They took with them the component needed to activate the transmitter, then waited for thirty minutes. If nothing came through, they disabled the radio, and that was that. Surely any instructions would come via that medium? This thought made up Sibbie's mind as to the action they should take. 'I think we'll have to radio HQ. Our orders were to inform them as soon as we can, if an emergency arises. I think this comes under the heading of an emergency. If that message is fake, then it means that Uncle Arnie – and our code – is compromised, and so are we.'

'But how?'

'The Maquis may have been infiltrated. We have no way of knowing.'

Fear showed in Marjie's eyes. And it matched Sibbie's fear. Thoughts of their instructions, if caught, came to her; although would they have to take the cyanide pill? They knew nothing and had been involved in nothing, so no matter how much they were tortured, they couldn't give away any information. But then she realized just how much they did know. They knew about the Maquis, and who the coordinator of the Resistance groups was. They knew Paulo, the leader of the Laurens de Hérault section, and that Jacques, Madame Bachelet's son, was a member of the Maquis; and, of course, they knew much about the workings of the espionage system. Information that would be catastrophic in the wrong hands, especially the radio codes used over the air. Her heart dropped.

She'd been shocked when, on their last briefing, the final item given to them was a pill that they were to keep on them at all times. 'If you are caught, you are to put this into your mouth and bite down on it. You will be dead within seconds. It is to protect you from torture, and especially the possibility of you giving information that would jeopardize our operations and compromise our agents in the field. Your captors will use vile methods to extract information from you, on the promise that you will go free if you give in; but you won't go free. As soon as they get the information they want, they will shoot you.'

Sibbie's blood had run cold. For the first time, the realization of what she had let herself in for truly hit her. But then the knowledge had come to her that she was ready to carry it all through. If she had been given this stark reality at the beginning of her training, she doubted she could have gone on. But as she had stood there and accepted the pill, and felt her first reaction of terror fading, she'd known that she had the courage to go forward.

Marjie cut into her thoughts. 'We have no contact network in place with the Maquis, Sibbie. All this time here – and nothing. Then this. Something is wrong, I can feel it.'

Madame surprised them then by saying, 'I have a contact. Leave it with me. I'll get an order ready for you to take to Monsieur Siet, and the message for him will be hidden within it. Oh, don't worry, it is nothing that can be suspected – no

202

note, just a certain number of an item, which will tell him there is something amiss and that he must come and see me. He will know if this is genuine, and what to do.'

Sibbie sighed with relief – not only that they had a way of verifying the message, but that Madame was clearly far more than they had first thought her to be. She was part of the Resistance, that was clear, otherwise she wouldn't be a party to such codes. The fact that she'd never revealed this, despite knowing why they were here, boded well.

In her fifties and elegant, Madame Bachelet had been widowed for ten years. Jacques was her only child. Still beautiful, with pearl-like skin that didn't sag, but was held taut and smooth by her high cheekbones, Madame must have been stunning as a young girl, Sibbie thought. Even in her wraparound apron, she looked sophisticated. Slim and with the figure of a much younger woman, she had very dark hair, which she wore swept back off her face and caught into a roll, rather than in a bun at the back of her head. Her eyes were fascinating; hazel-coloured, but with dark-brown flecks, they were large and bright and gave the impression that Madame knew everything and could see into your soul.

With the order ready, it was decided that Sibbie should take it to Monsieur Siet. She'd delivered his orders before, and wondered now how many of them had contained a code. She didn't have to ask why a code was needed. Monsieur Siet lived in a tenement block on the rue du Capitole near the railway station. In the overcrowded building there was never a moment when she had been there that she hadn't seen a lot of people, so it would have been dangerous to pass notes on or to speak anything other than casual greetings.

Never before had Sibbie felt this nervous when travelling around Narbonne. She often cycled around, enjoying the sights and smells; and despite the fear that accompanied the war, its people were lively and colourful and she felt it was a vibrant place. The *gendarmes* were a huge presence and were feared by everyone. It wasn't unusual to see them suddenly stop someone, search them and bundle them into their van. Sibbie always felt nervous when passing them, but so far they hadn't bothered with her.

The city of Narbonne itself was very attractive, with its magnificent cathedral dominating it from its high vantage point. The buildings that lined the streets were tall and elegant; mainly white, they had many windows and ornate facades. Their ground-floor rooms were shops and restaurants, with brightly coloured canopies extending over the tables and chairs set on the pavement.

The lovely River Aude rippled down from the Pyrenees through Carcassonne and reached the Mediterranean via Narbonne. Sibbie and Marjie often cycled along its route to the sandy beaches that dotted the coastline.

As Sibbie cycled down rue du Capitole, she began to feel less afraid. No one was taking any notice of her. No curious eyes were watching, there were no suspicious-looking figures on street corners and definitely no one following her. And, what was most reassuring, she passed a group of *gendarmes* and, apart from them glancing at her, none of them showed any interest in her.

Within an hour of Sibbie's return, a communication arrived to say everything was all right and the message was genuine. Mystified, but obeying orders, Sibbie and Marjie stood outside the cathedral at the allotted time and waited.

'I'm still nervous about this, Sibbie. How will we be picked up, and by whom? And why in broad daylight?'

Sibbie didn't have a chance to answer before a car pulled up in front of them. The driver – a man in his fifties wearing a trilby-type hat and a smart suit, and a stranger to them – wound his window down. 'Are you expecting Arnie?'

Sibbie nodded.

'Get in the back.'

Once they were settled, the driver set off at a normal pace. 'If we are stopped and questioned, which is unlikely, then I am Monsieur Dubret. I run a taxi service, which is often used by the officials. I am taking you to have tea with my daughter Renée, who is the same age as you. Renée met you in your aunt's shop and you became friends. She works in the office of the *gendarmes*. You know very little else about her, as your friendship is only just beginning. Understand?'

They both said, '*Oui*.' The cover story was simple to remember, and Sibbie could tell that, like her, Marjie had relaxed, although she did squeeze Sibbie's hand and give some indication of the excitement she was feeling. Sibbie understood, as she too was excited, in an anticipatory way. Although it would be lovely to see Uncle Arnie – and, hopefully, Uncle Cyrus – her main hope against hope was that Paulo would be present.

They were dropped off, a little over an hour later, near the edge of a forest that surrounded Marjie's former home close to Laurens. 'Follow that path and you will be met – good luck! Oh, by the way, you will become friends with my Renée, and she will be very useful to you. She learns much, in her job.'

'We will look forward to that, Monsieur Dubret. Please give our regards to Renée.'

The man smiled and drove off.

They hadn't gone far down the path when a low whistle attracted them. Turning towards the direction of the sound, Sibbie felt her heart soar. 'Paulo!' Then shyness overcame her. Never had she been in his presence knowing of his love for her. His arms opened and her shyness dissolved as she ran towards him. 'Sibbie, *mon Sibbie* – at last. I have dreamed of this moment, *mon amour*.'

For Sibbie, her life felt complete as Paulo held her close. The words she'd longed to say to him came naturally to her. 'I love you, Paulo. I love you.'

Paulo looked deep into her eyes. 'I have waited for so long to hear that. I wish things were different and we could be together, as we are meant to be. I love you so much, my Sibbie. Thoughts of you are the only thing that has kept me going.'

'Oh, Paulo, you have been in my mind and heart forever, but from the moment I received your letter, I have done everything to be near to you.'

'We're together now, darling. We'll work together to help bring this conflict to a close, and then it will be our time. But now we will have to join the others.'

Sibbie turned. 'Oh, where's Marjie? She was with me.'

'It was all arranged, to give us a few moments. As soon as you joined me, Marjie was beckoned away by her father and she will be enjoying a reunion with him.'

This warmed Sibbie's heart. 'I'm so glad to be here, Paulo, but why go against the orders of HQ? You frightened us by contacting us, and the message not coming through them.'

'It was your final test, darling. HQ needed to know that you were fully alert to anything that might be a trap. They instructed us that we were not to contact you for a while, and then to do so in an unconventional manner. If you simply obeyed, you would have been air-lifted out and found yourselves in a desk job somewhere in England. But you both did exactly what was expected of you. You questioned the implications of the order. Madame Bachelet was fully aware of the ruse and was instructed to further alarm you, if she could.'

This brought Sibbie such a sense of relief. 'Oh, thank God. I've been worried out of my mind, even suspecting Madame Bachelet and Monsieur Siet. And Madame did alarm us. She expressed concern that she hadn't been given a cover story.'

'Good. But don't worry – she had been given one. An old great-aunt of the family has fallen sick and needs help. You two are the only relatives who can help her. You will be back when she has recovered. I'm so sorry that you felt such panic; it was out of my control, and all I could do was pray that you came through the test – and you have. Oh, Sibbie, my Sibbie.'

Paulo's lips came down on hers. If she'd thought her world complete, she knew now that being in Paulo's arms was only part of that completion, for his kiss awoke longings in her that showed her there was more to learn, and that one day there would be a blossoming of her true self, and the fulfilment of who she was.

Clinging to Paulo and never wanting to let him go, she made her way with him to join the others. After a wonderful greeting from her Uncle Cyrus and Uncle Arnie, and catching them up with the news they had of Flors and Mags, there was a moment when they all fell silent.

Arnie broke the silence. 'Our world – our happy world – has tumbled around us. All we can do is fight to regain what we can of it. I think it's time we told the girls what we want of them.' All of them nodded. 'It is vital that we rescue my darling Ella and Lonia. We've had intelligence that the Jews in the camp where she is have been discovered, and are to be rounded up and taken to Drancy – a concentration camp in the north-east of Paris. It is known as a holding camp, and from there they . . . Oh God, they . . .'

Tears were streaming down Arnie's face. Paulo grabbed hold of him and supported him. Sibbie looked at Marjie. Her father held her in his arms, and both were crying. Sibbie's heart was breaking for them all. Tears stung her eyes, but she knew that the facts had to be faced, and she must be strong for them all. 'How and when will they transport them, Uncle Arnie? Have we information on this?'

Arnie straightened. Paulo wiped the tears that had been cascading down his own face and told her, 'My mama and Lonia could possibly be on the train that we know will leave Vittel in two days' time. We have to rescue them, and all the Jews, although we cannot offer much assistance to others, after this.'

Arnie had now composed himself. 'We know that the train will pass through Troyes at seven p.m. We plan to attack it, on the Paris side. We will set detonators to slow its progress, but not derail it, and then mount a surprise attack. You are both trained in this technique and we need you to carry out the detonation.'

'We carry plastic explosives, but we will have to work out how much is needed, so as not to blow the whole train.'

'I don't think that is possible, Marjie. Is there a bridge we can blow up? We could do it when the train is in view of it, although it would need to be from a distance, so that the train can stop in time.'

'Sibbie is right. I worked with explosives in the last war.' Cyrus held their attention, 'It is much better to create an obstruction that they know about, and have to halt. It is almost impossible to judge how to stop the train without causing a major derailment.'

'André will know if there is a bridge. He is from that area. You remember him, Marjie, he was at school with you.'

'Yes, I do of course. I haven't seen him since then, but it will be good to see him again.'

Arnie took charge once more, stopping any further reminiscences. 'Right, here is the plan. Paulo, you make contact with André. Find out where the best point is for us to disrupt the progress of the train. Also a good meeting point for all the Maquis who are willing to travel there and join in the attack. Each must make his or her own way. I will arrange for weapons and ammunition to be dispatched to that point. I will also make contact with the Resistance in the Troyes area – there is a good group there.'

'Communists.'

'Yes, communists, Paulo, but at the end of the day they want the same as us and are clever and ferocious fighters. We need them. We do not know how many guards will be on the train.'

Paulo nodded his head.

'Good Now, we must meet André tonight and I will arrange for him to be attached to this camp. We'll meet at Monsieur Bijour's farm. Sibbie, you and Marjella will come along with me and Cyrus. We are camped deep in the forest.' Smiling now, he joked, 'We have every modern convenience.'

Cyrus laughed. 'Ha! A hole in the ground, he means. But don't worry; we have prepared for you and have portioned off a bedroom space, with an en-suite hole.'

At this they all laughed. Paulo's hand came into Sibbie's. 'I can walk a little way with you, then I will have to cut off up a different path, but we will meet up in Troyes.' They had dropped back a little way when he spoke again. 'How long have you known that you loved me, Sibbie?'

'Mmm, I think I was thirteen, and Monty was teasing me and almost had me in tears. You stopped him, not in an angry way, but by making him see that he was causing me distress. Monty walked away, and you put your arm around me and asked if I was all right. From that moment on, I knew I wanted to marry you.'

'I have always felt a strong attachment to you, but I didn't imagine you could feel anything for me. When you reached sixteen, I vowed I would tell you, but I chickened out, for fear of your rejection. But you know now, and I am so happy that you love me, too.'

'Oh, Paulo, if only things were different.'

Paulo pulled her to him. They looked into each other's eyes. His kiss thrilled Sibbie, and yet lit a sadness in her heart. For their future was so uncertain, and their lives were in such danger, that they didn't know if they would ever be together as they wished to be.

# CHAPTER SEVENTEEN

# *Singapore*

## Daisy and Florrie

Daisy hurried down the ward. Most of the men were restless.

'Sister!'

'What is it, Captain Vincent?' She tried to keep her voice steady, although fear pulsated through her. Fear for Florrie; fear for Alex; and fear for these men, not to mention her colleagues and friends.

'Is this it?'

Daisy didn't have to ask what he meant. She took his hand. 'I'm sorry. I – I . . . look, there's every chance they'll take you prisoner.' It was a stupid supposition, which she didn't believe. The Japanese were so close, and the British were on the verge of surrender. When the island was conquered – and with all the hospital staff gone – these men didn't stand a chance. The ruthlessness of the Japs was well known. They wouldn't take as prisoners dying men, or men with missing limbs. And she doubted they'd even take those who were on the mend. Although she couldn't bear the thought, she knew that the fate of all of these men for whom she'd cared was certain death.

'We both know that's not so. Are you all being shipped out? Surely there's some plan in place?'

Daisy nodded.

'And no wounded are going?'

Daisy couldn't speak.

'Don't cry, Sister. As many of us as possible have to survive this. You must go. Don't ever look back with guilt. You are just a small cog, as I am; and these men are part of the greater aim that we're all fighting for. All that each of us can do is our best, but in the end we have to accept our fate.'

A voice from two beds down shook the feelings of acceptance that Captain Vincent had given her. 'Don't leave us, Sister – don't leave us! No. No! I don't want to die.'

Running to him, Daisy held him as best she could. 'Eeh, Corporal Lessings, try to calm yourself, lad.' But as she said the words, she knew they were futile. 'I won't leave. I'll stay with you.'

'No, Sister.' Captain Vincent was raised up on his elbow, looking over at them. The effort to lift himself must have cost him dearly, as he was very weak. 'You must go. All who have a chance of surviving must do so. Corporal Lessing, we'll all do what we can for each other. We've been in this together from the start, and we'll see it through till the end.'

'Aye, and so will I. I'm not going anywhere.' Daisy's heart thumped in her chest at this decision, but she knew it was the right one for her. Taking a deep breath, she went to the medicine cabinet and unlocked it. She would carry on as normal. Some of the patients were due their medication, while others needed their dressings changed. Then, if no orderlies appeared with breakfast, she'd go to the kitchen and cook it herself! But as she thought this, she realized the hopelessness of the situation. She couldn't look after the whole hospital.

The door to her office was flung open. 'Daisy darling, what are you doing?'

'Oh, Alex, I can't leave. Me conscience won't rest ever again. How can we leave these men – they're in our care?'

'We have to, please, Daisy. Florrie is out of her mind with worry about you. They're boarding the SS *Kuala* now. Our orders are to evacuate.'

'I knaw, but if we do, all these men will die. How can we leave them to that fate?'

'Darling, listen.' Alex had taken Daisy's hands and lowered his voice. 'They will die anyway – the Japanese will certainly kill them, then take you prisoner. What use will you be in a POW camp? The news that is filtering out is of horrific treatment of their prisoners. There are other men in other hospitals that we can help to save. We can't do that in a prisoner-of-war camp. We're not being selfish; we're not condemning these men to death. Our situation is hopeless. Our choices are that we stay and be taken prisoner, and these men die anyway; or we leave and they die, but we are able to continue to serve our country.'

Daisy knew Alex was right. 'Just help me to administer their painkillers and dress the wounds that need dressing, Alex, please. Together it won't take long, but it may be hours before the Japanese get here. I can't think of leaving the men in pain as their last medication wears off.'

Alex looked deep into her eyes. 'I can't deny you the very thing that I love you for: your caring and compassionate ways. Yes, I'll help you. There are hundreds of people to board yet, so we've got time.' As they filled the trays with the doses needed, Alex whispered, 'I almost feel like doubling the dose, so that none of them have to face their fate.'

Daisy understood. Part of her wanted to do the same, but they weren't killers; they were carers, the preservers of life, no matter what.

Once more the door to the ward swung open, and this time a desperate Florrie stood in the opening. 'Daisy! Daisy lass. I've been searching frantically for you. The nursing staff have all boarded. Come on, we've got to go.'

'Help us, Florrie. All the trays are marked with the names. And do it calmly, lass. As if you were administering medicine on an ordinary day. Then we'll go, I promise.'

Florrie hesitated. 'I – I . . . Aw, Daisy, it's hopeless.' The last word came out as a sob.

'Where there's life, Florrie. Remember that. We're nurses, and these men need us. We can give them that last bit of help.'

Florrie picked up a tray that was ready. Strength seemed to have come into her. 'Aye, we can, our Daisy.'

An explosion rocked the building and they all froze. Dust showered down from the ceiling.

'Oh God, they're attacking the hospital.'

'No, they aren't that near yet; it will have been a stray bomb. Let's hurry.'

Daisy followed the other two out of the office, all of them bearing trays. As she went from bed to bed, she felt as if she was betraying the terrified young men who'd fought so hard to keep the island from occupation.

By the end of the round, all three of them were in tears. As they reached the door, Alex turned and shouted, 'Good luck, fellows.'

He meant well, but the effect on Daisy was to make her

feel wretched, as if she was saying, 'I'm all right – you take care of yourselves.'

At the dock there was chaos, as so many people were trying to board ships: doctors, nurses, orderlies and even some patients who were able-bodied enough to mobilize themselves. No one was refused.

Once aboard, Florrie smiled. 'Eeh, Daisy, we made it!'

Daisy couldn't smile, but hugged her sister to her.

'Daisy, try not to dwell on leaving the men,' Alex said. 'This is war, and we could do nothing more for them. If we stayed, we would not only have sacrificed ourselves, but our talent, too. You have to think as we have always been taught – of those that we can save; and that will be many in the future, I'm sure, darling.'

'I'll try.'

Alex pulled Daisy to him. Letting go of Florrie and finding comfort in his strength, Daisy went willingly into his arms. But a voice calling out caught their attention.

They turned to see Giles running along the deck towards them, shouting, 'Florrie. Florrie!'

Her face lit up. 'Giles. Oh, Giles!'

'Florrie, I – I've been a cad. Forgive me. I've been desperate to find you. I thought I'd lost you, that you'd gone on another ship . . . Florrie, I love you – I do. And I know now that I can surmount any difficulty that we may face in the future.'

Daisy waited. Part of her didn't want Florrie to give in to the snobbish Giles, but looking at Florrie's face, she knew she would.

'Giles, oh, my Giles – there's nowt to forgive. I understood. I'm not much of a catch for the circles you move in.

But, you know, I can learn. I'll do owt. Cos I love you an' all, Giles. With all me heart, I love you.'

Giles giggled, then took Florrie in his arms. As he spoke, he warmed Daisy's heart. 'Don't ever change, my Florrie. I love you as you are, and if any of my friends reject you, then they reject me, too.' With this, he kissed Florrie on the lips. Daisy turned away and smiled up at Alex as she whispered, 'There's nowt like the closeness of death to open up your heart.'

'No, there isn't. And we did have a close shave, darling, especially with you insisting on staying that bit longer. But I love you for that. Oh, Daisy, as soon as we get home, will you marry me?'

'I will, and I'll be glad to. You're all I ever dreamed of.'

It was her turn to be kissed. The kiss took away her fear, and all the pain of having to leave. And Alex's whisper as he came out of the kiss thrilled her, when she read his meaning. 'Shall we go and find which cabins we've been allocated, and be together in mine in private for a while?'

She nodded. 'But I'll have to tell Florrie I'm going.'

'I'll do that.'

Alex tapped Giles on the shoulder and whispered something to him. Giles put his thumb up. 'See you later, mate.'

Daisy blushed as Giles gave her a knowing look. Her feelings were torn, as she realized that Alex must have told Giles what he had in mind, and this spoilt the moment for her. Turning back, she spoke to Florrie. 'Come on, Florrie lass. We'll go and find our cabin. We'll see you two later.'

'But . . .'

'Come on, lass.'

Florrie must have recognized that Daisy needed to get away and wanted her to follow, as she made no further protest until they were out of sight. 'What were all that about, Daisy? I'm not right pleased with you. I've only just got together with Giles, and you pull me away.'

'I'm sorry, lass. Just take it that I had to. I felt cheapened by sommat as happened.'

Florrie looked shocked, but didn't protest further.

As they stepped inside the ship and turned in the direction of the arrow pointing towards the cabins, Matron, looking more flustered than Daisy had ever seen her, stopped them. 'There you are! Thank God.'

'Sorry, Matron, we didn't knaw as you were looking for us.'

'It's chaos. I can't find half my nurses, and those I did find said that you and Florrie had stayed behind, Sister. I was terrified for you, but know that is your character, and I commend you for it. I wanted to myself, but had responsibility for all my staff. Now, the sisters and senior medics are all billeted up that way, and the nurses along here.'

'We want to be together, Matron, please. I don't mind going in a cabin in the nurses' quarter.'

'Very well, I understand. Of course. Take Florrie along with you – none of the first three cabins have been taken. Sister Bett is in the fourth one, awaiting someone to share with her, but there are only two bunks to a cabin.'

'I'll look in on her, Matron.'

Bett was composed and jolly, not a bit like she had been when the evacuation was first spoken of. After greeting them both with a hug and saying how glad she was they were safe, she told them, 'I ran to the kitchen before I left and grabbed a box of those biscuits I like. I was going to tuck in, but do you want to take some to your cabin?'

This made Daisy burst out laughing. 'Oh, Bett, you're incorrigible. Aye, I'd love a biscuit; it might settle my gurgling tummy. I've eaten nowt this morning.'

When the ship sailed out of port, Daisy felt they were truly safe. Florrie was asleep on her bunk, but Daisy couldn't rest. It felt to her as if she and Alex had had their first rift; but how could he make a joke about her with his friend? Not that she'd heard what he'd said, but it was obvious that Alex was warning Giles not to come to their cabin for a while. Giles's look had shrivelled her insides.

A knock on the door got her rushing to it, hoping it was Alex. It was. He took her arm and pulled her into the corridor. Already it was dark outside, and the empty corridor was dimly lit. 'Daisy, my love, I'm mortified. Forgive me. I didn't mean . . . I just meant for Giles to keep the coast clear for us, my darling. I could have killed him for looking like that. Please come on deck and talk to me.'

'I'll get my cloak.'

Alex held her hand as they walked. 'I need to find some-where we won't be seen, so that I can make everything right with you, my darling.'

Everything came right the moment he pulled her into a dark corner under a suspended lifeboat and kissed her.

As the kiss ended, Alex whispered, 'I know how it looked, but I—'

Putting her finger to his lips, Daisy hushed him. 'I knaw, I were silly even to think that of you. I just felt . . . well, it doesn't matter now. I love you, and that's all that matters.'

They clung together, both wanting to show the other how much they loved one another. Daisy yielded to Alex's loving of her, wanting him till the need was a burning ache as his hand crept up her thigh. And as he lifted her against the side of the ship and she wrapped her legs around him, she felt a moment of exquisite sensation as he entered her. Her cry of joy merged into the sound of the waves lapping against the side of the ship. Alex loved her fervently, giving all of himself to her, until she felt the moment she loved and craved – the moment of her release.

Clinging to Alex, not wanting the feeling to leave her and yet hardly able to bear it, she cried tears of joy into his neck. Alex stiffened and held her so close that she had difficulty in drawing breath.

'My darling. My world just came right, thank you.'

No sooner had she said this than a panicking crowd rushed by. Fear trembled through Daisy and she felt the same feeling shudder through Alex's body. Adjusting their clothing as quickly as they could, Alex stepped out from under the boat and pulled her with him. 'Something is amiss. Let's make our way back to our cabins and see if we can find out what.'

A man running by shouted, 'The Japs . . . The Japs – Christ, they're ahead '

'Florrie, I must get to Florrie.' Daisy's heart sank.

'Come on, darling, we'll get to her.'

'Torpedo!' The terrifying cry had hardly resounded around them when the ear-splitting explosion sent them flying through the air and crashing down onto the deck.

Alex cried out in pain, but the sound was drowned out when an aeroplane swooped so low that Daisy thought it would land on the ship. Looking up, she saw the pilot's grin, before he sent down a torrent of bullets that made her body dance.

Screams around her swirled in her head. 'A – Al – Alex.'

His name settled on her soul as it soared above her excruciating pain and took it away. Floating and unable to control her movements, or go back to Alex, Daisy couldn't understand why she felt so happy, so light. Her lips formed the words 'Goodbye, my love', but it was as if someone else had spoken them and they were a prayer, not a tearing apart. Then the earthly world lay far behind her and she was swathed in a beautiful light.

Confused and unable to see, for the choking smoke that engulfed him, Alex was surrounded by muffled screams. Lifting his hand, he reached out for Daisy. His hand sank into a warm, sticky pool of blood. 'Daisy?' Realization catapulted him to a sitting position. 'DAISY!' His scream rasped in his throat. The sounds of hell surrounded him – explosions, diving planes, rapid gunfire, screams and cries for help – as burning flames licked the deck, lighting up the tangled, bloodied body and beautiful face of his darling Daisy. Her unseeing eyes were staring at him, her hand outstretched towards him.

'NO! NO! No-o-ooo!'

Alex's agonized scream was lost in the sound of wave after wave of the ack-ack of gunfire and the explosion of torpedoes. Water swirled around him.

Getting up, he tried to move forward, but the slant of the ship was too great for him. *It's sinking. God, help me! Help me!* He couldn't stop the slide of his body. Choking on the salty water that threatened to engulf him, Alex knew he was going to die. The thought wasn't frightening, but a release that was all-consuming, as his head banged against something and he felt all sensation leave him, to be replaced with a feeling of weightlessness. He fought to feel again, but ahead of him he saw his Daisy, beckoning. She looked so beautiful. He wanted more than anything to be with her. Letting go of the will that had kept him earthbound, he drifted towards the love she was showering him in.

Florrie had woken to the sound of someone banging on her cabin door. Swinging her feet off her bunk, she felt freezing-cold water. Shock brought her fully awake and, with awareness, came the terrifying sound of anguished cries and, above them, the planes, the guns and the explosions. With the slant of the boat, she couldn't stand up. The door was flung open and Giles shot in.

'Florrie . . . the Japs . . . Oh God, Florrie!'

A lurch and Giles fell on top of her. Their bodies were flung onto her bed. 'Florrie. Oh, Florrie.'

Screaming above the terrible noise, she cried out for Daisy.

'They've gone, Florrie.' Giles's sobs registered his anguish and his fear, as he rolled his weight off her and pulled her towards him.

Florrie clung onto him. The angle of their bodies rushed the blood to her head. Water splashed onto her, making her feel so cold. 'Giles, we've to get out of here or we'll drown.'

He held her tighter. 'There's nowhere to go, Florrie, my darling. The corridor is blocked off both ways.'

'What! Oh, Giles . . . Oh God, help us. HELP US!'

'Florrie, Florrie, I'm here for you. I love you, I acted so stupidly. I – I'm sorry. Oh, my darling, if we were given the chance, I would make you so happy.'

'You have made me happy, Giles . . . I love yo – you.'

The rising water choked her as the last word was spluttered out. Panic gripped Florrie as she stretched her neck, but she couldn't get it above the water level. A sensation of falling seized her, and her body crashed into the cabin wall. Giles still held her, but one more violent lurching and her head split, with a blow that took her into a peaceful blackness. In the light in the far distance she saw Daisy. 'Eeh, our Daisy, you look beautiful, lass.'

Daisy's hand beckoned her. Florrie was filled with the greatest happiness she'd ever experienced in her life as her body floated towards her beloved sister.

# CHAPTER EIGHTEEN

# *Troyes, France*

## Sibbie and Marjie

The sound of the train bearing down on them terrified Marjie. But she carried on working away at attaching the detonators to the explosives they had taped to the bridge.

'Are you finished, Marjie? We have to blow it now!'

'Retreat!'

Looking up, Marjie made sure that Sibbie had followed her instruction, then set the detonator and ran for all she was worth into the long, thick brush. The thrust of the blast compelled her body the last few yards to safety. Still the train chugged forward, but as it came abreast to them, Marjie saw the driver lean out of his cab. She saw a look of horror cross his face, which was illuminated by the gas lights along the railway line, then the air was filled with the screeching of brakes as sparks flew from the wheels. Doors opened and soldiers tumbled out of the first and last carriages.

'Fire!'

On this command, Marjie cocked the machine gun she'd been allocated and fired, as did all her comrades. As some soldiers fell and others screamed in agony, her heart wanted to explode with the horror of it. A sob jolted her throat, but she swallowed hard. *I mustn't think of them as men – I mustn't. They are beasts who would kill all those I love.* With this, she released another round of bullets and knew she'd hit her target, as three soldiers' bodies were flung into a hideous pose before dropping to the ground, never to move again.

Screams and banging filled the air as those incarcerated in the carriages, sandwiched between those of the guards, cried desperately for release. Marjie realized that these carriages were no more than cattle trucks – no windows, just slits to let in air.

The cries of those trapped inside cut her in two, but she dared not go forward to release them, even though her heart wanted her to.

'Cover me!'

Arnie's command shot terror through her. There were still many soldiers and now they were organized, after their initial ambush, which had thrown them into chaotic panic. She wanted to shout, 'No, not yet', but Arnie was the commanding officer and she would not disobey him, even though she knew his action was driven by his emotions and not his reason.

Firing her gun sent her body into a tremble, but still she held fast. More soldiers fell, whether by her hand or by that of the many others shooting at the soldiers, Marjie didn't know.

In the shadows she saw Arnie making for the train. But then he stopped, crouched down and shot down at a row of kneeling soldiers.

Marjie's head reeled with the nightmare of it all, as bits of warm flesh hit her face from ten feet away. Cries, following a blast of fire from those at the rear of the train, made her aware that one of their number had been hit. She raised her gun and fired for all she was worth, tears streaming down her face. *Don't let it be Papa, Sibbie or Paulo, please. Please don't let it be any of them.*

As her prayer died, she saw a soldier throw a hand-grenade. Ducking, she crouched low. More prayers tumbled from her. A split second's silence registered, and then she heard an explosion, followed by screams of agony. Lifting her head, she called out, 'Papa . . . Papa!'

'Hush, darling girl. I'm all right.'

Crawling on her belly towards the voice, Marjie felt something in front of her and, putting out her hand, her fingers felt the still body of someone she did not know. Skirting around him, she made it to her father's side. 'Papa. Oh, Papa.'

His arm came round her, but only for a second and to lower her further to the ground. 'We'll be all right, my darling, we outnumber them. When Arnie gets behind them, it will confuse and divide them.'

This didn't reassure her, but only further fuelled her fear. However, she had no time to think about it, as a blast of firing rang out from her father's gun.

'Keep firing, Marjie – we've got them now.'

This command from her father brought her starkly back to the task in hand. Kneeling, she unloaded her gun, not letting herself feel for the young lives she was extinguishing. If she did so, she would be lost.

Instead she concentrated on the lives she was saving. And especially those of her dear Aunt Ella and the lovely little Lonia. This spurred her on and, seeing a German soldier make a dash for the carriage he'd alighted from, she gunned him down without a thought.

Another cry from behind reminded her of the grave reality – around her scores of people were injured or dying, and she just wanted it to end. Tears flowed down her face once more. *How did this happen? How did I turn into a killer?* The enormity of admitting what she was shocked Marjie.

Hearing her name brought her back to the horror of it all. Turning this way and that, she tried to see Sibbie, but couldn't. 'Sibbie, are you all right?'

Paulo's voice came back to her. 'Yes, we were checking on you.'

'Papa and I are all right, but I cannot see Arnie.' As she said this, an explosion ripped through the air, lighting up the figure of Arnie, flying backwards. 'Arnie. Oh God!'

'Stay down, Marjie. Please, keep low! I can see Arnie – he's all right. That's him firing from the back of the train.'

Another cry followed this: '*Nicht schießen! Nicht schießen!*'

Marjie held her breath. Peering down, she saw a lone soldier, whose arms were in the air. She closed her eyes, then opened them, as her momentary relief at it all being over left her, with the sound of a gun being cocked.

'No, Papa, no!'

A shot rang out. The soldier crumbled into a heap.

'Papa . . . Why?'

'We cannot take prisoners, Marjie, and we cannot let a German soldier loose, to inform his unit who ambushed them tonight, and how. Your name was called out. And so was Arnie's: valuable information for the enemy. Lessons must be learned from tonight.'

Marjie felt shame, and knew, too, that Sibbie had also let the side down. But although this told her that what her papa had done was necessary, she knew that as long as she lived she would never forget that lone soldier.

The sound of screams of joy brought her attention back to the train. Bodies were tumbling out of the now-open carriages and cries of freedom resounded around her. It was a strange sight to see hundreds of people disappearing into the forest. Marjie prayed they would find safety.

Taking her papa's hand, she whispered, 'I'm sorry, Papa. So very sorry. It was me who killed that surrendering soldier, not you.'

'No, my darling – it had to be done. Not only because names were compromised, which he may not have heard or remembered, but because what could we do with him?'

'Could we not have interrogated him and then handed him over to the authorities?'

'There are no authorities that we can trust, my dear. We cannot expose ourselves, or our operation, to anyone. As it is, they will know it is the work of the Resistance, but which faction and where they come from – they won't have a clue about that.'

'What about all these people?'

'They will make their own way. Hopefully, some of them will reach safety. This is as far as our responsibility towards them goes. Come now, let's see if Ella and little Lonia have been found.'

As Marjie went down the slope towards the train, Sibbie and Paulo caught up with her. Sibbie didn't speak, but simply slipped her hand into Marjie's free one, and together they descended on the carnage of their first mission.

'They're here – over here!' Arnie's joyous voice rang out.

As she ran towards the call, a feeling of great relief and happiness filled Marjie as she saw the huddle of love in front of her: Arnie, Ella and Lonia were in each others' arms.

After a moment of greetings, Arnie stood tall. 'Thank

much for you. Everything will get better. One day we'll all be happy again, and this will be behind us.'

Ella shook her head. 'Too much has happened. My life has been dogged by evil men, and yet all I ever wanted to do was help people.'

Marjie didn't know what she meant by this – had there been other times when her dear Aunt Ella had been violated? Maybe in the last war? Not knowing what to say, she wiped Ella's tears with her thumb. 'I promise you: everything can get better, and we'll fight to make it so. Don't give up, Aunt Ella. You and Mama and Aunt Mags were heroines in the last war. Dig into the spirit that fuelled you then. You can do it. For Lonia and Paulo and Arnie, you can.'

'My dear Marjella. I fear for you. Arnie tells me that he will arrange for me and Lonia to be air-lifted out and taken to England. Come with me, you and Sibbie. Come to where it is safe, with Mags and your mama . . . *Are* they safe? Is the North of England missing all the bombing?'

'Yes, you will be safe there. They have had bombing attacks, but they aren't a major target. And the attacks are few and far between. But I can't come. I am a serving officer in the British army and I have to do my duty. But don't worry about me. And don't tell Mama too much about the activities I'm engaged in. I don't want her to worry.'

Ella smiled, a weak, pitiful smile that didn't reach her eyes. Lifting her hand, she stroked a stray piece of hair from Marjella's forehead. 'My darling girl, so brave. I pray the evil of this world doesn't touch you as it has done me.'

Marjie couldn't stop the tears running down her face. A sob brought the rest of the room into focus. Her papa was holding Arnie, his best friend, as Arnie's body convulsed in agonizing cries. Aunt Ella looked round, but seemed unable to move. 'Go to him, Aunt Ella. Go to your Arnie. Don't punish him for what others have done to you.'

'Arnie. Arnie, my love.' He broke away from Papa's hold and went to Ella. To see them hold each other, really hold each other, with no resistance from Ella, had them all in tears. After a moment Paulo joined them. 'Mama, you're back now. When this is over, we will all help you to forget.'

Ella turned to her son. 'Paulo, my darling son, what happened to me is something you can never forget. You learn to live with it. It becomes something that happened to a former you. I will strive to do that, I promise.'

'We'll help you, my darling.' With this, Arnie held Ella close. And later, when they allocated the beds, and Ella said she wanted to sleep in Arnie's bed, Marjie felt like cheering. She caught Sibbie's eye, and Sibbie winked at her and gave her a smile that said, 'You did that.' Marjie's heart beat a little warmer, as she knew that she had.

Snuggled up to Sibbie in the bed they shared brought Marjie a little comfort. Sibbie lifting the blanket told her that her cousin wanted to chat, so together they pulled the thick woollen blanket over their heads.

'Marjie, are you all right?'

'Not really, Sibbie. Today shocked me.'

'It did me, too. I still feel shaky inside. But I've no regrets. You don't have any, do you?'

'Yes. The last soldier to die – he was surrendering, Sibbie.'

'Your papa did the only thing he could do. You have to think of that – and that alone.'

'I will try.'

'I was terrified, weren't you?'

'Yes, but it was as if all the training had prepared us for that moment, and I was a different person. Not the Marjella who grew up sheltered from harm and responsibility, but a hard murderer, to whom life meant nothing.'

'I understand, because I didn't think of the Germans as people – not at the time. Now I can't stop thinking about them, and about their mothers and fathers, brothers and sisters or wives and children. They are going to get the brown envelope that our own families dread – or whatever the Germans deliver to bereaved families.'

'Don't. Oh, Sibbie.'

'I'm glad I feel this way, though, as it proves that I am still a caring person. I haven't changed, and I'm only doing my duty.'

'Yes, and we wouldn't be doing any of this if the Germans hadn't invaded my country and were looking to invade yours.'

'I feel better now, do you, Marjie?'

'Yes. Try to get some sleep, Sibbie.'

They settled down again, Marjie with her arm around Sibbie. She didn't really feel better about it all, just better that Sibbie had found a way to deal with it. For herself, she wondered if she ever would deal with it; but no matter, for she would do it all again if the need arose.

They reached the Resistance camp the next day, and plans were made for Sibbie and Marjie to return to Madame Bachelet's shop. When the time arrived, Ella clung to Marjie, but Lonia was still distant, as if she couldn't let herself feel anything.

'Lonia, come and give me a hug.'

Little dark eyes, sunk into even darker sockets, stared back at Marjie, expressionless and yet telling of the girl's fear. Slowly Marjie persuaded Lonia to come into her arms and held her close. 'One day soon we'll run around the fields at home, pinching the grapes and being told off by your papa. And we'll hide behind the larger vines, so that he thinks we have left.'

The scene must have played out in Lonia's mind, as she joined in. 'Yes, and we'll move the baskets full of grapes that the workers have piled up, and see their astonished faces when they come to add more and the baskets aren't there.'

They both giggled at this. Lonia's giggles turned to tears. Ella grabbed her and enfolded her in a mother's love. She nodded at Marjie and whispered, 'Thank you for making her feel once more. Tears are good; they are a release, and are much better than the closing down that happened earlier. Go safely, my darling girl. I promise that Lonia and I will only tell your mama things that won't worry her too much.'

Kissing her aunt and Lonia, Marjie turned away as Paulo took his mama and his sister in his arms. Goodbyes were always painful, but now they ripped at her heart.

After hugging her own papa and Uncle Arnie, she and Sibbie set off. Paulo walked with them to the edge of the forest. There he took Sibbie in his arms while Marjie walked ahead, leaving them some privacy. She longed to be held by Wills, just as Paulo was holding Sibbie, but at the same time she was glad for them.

Turning around on her finger the lovely silver ring that Wills had bought her, she looked up towards the sky. Clouds drifted past, revealing and then covering blue patches here and there. The wind that rustled the trees chilled Marjie, but couldn't touch her inside, where she held Wills close to her heart. *Oh, Wills, my husband.*

When Sibbie joined her, she had tears in her eyes. Marjie didn't say anything, but held her hand. This gesture had become one they both knew communicated their feelings to the other. They walked to the main road in silence. Wearing the clothes in which they'd gone into the camp, they looked like two ordinary French girls out for a country walk.

Within hours they were back at Madame Bachelet's shop, having been picked up by the same taxi and delivered to town, as if they'd truly gone to a great-aunt's house.

'Welcome back, *mes chères*. It has been reported to me that you have done a good job and that all is well with your great-aunt, *non?*'

Marjie was shocked at this. Madame really must be quite a big cog in the organization. She made a note to ask Arnie the next time they saw him, as it was disconcerting to have someone who hadn't been introduced as a Resistance member clearly knowing vital information.

Within a few days, life settled down to a normal pace and the routine of the shop took precedence over everything else. With a few hours off, the girls were taking a walk by the riverside when Sibbie finally gave voice to the concerns that Marjie had been harbouring. 'I keep thinking that all is not well at home. And I wonder if my mother is getting letters from me, just as Aunt Flors was promised she would get ones from you.'

'Yes, they told us, didn't they, when we were training, that we mustn't worry about not being able to communicate with our families, because our families will think that we are writing to them?'

'I know. Yes, of course they did, but I think my mother will see through those fake letters and worry all the more.'

'Try not to think about it, Sibbie. Though why I'm saying

234

that, I don't know. I understand how you feel, as I so wanted to send a letter with Ella. I did give her a verbal message to take my love to my mama.'

'I did, too. But I had to ask Ella to tell Aunt Mags, and not to let my mum know that she'd heard from me. That would have been disastrous. Aunt Betsy would have marched to the War Office, waving a banner or something, and demanding that I be brought home immediately.'

They both laughed.

'Come on. I'll race you to that post there. The last one there has to wash the potatoes and bag them tonight.'

'Ha! It's your turn, Sibbie. You're just trying to duck out of it, knowing you're a faster runner than me.'

Sibbie took off all the same, laughing as she went as if she hadn't a care in the world. This lifted Marjie's spirits, and even though she hadn't a hope of winning, her giggles joined those of Sibbie.

Back at the shop, they tackled the potatoes together. Their mood had settled. 'Well, if you won't race me over who should do which chore, how about we see who fills the most bags of potatoes then?'

'And what's the prize this time?'

'Not a prize; the loser gets to take Monsieur Passat's grocery order.'

'Sibbie, you can't get out of every turn you have at the rotten jobs by challenging me.'

'He is horrible, though, isn't he? He seems to leer at you and has a way of taking the bags off you as if he is . . . Ugh! I hate going near him '

Marjie knew what Sibbie meant. 'He's a dirty old man, but probably harmless. All the same, let's ask Madame if we can do his deliveries together.'

Strangely, this wasn't granted by Madame. '*Non*, you are to go alone. Decide amongst yourselves which one. We must do nothing that draws attention to you. Delivering together will be looked upon as odd. But, if you have cause to, use one of your methods on him, so that it will look as if he died of natural causes.'

This alarmed Marjie. 'Why, Madame? And just who are you? You know so much, it is frightening. We should be told, if you are an agent.'

'I am someone to whom you have been entrusted by your government. I am informed of what they, and the Resistance, want me to know. And you should know better than to question me.'

Marjie apologized, but all the same, she decided to be very careful around Madame Bachelet.

# CHAPTER NINETEEN

# *Portpatrick*

## Betsy and Rosie

Rosie was enjoying the train journey, but was glad when they finally entered Scotland. Now, after changing trains a number of times, she was on the last leg of her trip, travelling from Stranraer to Portpatrick, and, having just passed through Colfin, knew that her station was next.

Excitement zinged through her, to see her ma at last and to have some 'normal' family life – though how normal it could be without Daisy and Florrie, and Sibbie and Billy, she didn't know. But she longed to be with her ma and Aunt Susan, and Roderick, although, from what Ma had told her, Roderick was like a bear with a sore head since he had worried about his flat feet. And yet Rosie hadn't heard better news in a long time, and suspected that a lot of Roderick's problems were down to him being a young lad thinking himself a man and dealing with the process growing up.

'Eeh, Ma, what's the flags out for?' Rosie giggled as she got off the train and saw a row of Union Jacks hanging up between two gas lights, and her ma waving a small flag as she greeted her.

'That's for your return, lass. By, it's grand to have you home.'

With this, Rosie found herself swept into her ma's arms and it felt good. So good she didn't want to leave the comfort of this safe place ever again.

'You can tell me all about it when we get home, lass.'

'About what, Ma? You don't want to hear about the gory business of working in a hospital, I can tell you. Naw, I've left all that behind for two weeks. You can tell me what's been happening up here instead.'

'I don't mean hospital life, but what's troubling you. Eeh, you can't fool me, lass. I knew, as soon as I got your letter. Sommat's up, and I want to knaw about it.'

Rosie tried to laugh, but the sound that came out was somewhere between a sob and a giggle.

'You're home now, me lass. Whatever it is, it'll be better for sharing, and don't forget what I told you: it'll be woman to woman, and though I might give advice, I won't be forcing me own feelings on you, naw matter what the trouble is. Now, let's get you indoors. I've the kettle on. I put it on the minute I heard the train approaching.'

'Is it just you that's in, Ma?'

'Aye, Angus and Roderick are out on the boat. And Susan is in the shop. You'll see them soon enough '

'How is Roderick – has he accepted his fate now?'

'If you mean not ever being allowed to go into the army, the lad'll never accept that. He's accepted that his job is as a fisherman, and is getting on with it. But the lad gives himself hell, trying to find sommat that'll develop his arches. He's designed and cut all manner of shapes out of wood to wear in his shoes. He seems to think that he can get them right by the time he's eighteen. Nowt can convince him otherwise.'

'Aw, poor Roderick. A lot of it's his age, Ma. He looks on the soldiers as real men, and he thinks he won't be one unless he can become a soldier. Happen the war'll be over afore he's eighteen anyroad, so just play along with him.'

'Aye, you're right, lass.'

'What about Daisy and Florrie and Billy? Have you heard from them? I've been worried sick, with the news coming out of the area where they are.'

'Naw. Our wireless has been on the blink. And the papers are a bit behind with their news, and Angus said he hadn't been able to get a copy of a daily for a few days.'

Rosie froze. 'Ma, I don't feel right about it. I've not heard owt for a couple of days, with travelling, but what billboards I've seen have spoken of our troops being about to surrender.'

'Naw. Naw, Rosie lass, don't say that.' Betsy plonked herself down on the nearest chair and stared at Rosie. 'Angus . . . he's been keeping me in the dark. Eeh, lass. Tell me what you knaw.'

'That's about it, Ma. The Japs are winning and are likely to occupy Singapore; they've already taken Malaya.'

Betsy paled. For a moment she didn't speak. Rosie rushed over to her. 'Oh, Ma, they'll be all right. I also saw where the evacuation of all medical staff was planned. I bet that has been done, and Daisy and Florrie are on their way home as we speak.'

'And Billy? What of Billy?'

'Naw news is good news – you knaw that, Ma. If owt has happened to Billy, you'd knaw about it.'

'Aye, that's what they say. That brown envelope is delivered quicker than owt, and families are informed within a very short time. I'll hang on to that then, lass. It's the only hope – that Daisy and Florrie are sailing the seas to us as we speak, and that Billy is still alive and not injured. But all the same, I'm taking that wireless down to Barry Macleod this afternoon when we go to see Susan. He'll soon fix it. I've said as we should, but Angus keeps making excuses. Well, he ain't expected home till late, so he won't be able to stop me.'

'Good idea – it's not good not hearing the news. We live on it, at the hospital. Every news bulletin is listened to and talked about. It keeps us all going at times, stuck on those wards as we are, because half of us want to be doing more.'

'Don't even think about it, Rosie lass. Please, don't. I can't take any more.'

'Aw, Ma, let me brew the tea and we'll talk of other things, eh?'

As Rosie poured the boiling water onto the tea leaves, the rich aroma surprised her. 'By, this is good stuff, Ma. Are you dealing on the black market then?'

'Naw. Angus gets it. Fishermen have allus bartered for stuff. Don't ask me where from, but a box of fish can buy any number of items that you can't get hold of.'

'Black market, like I say. Well, you be careful: they're clamping down heavily on those caught buying and selling stuff that's scarce and on ration, and swapping could come into that.'

'Just enjoy it and say nowt. And, Rosie, on the top shelf there's a baby-milk tin. Get that down and let's have a bit of sugar in our drink. I've had a bit of a shock today.'

Rosie did as she was bid, not even bothering to point out that hoarding sugar was an offence.

The tea tasted the best she'd had in a long time. A contentment entered her that overrode all the emotions and fears that had attacked her lately. The fire crackled a welcome from the hearth, and the feel, smell and familiarity of her home began to envelop her in love.

'Right, Rosie, we've talked about the others, but what about you? All troubles are halved when shared, I've allus taught you that.'

'Ma, sommat happened that I had naw control of and, if I tell you, you'll get upset. You've enough on your plate. It's gone now – it's in the past, and I won't let it happen again.'

'Well, if you had naw control, how is it that you're sure you will have control if it does happen again? Were it to do with a man?'

Rosie knew from old that to try to keep anything from her ma was a losing battle. 'I fell in love, Ma.'

'Is that all? By, luv, that'll happen a few times afore you're done. Who is he, and will I like him? He ain't naw doctor, is he, as some of them are a bit above us, Rosie.'

'Naw, he were a German pilot and . . . Oh, Ma, he – he died.'

The shock on her ma's face was gone in an instant as other emotions took their place, and Rosie could see she was fighting an inner battle. Without an unkind bone in her body, her ma would have been in a quandary as to what to say, as it was, but her promise to accept all and be there for Rosie would be very difficult for her in these circumstances.

'It's all right, Ma. I knaw as you wouldn't have liked it and are probably glad that he died, but you can't say so, for hurting me. I didn't want to tell you. I . . . Oh, Ma, it hurts. The pain's so deep, I don't knaw as I'll ever get to be me again.'

'Awe, Rosie lass. Come here and have a hug. That you

should fall in love with one of them as are killing our lads, I can't understand, but the pain of losing the man you love, I can. There's nowt like it, and it's a long battle back. I loved your da, so I knaw. But I've also come out the other side and found, not only love, but meself again. I knaw as it don't feel like it, but you will do the same, me little lass. You will.'

The love her ma surrounded her with helped Rosie. Aye, she would have liked her ma to say that she would have accepted Albie, but she'd known that wasn't going to happen. 'I love you, Ma, and I miss you and Daisy and Florrie every day. And our Billy an' all, little sod that he can be at times.'

'I knaw. Them being away and in danger is like a sore that you keep rubbing, and it don't get better, it gets worse. And aye, you're right about our Billy; he has many traits of his own da. Harold Roford were the Devil incarnate, but Billy ain't as bad as that, thank God, as Angus has been a good influence on him. But no matter that he is a sod at times, he's our sod, and we love and miss him. Eeh, Rosie lass, I just want you all home, and for us to be like we used to be.'

'Oh, Ma, why did all of this have to happen?'

'Greed – and the need to lord it over others. I sometimes think I knaw Hitler well, as Harold Roford was a Hitler type. They want what others have got, and will do owt to get it. The need to have power is what drives them.'

'You've never told me much about Harold Roford, though his shadow has seemed to hang over our family all me life.'

'He ain't someone as you want to talk about – that's why. He took all that your Aunt Mags had. He were in love with your Aunt Susan, but she had nowt, so he betrayed her and denied that Sibbie were his child; and he wormed his way into Mags's affections, but only because she were rich, or at least her father were, and she stood to inherit the lot. Anyroad, lass, it's a tale too long to tell, but you get the gist of it. Hearts were broken. But them hearts have mended now and are happy, and that's what'll happen to you, lass. It will, I promise.'

Rosie snuggled into her ma, trying to get comfort and feel some of what her ma had promised, but she couldn't. At this moment she couldn't see a time when her broken heart would mend.

At that moment the door opened and Angus and Roderick walked in. The greetings were a distraction. 'Eeh, our Rosie, it's good to see you, lass.'

'Ta, Roddie, and it's good to see you an' all. I were sorry to read about your disappointment, lad, but it gladdened me heart, too, because at least one of me siblings is safe from going to fight. Though I still worry about you. What you and Da do, going to sea to bring fish in for the nation, and manning the lifeboat, is dangerous and necessary work. I reckon as you're the most courageous of us all, and I'm proud of you.'

'Ta, Rosie.' She was rewarded by Roderick giving her a huge grin. 'I'm all right about it now. Well, in a way. It's hard to think of me brother and his mates fighting for our country, and I'll never be able to. But, like you say, the nation has to be fed, and aye, I do me bit in rescuing them as get into distress on the sea. The lifeboat is busier than it's ever been.'

'That's the way to look at it, Roddie. And, lad, stop trying to mend your flat feet; it can't be done and you're only causing yourself pain.'

'Has me ma told you about that? Ech, Ma, you can't

keep nowt to yourself. Well, except any chocolate that comes your way; aye, I knaw about that stash you have, an' all.'

They all laughed. Ma had always been known for her love of chocolate, but no doubt she needed it more than ever now.

A rap on the door brought their laughter to a halt. There was something about it – not just that no one they knew ever knocked on the door, but simply walked right in; somehow Rosie knew this caller was going to tear their hearts to shreds.

Angus opened the door.

'Telegram, sir.'

Ma's gasp cut right through Rosie.

It was as if they'd all been turned to stone, from the moment the knock on the door had interrupted them. The sound of Angus opening the telegram seemed to fill the space around Rosie. Her throat tightened and her head rocked on her shoulders in a gesture that said: No!

Angus's deep breath was pain-filled. He looked at Betsy and crumbled as his body sank into the nearest chair. No one spoke. Taking another deep breath, and with tears running down his face, he rose. 'Oh, me lassie, me lassie, how are we to bear this?'

Ma's head was rocking from side to side, just like Rosie's was. Her mouth was open and spittle ran down her chin. When her body began to tremble and her colour drained, Rosie was spurred into action. 'Roddie, help me, lad. Help me to help Ma.'

Together they held Ma, their arms entwined around her, holding each other's hands. 'Tell us, Da.' The term came naturally to Rosie now, though it was only recently that she'd called this lovely man that her ma had married 'Da'. And no one deserved the title more than him.

Angus's mouth opened, but nothing came out.

'Da? Please.'

'D – Daisy and . . . And Fl – Florrie. They're . . . Oh, God in heaven, I – I canna say it. I canna make it real.'

'Dead?' This was a shocked whisper from Ma.

Angus just stared.

'How? God . . . how? They were rescued, you told me. Evacuated, you said. Angus, tell me, what happened to me babbies?'

Ma's body sank and her weight bore down on Rosie, whose own body was folding. Then a wail came from Betsy that filled the room with the tangible pain that none of them had let in, at the initial shock.

'Ma . . . Ma . . .' The gasp that Roddie took after saying this was audible as a groan.

Nothing seemed real to Rosie. Her only reality was the need to help her ma and Roddie and Angus. 'Help me get Ma to the sofa, Roddie. Come on, lad. Do this for your ma.'

With Ma on the sofa, her face as white as a sheet, her mouth still slack and her eyes staring into nothing, Rosie felt extreme worry for her. She couldn't let in the terrible, devastating truth, because she had to care for her ma. 'Roddie lad, put the kettle on. Ma needs some very sweet tea – you knaw where she keeps her stash, lad. Go on, do it, Roddie. Ma's in shock. She could take very ill with it.'

'But . . . Rosie . . . I – I, oh God!' Roddie's face was wet with tears and his breathing came in great sobbing gasps.

'Roddie! Roddie lad, please, do as I say. In helping others, we find strength in ourselves.'

Roddie turned and picked up the kettle. Satisfied that she'd stopped him from breaking down completely, Rosie went to her ma. Grabbing the blanket that was always folded on the sofa for Betsy's legs, as she was one to feel the cold, Rosie wrapped it around her. 'Ma. Eeh, Ma, hold on, love. Don't let go completely. Our Daisy and our Florrie would want you to carry on.'

Angus moved at that moment and sat down next to Betsy. Thank goodness, Rosie thought, Angus had recovered himself and was ready to help his wife. 'Betsy, me wee lassie. Our lassies, oh God! Let me hold ye, me lassie, as me world is falling around me, and I knaw as yours is, tae.'

Ma didn't resist, and fell into Angus's arms. 'Help me, Angus, help me.'

'We'll help each other, me lassie. We'll tac this road together.'

Rosie felt her own tears leak from her broken heart, as she watched this beloved and devoted couple rocking together, as a child might do when extremely distressed. Sinking into the chair behind her, Rosie tried to take in what had happened. 'Was the ship attacked, Angus? Did the telegram say?'

Angus didn't speak for a moment. When he did, his voice shook. 'I knew the ship had been sunk. The news has been full of it on the radio. I – I . . . well, the moment I heard, I disabled our wireless. I tried to keep it from ye, Betsy, me lassie, in the hope that our wee lassies were among them as were saved. I ken I did wrong, but I didn't want ye worrying and waiting for news. When ye were coming, Rosie, I thought ye'd heard it too and were coming to be by ye Ma's side.'

'Naw, I – I, well, I had sommat on me mind, and I've been travelling. I tried not to see owt about the war.'

Roddie, moving as if he was a zombie, brought the tea over. Rosie busied herself pouring it, trying not to let in the horrific truth. 'Drink this, Ma, it's very strong and very sweet. Your body needs it, Ma.'

Still Betsy didn't speak. Sounds came from her – sounds of desperation and incomprehension – but no words.

Rosie helped her ma to drink her tea. Like a child, Betsy did just as Rosie told her to. When the tea had gone, Rosie took her ma into her arms – keeping the news at bay had defeated her. 'Ma, Ma. It's unbearable . . .' Sobs racked her body, and her heart split in two.

Betsy stroked her hair, her own tears spilling out now, her moans still the only sound that came from her, but at least she was reacting, and this comforted Rosie a little. Though she knew that life would never again be the same. Her darling Daisy and Florrie lost to her forever.

'Will I get me lasses back? I want them, I want me lasses. Angus, I want me lasses.'

This wail from her ma almost broke Rosie. 'Ma. Ma, please.'

'Oh, I knaw as they're gone, but I want to bury them here.'

'Ma, that won't be possible.' Though her own heart was breaking, Rosie tried to give some comfort to her mother. 'They were together, Ma. Aye, and with friends they would have made an' all, no doubt. They'll all go to heaven, and that means as they're here an' all – with us, all around us; we only have to speak to them, for them to hear. We'll have a service, though. How would that be, eh? We'll get Aunt Ciss and Uncle Patrick, and Aunt Mags and Uncle Jerome to come, and everyone from here, and we'll do them proud.'

'And Sibbie?'

'I don't knaw, Ma, but we'll try.'

'Maybe, hen, we'll have to wait until the war is over, afore we can have a proper service.'

At this from Angus, Rosie suspected that he was thinking, like her, that Sibbie and Marjella were carrying out special work they couldn't be released from.

'Naw, I want them as can come to be here now. I want me sister – get our Ciss for me, Angus, please. I've a phone number for her, it goes through t'office of the estate as Patrick works on.'

'We will, Ma; whatever you want, we'll do it.'

'Aye, me wee lassie, we will.'

Angus seemed to have gained strength as he said this. His hand came out to Rosie, and she took it and leaned her head on it. As she did so, she saw Roddie, sitting with his head in his hands, and her heart went out to him. 'Roddie, come over here, lad.'

With Roddie joining them, his da let go of Rosie's hand and stretched it out to his son. Roddie knelt, making it easier to comfort him, now that he was at the same level as them all. His arms came around them, his hand resting on his ma's head. And although there was little comfort to be had, with the enormity of this terrible news, they were a family, and just holding each other helped.

Days went by, with Rosie hardly noticing. Her nights were spent remembering and weeping, but during the day she was protected by her Aunt Susan, whose London grit helped her to cope, as she organized the day-to-day living. And then there was the constant flow of lovely folk from their community in Portpatrick who gave comfort.

It was five days later when the second brown envelope

came and, with it, a rich-looking envelope with a royal seal. They all stood together, holding hands. Rosie could feel her ma's body trembling, and the effort she was making to keep herself together. Angus tore open the brown envelope first and read aloud:

*'We regret to inform you that your son, Corporal William Roford, has been taken prisoner by the Japanese army.'*

Ma released a huge sigh that told of her relief.

*'Corporal Roford is being held in Malaya, but if moved, we will inform you. And we will do our best to get any letters from you to him, as well as any parcels you may want to send, but we must warn you that the Japanese do not always comply with the rules of war, and anything sent may not reach your son.*

*'At all times we will try to keep communications open and will inform you of your son's welfare, when we have news of how he is.'*

Ma stayed standing and, on hearing this, folded her arms. 'Our Billy's safe then? Thank God! By, lad'll have more parcels than he can cope with. We can look after him, Angus, even if it is from afar.'

It was as if Betsy couldn't let the true impact of this news into her heart, but was warding it off with bravado.

The rest of the letter was given over to telling them how to send letters and parcels to Billy, and although this was meant to be comforting, and seemed to be for Ma, Rosie derived no comfort from it. Tales of Japanese brutality were

249

rife, although Ma might not have heard of this or was pretending to ignore it.

In a strange way, thinking about this did provide comfort of a different kind to Rosie, as such notorious behaviour was known to be carried out particularly against women. *At least I can be thankful for one thing, in losing me darling Daisy and Florrie – they weren't taken prisoner, to suffer at the hands of the Japs. But what of Billy?* In her mind she pleaded fervently, *Oh, Billy lad, toe the line. Do all that is asked of you, lad.*

The second letter was a beautiful one from the King himself, mentioning his lovely wife, Queen Elizabeth, who joined with him in their sorrow to hear of the loss of Daisy and Florrie. Not that he named them like that, but no matter that he used his own posh words and gave them their full titles – Sister D. Bradshaw and Nurse F. Bradshaw – the letter did something for them all.

'There, the King and Queen themselves are feeling the loss of our Daisy and our Florrie, Ma.'

'They are, lass, and they have need to, as our lasses deserve their recognition. I'm framing that letter, Angus, and we'll have it on the wall to honour our lasses.'

Angus nodded. His arms came out and Ma went into them, her sobs shaking the very walls of the house. Rosie grabbed her coat and went outside, where she found Roddie.

'Eeh, lad, you'll catch your death. You've naw coat on.'

'At this moment I want to die, Rosie.'

'Naw, lad, you've got to live – for me, and Ma and your da. Aye, and our Billy an' all. When he gets home, he'll need his brother to be there for him. Remember, lad, you're having to bear this here, with your ma and da, and me and Aunt Susan, to help you. Billy'll knaw – if not now, then very soon – that his sisters have died, and will have to bear it in a living hell of his own.'

'Aye, Rosic . . . Rosie . . .'

She opened her arms and Roddie came and hugged her, and as big and strong as he was, his heart was broken, wetting her hair with his tears and opening up the rawness of her own wounds. Together, the brother and sister left behind sobbed out their grief.

CHAPTER TWENTY

# Blackburn and London

## Mags, Flors and Ella

'Flors, that telephone call I just took, you're never going to believe this – it was Ella!'

'What? But that's marvellous. Oh, Mags, where is she? Is she all right?'

'Yes, she's being cared for by the British Embassy; she says she was rescued and flown out of France, but couldn't give us any details of how or who by. They're taking her to hospital, but she wants to come here. I nearly screamed down the phone, I was so excited.'

'I'll fetch her, Mags. Ella can't travel by train. She . . . well, I told you what happened, and God knows what might have happened to her since then. She's going to need us.'

'I'll come, too. I can, as I have an excellent team at the mill who can take over from me. I'll get Bradshaw to drive us. But Ella's not able to come straight away, because apparently she is helping the embassy with information. Again she was unable to tell me more than that . . . Oh, there's the telephone again.'

Mags almost skipped into the hall as her excitement, mixed

with relief about Ella, gave her a feeling of euphoria. She hoped this was Jerome, so that she could share her wonderful news with him.

'Aunt Mags, is that you? Oh, Aunt Mags,' a tiny voice called out.

Mags felt a shiver run through her. 'Rosie?'

'Yes. Oh, Aunt Mags . . .'

'What is it, Rosie? Don't cry, my darling girl. I can't understand you. What's happened – is it Billy?'

'Naw, I mean, aye, but . . .'

What followed had Mags bending at the knees, with the weight of her grief. 'No. No. Oh, my darling, no!'

'What's wrong, Mags? Oh, my dear Mags, what's wrong?' Flors called out as she rushed over.

Putting her hand up to Flors, Mags spoke into the receiver. 'Rosie, I'll start out today. Tell Betsy – your ma – I'll be there tomorrow. Oh, my little one, my precious little one. We'll get through this, we will. Is your ma there?'

'Aye, but I don't think she can talk. She just wants you to come – we all do. I'll tell her you are coming.'

'Does your Aunt Ciss know?'

'Aye, we phoned the estate.'

'I'll go and see her before I set out. Thank God her sons, being farmers, are exempt from going to war, as your family is doing enough as it is. Can you stay with your ma, Rosie, or do you have to report for duty?'

'I can stay. I've been given indefinite compassionate leave. I need it, an' all. I've a lot to tell you, Aunt Mags. We all need you. We need your strength.'

Mags didn't feel strong. She wanted to curl up and scream against this cruel world and the loss of the lovely Daisy and Florrie, whom she'd known and loved since their birth.

253

Putting the phone down, after saying her goodbyes and reassuring Rosie that she would help them all she could, Mags turned to Flors.

'Come and sit down, Mags. I rang for tea to be served. Whatever has happened?'

Telling Flors made it all become true. Mags could no longer contain her grief and broke down. 'Betsy and I have been friends since we were thirteen.'

'I know.'

'We had an unlikely friendship, born of my loneliness and Betsy's lovely, kind nature. She was from a poor background and worked in the mill that my father owned at the time. I came to love her like the sister I never had. Her children are like mine. Oh, Flors, how am I to bear this, and how is Betsy to? I have to help her. I have to.'

'Of course. Look, I'll fetch Ella. I'd take her to my house, but London is no place to be at the moment. The Blitz may be over, but there's still a lot of bombing and suffering.'

'Maybe that's right where we need to be, Flors – all of us. We can't leave all this to our daughters and sons. Oh, I know my daughters are not old enough yet and are safe at school, but Sibbie is like my daughter; and your dear Marjella, I love her like a daughter, too. God knows what they are doing or where they are, but I fear for them every day.'

'I know what they are doing, Mags. I – I . . . well, I can't share it. I've signed the Official Secrets Act. But I am so worried about them; and about my darling Cyrus, and Freddy, Randolph and Monty. My heart is bleeding silent tears of anguish, but we have to keep strong. You're right, though. There must be something we can do. We'll talk about it. Let's get you to Scotland, and me to London and Ella, and then when we are all back here, we'll think of a way we can help. We'll all feel better for doing so.'

By the time Mags returned to Blackburn she felt drained. There was no way of helping Betsy, and that had left her with a feeling of hopelessness. But although it felt as if she couldn't make things better, Betsy had assured Mags that her coming, and bringing her sister Ciss to her, was all the help she needed. It was good to see Susan, too, though she couldn't reassure Mags about Sibbie's safety. And she saw that, in their own way, Betsy and Susan had been coping, doing their bit. She told Flors this, as they sat in the peaceful surroundings of Mags's sitting room, looking out onto the garden, which had almost shed the last remaining clumps of snow and was ready to welcome April and the spring.

'If a little corner of Scotland can do that much for the war effort, then I'm sure we can find a niche for us. It'll do us good. Keep our mind off everything,' Flors said.

'Is there any news of Ella? I hoped she would be here by now – it's been two weeks.'

'Yes, there is. Ella is sick. I only heard yesterday and wanted to go down at once, but knew you were coming home today, so I waited. Little Lonia is in a home. Oh, Mags, I know you have been through a lot, but I think we should go to London together. We can fight any red tape.'

'Red tape? Will there be any? Flors? Flors, what *is* going on?'

'I wish I could tell you. But all I can say is that if Ella was air-lifted out, then it would have been with the help of the French Resistance, as there is no other way.'

'Partisans, you mean? Aren't they dangerous?'

255

'Yes, they are, to the enemy, but Ella isn't an enemy of France.'

'Wait a minute. Why was she captured? And where are Arnie and Cyrus? Are they really hiding out till they can get here? And why, if you got out, didn't they?'

'Mags, you know better than to ask me. Anyway the fact that you are asking means that you have an idea what is going on. All I can say is that you're not wrong.'

'Oh, my God! They are working with the Resistance, too. Oh, Flors, you must be so worried. Look, I won't ask any more, of course I know better, but I am a shoulder to cry on, Flors. As you have always been for me, I am here for you.'

'I know. And I am in need of you, Mags, more than you know. Coming here has been my salvation. Look, now you know something of what is happening, I have other news. News that has increased my worries.'

'Oh, Flors, you were always the strongest of us all. How do you bear all that you have to?'

'I don't know. I suppose my childhood made me resilient. And my wonderful Nanny Pru, who always taught me to stand up to the world, has given me the mettle I need.'

Hardly daring to ask what Flors's worries were and why she needed her so much, Mags held her hand.

'I made a telephone call while you were away, Mags. Don't ask me where, but I was given some wonderful news, and some less good news. Firstly, Cyrus is coming home. He will be air-lifted out some time next week. I won't be able to see him for about a fortnight, but then I'll go down to London and prepare our house for him. I fled it, I'm afraid, almost without removing the dust sheets, though Mrs Larch – you remember I told you about her – did her best to make me, bless her.'

'I'm so pleased for you, Flors. To have Cyrus by your side will be a great help.'

'It will. I miss him so much.'

Mags was quiet for a moment. She didn't know whether to broach the subject of the true relationship between Flors and Cyrus or not, but surely it must be a worry to her, if it was found out.

'I know what you are thinking, Mags. And there are still a few people alive who know that Cyrus is my half-brother – something that has haunted us both, all our lives. But we were forced to come back here.'

'But to go to your old house together? Isn't that too risky?'

'Yes, you're right. Of course you are. Thinking about it, it would be better not to. I'll look for a rental on the other side of London from Brixton – somewhere we are not known. Cyrus is to be conscripted, but his work will be so secret that no newspapers will hear of him being home, so they won't dig up old news about our case.'

'Poor Flors, you had such an idyllic solution with your home in France. I could weep for you – for all of us – and for the world even.'

'I know. My next news did make we weep, and yet filled me with hope, when I heard that Randolph – my dear Randie has escaped. They are assuming he is safe, as nothing else has been reported. I don't know whether to laugh or cry about him, and have been that way since I heard.'

Mags could do nothing for the lump that had formed in her throat. Taking hold of Flors, she hugged her friend to her. Together, they rocked backwards and forwards. The feeling of how unfair this all was coursed through

Mags's mind. In their lifetime they'd only known patches of peace in the world. What had they done to deserve such a fate?

Their journey from Blackburn to London the next day was long and tiring, as there were many delays caused by blocked roads due to bomb damage, and re-routing off the main A5. When they finally reached Kensington, they were exhausted.

Their room at the Park Hotel, which Mags had booked by telephone, was a family room with a double and a single bed, so that Ella could join them as soon as she was released from hospital and they brought her here. Neither could believe that at last they were going to see Ella again.

Flors had told Mags all that had happened, and the horror at the thought of their dear friend almost being sent to a camp for Jews had trembled through her. Her heart went out to Ella, and Mags wanted to protect her from the world.

There was a shock waiting for them both at the sight of Ella, when they visited the hospital the next day. Always the smallest of the three of them, Ella now looked almost child-like with all the weight she'd lost. Her features, which were thin and defined, now looked skeletal, and her huge eyes stared out of sunken sockets.

Unable to find any words, all Mags could say was 'Ella! Ella, darling, we're here.'

On seeing them both, Ella's face became more recognizable, as it lit up with her lovely smile.

'You're going to be all right now, Ella. As soon as we can, we're taking you back to our hotel and we're going to look after you and make you well. We're applying to get

Lonia tomorrow. We'll keep her safe and we'll visit you every day, then get you home.' A tear plopped onto Ella's cheek as Flors told her this.

This loveliest of women had endured so much in her lifetime, and her suffering showed in her face at this moment, in a way Mags had never seen personified before.

'Ella, my dear friend, fight to get well. Don't lose your strong will. Think of the days when we will all be back together. We'll go back to our vineyard, and you'll be with Arnie and Paulo and Lonia. We'll sit out in the sun – well, under that canopy that the men fixed up for us – and drink tea. And Paulo and Sibbie will marry, and my boys will meet girls and marry, too. Then we will have lovely grandchildren playing around our feet. And Mags will visit. Oh, Ella, we have so much to look forward to.'

At Flors's words, a glimmer of hope seemed to come into Ella, as she nodded at each wonderful happening that Flors described. 'Help me, Flors, Mags . . . Help me.'

'Oh, Ella, we will. One or the other of us will be by your side at all times, once we have you out of here. Do all you can, my dear, to get well.'

Ella smiled at Mags. 'We've been through a lot in our lifetime and won through. We can again, can't we?'

Both Flors and Mags said 'Yes' together. Mags took hold of one of Ella's hands, and Flors went round the other side of the bed and took hold of her other hand as she said, 'Always, the three of us – together. No one can break us.'

At this, all three felt the tears spill over. Flors controlled hers first. 'Let's sit you up, darling. Then you can look around you, instead of staring up at the ceiling.'

As they lifted Ella, Mags was appalled to feel her bones jutting from her wasted body. Flors looked over at her, her face full of concern. Propping Ella up, Flors told her, 'That's better. Now, I'm going to leave you with Mags, Ella, and go and see the sister of the ward, and discuss how soon we can take you out of here.'

'No, I'll come with you, Flors. You'll be all right for a moment, won't you, Ella?'

At Ella's nod, Mags walked away with Flors. 'My God, Flors, what do you think is wrong?'

'I would say ill-treatment, mental torment, a broken heart – all things that can be mended by us, Mags, but not in these clinical conditions. We need Ella out of here, and with Lonia.'

'Flors, you are a very special person. You have been through some of what Ella has, with what those soldiers did to you, and yet you haven't crumbled.'

'I nearly did. Cyrus and I had a battle to get through, as he was so hurt by it all, but it is as I said: the rejection of me by my family, as a child, helped to shape me to fight back, no matter what I had to face. We've got to help Ella do that.'

The sister surprised them by agreeing with them. 'There is nothing clinically wrong with Mrs Smith-Palmer; she needs building up, and help to come to terms with what she's been through. Your idea might be just the thing for her. I will speak to the doctor and, hopefully, we can discharge her into your care tomorrow.'

Mags and Flors hugged each other and Mags felt such relief that she hugged the sister, too. The sister laughed as she tried to hold on to her headdress. 'My, that wasn't expected, but I think you will both be exactly the tonic my patient needs.'

'Mags! You and your hugs!'

They both giggled, but then Mags became serious. 'We've

a lot to do, though, Flors. We can't take Ella back to a hotel, not as she is, and yet we have to make everything happen quickly.'

'I agree. I think, as I know London, that I should leave now, and you should stay with Ella, as we promised her that we wouldn't leave her. I'll sort something out for us, although it isn't going to be easy. London is broken; well, its people aren't, they are amazing, but there cannot be many places to rent. I think we'll have to go back to my house. There's very few people left around there who remember everything from twenty years ago. We'll have to take the chance, in the immediate future.'

'I agree, but, Flors, I think Ella would fare so much better at my house. She will be in the countryside, there's someone to look after her all the time and, especially, where Lonia is concerned. If Lonia is traumatized, and there's a fair bet that she is, then she doesn't need to be around death and destruction – the bombing raids and the extreme shortages that the poor Londoners are experiencing.'

'You're right. Yes, that is the best solution. But I do need to be here, as these are my people. I want to help them, and the war effort; and besides, Cyrus will be here soon and working in London. Oh, Mags, will you be able to manage without me? Will Ella?'

'It isn't what I want, and I know Ella will feel the same, but it is the only solution, Flors. Why not spend your time today finding out how we can get Lonia released to us, and then come back here and we'll work it out from there?'

'I will. Thank you, Mags. Sometimes I think I can conquer the world on my own, but I realize that I can't, and compromises have to be made.'

Back at Ella's side, they told her the plan. 'I would love

that, Mags, thank you. I've a lovely memory of visiting your home when we were younger. We sat in the garden for hours, laughing and chattering. The sun was warm, the trees rustling in the breeze, birds chirped, and all to the beautiful backdrop of the dramatic scenery you have in the North.'

'Well, it won't be long before we can sit in the garden, as already the trees are budding and early spring bulbs are pushing through. The birds are in abundance, too, fighting over a piece of flotsam as they build their nests, or over the lady they want to share it with.' Ella laughed at this, and Mags felt her heart gladden. 'Oh, and we have a summerhouse – a new one, as the old one was tumbling down. I love sitting in there in the afternoons and have my tea served there most days. There's a rocking chair in there, you'll love that.'

'I will, and Lonia will.'

'She will, and children thrive in our neck of the woods.'

Just talking about the hopeful future for Ella was having an effect. There was a marked difference in her. Her face had filled with colour and her eyes had renewed hope.

'Well, I'll leave you two to talk. I have a mission to accomplish.'

As Flors left, Ella surprised Mags by giggling. 'They'd better watch out at that home – Flors is coming.'

Mags giggled with her at this, then took Ella's hand. 'Everything is going to turn out all right, Ella. I promise.'

Flors didn't find her mission easy. Seeing Lonia was heart-breaking. The funny, adorable little minx that Lonia had been was no longer. Her eyes were inexpressive, her tears never far away, her spirit all but dead. But if anything could be worse than all this, it was the awful silence. Lonia wouldn't utter a word.

Even seeing Flors didn't lift her, though Flors could tell that Lonia did gain a little hope, as she clung to Flors's neck and wouldn't let go until Flors prised her away. 'Darling, believe me, I'm going to make everything right. Your mama is getting better, and we have plans for you both.' She told Lonia about Mags's home. 'You love Mags, don't you? When she visits us in France, you hardly leave her side. And her girls, Beth and Belinda. They will be home from school for the Easter holidays soon, and you will have lots of fun with them, like you do in France.'

A glimmer of hope entered Flors as Lonia nodded at this and, for a fleeting second, a small smile visited her lips.

Tackling the matron of the home wasn't easy, either. 'Taking a child from here isn't simply a matter of turning up and saying you can give her a home, Mrs Harpinham. There are legal requirements.'

'I expected as much, but I am not asking to adopt the child, just to take her back to her mother.'

'But I understand the mother isn't well enough to take care of her child.'

'Lonia and her mama will be in safe hands, very comfortable and cared for. One cannot get better without the other – they need to be together. Don't you think they've been through enough? Having to run away from their home and their family, being captured and put into a concentration camp where they faced death, as they are of Jewish descent? Please, Matron, if you never do another thing for a child, move heaven and earth for this one.'

'All of the children in my care have been through hell, Mrs Harpinham.'

'Well, now that you have a chance to change that for one of them, wouldn't you want to do that? Wouldn't you want at least one of the children in your care to win through and be back with her parents – loved and cared for, and recovering from all she has been through?' Flors told Matron of the plan that she and Mags had for Lonia and Ella, and how Mags's home would be a haven for them both.

Matron sighed. 'Yes, of course. Look, I will do my best, but the process isn't short. I will need to know all about this Mags – her full name for a start.'

'She's Mrs Margaret Cadley.'

'Well, she needs to be checked out – we will have to speak to her local clergy and her doctor, and references will be required.'

'What? Lonia is going to be in the care of her own mama, assisted by Mags, until she is stronger. You cannot need to check out the child's own mother, surely?'

'I need authority.'

'Is authority from the War Office enough? They put her into your care, through their welfare system, didn't they?'

'Well, yes, of course. But—'

'Then may I use your telephone?'

Getting through to William Parsons posed even more difficulties, but at last Flors heard his voice. 'Captain Parsons, it's Flors Harpinham. I need your help.'

On explaining the situation to Wills, he said immediately that he would help and agreed to send a communication at once to the home and to the hospital to inform them of his decision. 'Putting Mrs Smith-Palmer's child in the home was our only option when her mother collapsed. I'm sorry, but you were up in the North, and we couldn't care for her.'

'I understand. Thank you for helping me.' Flors wanted so much to ask if there was further news on Randolph, and to be reassured that Cyrus was still coming back to her. And to ask how Marjella and Sibbie were, and Arnie and Paulo, but she knew she must not do so.

'That's all right . . . Erm, Mrs Harpinham, I meant to tell you that the delivery you are waiting for will be here soon.'

Flors caught her breath. 'Oh? That's wonderful news. I will wait at my home address for it. Thank you.'

The telephone went dead. Flors wanted to jump for joy. *Cyrus, my Cyrus. Please, God, don't let it be long before I can hold him. I need him so much.*

As she left the home, Flors's heart sang. Lonia was smiling properly for the first time as they made their way back to the hospital. When they arrived there, the loving reunion between Ella and Lonia was a joy to watch.

Holding hands, Flors, Mags and Ella looked at each other as Mags said, 'Together – and with Flors at our helm – we can achieve anything. Just as we did back in 1914. Did I ever tell you girls that I love you as if you were my sisters?'

'Mmm, a few times, Mags.' Flors winked at Ella as she said this, and all three burst into laughter. Lonia seemed to come to life at this – she giggled and clapped her hands. 'I love you all too, and as if you were my sisters.' This increased their laughter, making tears run from their eyes. And although some were tears of joy, Flors knew that her own tears and Ella's were tinged with sadness, too. Ella brushed hers away. 'Oh, Lonia, darling, we're going to be all right.'

'We are, Mama. We always are, with Aunt Flors.'

Flors's tears of joy increased, blocking out the sadness. Their Lonia – the little girl with cheek, spirit and a way of making everyone laugh – was back, and Flors thanked God for it.

CHAPTER TWENTY-ONE

# Narbonne, France

## Sibbie and Marjie

'Your way of dealing with Monsieur Passat has worked. That little French boy you bribed to take the groceries up to Monsieur's apartment is waiting every time I go to deliver now. Costing me a fortune, though, Marjie.'

'I know, Sibbie – he's a little devil. One centime isn't enough for him. I have to give him an apple or something, as well.'

'Ha! He's a minx. In the three or so weeks he's been working for us, he's done well out of us.'

'He has, but he's also saved us from a pervert.'

They were getting ready for a rare evening out, at the insistence of Madame Bachelet. 'You are young and should enjoy life more. There's a local dance, and lots of young people will be there. Go. Here, I have tickets for you.'

The girls hadn't been keen. The only dance they wanted to go to was one with Paulo and Wills, and that couldn't happen for a long time.

The dance was being held in the municipal buildings attached to the public swimming pool, about a mile from their home. While cycling to it, they were stopped and their pupils checked, but as this had happened many times before, they had taken it in their stride, just as they did the banter of the *gendarme*, who had flirted with them.

The hall was drab and cold, not at all inviting and painted a dull yellow. The lighting was dim, though the music, played by a trio – pianist, cellist and saxophonist – did excite them as they played a lively jazz number, and the joviality of the young people lifted them. 'Let's dance, Sibbie. All the girls are dancing together. I'll be the woman, though. I couldn't take the man's part.'

'That's fine. Me and Daisy always took the male lead with Florrie and Rosie, so I'm used to that. I wonder how they all are. It's horrid not having any contact with everyone.'

'I know, I long to hear from Mama, and Wills, but I'm lucky to have Papa here. Anyway, don't let's think about it tonight. Come on.'

They giggled as they shimmied across the room, but then the music changed and a slower number was playing. Sibbie took up the position of the man as they went into a waltz. They'd only done a few steps when Marjie complained, 'Ouch, you stood on my toe.'

'Oops, sorry, Marjie. I'm out of practice. Don't think we'll win any championships, do you?'

They both laughed and Marjie felt the pressure of her worries lift off her. They'd received a message the night before that there was to be another mission, and were told it would be in three days' time and they would be contacted by the Maquis. The thought of this didn't sit easy with her, but neither did the fact that today Madame Bachelet had told them she would be arranging the details of their travel.

Marjie still felt uneasy about Madame, but didn't know why. It was feasible that her son had given her the message, but nothing formal concerning such an arrangement had been discussed with them. Putting it out of her mind for the moment, she concentrated on the dance, until Sibbie surprised her by saying that she thought they should sit down.

'We're being watched.'

'What? Who by, Sibbie?'

Sibbie indicated two men slouched against the far wall. The feeling of unease that Marjie harboured deepened.

As they sat down on one of the many benches that stood against the walls, Sibbie whispered, 'I'm not happy here, Marjie.'

'No, I'm not, either. I hadn't noticed them, but now that you say . . .'

'Oh, I don't know – maybe we're paranoid and they just fancy us.'

'I know what you mean, and it would be a relief at this moment if that was the case, but why aren't they approaching us and asking us to dance?'

'Let's dance again, only this time towards the exit. If they are watching us, then they will do something.'

As they reached the door, they stopped dancing and stood for a moment, as if talking. Sibbie was facing the men. 'They don't seem bothered and are talking amongst themselves now.'

'Could be a ploy, as they may have noticed that we spotted them. Shall we slip through the door and see if that alerts them into action?'

Shivering while they waited to see if anything happened – and with the excuse that, if challenged, they would say they had wanted some fresh air – they decided they were being silly, after no one followed them out. 'The evening's spoilt now. I'd rather go home, Sibbie. We could tell Madame that we were too tired to enjoy it.'

'Good idea. We'll fetch our coats and have one more check, as we do so.'

They laughed at themselves as they saw that the two men they'd been afraid of were dancing with other girls. 'Ha, it's getting to us, girl. But even though there's no threat now, I still think I'd like to go. I feel unnerved. Come on, let's ride back by the river, I love that route. And in this moonlight it'll be lovely.'

'No, Sibbie, I just want to go home. I don't feel safe.'

'But that is the safest way, Marjie. I know it takes longer, but we miss the checkpoint on the main route. If the feeling we have is right and there is something amiss, the *gendarmes* may have been alerted.'

'Yes, you're right. By the river it is, then. Sibbie, what's spooking you in particular?'

'Madame. I haven't said anything, but I feel there's something not quite right.'

'That's exactly how I feel. Why this dance? She's never suggested that we go out before, and she was so insistent. She seems to know too much, too.'

As they rode by the river, the sound of the lapping water in the quietness of the evening further enhanced their wariness. They rode their bicycles in silence, cutting behind the cathedral and through a dark, narrow street to reach the shop.

'That's odd, Sibbie, there isn't a light in the place. Madame didn't say she was going out, did she?'

'No, let's pull up a mo.'

They stood on the deserted pavement, looking around them. Nothing seemed untoward, and yet everything felt sinister. Marjie felt the muscles in her stomach contract. 'I don't like it, Sibbie.'

'No, neither do I. I think we should go in the back way.' Sibbie's whisper held her fear, and her head bobbed this way and that. Every shadow seemed to hold danger. 'If we creep up the fire escape and get in through the attic room, then we can get to our room and lock the door. At least then, if anything happens, we can be ready to defend ourselves.'

Marjie's unease increased as they reached the back gate and saw dim rays of light coming through the broken slats of the attic-window shutters. Leaning their bikes against the wall, they signalled to each other the code for arming themselves.

In the dim light the moon provided, Marjie searched in her bag. Her hand clutched the innocent-looking pen that, on touching the ink-release button, flicked open to reveal a sharp, deadly blade. When she showed it to Sibbie, Sibbie nodded and did the same.

The gate creaked as they opened it, freezing them to the spot for a moment. Without opening it any further, they held it still while they squeezed through it, then Sibbie held the gate while Marjie moved the wooden wedge into place. This done, they crept across the yard and began to ascend the wooden steps, grateful for the sound of the rustling branches of the tree that stood in the yard next door, as it masked the tiny creaks of their progress.

As they neared the top, voices came to them; one was Madame's distinct tone. Speaking in German, she was giving every detail of the forthcoming mission – details they hadn't yet been provided with.

Marjie knew what they had to do. Without thinking about

the horror of it, she signalled to Sibbie, who gave the thumbs-up sign.

With her heart pounding, Marjie grabbed the door handle. A moment of doubt assailed her. Never before had they killed in close quarters. The horror of shooting the German soldiers came to her, but then so did the thought of her comrades being ambushed and killed.

When she flung the door open, two shadowy figures turned towards her. 'What? Who?'

Blotting out Madame's terrified voice, Marjie leapt forward and, in an instant, had stuck her knife deep into the woman's heart. Looking up, she saw that the German had backed off towards the wall. Sibbie dashed by her, but he had recovered and grabbed Sibbie's arm, bending it backwards. Her cry of pain, and seeing the German go for his gun, spurred Marjie on. Stepping over Madame's dead body, she lunged forward. Her knife stabbed into his heart.

'Quick, Sibbie. We have to get our things and get out of here.'

'No. That would implicate us and surround us with suspicion. The mission isn't taking place for another week, so that gives us time to let HQ know that it has been betrayed.'

'You think we should stay here? But—'

'Yes. We mustn't be suspected of carrying out these murders. If we are, our cover is blown. We have to burn our coats in the big incinerator by the shed, then clean ourselves up. Madame has a number of coats – we can take two of them. Then go to the door and scream the place down, as if we have just discovered Madame and this other man dead in the attic.'

Marjie knew Sibbie was right. Shaking from her reaction,

her mind had gone into flight mode, but now she could see the sense in braving this out.

Working in silence, they dismantled the radio and hid its components in their bikes – in the saddle and the hollow handlebars. Their coats they pushed into the ever-burning incinerator. Back in their room, they washed in ice-cold water and, with only the light from the moon shining through the window, as they dared not show any signs of being home, they made their way to Madame's room, where they each donned a coat: Sibbie a long, plain grey coat that Madame wore on everyday errands, and Marjie her church-going coat, which was long, black and sported a fur collar.

'Right, our story? Any ideas, Marjie?'

'Yes, I've been mulling it over. We went to the dance and felt hot and stuffy, so as we weren't expected back, we rode the long way by the river. When we found the house in darkness, we thought Madame had retired early. Not wanting to disturb her, we decided to come in the back way, as then we wouldn't have to pass her bedroom door.'

'Brilliant. And we can say that we will go to our great-aunt's to stay.'

'What if they want an address?'

Marjie thought for a moment. 'We could give my old address. I doubt they would ever go and check up, as they would have no reason to. But we must get to Arnie and Papa quickly, to warn them about Madame's son. He must have given his mother the information, when he was only supposed to have given her the arrangements for our pick-up.'

'Oh God, Marjie. What if she has passed on information about us and that is why we have been allowed to travel around freely?'

'It's a possibility. We may be compromised. Arnie will

seek that information from Jacques. We just have to get to them – come on, let the first step of our plan begin.'

Having a plan gave them confidence. Their screams brought neighbours out of their houses and a nearby patrol of *gendarmes* rushing to them. Acting distraught, the girls were taken to a neighbour's house and were given hot cocoa to drink.

The *gendarmes* didn't ask the questions they expected, but from what Marjie overheard them saying to each other, they seemed more concerned with covering their own backs. This made Marjie think that perhaps the *gendarmes* should have been watching the property while the German was in there with Madame, but had not been at their post.

Nothing indicated that the *gendarmes* knew who they really were, or why they were here. The least nervous of the *gendarmes* told Marjie and Sibbie that they would no longer be needed, and that it was thought the German who had died must have been a friend of Madame's. That many romantic liaisons between the Germans and French women were conducted in secret. 'There seems no other cause than that they must have been found out, and that their deaths were probably due to reprisals by criminal factions who are traitors to the government.'

To Sibbie and Marjie, this cover-up story was one they were very grateful for and showed that they weren't under any suspicion. When the *gendarmes* told them they were free to go, they were asked if they had any relatives they could go to. They told their story.

Marjie was proud of Sibbie's composure, and grateful for it, as she felt that if she had to talk, she'd be sick. 'Our great-aunt lives in Hérault; we can catch the train to Béziers in the morning and then cycle the rest of the way.'

The neighbour helped, by saying the girls could stay on her sofas until morning. 'We will take care of them.'

The *gendarmes* seemed pleased with this arrangement and left.

The next morning Sibbie and Marjie were waved on past the checkpoint and had no problem with the *gendarmes* on the train. It was obvious that word had been passed to let them make their way without hindrance.

They hadn't discussed anything to do with the incident, or what their next move was, for fear of being overheard, but now, having reached Hérault and walked some way into the forest, they sat on a fallen tree in an open brush area and discussed what to do next. They both agreed they should make contact with the Resistance.

Practised at building their radio, contact was soon made with HQ, using the code they'd been given for an emergency. Telling HQ what had happened and giving their current position, they waited.

Pushing their bikes had exhausted them. 'Sibbie, we're not too far away now; once we go through this next clump of trees, we will hit the road, and crossing that will put us into the forest where Paulo and Arnie are hiding. But we're safe here, so let's rest while we await instructions.'

They lay down, head-to-head on the smooth tree trunk, with the transmitter between them.

Sibbie shivered. 'It's so cold. I wish we could lie closer to each other for warmth.'

'There is nowhere – it's rough, rocky terrain in these clearings in the forest. But if we go into the trees, where we might find a softer bed, our radio won't work.'

Hugging herself, to combat the cold and the desolation

she felt, Marjie willed the radio to signal a message coming through. When it did, sometime later, she jumped and nearly screamed with fright, because with the sun coming out at last, both girls had been warmed enough to be lulled into a light sleep.

Sibbie giggled as she turned the radio towards her and put on the headphones. The sound set Marjie off giggling, too. 'The blooming thing always catches me unawares.'

'Shush, Marjie.'

After a moment Sibbie said, 'They've made contact with the Maquis!' Then relief and something akin to joy lit her face. 'We're going to be picked up; we've to make our way to the road, keeping in a northerly direction. Once on the road, we're to head east until we meet up with a farm truck. The driver will wave to us, and when we wave back, he will turn round and pick us up.'

Seeing Sibbie go into Paulo's arms, once they arrived, gave Marjie a feeling of gladness, and yet longing swept over her that was never far away, as she wished with all her heart that she could feel her Wills's arms around her. Papa's arms didn't compensate, though it was good to see him, and she soaked up the comfort he gave.

'You did an excellent job, Sibbie and Marjella. A traitor taken out and an ambush thwarted. And all without being compromised.'

'What about Jacques?'

'It has been taken care of. Don't worry yourself about it. Now, I have news, darling. I'll be seeing Mama very soon.'

'When, Papa? Oh, that's wonderful.'

Marjie listened to details of how her father was going to be air-lifted out, smiling with happiness as she did so. 'Oh,

Papa, I'm so glad. I will miss you, but Mama needs you by her side; and to know that you will be working in HQ, and will have our backs, is very comforting.'

'Marjella, I received other news, too.'

As Randie's situation was explained to her, Marjie felt a mixture of feelings. Fear for her brother vied with relief that he was alive, and had escaped the prisoner-of-war camp that he must have been held in, but where was he now? Her father's words didn't bring much comfort, as everything Randie did would be fraught with danger.

'We are sure he will make his way here. He knew of the Maquis before he left, and his regiment doesn't exist any more, having been taken over by the Vichy government. So Randie would seek to join the Resistance or re-join the Allies. We're playing a waiting game until HQ, or Randolph, contacts us.'

Paulo then offered, 'In the meantime we have our next mission to plan. But first of all, you two need to eat and rest. Gisele has brought us some milk and eggs, so that we can make you an omelette.'

'Who is Gisele, Paulo?'

'You remember her, Marjie? She lives in Laurens village – a cheeky youngster, always up to something or other. We used to tease her.'

'But she can't be more than sixteen, and yet she risks her life to help you?'

'She does, and most days, though she is rarely checked by the *gendarmes*. She's still small and rides around on her bike in her old school uniform, so she is of no interest to them. On one occasion she was stopped by a German patrol. She had some meat in her basket. They laughed and said, "Ach, black market!" Gisele was terrified they would lift up the meat, as under it she had two handguns, which she'd stolen for us.'

'She is very brave. But when I think of her previous nature, she lived on her wits and didn't seem afraid of anything.'

'Yes, Marjie, Gisele is brave and is a valued and very useful Resistance worker. She types our pamphlets and is responsible for finding our provisions and getting us our papers. As you know, everything is bought with supply coupons. Gisele organizes others to carry out raids on the town hall to get to these golden tickets. She steals everything she can: tickets, stamps and identity cards. The most insignificant documents that she comes across, when on these raids, she will bring, and a lot of them prove useful to our organization. Villagers support us through her, too. They give Gisele supplies to bring to us – all kinds of forbidden treasures, which she hides in the panniers of her bike: foods such as eggs and meat, but also weapons, incendiary fuses and dynamite.'

'Oh, Paulo, she is in so much danger. I can't wait to see Gisele, to thank her.'

'I don't think that's wise just yet. I need to prepare her and brief her on your cover names, and so on. We shouldn't take her by surprise without arming her with the information she will need to maintain your cover. She always gives a low whistle to alert us that it is her approaching, and I think it best that you hide then. We will gauge when the time is right for you to meet, as we are always mindful of Gisele's young age and of how frightened she is sometimes. She tells us that a soldier only has to be walking down her street for her to have a fit of nerves, thinking they are coming for her.'

The idea that the lovely imp of a girl that Marjie remembered should live her life in fear saddened her. And yet she felt such admiration for Gisele.

Paulo brought her out of these thoughts. 'Mmm, I can smell your meal cooking, and you look all in. Let's get you two rested. You can sleep in my sleeping bag, Sibbie. I have made a soft under-cushion for myself by piling up bracken into a bed shape; it is all dried out now and makes a good mattress.'

'And you can sleep in mine, darling.'

'Thanks, Papa. If we are to stay here, then I will commandeer that, the moment you leave.'

'Ah, glad to get rid of me, are you?'

'Yes. I want you safe, and I want you to be with Mama. I won't worry so much about her then.'

Her papa squeezed Marjie to him. 'But we will worry about you, my darling girl. We will also be very proud of you.'

When they woke it was late afternoon and the still atmosphere had a chill to it that made Sibbie not want to get out of the cosy sleeping bag. Opening her eyes, she saw Paulo sitting on a log just inside his tent, gazing down at her.

'That's a lovely smile to wake up to.' Her hand crept out of the bag and reached for his. 'I love you.'

'Thank you. I am honoured to have your love.' His rakish smile matched his looks, as his black hair fell untidily over his forehead. Running his fingers through it, as he did now, was a gesture that she'd seen him do so often. His dark eyes twinkled as he whispered, 'I wish I could get in there with you.'

'There's no room – you would squash me.'

'Ha, wouldn't you like that?'

Sibbie felt herself blush as she yearned for that to happen. Paulo's expression showed that he'd read her thoughts. He leaned forward. 'One day, my darling Sibbie.' His lips pressed on hers and his tongue gently prised open her mouth. Sibbie melted into the sensation and longed for that 'one day' to be now.

As they came out of the kiss, Paulo's sigh was heavy with feelings that matched her own. Holding her eyes with his for a moment, he whispered, 'I love you, my Sibbie.' Then abruptly he stood up. 'I'll leave you to get dressed, before someone comes looking to see if I'm up to no good.'

His laughter lightened the atmosphere and she giggled at him. When he left, Sibbie wondered what it would be like to make love to Paulo. Unable to control her feelings, she made herself scramble out of the sleeping bag and dress.

As she emerged from the tent she met Marjie. 'You slept well, sleepyhead.' They hugged one another.

'I'm glad to be here, Marjie. I know there's more danger for us, but I sometimes felt a bit of a phoney agent, working in a shop and waiting for orders.'

'Me too. Now that we are, where we are more in the thick of things, we can be useful in so many ways.'

'Shush!'

The urgent whisper tightened Sibbie's stomach muscles. She saw the same streak of fear attack Marjie, as her head shot round and her eyes widened.

André stood a few feet from them, his finger on his lips. Pointing, he mouthed that someone was coming.

Standing as still as statues, they registered that everyone else was lying down, holding guns that were pointed in the same direction. Sibbie felt useless, as she wasn't ready for such an event and hadn't thought, or been told, they would need to be. The sound of footsteps crunching the under-growth further enhanced her anxiety.

But then there was a low whistle, and everyone relaxed. André laughed. 'That minx, Gisele. She left it late to signal. Hurry, get out of sight.'

Sibbie and Marjie darted into Cyrus's tent, but came out again at the sound of Cyrus's astonished voice. 'Randolph! Randie, my boy. Oh, my boy, let me help you.'

# PART FIVE

## Britain and France, 1942–43

~

*Heroes and Traitors*

## CHAPTER TWENTY-TWO

# *Hérault, France*

## Sibbie and Marjie

'Randie, you're safe now.' Marjie said the words, but in her heart she knew that her lovely brother, only a year older than she was, wasn't well and didn't feel safe. All he'd been through at the hands of the Germans had taken its toll. Tucking the blanket further around him, she asked, 'Do you want to talk about what happened to you? It may help you.'

Randie lay on the bed of their father's tent while Marjie tended to him. He'd been bitten by all manner of insects and fleas, he had a fever and was half-starved, but worse than that was his apparent mental fragility.

Randie nodded. 'I – I kept my courage all that time, Marjie, but now I can't settle my mind. I wish we knew more about how Freddy really is.'

'I have a friend in England who is trying to find out for us and will let us know as soon as he can – well, he is more than a friend; we are engaged to be married and—'

'Oh, Marjie, that's good news, although you're too young – you're just my little sis.'

'Ha, I've aged while you've been away. I've done things I never dreamed I would. Some of it will haunt me forever.'

Randie's hand came out from the bedcover and reached for hers. She took it gladly, as Randie hadn't made many gestures towards her and Papa, hardly wanting them even to hug him. 'Will we ever get back to how we were, Marjie?'

'We will. But only if we learn to cope with what has happened and is happening. None of this is our fault. None of us planned to become killers, to be torn away from our home and forced to fight for our own and our countrymen's freedom. But we've risen to the challenge. Yes, we've been broken in the process, but we're alive, Randie.'

'Oh, Marjie, I need help to come to terms with it all. I – I need Mama . . .'

Marjie's heart was breaking as she saw the tears running down Randie's face.

'It was like a horror film, Marjie. The terrible battle, seeing friends shot to pieces, not knowing if Freddy was all right, falling over dead body after dead body. Then I landed in the mud, crushed by another soldier behind me who'd been shot – his whole weight was on top of me. I just waited as he took his final breaths.'

Sweat stood out on Randie's face and his trembling increased, but Marjie didn't react. She stayed quiet and waited.

'I don't know how long I lay there, hardly able to breathe. Then all went quiet. The gunfire seemed a long way away. I thought I could push the body off me and lie there till dark, then re-join my regiment. But when I rolled over, I – I was staring down the barrel of a gun. A – a German gun.'

The trembling became worse, and Marjie felt afraid for Randie, but knew she must let him talk.

'We – other prisoners and I – were marched for miles. If we stumbled, we were hit with the butt of a gun or kicked. Then when we reached the camp we were tortured, but I didn't tell them anything they wanted to know, Marjie. I – I just kept thinking of you all. I hung on to the days we'd had together, beautiful days as a family surrounded by love. Oh, Marjie . . . Marjie, they hurt me so badly.'

She got up from the log she'd been sitting on and held her brother to her. 'You're all right now, my brave brother. You're with me and Papa.' They hadn't told Randie yet that Cyrus was to be air-lifted out the next day. And they were hoping against hope that Randie could be, too. Sibbie had radioed HQ and made the request, but they were still awaiting the answer.

'Tell me about your escape, but only if it is helping you. We can stop when you want to.'

'Yes, it is helping. It's getting it out of my head.' His hand squeezed Marjie's even tighter. 'I was in solitary – a box; it was dark and there was no room to move. I don't know how long for, but then suddenly it was opened and I was grabbed by the hand. I could hardly walk and collapsed on the floor. Strong arms lifted me and ran with me. My mouth was so dry, I couldn't speak to ask what was happening. This went on for a long time. Then I was put down and given a drink. And I asked who the man was. It was a man called Maximilian, a circus strongman; we'd made friends back in our training days. I don't know how he got free from his cell or managed to open the box I was in. I – I never got the chance to ask, I was too weak and slept as he carried me all night.

'We sheltered in an old barn that housed hayricks and Maximilian said he would get us food. He went out and didn't come back. I heard Germans shouting to one another, and shots. I crawled under the hay. They came in . . . they were so close, I could almost touch them. They dug their bayonets into the hay, but missed me. When they left, I waited for hours until it was dark and then started my journey home. I never knew what happened to Maximilian.' A sob escaped Randie, but soon turned into a torrent of weeping and calling out incoherently. Marjie clung to him.

'Marjella, what has happened? Randolph! Randie, my son, Papa is here.'

'He has talked, Papa. He has told me all he has been through.'

'That is good, darling. You'll be all right, Randie; now you can begin to face it all and come to terms with it. You will, son, you will.'

They held each other, the three of them, trying to glean comfort from being together. Trying to come to a place of understanding of all they had had to face, and of what the future held.

As Sibbie entered, they looked up in silent expectation.

'Marjie, the plane's due.'

Marjie let go of her papa and Randie and, hardly daring to ask, whispered, 'What did they say, Sibbie?'

'Yes, they will lift Randie out as well.'

Randie released a sound that was between a gasp of joy and a sob. Papa did the same. 'You're going to be all right, Randie, my son. Mama and I will take care of you.'

'Thank God. Oh, Randie, you're going to Mama.' For a moment Marjie found it difficult to swallow, as a loneliness crept over her, but then she thought, *I'll be all right. I have Sibbie, and Paulo and Uncle Arnie. I'm glad Randie is going. Now I will have three members of my family safe and sound. I just wish I could hear about Freddy. Dear God, take care of him and Monty. God knows what's happening to poor, misguided Monty.*

\* \* \*

The night of the air-lift, Sibbie, Marjie, Arnie, Paulo, Randie and Cyrus set off for the field that had been earmarked for the aircraft to land. Spotters had gone before them. Marjie had counted a dozen or so men trudging out of camp, making their way to various outposts, all of them armed, all intent on safeguarding the mission by giving an early warning of anything amiss.

Thankfully, it was a clear night with little wind. The planes would always come in low to avoid detection, which was difficult enough, without bad weather. They trudged in silence, through the forest and over rough terrain in the clearings. Marjie walked between her father and her brother whenever the space between the trees allowed.

When they came to the edge of the forest there was a sense of being exposed, but lookouts had gone ahead of them and no concerns were reported. Sibbie had the radio, as the pilot would contact them, once he was near enough and was descending. The rest of them carried torches that would line the route and would be lit as the plane approached.

Nothing seemed untoward, and preparing the landing strip – which meant clearing it of debris and lining it with torches – kept them busy and didn't give Marjie any time to dwell on the goodbyes that lay ahead of her.

They worked in silence – a silence that a distant drone encroached upon. 'It's the plane. I'll make contact.' They all waited while Sibbie manned the radio. A crackly voice came over it, asking them to light the torches for the approach and to have the cargo ready. Marjie smiled at her papa and brother being called 'cargo'.

Running down the length of the landing strip with a lighted torch, she lit the four torches she was responsible for, and as she ran back saw that the others had done the same and the runway was now an illuminated causeway.

Crouching with her papa, Marjie felt his arm come around her. 'Stay safe, my darling.'

'I will, Papa.'

Randie crawled forward and held her to him. 'I'll be back, Marjie, I promise you. I'll get well and I'll come back.'

'I know you will, Randie, and I'll hang on to that day, keeping it as a ray of hope in my future. Together, we'll work for the freedom of our beloved France.' They clung together.

Papa encircled them both. 'My children, I am so proud of you both.'

The engine noise increased. The plane was here.

'Go – go on, both of you – take my love with you and give it to Mama. I wish I could send it to Aunt Ella and Aunt Mags and everyone, too.'

Her father and Randie left Marjie then. They made a beautiful picture, father helping son to safety.

'Tell Mama that I love her more than life.'

This whisper was spoken into the darkness. They were gone. Marjie could see them boarding, and then the plane lifted off the ground. A tear seeped out of her eye as loneliness engulfed her. An arm came round her. She rested her head on Sibbie's shoulder.

'You still have me, Marjie – nothing will part us. Well, until this is all over, and then I'm off with my Paulo.'

Marjie giggled. 'And I'm off with my Wills. And we're going to make lots of babies, and keep them safe, and there'll be no more wars.'

'Lots, eh? I bet me and Paulo make more.' They collapsed in laughter. The ground beneath them felt damp and cold, but they didn't care. A shout brought them out of their fun-making world to the reality of the tasks ahead. As they ran to help dismantle the runway, they didn't hear the pilot radioing in to their deserted radio that he'd seen a German convoy heading towards them.

As they doused the last flame, a shot rang out. Marjie froze. Sibbie moved nearer to her. Within seconds they were lying face-down on the ground.

'Can you see anything, Sibbie?'

Before she could answer, the sound of many trucks filled the space around them. 'Come on, Marjie, we have to run!'

'Take cover!'

At this shout from Arnie, Marjie grabbed Sibbie and joined the many men running for the shelter of the trees. When they reached the safety of the cover that the woodland offered, they were joined by ten or so other Resistance fighters and looked for Paulo. He pushed himself through the others to reach their side.

Arnie shouted more orders. 'Load your weapons and spread out. Try to make it back to camp. Let's hope that shot didn't hit any of our spotters, although it is a worry that they haven't been able to warn us. Good luck, everyone. Sibbie, Marjie, Paulo, keep with me.'

Sibbie grabbed the radio.

'We'll hide that, Sibbie – we've no time to dismantle it, and carrying it will slow us down.' Paulo took the radio and ran with it to where there was a thick growth of bracken, which they'd seen in the torchlight on their approach.

With this done, Paulo re-joined them, to the sound of gunfire splitting the night air. Arnie shouted more orders. 'There sound like too many for us to stand and fight, so run for all your worth back to camp. Keep your weapons at the ready, in case the Germans break through the spotters.'

As they set off, Marjie prayed that the spotters would win through and get away.

Panting for breath, they ran, until a shot rang out that told them the Germans were close. 'Bed in and keep quiet.'

At this command from Arnie, they scattered into the brush. Marjie lay down, her body shivering with cold and fear. Silence fell. She strained her eyes to try to see where the others were. A whispered 'Is everyone all right?' came from her left.

'Yes, Paulo,' came from Arnie.

Then Paulo addressed her. 'Sibbie's with me. Are you all right, Marjie?'

'Yes, Paulo. I'm over to your right.'

'Everyone, keep down and stay quiet.' Arnie's voice always reassured, but at this moment nothing could take away Marjie's extreme fear.

Torches approached from behind Sibbie and Paulo, but before Marjie could warn them, a shout in French, with a German accent, echoed around her: 'Don't move.'

Terror deeper than any she'd ever felt overcame Marjie. From her vantage point she could see that the soldier had been joined by another, and that both had their guns trained on Sibbie and Paulo. The voice she'd heard previously cut through her, as he addressed them once more.

'Stand up, dogs!'

A silent scream pierced Marjie's head, as she saw Sibbie and Paulo stand with their hands held high above their shoulders. Her instinct made her wish to give vent to the scream, but her training officer's voice echoed through her: *You can hear your comrade screaming, you are near, the Germans have her: what do you do, eh? Tell me! . . . You remain totally silent, that's what you do! No heroics. YOU MUST*

*NOT BE CAPTURED, TOO. You must survive, to report back and continue the work your comrade cannot now do. It will be decided later whether a rescue can be attempted.* And even though she had her gun at the ready and could clearly see the German, Marjie knew that to shoot would mean that she would give away the fact that there were more of them. She had to remain still.

The German soldier barked out, 'Where are the others? You are not alone. We know that. It takes many of you to set up the facility for a plane to land. We have killed your filthy comrades, but we know there are more.'

Sibbie answered him. Her voice sounded strong, and this reassured Marjie a little. 'We are the only two who ran this way; the others ran the other way.'

'You're lying, dog.' Sibbie's cry of pain, and Paulo's protest, brought silent tears to Marjie's face.

In German, the soldier who had done all the talking now said, 'Search around – find the dogs!'

Marjie held her breath and prayed. Her prayers were for Sibbie and Paulo, and for herself and Arnie. Creeping backwards, she found herself sliding and slowly her body went into a dip in the ground, as the torchlight passed by her.

She could see the soldier's muddied boots as he trod close to her head, but he didn't detect her. When he had passed by, she released the breath that she hadn't been conscious of holding. Then she was filled with relief, though she still felt fear for Sibbie and Paulo, when another German voice shouted, 'Nothing! There's no one here.'

'Well, we have our prize, and these two dogs, who will tell us all we want to know . . . DO YOU HEAR THAT, COWARDS? HIDING AND LETTING YOUR COMRADES TAKE THE RAP FOR YOU IS NOT HEROISM!'

The soldier's yell resounded in the silence, giving Marjie the sense of betraying Sibbie and Paulo, but she remained still, weeping soundlessly.

'WELL, HEAR ME. THEY WILL TELL US WHO YOU ARE AND WHAT YOU PLAN. AND SOON! WE WILL TORTURE THEM TO WITHIN AN INCH OF THEIR LIVES! YOU WILL NEVER WIN. HEIL HITLER!'

As both Sibbie and Paulo let out cries of pain, Marjie's tears soaked her face. She rested her forehead on the cold, wet bracken. Despair engulfed her, but then Sibbie's voice rang out, strong and courageous. 'You will never beat us, never – German pigs. You didn't beat our parents and you won't beat us!'

This earned her another blow, and a pain-filled scream reverberated through the woods.

Paulo shouted, 'And you won't break us. We'll never tell you anything, you filthy, vicious PIGS!'

Marjie cringed as he hollered out in pain and must have been knocked to the ground, because he was then told to get up and Sibbie was screaming, 'Don't – don't kick him. Oh, Paulo, my darling.'

Marjie felt a moment of horror then as the German said, 'Ha, lovers, eh? Well now, won't that be useful information.'

As their voices faded, Marjie crawled out of her hole in the ground. A desperate whisper came to her. 'Stay down, Marjie.'

She lay there for a long time, allowing her heart to bleed. At last Arnie rose from his hiding place and came over to her. Lying next to her, he held her. 'Well done, Marjie. My God, that wasn't easy. But there were too many of them, and more searching further, who would have been down upon us and outnumbered us. We had to do as we did. Our beloved Paulo, and darling Sibbie, will know that. They would have done the same. They sent us a message in the last words we heard them speak.'

Though Arnie didn't mean they would be the last words she'd ever hear her lovely Sibbie and Paulo speak, something in Marjie prepared her for that being so, although in her mind she screamed against the thought.

Back in the camp, those that were left of them – a band of thirteen bedraggled and battle-weary men, and Marjie – knelt in a circle and prayed together. They prayed for Sibbie and Paulo, for all those who had fallen, naming each one; and they prayed for their mothers, who had yet to learn that their sons had been killed. Then they prayed for themselves and their country. Arnie and André knelt each side of Marjie.

At the end of the prayers, Arnie instructed one of the men to make some coffee, as he wanted to talk to them.

'I'll do that.' Marjie, desperate for a distraction, went to the kitchen area and filled the iron pot with water from a bowser. She stood it on the huge wood-fuelled stove with its cleverly adapted chimney, which puffed out the smoke at a sideways angle, meaning that it had almost petered out by the time it made its way skywards.

As they sat drinking their coffee, they listened to Arnie. 'Our own intelligence in these situations informs us that Sibbie and Paulo will most likely be taken to Gestapo HQ in Paris. We will find out the exact plans and details from Elianna, our contact in the offices of the *gendarmes* in Narbonne, as it is certain they will initially be taken to the cells there. They are too important to the Germans to be interrogated there, and will be seen as the Gestapo's responsibility. I will do my utmost to mobilize men along the route to Paris. I have several factions of the Freedom Army who work and camp in those areas. This will mean that I have to leave for a time, in order to organize this, and to work alongside those who will mastermind a rescue of Sibbie and Paulo.'

Just hearing this lifted Marjie's heart. She'd thought all was lost, but now she knew there was hope, and for the first time she realized she had done the right thing in not trying to fight the Germans, but staying undercover. With them all captured or dead, there would have been no hope. But although this reassured her, there was one thing preying on her mind. Would Sibbie bite into her cyanide pill? *Please don't, Sibbie, please.*

'And so the obvious question now is: who betrayed us?' Arnie looked around the group. 'I want you to know that I don't for a minute think it is one of you. But then did any of us ever suspect Jacques? The threat he posed is now removed, with his own and his mother's death, so who is our second traitor? The Germans knew exactly where to find our landing strip, and that we would be there at that time, although it must have been an approximate time, as they weren't there when we arrived. Or the traitor deliberately gave them the wrong time, in the hope of us having gone. If that was the case, then it was someone who cares about us, but cared more about what the Germans offered them. Be mindful that such a person is out there and does have knowledge of us.'

'Gisele?'

'I hope not, and cannot think it would be her, André, but we have to suspect everyone.'

Marjie asked, 'Did she know about the pick-up?'

'I don't know. She shouldn't have done, but we're never

guarded around Gisele. And she is a very clever young lady – always has been. If she wanted to know something, she could find it out. Can any of you remember her asking when Cyrus was leaving?'

No one answered Arnie for a moment, then André said, 'Juan was very friendly with her. It's possible.'

Juan was one of those whose names had been called out in the roll call of the dead. 'He was only injured; we could have got him back, but as we were hiding, a German soldier shot all those who were injured. Whoever betrayed us has blood on their hands.'

'It is terrible. I feel so bad that we can't go back and bury them. But it is too dangerous. All we can do is to tell the families, but that will take time, as some come from far afield.'

'Gisele should be made to inform them – we would normally ask her to. Maybe she will show some shame and then we will know it is her.'

'You are right, André. If Gisele is the traitor, we need to know.'

Marjie could see that the implications of this were very difficult for Arnie and all of the men to bear, as it was for her, when she thought of the time before she'd left for England, when Gisele had been a funny and special part of their lives.

'Let's sleep on it. Goodnight, everyone.'

The men took this as a command from Arnie, and all but those on lookout duty dispersed and went to their tents, or whatever they had put together to sleep under. Left alone with her uncle, Marjie kissed him goodnight, then whispered, 'How am I going to cope without Sibbie?'

'You will, Marjie. I need you to be strong. We'll talk in

the morning. But, Marjie, I need you to take over here. The men will accept you as their leader. You will need to guide them in the next mission. I have the details and it is to take place in three days' time.'

'I can do that, Uncle, and I know you will return with Sibbie and Paulo.'

Arnie held her in the kind of hug he'd always given her, and for a moment Marjie felt like a child again. Her heart so wished that she was, and that all of this had never happened.

## CHAPTER TWENTY-THREE

# *London*

## Flors

Flors stood in King's Cross station. Her stomach nerves clutched tightly with excitement. Trains came in and went out, whistles blew, flags waved and crowds arrived or departed, all seeming to have a purpose. Most of the men were in uniform: someone's son, husband, brother or boyfriend. Girls and older women saw them off or greeted them. The smell of fumes and the clouds of smoke puffed out from the trains rasped her throat, but somehow also added to the atmosphere of eager anticipation, although around her many tears were being shed.

Conscious of the officials waiting a few yards away from her, Flors thought of the moment when Wills had rung her to tell her that Randie was safe, and that Cyrus would bring him to her. Happiness had vied with anguish at being told he was well physically, but was mentally traumatized. Happiness had won over, because she'd seen this happen so often and she knew that, in time, there could be healing. But then Wills told her that he'd arranged for her to have a moment or two with Cyrus, before they took him for debriefing. *A moment or two! I want more than that. I want my darling by my side, never to leave me again.*

At last the announcement came that the train from Nottingham was about to arrive.

In the time since Mags had taken Ella to Blackburn, Flors had been very lonely, but had kept busy. Both women had telephoned her regularly. Ella was making progress and they were planning to go to Scotland to see Mags's friends. Flors had wondered at the wisdom of this, but then her friends needed help, and maybe that would do Ella good – bring out her caring nature and help her to focus on something different, after all she had been through. That was always a good healer.

Flors had thrown herself into finding an apartment to rent, with the help of Wills, and had now moved in and settled down. It was a few minutes' walk from Baker Street HQ, on Chiltern Street. She hadn't yet done anything with her own house, but thought she might rent it out again, or even sell it and look for a home that she and Cyrus and their family could make their own until – if ever – they could return to their home in France.

Wills had endeared himself to her, and she was growing very fond of him. It had been a comfort having the man who would marry her daughter by her side; almost like having her own family taking care of her. She could see why Marjella loved him.

There had been awkward moments when Wills had questioned why Flors hadn't wanted to go back to her own home, but she'd passed over it by saying that one should never go back, and that there were so many sad memories there for her that she couldn't settle.

The worst of all the memories she had of that house was

of losing their darling first child, Alice. Visiting her grave and Nanny Pru's had been heartbreaking, and yet uplifting to see that those in the street who were still alive had kept their promise to keep the graves tidy for her.

Shaking these memories from her, Flors scanned the faces of everyone getting off the train. At last she caught sight of them. Straightening her pencil skirt and touching her hair, she felt glad she'd bought a new costume for the occasion. Light-grey, with a box jacket, she'd teamed the skirt with a pink silk blouse, wrist-length gloves and a clutch bag. Her shoes were black with a small heel, and she had her fox-fur stole, with the fox's head still attached – the height of fashion – draped over her shoulders. It warded off the slight chill that still hung around, even though it was mid-May. Flors felt she looked good, and that gave her confidence.

As they neared, she felt a pang of concern. What if Cyrus had been thinking about everything and was hurting all over again? How would she handle it, if he rejected her? But these thoughts left her as her beloved husband and son caught sight of her. Cyrus's face lit up and his movements quickened towards her.

A moment's concern for her darling Randie attacked her, as he looked so fragile, but then he smiled and waved and dispelled her worry. In no time she was enclosed in Cyrus's arms, and then in Randie's. 'Oh, my darlings, I cannot believe you are here.'

'No, neither can we, darling. Oh, Flors, I've missed you so much.'

His kiss told her how much, and awoke her need for her darling Cyrus. 'I wish you hadn't to go with those men for a debriefing, but it has to be done. I hope you're not away too long, my darling I'll be counting the hours.'

'I'll tell them all I know as quickly as I can.'

With this he released her, and she was able to hold Randie to her again. 'My darling, everything will be all right. We'll make it so. I'll help you to get well and strong again. I can't erase your memories, but perhaps I can help you to live with it all.'

She was rewarded with a watery smile that tore at her heart. Her Randie, her big strong son – the adventurous one, the one always ready to take on a challenge – reduced to this. War wasn't only pointless; it was the cruellest action she knew of.

Cyrus drew her attention away from these thoughts. 'Flors, my darling, there is something I have to tell you. Whether HQ will be able to put our minds at rest, my darling, I don't know. But something bad happened as we left. It has affected Randie greatly, as it has me.'

Flors listened with horror as Cyrus told her of them seeing the Germans from the air. 'They were closing in on the Resistance. We tried to warn them on the radio, but they did not hear us. They were all engaged in breaking down the temporary runway.'

'Oh my God, Cyrus! No! Oh, I hope they are all right.'

'Flors, I – I . . . well, I have to tell you that Sibbie, Paulo, Arnie and our darling Marjella were among them. We had to leave, so we didn't see what happened, but I'm hoping that news of them has got through to HQ, and that it is good news.'

The horror turned to inner terror. 'Oh, Cyrus, no! I can't bear it – I can't.'

'You can, my darling, Flors. I don't know anyone stronger. Stay strong for Randie. As he is already traumatized, this has added to his mental torture.'

Flors took a deep breath. 'I will, my darling, I promise you. But the moment you can, please let me know.'

The officials came forward then: nameless men, distinguished only by their deadpan expressions. 'Mr Harpinham, sir. We need to go.'

Cyrus nodded, then turned to Flors and held her to him. 'Stay strong, darling. Look after our son.'

'Goodbye, my darling. Let us know any news as soon as you have it. Oh, Cyrus, I forgot. This is my telephone number. I'm not at home. I've rented us an apartment. I was afraid . . . I mean, I – I couldn't live back at the house; the memories . . .'

'I understand, darling. I'll telephone you as often as I can.'

'Sir, please, you must come now. You are expected at HQ. A meeting has been set up. We will look after him, Mrs Harpinham, but please let him come now.'

Flors watched them go. Randie's hand came into hers and she clutched it, remembering an old maxim that if someone shows they are afraid, it makes you stronger. 'Thank you, my darling. I need your support at this moment. Help me, my darling son, help me.'

This did the trick. Randie's arm came round her, and his voice had the strength that she knew he possessed. 'I'm here now, Mama. We'll get through this. We will.'

Smiling to herself, Flors allowed her head to fall onto his shoulder. 'Oh, Randie, I can't tell you what it means to me to have you with me. I've been so worried about you, and Marjie, Monty and Freddy. And now this. How are we to get through it all?'

'We will – we'll pray for good news. They may all have got away in time; they are very organized and focused. Most are from around there and, like all of us, know the forests like the back of their hands. The Germans wouldn't have a chance of finding them and would be lost in no time, as every tree looks the same and there are no marked paths. I really think they all got away.'

This was reassuring to Flors and she tried to latch onto Randie's confidence, glad that he'd found a way of dealing with it.

'Thank you, darling. I feel a little better about the news now.'

'Have you heard anything from Freddy, Mama?'

'No, not from him, but there is some hope that we will find out where he is. Did Marjie tell you about Wills?'

'She did. Fancy our Marjie being smitten like that. And yes, she did say that he was trying to find out where Freddy is. But you haven't heard anything yet?'

'No, not yet, but I think we will, darling. In fact I am sure of it.'

They had reached the station steps and started to ascend them. Once outside, Randie expressed his shock at the destruction all around them. 'Are there still bombs dropping, Mama?'

'Yes, there are still a few raids, but not many. The Blitz did most of this. My people have suffered terribly.'

'Your people?'

'Yes, son. Have you forgotten that your father and I are both Londoners?'

'No, but I didn't think you thought of them as your people, or of this city as your true home.'

'Your heart never leaves your beginnings, darling.'

'France will always be my country. I hate what is happening to her.'

'I do, too, and my heart bleeds for the French people, but when I came here and saw all of this, and the poverty it has caused – the homelessness and the destruction – then I was torn in two. I have to do something, Randie. I haven't thought what yet, but I will call into the Red Cross and see if they need volunteers. Look, let's go to a tea shop I know and have a hot bun and a cup of tea. We can chat, and you can get a little used to your surroundings.'

'Tea? You know I never liked tea, Mama. Do they have coffee?'

'Ha, of course they do, darling. Well, that chicory stuff that you have from a bottle – ugh! But even before the shortages, it was pretty much all you could get in Britain. Though wait a minute, there's a French bistro. They used to open in the afternoon for coffee. All the Europeans who lived in London at the time frequented it, and the bistro imported coffee for them.'

'That sounds better. How far is it?'

'Only just round the corner. Come on.'

The bistro was still there. *Chez Nous* displayed its sign with pride. To Flors, it was a little part of France: the blind that extended over the pavement, the green gingham half-curtain, the writing on the window that proclaimed: '*Vrais grains de café* – Real coffee beans'. Inside, onions and garlic bulbs hung from a beam, and the French flag was proudly displayed on the roughly plastered whitewashed wall.

The owner reminded Flors of the previous owner, in her day, and she assumed he was his son.

'Monsieur Benoît?'

'*Oui*, Madame – you're from France?'

Speaking in French, Flors told him that she was originally from London, but had lived in France for more than twenty

303

years. Then she asked after his father. Finding out that Monsieur Benoît senior was alive and well, and enjoying his retirement, made Flors feel very happy. She couldn't have said why, but then any good news was so rare that it was good to hear some.

'This is my very brave son, Randolph, a French soldier, who fought and was captured, and escaped. He is desperate for a coffee. Do you have any – I mean, real coffee?'

'*Mais oui*, Madame, and it iz on the house for a French soldier. Let me shake your hand, Monsieur.'

Randie laughed, that deep lovely laugh that mimicked Cyrus's. 'Mama, it didn't take you long to embarrass me.'

'Ha, I'm proud of you, and I am allowed to embarrass you, darling.'

They laughed together and Flors knew in that moment that her beloved son was going to be all right. Now she just needed to feel the same about her other beloved sons, Freddy and Monty, and especially her beloved daughter Marjella, for whom she felt great fear. *Please, God, if you never do anything ever again for me, look after them all . . . please.*

By the time Cyrus was back with them, having been given two weeks off before he started working as an advisor of strategy, responsible for planning operations in southern France, Randie was coping much better and was talking of returning to France and joining the Resistance.

When he retired after dinner, saying that he would be in his room as he needed to think his future through, Flors felt dread that Randie would announce that he was going for sure and ask his father to arrange it.

'Is it possible Randie will be allowed to go back?'

'It is, darling. After what happened, Paulo's group is very

much depleted. I have much to tell you, darling, and I can't say how glad I am that I am able to. M told me that as you had been vetted and had signed the Official Secrets Act, it was all right for me to discuss these concerns with you and seek your advice. He thinks highly of you, and it wouldn't surprise me if he isn't planning on recruiting you to work alongside me.'

'I would like that. I need to do something, but I have been occupied first with settling myself and then dear Ella, and finding this place, and now with taking care of Randie, though he has made remarkable progress.'

'That's your magic, darling.'

'Well, I hope it is a bit of that, but it's also his own strength. This time away from France and in safety has given him a clear head, to think through what happened and come to terms with it. I also think he realizes it was no mean feat to escape from a prison camp and survive weeks of being hunted, and having to fend completely for himself. This is what is leading him to want to return. It breaks my heart, but I would support him in whatever he decides.'

Cyrus reached for her hand. 'It will be difficult, but we must.'

Sighing in a meaningful way, Flors said, 'I know. Now, what did you want to tell me, darling?'

Coming to terms with what Cyrus told her about Sibbie and Paulo's capture was extremely difficult, but although Flors felt like screaming and crying out her anguish, she remained calm. 'Can I be the one to tell Ella and Susan?'

'No. I'm sorry, darling, but we cannot tell anyone, not even Randie. He did ask, but I said that details hadn't yet come in. You see, there is a suspicion hanging over everyone.'

'Surely not their own mothers, and Randie?'

'That's how it works. Certain information can only be given to those who are vetted and have been sworn to secrecy, especially so when a traitor is involved.'

'Ella! My God, do you think she told the Germans things when they held her captive and interrogated her? Do you think that is what is troubling her?'

'It's a possibility, especially as they could have threatened to kill Lonia. But if she did give information about the camp, she knew very little, and at the time she didn't even know that I hadn't come back to England with you, so she couldn't have given that information.'

'And Randie wouldn't, nor could he, as he had no one to give it to.'

'In M's eyes, Randie isn't altogether in the clear . . . They want to question him, Flors.'

'What? Why?'

'They want to make sure he didn't bargain his way out of the prison camp.'

'You mean they think he led the Germans to you – his own father – and to Marjie, his beloved sister? Rubbish! Randie would never do such a thing.'

'I know, and I think I have convinced them, in fact I am sure of it, but they have certain procedures. Randie will be fine. He only has to tell them how it happened, and then he can talk to them about going back. They may even recruit him and train him to work in special operations, because with Sibbie captured and HQ not knowing her fate, or whether she is compromised, they have to be ready with a replacement.'

'Oh, Cyrus, I don't like all this clandestine business, and yet I know how necessary it is. I would be involved tomorrow, if asked. But it is hard being made to suspect your own.'

'It is and . . . well, there's something else. They asked me about Monty.'

Flors felt as though she'd been punched; she couldn't have said why, but the mention of Monty in the same conversation as betrayal worried her.

'They can't trace him in any of the labour-intensive camps, which is where most of those sent on forced labour go. I don't know how they know these things, or get intelligence from such places, but Monty was known about, but isn't now.'

'Oh God! No! Not Monty.'

Somehow she just couldn't defend him, her youngest and precious son, as she had Randie. Her whole instinct told her that Monty could do such a thing – even knowing, as he did, that Paulo was involved. She hated herself for these thoughts, but knew the truth of them. If Monty found the going tough in Germany, he would want to get out. Betraying the Maquis, about whom he knew quite a lot, would buy him that ticket. She looked at Cyrus and saw his pain. 'You believe it is a possibility, don't you?'

'I want to save him, Flors.'

'Oh, Cyrus, how can we? What can we do? If – if Monty is the traitor . . . Oh God! What will happen to him?'

'HQ will inform Arnie of their suspicions so that he is aware, if Monty suddenly turns up, and that is where our hope lies. Arnie may tell Marjie, but I don't think he will tell the others. I hope he can get Marjie to do something, but what I don't know. I only know that if there is something to be done, Arnie will do it. However, he has his hands full planning to rescue Sibbie and Paulo. He contacted HQ and needs various things, but does not want to source them locally, now that they know there is a traitor amongst them. There is to be a drop, but only he and Marjie will know about it. It will be parachuted in.'

Cyrus walked round to Flors's side. 'Darling, I know what you are thinking, and I did too, but I have thought again. Monty loved Paulo, almost more than he loved his own brothers and sister. I cannot believe that he would put Paulo in danger to save his own skin. And besides, he couldn't have possibly known there was to be a pick-up that night. If he did, then he would know that it was me and Randie who were being picked up.'

Flors thought for a moment, but didn't say what came to her mind: Cyrus had said that the Germans had been seen, once the plane was in the air. Why the delay? Why hadn't they been waiting for the plane to arrive? If Monty was the traitor, this would be him safeguarding his father. Shaking these thoughts away, she took Cyrus's outstretched hands and went with him to the sofa. There they sat, holding each other close. Expressing their fear for their children and, yes, of their children, because if this was the work of Monty, then they had created a monster.

'Is this our punishment, Cyrus?'

'Don't, Flors, my darling. Yes, we share the same father, but we didn't know that when we married. All we're guilty of is loving each other so much that we couldn't ever part and *not* live as man and wife.'

This did not placate Flors, because she knew this wasn't all they had done. They had sinned and lived a lie. No matter how you tried to justify what they did, incest was wrong.

A heavy feeling settled in her stomach. *What will become of us?*

# CHAPTER TWENTY-FOUR

# *The South of France*

## Marjie

The mission was unusual: to assist in the safe transport of fifteen Jewish children. Taken from their school in Paris by their teacher, Marianne Gamzon, they were destined to be housed in many different homes in the South of France.

Marjie met up with Marianne in a Catholic church in Lyon.

'Madame, I am Margarita Barrault – I'm called Marjie, for short.'

'But you look so young, and this is a dangerous mission.'

Marianne was in her late thirties or early forties, petite with lovely features, especially her black-as-coal eyes.

'Please don't worry as I am highly trained. How old are the children?'

'They are all ten or eleven.'

'Oh, that's good. I was worried they would be infants, and that would have been difficult, as they will walk a lot of the way through forests and remote countryside that has no access from the road. We do have a number of safe houses along the way, ready to take them in so that they can be fed and can get some rest. And often the farmers will take them on tractors and trailers over their fields to the next wooded area on our route.'

'But that is marvellous. Each child will have a box in which they will have supplies for two days, but nothing more. I cannot come with you, as I have many more children in my school. I have to get them all dispatched as quickly as possible now. The round-up of the Jews is becoming intense.'

'Will you be safe?'

'None of us are safe. But I hope to have all the children safe by the end of the week. They are going to Christian families in the South of France, all arranged by the Christian Fellowship. And contacted by London, as no doubt you were. My uncle works in the embassy in London and arranged everything.'

'I can only say that I have been charged with the first leg of the children's journey from here. I will hand them over to members of the Fellowship in Avignon.'

'I will pray for you and the children, and for all the good people who are helping us, as you are all putting yourselves in extreme danger. The penalty for harbouring or helping Jews is death.'

'I know. And I will pray that you are not taken.'

'It is more than possible, but as long as the children are safe, that's all that matters. Here is a list of their names. One – her name is Lysette – is not well, and she desperately needs to get to the doctor; the Fellowship are expecting her.'

'We will take care of her. Now, the first leg is in an hour, so where are the children?'

'They are in with the Catholic priest.' Marianne laughed. 'He has been teaching them a little about what Jesus means to you Christians, and about Jesus's mother, Mary. I hope he isn't managing to convert any of them.'

Marjie laughed, too. 'It is good that they will be prepared a little in the faith and so, if questioned, can answer the basic questions that a Christian child would know.'

'Yes, of course. So, what is the plan?'

'It is best that I don't tell you.' Marjie smiled at Marianne to soften having to say this. She liked her and thought that if they had met in another lifetime, they could have been friends. 'But please don't worry. Not long ago a whole trainload of Jewish people were rescued. That mission was far more dangerous. The children will be in Avignon in a week, I promise.'

'That is good. Thank you, Marjie. And I understand – I shouldn't have asked. I know they will be safe in your hands.' At this, Marianne kissed Marjie's cheeks and looked deep into her eyes. 'You are all so brave.'

Brave? Margie didn't feel brave. She just hoped their mission to rescue the children worked.

As she waited for everything to fall into place, she went through the plan in her head. A truck that disposed of waste was to call for them in an hour. The priest would direct the driver and his mate to pick up a couple of deliberately stained and torn mattresses from around the back of the church. She would then guide the children to walk behind the mattresses, out of sight from any prying eyes, and help them into the truck, where there would be blankets for her and the children to lie on. The mattresses and a few cardboard boxes would be placed over them.

This part worried Marjie, since they would have to remain like that for three hours, as the truck took them near to Valence. The first safe house was just a mile across fields from where they would be dropped off. Then tomorrow they were set to start a cross-country trek.

She was comforted by the thought that many of the local members of the Resistance would be in hiding, guarding them along the way, and that André would be with her once she reached Valence. He would be able to reassure the children, as he had been training to be a teacher before he was directed to go on Germany's forced-labour programme, from which he absconded and joined the Resistance.

Marjie sighed. She had tried to sound confident that they would save the children, but she knew the plan was precarious, especially with a sick child to care for.

Once they were on the road, a new confidence took hold of Marjie. Everything had gone smoothly so far. But after travelling a little way, she began to worry about the children, who all seemed so small and vulnerable. It was stuffy under the sprung mattresses, which were balanced on upturned crates mere inches above their faces. For long periods of time, she held up the one she was under, trying to create more air-flow around Lysette, the frail child who lay next to her, whose body felt hot and sweaty. Marianne had told her that the child's kidneys weren't working properly. She'd given Marjie Lysette's medication, which was to be administered on a regular basis. Marjie had felt pity when Marianne had told her how difficult it had been to get the help that Lysette needed. That a child, no matter what her parents' origins were, should be denied access to medical care tore at her heart.

As the journey progressed, Marjie marvelled at the children's resilience when they relaxed and began to chat and giggle. It was as if they had been well prepared, for they all knew the risks and didn't show any reluctance to talk about what was happening.

At last the truck came to a halt and Marjie felt the mattresses being lifted off.

'André, thank goodness. That was terrible. I fear for the children – we need to check each one and give them all a drink.'

'We have to get them away from the road first. Come, children. You are going on the next leg of your adventure. Hurry, climb the fence and then there is a stream across the field, and you can all paddle and quench your thirst. It is good mountain water.'

The children did as André said, except for the listless Lysette. 'You will have to carry this little girl, André. Her name is Lysette and she isn't well.'

André looked at the child and whispered, 'She is very yellow. Why have they sent a sick child?'

'André, she needs saving more than all of them. She needs medical help and she won't get it in a hospital in Paris, where she is from; or in Lyon, where I picked them up. She is Jewish, remember?'

'I'm sorry. What was I thinking? Of course she won't.' Taking Lysette, André held her close to him. 'You're going to be all right, little one.'

Once the children had stamped the stiffness out of their legs, they ran ahead as if this really was an exciting adventure. 'Well, if they keep up this eagerness and mood, we are in for an easy trip, Marjie.'

'Don't speak too soon, for nothing is easy today.'

'No, but we can make it fun.' André pulled a face, which made Marjie laugh.

When they reached the water, they heard a mass of voices saying they wanted to pee. André took the boys behind a bush, while Marjie saw to it that the girls found some privacy

313

in a clump of trees. Once they'd all splashed around in the water for a while, they set off again.

'You will be sleeping in a lovely barn that smells of fresh hay tonight, children, but first you will sample Madame Dinlet's delicious stew.'

As they walked, they got to know the children one by one, asking them their names and their favourite toys. Most of the children had these with them: teddy bears and knitted dolls for the girls, and wooden toys for the boys. Marjie began to relax and enjoy the assignment, but was glad when the children were all bedded down.

Sitting on a bail of straw in the farmyard, with her coat pulled around her against the intrusion of the chill of the night air, she allowed herself for the first time to think of Sibbie and Paulo. She tried to imagine what was happening to them, and wondered if Arnie had been able to get the intelligence that he needed to plan a rescue.

André came and sat next to her, his body a little closer than she liked. Marjie hitched herself along, to put a little space between them.

'I didn't mean to make you uncomfortable, Marjie. I'm sorry.'

'No – no, I . . . well, I thought you needed more room.'

André stood up and looked down at her. She couldn't see his expression, but a feeling overcame her that made her want to be anywhere other than here. She didn't want to hear what she guessed was coming.

'Marjie, I want to talk to you. I want to tell you that I'm very fond of you . . . In love with you.'

'Oh, André, I'm sorry. I like you, of course, and respect you, but I am betrothed.'

There was a silence.

'What? Oh, Marjie, please forget I said anything. I . . . well, I should have found out. No one told me – not Paulo, Sibbie or anyone. I feel such a fool now.'

'Please don't. I'm very fond of you, André. But only as a good friend. I hope we can carry on as normal. None of this will affect me; if anything, I am very flattered.'

André gave a little laugh. 'Of course. Now can I sit next to you, and I promise not to misbehave.'

Marjie giggled and felt they had ridden that little blip easily, but then André was an easy person to get along with.

'Tell me about your fiancé.'

Sitting there as the moon came up, Marjie opened her heart. Wills came alive to her as she talked, but part of her realized how little she knew about him, and yet how much.

'He's a lucky man, Marjie. I envy him.'

'There will be someone for you. And when it happens, it will be like a bolt out of the blue. Not some old school friend that you're very fond of, and mistake your feelings for.'

'I know, I . . . Anyway, I'm turning in, as we have a long journey tomorrow.'

'I don't think I can sleep. I'll stay out here a little longer, then check on the children, before I bed down. I'm worried about Lysette.'

'Oh, I forgot to tell you. Madame is keeping her indoors with her. It turns out that she used to be a nurse, so will take good care of her.'

'Thank you, André, goodnight.'

Once André was gone, Marjie thought of Sibbie and Paulo. She longed to know how they were, and uttered fervent prayers that broke the shield she had put up. Slipping onto the floor, she leaned her head on the straw bail and her heart broke.

The journey was made much shorter the next day, as Madame Dinlet drove them in a tractor and trailer for many miles until they reached another safe house, some twenty miles away. She'd made several stops at farms to refuel, and bedded down with them that night in the home of Monsieur Lavet, another farmer.

Lysette had deteriorated. The concern for her life was very real.

'I will fetch my doctor to her. He, too, is a Jew, so you will all be safe. He will know what to do.'

'Thank you, Monsieur. Thank you.'

Holding Lysette, Marjie felt so helpless, as the child seemed to be slipping away. The other children were sitting on chairs and a variety of crates around the warm kitchen, eating large chunks of bread.

'Poor Lysette, I know you feel poorly, but could you try to sip this water, little one?'

Lysette opened her eyes, then closed them, never to open them again. Marjie gasped at how quickly she'd been taken. Rising from the table, she calmly asked Madame Dinlet to follow her into the next room. There she found a small sitting room, with a huge sofa taking up most of the floor space, and a long low table with books on it standing in the centre.

'Madame, she has gone.'

'Oh no, poor little child.'

Taking Lysette, Madame placed her on the table. 'We need something to cover her. Oh, that blanket – there over the arm of the chair – would you pass it?'

Once Lysette was covered, Marjie's body shuddered. And she found that she couldn't stop the deluge of tears that flowed down her face.

Madame Dinlet, too, was crying. 'She was the reason I took this long journey. I hoped to save her. But look at her – she looks so peaceful. Maybe she is in a better place, and she is out of danger.' Taking the cover off Lysette's face, Madame stroked the child's hair. 'You came into my life for just a few short hours, little one, but I gave you my love, so take that with you.' Turning to Marjie she said, 'Come, you must be brave for the other children. We will tell them that Lysette is resting until the doctor comes, and then he will take her to hospital. It is good that he is a Jew, as he will see that she is laid to rest according to their traditions.'

This gave Marjie a little comfort, and she found the strength to straighten her body and go through to check on the other children. As she got to the door, André came through it. Marjie shook her head. The colour drained from André's face and tears sprang into his eyes.

'Take a minute with her, André. I'll see to the children.'

The rest of the journey went well. Marjie had never felt more relieved than when she reached the house outside Avignon and met the leader of the Christian Fellowship, a kindly man who took charge of the children, with his entourage of jolly women helpers.

It was a tearful goodbye, with some of the girls clinging to her, but once she'd left them, the feeling Marjie had was one of great happiness that she'd helped just a few of the Jewish population to safety. She knew she'd done it for her Aunt Ella.

Before she could travel back to Hérault, Marjie had to

put on a disguise again. It had been wonderful not to have to bother with it as she travelled across the countryside, but now she was to go by train, as she and André had to get back as quickly as they could to the safety of the camp. The leader of the Fellowship had given them the address of a house where everything would be ready for them.

To their surprise, a *gendarme* uniform and papers were ready for André, and a clean outfit for herself – a woollen dress that belonged to the lady of the house. It was a little big for Marjie, but she pulled it in with the belt. A drab plum colour, it had a rounded neckline with a straight skirt that fell to her calves. A headscarf and fur jacket completed the outfit, as did her disguise glasses, which she had in her bag. Combing her hair back off her face and donning a small-brimmed felt hat made her look a lot older.

Their papers declared them to be man and wife. Their story was that they had visited an uncle, but that André was on duty as soon as he arrived home, so he had taken his uniform with him.

As it turned out, they didn't need a cover story, because everyone they met either showed no interest in them or seemed afraid of André. The few officials saluted or made some gesture to recognize him as one of their own.

'A useful disguise, I think, Marjie. We'll keep these outfits in good condition, as they may come in handy again.'

Marjie didn't answer; she couldn't. Nor could she believe what she was seeing. Her brother Monty was sitting on a bench seat on the station platform! Her first reaction was one of joy. She wanted to push her way off the train and run to him before he disappeared. But then she remembered that if she did so, she would expose herself for who she really was.

As the train pulled into the station in Narbonne, they stood up and went to the door. Marjie looked through the window, along the platform. A group of *gendarmes* were a little way along it, scrutinizing intently all those getting off. Looking back at Monty, she saw that he was doing the same. *It's as if he is expecting someone . . . Me? Oh my God!*

Turning to face André, she whispered, 'Don't question me, just turn around and go as fast as you can to the end of the train. Go into the guard's van. I'll be just behind you. Once there, jump and then run for all you're worth – don't look back.'

André did as she bade him. With her heart pounding, Marjie kept up with him. The part of the train they entered at the back had a kind of balcony-like structure. Thank God the guard had alighted, because sometimes, she knew, they would lean out from there to direct the train driver by waving their flag or blowing their whistle.

André jumped onto the railway line and took off. Marjie followed him. High walls prevented them from getting off the track. Running along it, Marjie prayed that another train wouldn't appear, and the one they had just left wouldn't move, exposing them to those who, she was certain, would try to capture them.

'Marjie, there, in that siding – there's an old engine. I'll make for that. We'll hide behind it and you can tell me what this is all about.'

Once out of sight, they leaned heavily on the engine wheels, gasping for breath. André recovered first. 'What's wrong, Marjie, what did you see?'

'My youngest brother, who is meant to be doing forced labour in Germany—'

'Your brother? But I don't understand. Oh, I see – of

course you couldn't risk being recognized. Well done, Marjie. But a bit elaborate, don't you think? You could just have kept your head turned away from him.'

Marjie felt conflicted; if she told André what she suspected, she might as well sign Monty's death warrant.

Her heart pounded as indecision divided her loyalties. Would André remain as alert as he could, if he knew the truth? Desperate to save her brother's life, and yet to protect herself and André, Marjie frantically sought a reason why they should get away from here as quickly as possible. *Suppose the driver had been looking and saw us running. Oh, what shall I do?*

Making her mind up, she told André, 'It is vitally important that I am not recognized. My cover will be blown and our safety, and that of our comrades, will be compromised. We need a plan to get away from here without being seen, because we will draw suspicion anyway – a *gendarme* and a woman walking on the train tracks.'

'Yes, you're right. Maybe you should have done as I said, because now we are in a position that it is difficult to get out of.'

Opening her handbag, Marjie took the gun from her make-up case and assembled it. This only took seconds, with all the practice she'd had. 'Take this, André.' Bending down, she took off her boot and accessed the bullets and handed them to him. As André took them, his frown told her that he thought her completely mad. 'Just do as I say, André. There are times when you shouldn't question me, and this is one of them. I am in charge of this operation until we reach the safety of our camp.' However, now Marjie wondered if even that was safe.

André loaded the gun. Marjie accessed the knife from the

inner cushion of her boot, before quickly putting it back on.

'Now, this wall gets lower a short way along. Follow me. But keep close to the engine at all times.'

The sound of the guard's whistle reached them, giving Marjie a small amount of relief. Had the *gendarmes* searched the train and allowed it to go on its way? Would she be better to hide in the old engine than risk being seen?

At that moment the gods were with her, as another train approached in the distance. Stopping her progress, she waited. Once the train approached the station, she knew the old engine would shield her if she made a run for it, but what of the passengers? Would they be too busy getting ready to get off the train to notice her? Unsure, she stayed still. Looking back, she saw that André was close behind her and thanked God that he'd decided to let her dictate what they did.

The last of the carriages was passing them now. Marjie leaned out and checked the windows: no one was in the carriage. But she darted back as the guard's van came into view. Having just caught sight of the guard, she'd seen that his attention was taken on the other side, watching the train as it slowed into the station.

'Now! Run!' When they reached the shorter section of wall, she shouted, 'Give me a leg up, André.'

As he bent and cupped his hands for her, Marjie stepped on them, her eyes fixed on the top of the wall. Grabbing it, she threw her bag over and then scrambled over the top. Below her was a deeper drop than she'd anticipated, but she bent her knees and rolled as she landed. But then she couldn't stop rolling, as the bank sloped steeply down. At the bottom was a road that she was unfamiliar with, and across from it a row of houses. As André came over the wall, she shouted, 'Grab my bag! Then act as if you are chasing me, but not catching me!'

Taking off, Marjie prayed that if anyone saw them, they wouldn't raise the alarm or try to help her. Most people hated the regime that ruled them and were afraid to interfere with anything the *gendarmes* did. They were more likely to keep away from the window than watch the drama they thought was unfolding outside their home.

Ahead, Marjie could see that the houses came to an end and, just past them, parkland led to a clump of trees. She made a run for it.

# CHAPTER TWENTY-FIVE

# *Portpatrick*

## Mags, Ella, Betsy and Rosie

Mags held Betsy to her. That her lovely friend should be suffering as she was cut at Mags's heart. There were no words.

She and Ella had travelled to Portpatrick by car. Their driver was unloading their cases, and Ella stood where she'd alighted on the other side of the car.

Stroking Betsy's hair, Mags noticed that it had lost its vibrant chestnut sheen and was peppered with grey strands. 'I'm sorry that I haven't been able to come to you sooner than this, my dear Betsy, but you have been in my thoughts.'

'I knaw, lass. And I've looked forward every evening to your phone calls. They, and our Rosie, are what has kept me going.'

'Well, I'm here now, Betsy, and if there is anything I can do, I will. This is my friend Ella.'

Betsy wiped her eyes on her apron and went towards Ella. 'Eeh, lass, it's good to meet you at last. I knaws all about you. You're a heroine, just like my Mags. And I'm right sorry for what you've been through, lass. If I could get hold of that Hitler, I'd string him up by his . . . Aye, well, I won't say it, as you're a lady; and I wouldn't in front of your little one, anyroad. But by, I wished it could happen.'

Mags noticed that Ella showed no surprise at the hug Betsy gave her and was glad to see her laugh out loud. Ella was getting used to the northern way of greeting. Mags smiled to herself as a memory came to her of the first time she'd met Ella all those years ago, on King's Cross station as they had waited to be taken to Belgium in 1914. Three Voluntary Aid nurses – herself, Ella and Flors – young and excited, without any fear of what lay ahead of them, but sure they could conquer the world. She'd surprised them both by hugging them, when they had offered a formal handshake.

When Betsy turned her attention to Lonia and gestured to her to come and have a hug, Lonia went willingly into Betsy's arms.

'By, you're a bonny lass. I'm pleased to meet you.'

'My name's Lonia, and I'm to call you "Aunty Betsy". I like that name. Were you named after someone? I was named after my mama's nanny. I never met her, but Mama says she was a lovely lady and I should be honoured to have her name.'

'It's a lovely name an' all. I'm named after me ma. And she were a lovely lady an' all. Weren't she, Mags?'

'She was. And is still missed. By the way, Ciss sends her love.'

Looking at Lonia, Betsy said, 'That's me sister, you knaw.'

'I haven't got a sister. I've got a brother. Well, he's a half-brother as we have different papas. He's called Paulo, but his papa died.'

'Oh dear, what Mags hasn't told you about me, Betsy, you'll learn from Lonia.'

324

They all laughed at this, from Ella.

'Well, come on in. I've got the pot on the go and I've baked some raspberry buns with home-made jam. Mind, it's a bit runny without the proper amount of sugar, and it's seeped into the cake mixture and made it pink an' all, so they look unusual, but they taste nice.'

Mags walked through the gate. The early summer flowers were blooming, and the rose bushes by the front wall had many buds, as well as one or two flowers that had been teased open by the warmth of the sun. Turning as she reached the top of the slope that brought her to the house, she looked out over the beautiful view across the port and the calm sea. Even though she was blissfully happy with Jerome and loved him dearly, here she was reminded of her Montel, who always held a special place in her heart. Tomorrow she would visit his grave and chat with him, as she was used to doing every time she visited.

Not letting her mind go further into the past, Mags called out, 'I'll just let our driver in, so he can unload the car, and then I'll be with you.'

'Will he want a cuppa?'

Conscious that her driver would be embarrassed to drink tea in her company, she refused this offer from Betsy on his behalf. 'No, he'll go over to the inn you booked him into, and most likely enjoy a beer. He's going back to Blackburn tomorrow.'

When they were seated with their steaming hot tea, and had sampled the buns, Betsy asked after Jerome and the girls.

'You will see for yourself, in a week's time. Jerome is coming to pick us up and is bringing the girls. They are staying for a couple of days.'

'Eeh, that's grand. Neither of you gets enough breaks – what with you and that mill, and Jerome and his vetting.'

Mags laughed at this. 'Vetting? You make him sound like someone who ticks people off for approval.'

'Ha, you knaws what I mean – doing all his vet work.'

'I do, and it describes it very well. Anyway, as always, Jerome's in the best of health. We are lucky as we don't experience the shortages that many do.'

'Oh, aye?' Betsy gave a half-smile and winked. 'Well, we do all right along them lines an' all.'

Mags felt a pang of irritation at the insinuation that she was getting what she shouldn't as she didn't approve of trading on the black market, but realized Betsy meant that Angus did more than talk to the fishermen from Fleetwood.

'No, I meant that, because of his work, there is often a gift of a couple of eggs or some other farm produce by way of payment.'

'Well, we'll leave it at that – we all have to take what we can get, no matter how we come to get it. Anyroad, as I said, it's good to have you here. So, the girls will be free to come up with Jerome? By, it'll be good to see them.'

Mags didn't like Betsy suggesting that these gifts were no better than items obtained on the black market, but then had to admit that maybe they weren't. Deciding it best to ignore it, she laughed as she told Betsy: 'Yes, and they are looking forward to seeing you, too. Both are excited at the moment – Beth because she is looking forward to finishing her schooling, and Belinda because it is the school holidays. She always hates being away from home.'

'I can understand that. Having you here brings me proper home to me, and I feel the sadness of not being where me heart is – back in me beloved Blackburn. Anyroad, as I can't be there, I have to say as there's no better alternative than here in Portpatrick, and I hope as you being here, Ella, will help you to recover.'

Mags's annoyance had passed and she wanted to take Betsy in her arms and hold her again for the welcome she gave.

Ella further cemented this as she said, 'Thank you, Betsy. I'm sure it will. I feel lifted already. I – I . . . well, I wanted to say how sorry I am for your loss. I . . . I don't mean to dampen the atmosphere, but I feel so much for you. I feel akin to your girls, as I was out in the Somme and various war-torn places for the duration of the last war. They are heroines, Betsy, and when the time comes that you can think a little beyond your grief, you will feel so much pride in them.'

'I knaw. Ta, lass. I try to see it that they were doing their duty, as I do me son, Billy, who's a POW. But it's hard. Your son, as Lonia told me of – Paulo? He's doing his bit and all, isn't he?'

'He is. And my husband, Arnie. I can't talk much about what they do, but they are in danger every day.'

'It's a rum do, the lot of it. There we were, all going on nicely putting the last war behind us and getting on our feet, and it all starts again. Have you heard owt about Sibbie and Marjella, Mags?'

'No and, like you all, I feel no news is good news, so I try not to worry. Are Susan and Rosie in the shop?'

'Aye. Rosie is worrying me. She's still on compassionate leave, but I reckon as she'd be better occupied going back. She's needed there, and it would do her good. Besides, she stops me doing owt, and I need to be busy.'

'Grief affects us all in different ways, Betsy.'

'I knaw, Mags.'

'But, having said that, I agree with you. I'll talk to her. She may take my advice.'

'Ta, love. Me girls allus listened to you, they love you dearly.' With this, Betsy coughed. It was meant to cover up a sob, but it did a poor job and tears plopped onto her cheeks.

Before anyone could do anything, Lonia got down from the chair she'd been sitting on at the table, drinking the juice Betsy had given her and listening to the women talking. She ran to Betsy. 'Don't be sad, Betsy. I know your Daisy and Florrie died, but they are in heaven. My puppy died. It was run over, and Mama said it is far happier than it was here, as it is in a beautiful place.'

Betsy smiled through her tears at Lonia. 'Ta, lass, I knaw as that's right, but I miss them.'

'I miss my puppy.'

Lonia put her head on Betsy's lap. Betsy stroked her hair.

'And I miss my daddy and Paulo, and Marjella . . . and everyone, but although that hurts, it's not the same hurt, as I know I'm going to see them again. I just have to be patient.'

'Aw, lass. Me and you are in the same boat.'

'What does that mean, Aunt Betsy?'

'It means our troubles are the same, lass, as I have a son, Billy, who I miss, but I knaw I'm going to see him again. And when your Aunt Mags ain't here, I miss her an' all, but I'm going to see her again. When they go to heaven, well . . .'

'We still might see them again. Mama says we have to hope, and keep remembering them. I'll never forget Butty.'

'Butty? That's an unusual name.'

Lonia laughed. 'It was meant to be Bunty, but I couldn't say that then, as I was only little.'

Mags had tears in her eyes, listening to them. This child of Ella's was like a grown-up in a small body. But then Lonia had spent her life around grown-ups and had learned how to please them. She was adorable and caring, just like Ella. She and Betsy seemed to have become friends in a special way, and that pleased Mags. She could see it gave comfort to Betsy, too.

They walked to the shop as soon as Betsy had cleared the pots and Mags and Ella had freshened up. The sun was high in the sky on this lovely May afternoon, though the breeze coming off the sea still had a chill to it.

Mags had donned her flared-bottom trousers and they were flapping around her legs. Her Fair Isle jumper had been knitted by the local women and she loved it. It had been the buying of one of these jumpers, when she'd first come to Portpatrick, that had led her to employ the women to knit items for the shop, which she and Betsy had originally started along with dear Montel. 'I'm excited to see your new lines, Betsy. Ella's in the market for a Fair Isle jumper like mine. She's had to borrow warm clothing from me and it's far too big for her.'

'I love them. I saw in a magazine that all the film stars are wearing them. There was a picture of Rita Hayworth in one, and she looked gorgeous, as you do, Mags.'

Betsy chimed in, 'I'm too busty for them, but they are popular. The fishermen love them.' They laughed at this and Betsy reddened. 'Eeh, I didn't mean it like that. It's your minds.' This made them giggle even more.

Lonia made things worse. 'The fishermen like your busty? What's a busty?'

Mags thought she would burst and had to bend over double to stop her stomach hurting. Lonia skipped ahead. You never knew, with that one, if she was being cheeky or not, as she had a talent for making fun.

As they turned onto the road that ran along the sea wall, Ella gasped. 'Oh, it is so beautiful!'

Mags beamed. She loved it when others praised her beloved Portpatrick. It was a timeless place, with nothing changing, year in, year out. Just the folk that peopled it, as they gave way to another generation.

Ella loved the shop, and especially the intricately designed Fair Isle jumper she bought. And she took to Susan and Rosie immediately, chatting away with them both.

'So, you're a nurse, Rosie. We'll have a lot in common.'

'Aye, but you nursed in the thick of things. I haven't, and it makes me feel a bit of a fraud.'

'No, don't feel like that. If all nurses went abroad, who would look after the people here, and who would nurse the returning wounded? Your job is of great value. Look, I wanted to talk to you. Are you able to go for a walk with me?'

'Aye, I don't see why not. Ma, me and Ella are going for a walk – we want to talk nursing and it'll bore you all.'

Betsy smiled over at Ella. A smile that said she was grateful to her.

Outside, Rosie took a defensive stance. 'I hope this isn't set up by me ma. She's allus on at me to get back to work.'

'No. I promise you. It's prompted by something in me, and I wanted to ask you a few questions. You see, I feel that I will go mad if I don't do something. There is so much tugging at me. I wanted to ask you if you thought there was room in today's world for someone who has masses of experience in nursing wounded and working as a theatre nurse, but no formal qualifications, and very little in the way of hospital-ward work?'

'You! Eeh, Ella, are you sure? We all knaws what you've

been through. Are you ready to face what we have to face on a day-to-day basis? It brings the horror of war home to you.'

'I know it does. And yes, I've always found solace and lessened my problems by helping others.'

'Eeh, I never looked at it like that. I just loved nursing, but aye, it does help you put things into perspective.'

'It does, and in that I do agree that you would be better off back in the ward. Having said that, it is something I truly believe, and not something I was set up to say. Your mother has voiced her worries over you, but I don't think she'd ever ask a virtual stranger to talk about that with you. Ha, I should watch out for your Aunt Mags, though – she might broach it.'

They giggled. 'I have to watch out for them two all the time. They hatch many a plot to get me and me sis— Oh, I . . .' Rosie drew in a massive breath.

'It's all right, Rosie. That shows they are still with you. Talking about them in everyday conversation will help you. I know how hard it is for you.'

Rosie swallowed. 'It is. Oh, Ella. Me ma says she wants me to go to work, but I don't knaw if she really does. How will she cope?'

'I would say a lot better than you think, as she'll know that at least one of her girls is all right.'

'You're making me see everything differently, Ella. I feel you understand.'

'How about you ask to be transferred back to a hospital nearer here? You could come home when you want to, then.'

'I've thought about that, as there's another reason I don't want to go back to Herne Bay.'

'Oh, do you want to talk about it?'

'I – I, yes, I do. But you will think less of me.'

'Why should I? No matter what it is, I will understand. There's not a situation you could tell me about that would shock me, but it may help you to get it off your chest.'

Rosie was quiet for a moment, then blurted out, 'I fell in love with a German. I shouldn't have, but I couldn't help meself. It just happened. But . . . he died.'

Ella reached out for Rosie, who came gladly into her arms.

'Naw one knaws. Not up here, they don't – well, except for me Ma.'

'Does that mean you're ashamed, Rosie?'

'Naw, I'm not ashamed. Albie were a lovely man; he didn't want to fight a war, but had no choice.'

'Then keep his memory inside you. Only share it if you think you will have understanding, as you don't want to be in the position of having to defend yourself. I understand, and I know the pain of losing the man you love. We can't choose who they are, or where they are from, or anything about them. Yes, we have preferences, but that's all they are. The reality hits you like a ton of bricks. Albie sounds like a nice person. He must have been, for you to love him.'

Rosie wept for a little while, then lifted her head. 'Ta, Ella, I feel better about it now. I'll do as you say, and I'll ask for that transfer.' She wiped her eyes and blew her nose loudly. 'You knaw, I have some advice for you an' all. Why not volunteer? I mean, if you don't need the money. There's a lot of volunteers in the hospital. They don't do much medical stuff, but they make the patients more comfortable, making beds, doing bedpans, serving meals – that sort of thing.'

'Yes, I like that idea. Thank you. Rosie. And you know what? I love it up here. I might just volunteer in the hospital that you land up in. I think it would be good for Lonia up here, too.'

'That'd be grand, Ella. I reckon as me and you could become real friends.' With this, Rosie hugged Ella, and Ella knew she could love this young woman like a younger sister, in the way that she'd been denied loving her own sister for so long. At this thought she drew in her breath.

'Are you all right, Ella? I ain't upset you, have I?'

'I – I have something I haven't been able to talk about, Rosie. And, like you, I believe everyone will think less of me if they know. You see, I – I was interrogated.' Never thinking she would tell anyone this in a million years, Ella related how she'd betrayed her own family. 'But they were going to hurt Lonia and . . . and they told me my sister had perished. Oh, I – I—'

'Eeh, Ella lass, don't.' Rosie held her. 'Sit down, lass.'

They sat on the grass. Rosie holding Ella and rocking her in her arms helped.

'I don't see that as a betrayal, Ella, and I knaw as no one else will. If it was just yourself that you were sacrificing, then that's your choice; but you had no choice – you couldn't sacrifice your child, and no one would expect you to. Talk to Aunt Mags, she'll understand. And I'm sorry about your sister; there's nowt more painful than losing your sister.'

They sat in silence then, holding each other and gazing out to sea. Two women joined in their grief, and by kindred natures, and each knew they had found a friend for life. For Ella, being with Rosie had released so much pain. She'd set out to help this young woman and, in doing so, had found help for herself

# CHAPTER TWENTY-SIX

## The South of France

### Sibbie and Marjie

Marjie's head ached. There had been no word from Arnie by the time she and André had reached camp two days ago. She paced up and down, feeling on edge.

'You can't alter things by worrying about them, Marjie.'

'I know, André, but why no word? It's driving me mad not knowing if Sibbie and Paulo are safe.' She wouldn't say that part of her anguish was caused by fear over what Monty might do next. What if he led the Germans to this camp and she hadn't done anything, after suspecting him? Hadn't even discussed her concerns with anyone? But how did you do that, when you knew the outcome would be your own dear brother's death?

'Marjie, something spooked you – what was it?'

'Please stop questioning me, André.'

'You don't trust me. That's it, isn't it?'

'No . . . Look, I do have something on my mind, but I need to discuss it with Arnie first.'

A low whistle told them that Gisele was approaching. Marjie didn't need to hide from her any longer, for Arnie had briefed Gisele and the two girls had met. Gisele had been just as pleased to see Marjie as Marjie was to see her, and they'd chatted and laughed together. But her approach heightened the already tense atmosphere in the camp, as this was the first time they'd seen Gisele since the betrayal.

André looked uncomfortable, and several of the men who'd sat apart from Marjie and André now became alert and hostile. One spat on the ground. Others moved away, making for their tents, or stood leaning on a tree, but not facing the group to greet Gisele, as they normally would.

'André, fetch them back. Tell them that we must act normally. If Gisele is the traitor, we don't want her alert to the fact that we suspect her. That could lead to her doing something desperate, to save her skin. Maybe even exposing the camp and having us all killed.'

André nodded, then acted swiftly. By the time Gisele entered the camp everything appeared normal, even if their greeting didn't hold the usual banter they exchanged with her. Gisele didn't act as if she knew something was wrong, and probably took the atmosphere as normal in the circumstances, as her first question showed. 'What happened, André? How did Raphael and Juan come to get killed? The whole village is in mourning. I wanted to come before now, but I was afraid to. I – I thought I might be being watched. There's a large *gendarme* presence, and the villagers are very frightened. They asked me to see if the group can do anything?'

This alarmed Marjie. The village of Laurens lay within ten miles of them. 'It was the night of my papa's pick-up. Germans suddenly surrounded us. Sibbie and Paulo have been captured, Gisele.'

The colour drained from Gisele's face. 'No! But I – I . . . No! Not Paulo, no.' Tears ran down her face. Marjie wanted to comfort her, but found she couldn't move. Gisele had known Paulo all her life and had a special relationship with him. He'd been like a big brother to her. But then the thought came to Marjie that Monty had been even more than special to her. Gisele adored Monty and would do anything for him. What if he had approached her for information?

Dropping her bike, Gisele looked round at the unmoving faces. 'There must have been a traitor, otherwise how did the Germans know? You all suspect me, don't you?'

One or two of the Resistance group shuffled about, looking uncomfortable.

Gisele looked around her, her face betraying her fear.

'Who else knows as much as you do, to be able to inform on us, Gisele?'

'I wouldn't, André, I . . . You all know me. Some of you since I was a child. You know I couldn't tell the Germans.' Gisele looked as though something had dawned on her.

'Have you spoken to anyone, Gisele? I mean, unwittingly? Has anyone approached you?'

Gisele stared at Marjie. 'I – I, oh God, Marjella, it's . . . Oh, Marjella, I must speak with you.'

Marjie realized that Gisele, like herself, was protecting Monty. That she must have been tricked by him and was now desperate not to inform on the young man she loved. *Oh, Monty. Monty, what have you done?*

The mood became angry. 'We trusted you, Gisele. All those men . . .'

'Henrick, I . . . Please believe me, this isn't my fault. I must speak with Marjie. Marjie, please!'

'What can you tell Marjie that you can't tell us?'

'I must tell her first, André. Look, all of you: something has happened. It wasn't my doing. I – I trusted someone you would all have trusted. Just give me a chance to tell Marjie first, please.'

Marjie felt her heart sink, while her mind screamed at the danger Monty was in. As yet she hadn't allowed herself to think of him deserving it; only of the devastation it would bring to her and her beloved family.

'Come with me, Gisele. Everyone, please stay here. Let Gisele do this as she wishes – needs – to. I promise you, I will do what is right by you all.'

Marjie and Gisele walked away. When she knew they were out of earshot, Marjie stopped and turned to Gisele. She wanted to ask if it was Monty, but didn't want to give away the fact that she knew. Looking into Gisele's face, it was as if she was seeing her for the first time. This wasn't the cheeky kid she'd once known, but a very beautiful young woman. Gisele's fair hair, which had always been a tangled mess, due to her tomboy ways, now shone and was fashioned with the front rolled and held in a clip, and the back falling to her shoulders, where it neatly curled under. Her eyes – the lightest-blue eyes Marjie had ever seen – were large and enhanced by the black pupil in their centre. Her features were clear-cut, and her skin creamy. Gisele was about the same height as Marjie, with a slight figure that wore clothes as if they were top designer outfits, not hand me downs or giveaways.

'Tell me, Gisele. Who was it?'

'Monty.'

Even though she knew, Marjie drew in a breath that spoke of her shock. 'How? I mean . . .' Her thoughts were thrown into a turmoil. *It's true then, I wasn't mistaken. Oh, I so wanted to be.* 'How did Monty get here? What has he asked you about? And why – why would my brother . . . Oh God!'

'I'm sorry, Marjie. I never dreamed Monty would do this. He told me he had escaped, that he'd been through hell and was sorry he ever believed it was for the good of the country that we honoured the Germans and lived under their occupation, and that they would make everything better in France. He wanted to know where his family were, and why his home was deserted. He was broken-hearted when I told him they had been forced to flee. He broke down and said he was desperate to put everything right. That he wanted to make contact with Paulo and join the Resistance to help the cause.

'I had no reason not to believe him. Monty is part of your family. I told him that I was part of the Maquis group and what I did, and that his father and you and Arnie were all in the camp. Oh, Marjie, I told Monty he would need to hurry if he wanted to see his father, as he was being air-lifted out. He wanted to know when. Then he . . . he told me he loved me. I went with Monty to your home, and we . . . Oh, Marjie, please don't condemn me, I couldn't help myself. I love Monty. I can't bear anything to happen to him. Oh, Marjie.'

As Marjie looked at the distraught Gisele, she realized what it was that had made her suddenly appear so different. Gisele was truly a woman now, made so by Monty, the man she loved . . . a traitor!

Trembling, Marjie asked, 'Did it not alarm you, when he wanted details? You must have told him when and where my father and brother were to be picked up.'

'Your brother?'

'Oh, I mean Randie escaped too and came here.'

'And now he is in England? But that is wonderful.'

'It is, Gisele, but tell me: do you know why Monty wanted the details?'

'He said he had to know as he must go there, otherwise he might miss his father.'

'Oh, Gisele, I can't believe all this . . . I don't want to. Not Monty. Oh God, make this go away!'

'Marjie, don't cry. I'm so sorry. I'm scared. What are we going to do?'

Marjie opened her arms to Gisele, who suddenly seemed so young, so vulnerable, and yet they owed her so much. 'I don't know what to do. I want to wait until Arnie comes back. Monty can't know about Arnie's mission, can he?'

'What mission?'

'I can't tell you, Gisele. Not now. But as you don't know, it is unlikely that Monty can know.'

'Marjie, I had no idea what I was doing, by telling Monty what I did. I swear. I believed him. I had no reason not to. I would never have told him anything if I'd thought this would happen.'

'I know. I'm not showing a lack of trust in you; it's just that what you don't know, well . . . sometimes it is better not to know. Oh, Gisele, we cannot trust anyone. But I understand. You haven't had the benefit of the training I have had. Did Monty want to know anything else? Have you seen him since? Did you know he hadn't made contact with us?'

'Yes. I saw him again. Monty told me he'd been unwell and hadn't been able to go and see his father. That he had decided to wait, after he heard about the deaths of Raphael and Juan. He said he was afraid something must have gone wrong, and that if he tried to come to you, someone might follow him. He asked me to go and visit him at your home. I – I went. We had such a wonderful time, I stayed . . . Monty made me promise not to visit the camp until I was contacted.

He felt I might be being watched, too. He asked if there was any other way that he could make contact with you, Marjie. I told him that until I went into the camp and asked you, I wouldn't know. Monty then changed his mind about me not coming here, and asked me to bring this note to you.'

Gisele fished in her pocket and brought out the note. As Marjie took it, part of her was consumed with relief. It must have been a coincidence that Monty was on the station when they arrived. 'Gisele, has Monty travelled anywhere? I mean, has he done anything that you thought unusual? I want so much to give him the benefit of the doubt. But I have to know how he acted and what he has been doing.'

'Yes, he caught the train to Montpellier. He said he had to do some shopping.'

Marjie released a sigh. *So Monty hasn't betrayed me. His presence, and that of the* gendarmes, *was a coincidence. But would he have betrayed me, if he had known I was likely to be on that train?* Marjie couldn't honestly say that he wouldn't.

Wanting to read Monty's note, but conscious of how long they had been away from the group, she decided to wait until later. For a moment she was silent, her mind giving her many solutions about how to go forward. 'Gisele, my instinct is to keep you here until Arnie comes back – not only to keep you safe, but to put the minds of the men at ease. However, I think it better that you go back and act normally, otherwise it may raise Monty's suspicions and force him to do something that would be disastrous to us all. We'll go back to the group now, and I will appease the men, then read Monty's note and decide the best action to take.'

The men weren't easy to appease, as Marjie told them they did have a possible suspect. That it wasn't Gisele, and that things would be worse for them all if they did any harm to Gisele or tried to detain her.

'Are you mad, Marjie? If she has compromised us, what is there to stop her doing so again?'

'I trust her, André. Gisele has been very honest with me and has helped to reveal who is working against us. I want to wait for Arnie's return. It is his decision as to what should be done. I'm going to contact HQ. I will tell them it is imperative that Arnie is contacted. They know we have been betrayed. I will tell them we think we know who by, and that we need Arnie to give us the way forward.'

Going to the tent containing the radio, Marjie pulled out Monty's note.

*Dearest Marjie,*

*By now you will know that I have escaped. Now I just want to fight this hateful regime that has occupied our country.*

*I'm amazed that you were able to make your way back, and bring a friend. You are so brave, dearest sister. And I cannot believe that Papa was here with the Resistance and was air-lifted out. This means that you are very organized now and have backing from Britain. With that in place, we must surely win through.*

*Please tell Paulo that I cannot wait to see him, and tell Uncle Arnie, too. I need to be with family, Marjie. Please make arrangements for me to come to you very soon.*

*Love, Monty x*

*Oh, Monty. Monty, I don't know what to believe.*

Setting up the radio, Marjie was about to make contact when she stopped. If they were compromised, someone could be waiting to detect radio activity and would track them down. They had to move camp – it was the only way. She could contact HQ once they were settled, and they would let Arnie know where they were.

Sitting back, she sighed. She'd hardly dared think about Sibbie and Paulo, holding on to the hope that Arnie would save them. Every part of her prayed that would be so.

Penning a quick note, she wrote:

*Dearest Monty,*
*It did my heart good to hear from you, and to know that you are safe in our home. I will contact you soon. Just be patient, and before long you will be with us.*
*I love you, my brother. Paulo and Uncle Arnie send their love, and are making arrangements to fetch you in. Until we meet, dearest Monty.*
*Your loving sister, Marjie x*

Swallowing hard to stop the tears, she called out to Gisele to come in to her. When she did so, Gisele looked even more fearful. 'They are all very hostile towards me, Marjie. They may not let me leave.'

'They will – don't worry. Here, take this note for Monty. Hide it from the others. And, Gisele, do you have a relative – someone who lives far away from here – that you can go to?'

'Yes, my aunt lives over the border near Girona in Spain – my uncle is a fisherman. Why must I go? Oh, Marjie, I don't want to, please.'

'You must, it is the only way you will be safe. The Germans know about you now. They will watch you. And if Monty is the person we think he is, then once you don't give him any information, he will turn you in.'

'No! He would never do that. I can't leave him, I can't.'

'Gisele, staying here will sign your own death warrant. I won't be able to save you. You know too much about the Resistance: how they work, where they are, their missions. And, Gisele, if our organization doesn't kill you, then the Germans will. But they won't just shoot you – they will torture you and then, when you are of no further use, they will shoot you anyway.'

Gisele's large eyes filled with terror as she stared at Marjie. Her voice was a shocked whisper. 'I'll go, I promise. But, Marjie, take care of Monty. He is your brother. Don't let them kill him. I can only survive knowing that one day he and I will be together.'

'I will do all I can. Yes, he is my brother, and I love him very much. Arnie will get him away somewhere, I'm sure.'

Back with the group, Marjie could feel the ugly mood that had descended. She told them of her decision not to use the radio, and of her plan to move camp. All agreed. But when Marjie told them that Gisele was to leave, and about her plans for her to disappear, they were not in agreement.

'She has betrayed us. How do we know she won't do so again?'

It was a usually quiet member of the group, called Louis, who had said this. Marjie told them all, 'I cannot give you the details of what I know – you will have to trust me – but Gisele isn't a traitor. What happened was a misjudgement on her part, but she poses no danger to us, and never has.

She is going away so that nothing like this can happen again, and for her own safety.'

Ethan, a sullen man who was always disgruntled, spoke then. 'If that is the way of it, then I think we need to escort her to where she is going. She needs our protection.'

Marjie was nervous about this. She looked over towards André. She could trust him. When he spoke, he put her mind at rest. 'I agree, but I am going to be part of the party that escorts her. I agree with Marjie. Gisele, whatever she has done, deserves our protection.'

At this, Marjie agreed. She knew she could trust André. Gisele, too, relaxed as he told her, 'Gisele, this will have to happen soon. We will make the arrangements. You need to get ready to go tonight. Be by the river in Laurens at midnight. Wait near the bridge, in the shadow of Monsieur Vandaise's house.'

Gisele nodded. Her eyes travelled around the group as she picked up her bike.

Marjie spoke to her as she prepared to leave. 'Goodbye, Gisele. Thank you for all you have done for us. You are very courageous, and we are going to miss you. Safe journey and, when this is all over, I hope we meet again.'

None of the rest of the group uttered a word as Gisele left.

Sibbie tried to keep her eyes on Paulo. The lorry transporting them rocked from side to side. They lay on the hard, slatted floor, bound and gagged. Breathing was difficult through her smashed nose. Her arms hurt, from the many burns inflicted by her interrogator's cigarette, and her hands smarted where some of her nails had been yanked out. But she hadn't given in. Even when the pain engulfed her in agony.

After discovering some of the weapons she had secreted around her body, and finding her cyanide pill, the Germans had deduced that Sibbie was a British agent and must have decided that she should be sent to the Gestapo. Her German torturer had taken great pleasure in telling her of their decision, and had described horrible tortures that she didn't know if she could endure. 'Your hands will be plunged into boiling oil – oh yes, let's see if you keep quiet after that, you English pig.' He'd gone on to say that they would cut her feet off, very slowly, with a hacksaw. Sibbie's mind had screamed in terror at the thought, but still she hadn't given in.

Her heart ached as she looked at her beloved Paulo. His eyes were full of pain. Looking out from blackened, swollen sockets, they seemed to be pleading with her. She knew that his leg was smashed, as she'd seen the bone jagging out from it. Fear clenched her, as she knew he could die if it wasn't tended to. *Oh, Paulo, if only we could speak to each other.*

The horrendous sound of an explosion smashed through the air around her, freezing her thoughts as the truck veered off the road and down the verge. Her body rolled uncontrollably on top of Paulo's. She tried to lift herself off him, knowing that she was adding to his pain, but couldn't.

Gunfire resounded around her. Panic-stricken, Sibbie made an extreme effort to lift herself. In doing so, she caught sight of Paulo; his face was blue, he couldn't breathe! *Help me. Oh God, help me.*

At that moment strong arms lifted her, and she looked into Arnie's beloved face. The strip of plaster that held her mouth closed stung as he ripped it off. 'I'm sorry, my darling girl, but that is the only way. I'm going to lift you out, and then see to Paulo.'

'Hurry, he isn't breathing, Oh, Uncle Arnie, save him – save him.'

Someone took her from Arnie and carried her away from the lorry. She was conscious of dead German soldiers as he stepped over them. 'You're safe now.'

Safe? Without her darling Paulo? *Please don't let him die.*

'I'm going to untie you. I'll try not to hurt you. We have a doctor in our camp, he is a freedom-fighter, too. He will help you.'

'Where are we? We don't seem to have travelled far.'

'Just south of Lyon.'

Once free, Sibbie tried to stand and go to Paulo, but her legs wouldn't hold her. 'Help me, I must get to Paulo's side.'

'Arnie is bringing him out now. Sit still. Our main objective is to get out of here as fast as we can. It's too dangerous to stay on the road for long.'

Sibbie looked towards where Arnie was carrying Paulo's limp body and heard Arnie shout, 'Paulo's alive! Carry Sibbie, Pierre. We must hurry.'

The journey across fields and rough terrain seemed endless to Sibbie. Along the way, Arnie and Pierre swapped the burden of carrying Sibbie and Paulo with two other members of this faction of the Resistance movement.

Once in the camp of the faction, which she knew to be the communists, Sibbie again asked after Paulo, as he was taken into a different tent to her. Pierre told her to hush, and that the doctor, who was called Michel, was also a surgeon and was doing all he could. As he spoke, Pierre bathed her wounds. His touch was gentle – her pain excruciating. 'I, too, trained to be a doctor, and at the same hospital as Michel. We now work for the Resistance and carry out many procedures in the special tent where Michel is working on Paulo. He is in the very best of hands.'

At Sibbie wincing as he bathed her hands, Pierre said, 'How can anyone do this to another human being? But you will heal, I promise you. I have some morphine. I'll give you that.'

'No, not yet. I want to be awake, I need to know how Paulo is. I can stand the pain; it is more comfortable now, thank you.'

After a few moments Arnie came and knelt by the pallet bed they had lain Sibbie on. Tears ran down his face. 'Paulo is very ill. The doctor has said it is touch and go. I think he will benefit from having you by his side. How are you, my dear?'

'I am in pain, but my heart hurts the worst. Don't let me lose my Paulo.'

'Everything that the doctor can do is being done, Sibbie. He has limited resources, but he has set Paulo's leg. Paulo needs an operation, but that isn't possible. Hospitals will be searched, once they know you are free. But Paulo is strong. If he survives this, we will request that you are both air-lifted out. But in any case you will be, I promise.'

'Oh, Uncle Arnie. Take me to Paulo.'

Once she was lying next to Paulo, Sibbie put her hand out towards him and touched his arm. Paulo didn't stir. 'Get well, my darling. Please get well.'

## CHAPTER TWENTY-SEVEN

# The South of France

## Marjie

As soon as Gisele had left, Marjie instructed that they strike camp.

'Where are we going?'

'I think we should move west towards the Pyrenees, Louis.'

'It is where we should have gone in the beginning. The mountains will give us more protection, but back then it was the terrain of the communist freedom-fighters and there was a lot of aggravation between us. But since the British agents have united us and we all work together now, I don't see any objection.'

'Thank you, Louis. Now, there's a lot to carry, but we can only take a backpack each.'

André spoke then, taking charge. 'First, we must roll the tents; and you, Marjie, must dismantle the radio. Then we must destroy everything that has been built here, and scatter it so that we leave the area looking as if it is untouched.'

'It is still too much for so few of us to carry. I'll go to my father's farm and borrow a tractor and trailer. I will bring some straw bales to hide everything beneath.'

'That's excellent, Louis. Well, let's get to work. There's

not much daylight left, and André and Ethan will have to leave by eight to pick up the truck to collect Gisele.'

André had told Marjie that they kept a small, old truck stored at one of the safe houses. If challenged, the two men would pass themselves off as workmen whose job it was to clear ditches. They would say they had to be in Perpignan early in the morning. Once on the border with Spain, Gisele would be on her own. She, and all those who lived close by, had sneaked through on many occasions when they were youngsters. Marjie remembered her brothers doing it once and having a wonderful adventure. They'd caught the train to Perpignan and then followed a mountain route to Spain. She felt confident that Gisele would be in Spain by tomorrow morning.

By noon the next day Marjie and her companions had reached a safe house, very near the mountains. Here they had agreed to wait for André and Ethan to join them. Marjie couldn't wait to hear that Gisele was safe.

Setting up the radio, she contacted HQ. When she deciphered the message that came back, her heart banged loudly in her chest. Sibbie was safe. Arnie would be informed of their new camp and instructed to make contact. No mention of Paulo, but then he wasn't an agent, so maybe they wouldn't give any details of whether or not he was all right.

*Thank God. Now all I want is for Arnie to come and tell me that Paulo, too, is safe.*

Within an hour André turned up. His face was ashen. Marjie stared at him. 'What's happened? Where's Ethan? Is . . . Gisele all right?'

'I want to speak to you in private, Marjie. Please come with me.'

349

Marjie felt sick to her stomach – something had gone wrong. *Please don't let it involve Monty.*

Once they were out of sight and earshot of the others, André said, 'Gisele's in the truck. She is responsible for the death of Ethan and is a traitor to our cause.'

'What? No. No, André, tell me it isn't true. What happened?'

'When we neared the Spanish border, someone fired a shot at us, which hit Ethan and killed him. I stopped and a man came out from behind the rock the shot was fired from, shouting to Gisele to jump off the back of the truck. He had his gun trained on me. I ducked, set the truck in gear and raced towards him. He disappeared behind the rock and I turned the wheel violently, just missing the rock. Gisele fell backwards and must have banged her head. It knocked her unconscious. I drove like a madman, swaying all over the road, trying to miss the shots he fired at us. When I had gone a good few kilometres, I stopped to check on Gisele. She was coming to and didn't make any sense. I tied her up. I brought her back here, because we must make her talk. We must know who her accomplice is, so that we can deal with him. Everything is at risk.'

Shocked to her core, Marjie frantically racked her brain for a solution. She'd made a mistake, she knew that. If the real traitor hadn't been her brother, then she would have dealt with the whole situation differently. She should have done, for she knew how powerful love could be. She should have known that sending Gisele back to Monty would give him time to manipulate her, using Gisele's feelings for him. But she had trusted Gisele.

'What do you think we should do, André?'

'We need to know who her accomplice is. Louis will get it out of her. He is sadistic, he'll make her talk.'

Taking a deep breath, Marjie took the most difficult decision she'd ever taken in her life. 'I know who it is.'

'Marjie?'

'I told you before that I did – well, in a non-specific way – but I made a mistake. I should have told you. I just couldn't handle it, and I wanted to wait for Arnie.'

'He left you in charge, Marjie. Yes, you should have told us. You must tell us now, so that we can deal with the traitor.'

'Oh, André . . . it's—'

'Marjie, you're crying. Oh, Marjie darling. What is it? Do you know him well?'

The endearment, and André taking her hands, undid her completely. Her sobs racked her body as she thought of her mama and papa, of Freddy and Randie. How could she ever face them again, if she had to order the death of their son and brother – her own dear brother?

She didn't resist when André pulled her to him, but clung to him for support. 'Oh, André, help me. Help me!'

'I will, my darling. I am here for you. We'll work this out. Is it someone you love?'

Unable to reject André's love, Marjie didn't pull away from him. At this moment he was her rock. 'Yes . . . more than life itself. I tended him when we were children, watched out for him, covered up his naughtiness, often taking a telling-off for him. I adored him, and still do. It – it's . . . Oh, André, it's my darling brother, Monty.'

'Good God! Monty?'

'Yes. He wrote to me. Gisele brought the letter to me yesterday. Oh, André, I think he traded all of us for his own freedom. He used Gisele. She's always adored him and hung on his every word, and she is now in love with him. What happened tonight, she wouldn't have wanted. I'm sure of that. She probably told Monty where she was going, and he got out of her when and how. Gisele wouldn't have set an ambush – Monty would have done that.'

'But for what purpose? I mean, if he wanted Gisele, he could have stopped her rendezvousing with us. Unless . . . Marjie, there could have been Germans waiting for us ahead. But Monty chickened out, where Gisele was concerned, and thought to get her off the truck before we reached the real ambush. Not good thinking on his part, as we were hardly going to go on without her.'

Composing herself, Marjie thought about this. Monty was never the brightest boy – but such thinking was stupid, even for him. But then, she knew Monty. Knew him well. 'André, knowing Monty, I think he wanted to stop working as a traitor. I wouldn't put it past him to have bargained with the Germans to deliver freedom-fighters to them, in exchange for his own safe passage to Spain, but then, as you say, to have had a change of heart and rescued Gisele. He probably hoped to kill you all in the process as he would have been afraid that you would betray his actions if the Germans did capture you.'

'But what of Gisele? She has to be disposed of. She knows too much, Marjie. We have no choice.'

'No! Oh, André, no, please. There must be another way. Think about it. Gisele has known Monty all her life, she is in love with him and had no reason not to trust him. He had been through hell and had escaped. He asked her about Paulo as he said he wanted to join the Resistance. How could she know it was a trick? And so she told Monty where Paulo was, and about me and his father. Then she told him about his father being air-lifted out, and that he must hurry if he wanted to see him. Gisele has done nothing that all of us wouldn't do, but for our training. Remember, she hasn't had the benefit of that.

'We must save her, André. We must. She's just a young girl, and she has put her life on the line for this cause almost every day, bringing supplies and vital papers – weapons even. She organized the stealing of everything that was needed. The cause has used this young girl, and she rose to the challenge. We cannot order her death because of this one time she's made a bad judgement. The fault is that of the cause, for not training Gisele in clandestine methods. She has done everything using her own wits. That let her down when she fell in love.'

'You're right, my love. But . . .'

Now that she was in charge of her emotions, the endearment sank into Marjie's conscious thinking and she pulled away from André. 'I'm – I'm sorry, André, please don't call me that. I didn't mean to give you the wrong impression. I needed you as a friend, a very dear and trusted friend. I'm so sorry, I—'

'No, no, it's my fault. I shouldn't . . . I mean, I misread you coming to me. Please forgive me. I love you, you know that. I love you so deeply, Marjie, that I don't know how I am going to live without you, or how I am managing to live so closely to you, knowing that you don't – and can never – love me back.'

Marjie didn't know what to say. She looked away.

'Forget it. Please, Marjie. Let's concentrate on the problem we have, and forget I ever showed, or talked about, my feelings for you.'

It wasn't easy. Marjie wanted to say that if she had never met Wills, she could have seen herself falling in love with

André, but she knew that wouldn't help, so she turned the conversation back to Gisele. 'Yes, that's best. I thank you for the honour of what you've just said, but we do have to forget it, if we are to carry on working together. And at the moment we need to find a solution to the problem of Gisele.'

'While Monty is alive, she represents a great danger to us. To save both us and Gisele . . . I'm sorry, Marjie, but we have to kill your brother.'

Pain shot through Marjie's heart, but she knew he was right, and she had to agree. But how could she? *Oh, Mama, Papa, help me.*

'Marjie?'

She nodded, and as she did so, she drew in a gasp of air that rasped her throat. 'May God – and my family – forgive me, but yes, André, it has to be done.'

'Oh, Marjie, I'm so sorry. I wish I could help you, or that there is another way, but there isn't. What about Gisele?'

'She stays here until we can get her to Spain. Please, André, help me in this. I cannot bear for such a brave young girl as Gisele to lose her life for what my brother did to her.'

'Yes, I agree. But what about the others? When they hear what happened, they will want Gisele dead.'

'Then we must not tell them. Where have you left the truck?'

'A little way down the lane. No one has gone to it, as they would have had to pass by us.'

'Good. You go and set Gisele free, and I will tell the others you were stopped by a checkpoint and weren't believed. That you were shot at, and Ethan was killed. I will tell them that you have Gisele, but didn't want to bring her back in, because of the mood they showed towards her

354

before. I will tell them that anyone who lays a finger on her will be shot; and that you now know who the traitor is and are dealing with him.'

'On my own?'

'I know that's difficult, but . . . Well, I don't want everyone to know who it is. Most of them do know Monty.'

'I'll go to the communist camp and tell them that I know of a traitor and where he can be found. I will tell them that he is known to us, so it is difficult for us to kill him. They will do it, and we won't know anything about it.'

'Yes, that is best. Oh God, I can't believe I'm saying that about my own brother. I can't bear to lose Monty. I want to see him. I want—'

'No, Marjie, you must be strong. Don't think of him as your brother, but as a traitor who didn't care if you were killed or not. A man who set the Germans on his own kin – and on Paulo, his faithful friend. And who could even have killed his own father; Monty couldn't know the plane would be on time – what if it had been late?'

'And all to ingratiate himself with the enemy. But despite knowing all that, André, the pain of what I'm agreeing to is unbearable.'

When Arnie contacted them later that day to say he was on his way, Marjie and André decided that the group would stay on at the safe house until Arnie arrived. His message was short, but did include an update: 'Sibbie all right. Paulo still very sick. Plane lifting them tomorrow for UK. Pray for Paulo.'

To Marjie, this was all too much. She bent her head and wept as she'd never done before. She wept for her mama and papa. *Forgive me. Forgive me. Oh God, I want to be with*

355

*them, I want to be home.* And she wept for Sibbie and Paulo. *I feel so alone, so alone. I miss you, Sibbie. And, dear Paulo, please get better – please!* But most of all she wept for Monty, who was so dear to her. *Why, Monty? Why? I love you so much – I don't want you to die. Why did you do it? What makes you like you are? Oh, my precious brother, forgive me, and help me to forgive you.*

Arnie looked haggard when he eventually arrived. It had been a long trek, as he explained. 'The first twenty miles I rode pillion on the back of one of the communist freedom-fighters' motorbikes, then I did a good few miles by rail, posing as a businessman, and finally in the back of the van of a market gardener – a contact at one of the safe houses I stayed in. I feel smelly and very tired.'

They all gathered to greet him. 'There's a room in the house, Uncle Arnie,' Marjie said. 'I've slept in it for the last couple of nights, but I want you to have a proper bed. I'll bunk in the barn with the men.'

'You won't, young lady. I'll decide who sleeps where, now I'm here. I only put you in charge in my absence, you know.' Arnie laughed as he said this, and although it was difficult for Marjie even to smile, she did manage a small one.

'You look tired, Marjie. What's wrong?'

'Oh, nothing.' She and André hadn't yet told the others about Monty, and Marjie never wanted to. They'd had a fight on their hands over Gisele, but in the end the men had accepted that she was staying until they could arrange to take her to Spain.

With Arnie cocking a knowing eyebrow at her, Marjie told him, 'I do have something on my mind that I need to tell you about, but I haven't been sleeping well since I heard about Sibbie and Paulo. I'm so glad they've been taken back to Britain. But so worried for them, and about them.'

'My dear, you have to accept that things don't look good for Paulo. Both of them were horribly tortured, but Paulo had limbs broken and suffered internal injuries. Neither of them gave in. But they were being taken to the Gestapo, who are known to extract information using horrendous torture. We saved them from that, but whether we are too late with Paulo, I'm not sure. He'll get proper treatment in England, so it is possible he will live, but I am very afraid for him.'

'Can we have a minute alone, Uncle Arnie?'

'My dear. What is it? You're crying!'

Brushing her tears away, Marjie took Arnie inside and asked the farmer's wife, Madame Dupret, where they could talk in private. Madame showed them into her best room.

'*Non*, Madame, I am very dirty.'

But Madame wouldn't hear of Arnie using any other room. 'You are zee most important man. I cannot treat you like you are less so.'

When Madame had left, Arnie asked, 'Why does she look on me like that?'

But Marjie couldn't answer. As soon as the door closed on them, she turned to Arnie. 'Oh, Uncle Arnie, help me – help me.'

'My dear Marjie. What is it?' His arms opened to her and she went into them, so grateful for the warmth and love of his hug.

Once she'd controlled herself, she told him all that had happened, finishing with the worst news in the world. 'They're . . . they're going to kill Monty, and I sanctioned it! I put a death sentence on my own darling brother. Oh God! Oh, Uncle Arnie, help me.'

Shock held Arnie silent for a moment. He stared down at her. 'My God! Why didn't you ask me?'

'I couldn't. I dared not use the radio and, in any case, how can you explain all that over the air? I tried to deal with it by getting Gisele away, and waiting for a decision from you, but Monty acted again.' She told him about the failed trip to take Gisele to the border with Spain. 'Oh, Uncle Arnie, Gisele hasn't been well since. I – I've kept her away from the others, as I'm sure they would kill her.'

'Where is she?'

'She's in an attic room; it's a sort of makeshift guest room. I told Madame that Gisele has a fever that is infectious. I have a key, so that no one can get to her, and I look after her. I think she's concussed and could have cracked her skull in the fall.'

'Oh, Marjie, this is awful. But, my dear, you have done the right thing in ordering that Monty be dealt with, and in moving camp. There is no alternative. I'm shocked about Gisele. And, well . . . Oh, I don't know. This is a stinking mess.'

'She's so young, Uncle Arnie.' Marjie laid out the case for Gisele as she had done to André, reminding him of Gisele's work for the cause, and how she thought Gisele innocent in it all – trusting someone she'd known all her life and was deeply in love with. 'Please, Uncle. It is enough that my darling Monty pays the ultimate price, but not Gisele, too – she doesn't deserve to.'

'I understand her part, and we are at fault. We took all she could do for us and never trained her in how to deal with anyone – even those she knew – wanting information. Of course she knew that, if caught, she would face torturous interrogation and certain death. But, as you say, Gisele is courageous and she accepted that. And, I believe, she would rather die than give us away intentionally.'

'Thank you – thank you so much. And you agree that it is possible the Germans may have known the source of Monty's information and that, once they lose Monty, Gisele will be a target for the information they can no longer get through him?'

'Yes, I do. But if we are going to save her, it is vital that we get her to her aunt's in Spain as soon as possible. However, if you are right in your suspicion about what is wrong with Gisele, then we need a doctor. The communist groups are well organized and have recruited doctors of the same persuasion to join their cause. I'll see about Gisele getting help. Did her parents know she was leaving?'

'Yes, it was all arranged very quickly, and they probably think she is in Spain now.' Talking about the practicalities of what was going to happen to Gisele had distracted Marjie from her grief, but once she felt happy that Arnie was on the same side as her, where Gisele was concerned, pain flooded back into her. 'I'm so relieved, for Gisele; but how am I going to cope with what I've done to Monty? How will my mama and papa, and Freddy and Randie, ever forgive me? How am I going to live with myself? Oh, Uncle Arnie, I can't bear it all.'

'It is a terrible burden, Marjie, my dear. But you must look at what you will have achieved, not at what you had to do. You have stopped someone who informed on our comrades and caused their deaths, and the capture of Sibbie and Paulo – and Monty may yet have killed Paulo. Monty is someone who would have sacrificed André, and who killed Ethan. Someone who wouldn't have been allowed to stop there, as the Germans wouldn't have let go of such an asset.

They would have wanted more, and Monty would be able to give it, or could have done. He might eventually have forced Gisele to give information about our supplies, our positions, everything; and that wouldn't only be disastrous for us, but for France, too. At the moment we are the only hope for the French people, and we have much work to do to disrupt the Germans' ability to transport armoury, tanks, military men and, not least, the poor Jews to the extermination camps.'

'I know. Thanks, Uncle. I just wish it made me feel better.'

'Nothing can do that, my dear. It is a terrible burden for you to shoulder. But listen to me. I love Monty like a son, and this is breaking my heart, too, but your decision is the one I would have taken. I am sanctioning it, and therefore I am taking responsibility for it.'

Marjie couldn't speak. Some easing of her conscience settled in her, at these last words of Arnie's, and she knew that with him by her side, there might be a chance to make her family understand, although there wasn't anything in the world that could really help her. How could there be?

# CHAPTER TWENTY-EIGHT

# *London*

## Ella, Flors and Sibbie

Flors screamed with joy as she opened the letter that had dropped through the letter box of their apartment. Seeing the War Office stamp, she'd picked it up tentatively, wondering if the news was good or bad. She now worked alongside Cyrus in the Baker Street offices of the Special Operations Executive headquarters and knew most of what was happening, but not all that the War Office was party to.

Her mind had been centred of late on messages coming in that the Hérault faction of the Resistance had moved camp, due to being compromised by a traitor whom they were seeking. And she'd been full of anguish about Sibbie and Paulo, especially Paulo. Anticipating their arrival today, she and Cyrus had been getting ready to go to the hospital to greet them. But now her heart didn't know which emotion to follow as part of her world came right, for the letter was from her darling eldest son, Freddy.

'Cyrus. Cyrus!'

He came through to the hall from their bedroom, looking handsome in his pin-striped business suit – a change from his officer's uniform, which also suited him so well. But then her Cyrus looked beautiful in anything.

'What a wonderful sound, darling. To hear you so happy has lifted me. Is it Freddy?'

'Yes, a letter from Freddy at last. I'll read it out:

*'Dearest Mama and Papa,*
   *I am so happy and relieved to know that you are both all right.'*

It was obvious that his letter had been vetted, as the first sheet had been cut off at this point and was shorter than the others. She guessed that Freddy had asked about all of his siblings and Paulo, as well as Ella, Arnie and Lonia. She read on:

*'Oh, Mama and Papa, when you eventually go home you will find a hundred letters from me – that's if they ever reached there. I have been desperate to hear news of you all. When the War Office contacted me, I was over the moon.*

   *'I am doing all right. I expect you know all my news by now. I have many friends and we keep each other going; a lot of the time is spent playing football, which I love. There is a British coach here, and he told me that I am good enough to play professionally – how about that?*

   *'Well, Mama and Papa, write soon and, if you can, send me a woolly jumper as it gets very cold at night. And some cigarettes. I know I shouldn't have, but with everything else, I have begun to smoke, but have to pinch from my mates because, not declaring myself a smoker, I don't have a ration of them. Oh, and some*

362

*boiled sweets; the ones I love, which Aunt Mags used to*
*bring over to France for me – happy days, but they will*
*come back and we will win this war.*

  *'Keep faith, Mama and Papa, I love you both very*
*much. Give my love to everyone and tell them that I*
*pray for them all every night, as I do for you, Mama*
*and Papa. I miss you all so much, but know that we*
*will all be together again sometime in the future.*

  *'Your loving son, Freddy x'*

Tears were flowing down Flors's face as she finished the
letter.

Cyrus's arm came round her and his love reassured her,
as it always did. 'You'd better get knitting, Mama!'

Laughing through her tears, she pushed him playfully on
the shoulder. 'I'll get Mags to send me down one of those
fishermen's jumpers from her friend's shop in Scotland. She'll
be telephoning tonight. But cigarettes – ugh, I don't like
to think of Freddy smoking.'

'I expect he needs something to help him, and smoking
is very soothing on the nerves. I always turn to my Senior
Service cigarettes when I'm stressed.'

'I know you do. Well, I'll let you buy them for him. I
hate the things and don't fancy going into a tobacconist's
to buy them.'

'You're delegating well, darling.'

'Ha, it's my nature. I'll get the boiled sweets, if they are
available, and any other treats that I think I can get into the
permitted parcel size that the Red Cross will deliver.'

'That's settled, then. Oh, I'm so happy to hear from our
Freddy at last. And Randie will be home in a couple of days
– he's doing well with his training.'

'Don't remind me. I can't bear to think of him going out on operations. Oh, Cyrus, every day I worry that we will hear the news about one of them that we are dreading. But, more than that, I am so anxious about Monty, and the news that a traitor has been identified. If it is him, then . . . oh God!'

Cyrus could offer Flors no comfort on this, so instead he sought to distract her. 'Well, let's concentrate on our darling Sibbie and Paulo for now. And pray they are going to get better. Mags is on her way down, with Ella and Susan. We need to be there when they arrive.'

'I feel so much for Ella and Susan, darling. The shock for Susan must have been tremendous. For Ella, too, but at least she knew what Paulo was doing and the risks he was taking. But Susan had no idea that her daughter wasn't doing important work somewhere in the South of England. And I feel so guilty about the letters we have had to send to Susan as if they were from Sibbie.'

'I do, too, but it is the way of things, and is not of our doing, darling. Although I can imagine how we would feel if we didn't know and then were suddenly faced with this!'

Flors shuddered. All her nightmares were wrapped up in something bad happening to her children. But at least, she thought, Mags – who looked on Sibbie as if she were her own daughter – had half-guessed what work Sibbie was doing, so wouldn't feel the shock about her that Susan would.

When they arrived at the Military Hospital in Millbank, a young WRAC member, who worked as a driver to M, was there to greet them and saluted Cyrus. 'Hello, sir, ma'am. M assigned me to meet the plane bringing Agent S and

Resistance fighter Paulo Rennaise in. I escorted the ambulance to the hospital. I'm sorry, but they told me to let you know that you need to hurry . . . It isn't looking good for Paulo.'

Flors gasped. Taking Cyrus's hand gave her no comfort, as her mind showed Flors her darling friend Ella, and all she had been through. Yes, Ella would have been shocked that her Paulo was injured, but she would have put aside her plans to volunteer at the hospital in Scotland and would have found a way to cope, in nursing him back to health. But Paulo dying? *No . . . no, that can't happen!*

Cyrus didn't speak, and his face was ashen.

At the end of a long corridor, they were shown into a side ward. The scene that met them broke Flors's heart. A bruised and battered Sibbie sat, holding Paulo's hand. Paulo looked so close to death that his face was an expressionless yellow mask, which didn't appear like him. His jaw was jutting out to one side, despite the bandage wrapped around his chin and taped at the top of his head, indicating that it was broken. His closed eyes sank deep into bruised and blackened sockets, with one cheek distorted and swollen.

'Sibbie. Oh, Sibbie, my darling niece. I – I . . . oh God! That this should happen, my poor, poor darling.'

Sibbie rose and came into Flors's open arms. The hug Flors gave made Sibbie wince.

'You're in pain! My brave, brave girl. You should be in bed, too. How could anyone do this to you both?'

Sibbie didn't speak; her lovely dark eyes were bloodshot and looked up at Flors from swollen black and yellow sockets. Through her hair, raw patches of skin showed, where chunks had been pulled out. Her fingers were bound in plasters, and Flors could feel that her body was encased in bandages, while blisters covered her arms. 'Are your ribs broken, my darling?'

'Yes, they are so painful.'

'You must rest, Sibbie.'

'I can't leave Paulo. I love him so very much. We love each other. We . . . we're going to be married.'

Flors's heart broke for this very dear young couple. She and Ella had known for a long time that they loved each other and had waited for the moment when they acknowledged their love. She was glad that moment had happened, but felt so very sad, too.

She looked around the room. It was big enough to fit in another bed, which, when Sibbie or Paulo weren't being tended to, could be pushed close to the existing bed. 'Sit down, darling. I'll go and see the sister of the ward.' Turning to Cyrus, Flors saw the hurt and the deep love in his eyes, before he gently supported Sibbie as she painfully lowered herself back into the hard wooden chair, which must be so uncomfortable for her.

Finding the ward sister, Flors introduced herself and then asked about Sibbie's bed being moved into the same side ward as Paulo. 'Hmm, unconventional, but do-able, I suppose, in the circumstances. Those two are heroes and deserve us to go the extra mile for them, bless them.'

'Thank you, Sister . . . ?'

'Sister Baker – Annie Baker.'

'Well, I'm very grateful to you, Sister Baker; that's very kind of you.'

'Not at all, I learned a long time ago that medical intervention is all well and good, but we should take note of emotional needs, too.'

'Sister, is there no hope for Paulo?'

'Where there's life, there's always hope, my dear. That young man has suffered internal bleeding from heavy blows, and had the blood supply to his leg cut off for too long. The surgeons have done what they can to make him comfortable, but he is very poorly.'

'Has he been given blood?'

'Yes, what we had of his type sustained him through his operation, but he has a rare Rhesus negative blood group, and that is inhibiting our ability to give him what he needs. He needs more radical surgery. I'm sorry, but his leg requires amputation, as it is gangrenous, and it is this that will kill him; but we didn't have enough of his blood type to get him safely through the operation. We have tested all the nurses and doctors, and even the patients, but none have the same type. And we have sent out a request to all the hospitals in London to see if they have any – but nothing. Without it, he has very little chance of survival.'

'Rhesus negative? I've never heard of that. In my day, we simply gave blood.'

'You were a nurse?'

'A Voluntary Aid nurse in the last war.'

'I was, too. There have been a lot of advances since those days, when blood was just blood to us. We now know that a patient must have compatible blood; and further to that, we are finding that there are a few people who have an extremely rare blood group. We have tested many medical staff, in the hope of one of them being of the same type as Paulo, but no luck yet.'

'So Paulo's life depends on something you can't locate. That's terrible. Will you test me and my husband, please? And his mother is on the way – is there a chance she might have the same blood type?'

'Yes, of course we will test you both. I'll send a nurse to take a sample from you. But there is a much greater chance that his mother and any siblings will have the same blood type, so when will she arrive? Time isn't on our side.'

'She is on her way. Paulo has a sister, too; well, a half-sister, but I don't know if they are bringing her, as she is only nine.'

'Then we have double the hope, as she is much more likely to be a match, or to have compatible blood.'

'I'll make a telephone call and check if Paulo's sister, Lonia, is on her way; if not, I'll make sure she is brought down very soon.'

'Lonia's an unusual name.'

'It's of Polish origin. Paulo and Lonia's mother is Polish.'

'Hmm, it might be worth me talking to the doctors about the possibility of testing Polish airmen based at Northolt, and any French officers. I say "officers" because they are usually in one place that has been designated especially to take officers – a stately home or something like that – though I would need to find out where, whereas the lower ranks of French soldiers are taken wherever they can be found a bed. It's a long shot, as we know so little about blood groups and hereditary traits, but we're learning all the time. And desperate situations call for desperate measures, as you well know.'

Flors nodded. Hope had risen in her, with the spirit of determination that she saw in Sister Baker. 'May I use your telephone, Sister?'

When given permission, Flors asked the operator to put her through to Mags's number in Scotland, in the hope that her friend, Betsy, would answer.

'Hello, Stranraer three-o-three.'

'Is that you, Betsy? This is Flors, Mags's friend.'

'Aye, Betsy here. Is owt wrong? Is Mags all right?'

'I'm sure she's fine; she hasn't arrived yet, though. When did they leave, and have they brought Lonia with them?'

'They've been gone a good few hours. They should be on the train to London by now. And aye, they have the lass with them. Poor Ella thought it best, as it would do Paulo good to see Lonia – she's a tonic that one. How is he, have you seen him?'

'Yes, he's very ill and needs all our prayers. But thank God Lonia is coming. There's a problem with his blood type; it's hard to explain, but between them, Ella and Lonia may be the answer to saving Paulo.'

'Ech, that sounds complicated to me. But whatever you're talking about, I'll pray it is so, and I'll pray for the lad. And I'm sorry – very sorry – about the circumstances. Me heart's with you all.'

'Thank you, Betsy. It's nice to talk to you. I've heard so much about you.'

'By, I hope it's all been good. Not that it could be.' Betsy laughed, but then became serious again. 'How's me Sibbie? Is she going to be all right?'

'Physically, yes, but emotionally we've yet to see. She's being very brave, but . . . well, she and Paulo are in love.'

'Dear God, poor lass. We're mystified here as to how it could all happen. We thought . . . Aye, well, there's a lot going on as we don't knaw of, and shouldn't ask after. But give her me love. Me heart's breaking for her.'

'I will, Betsy. I'll say goodbye now, but I hope it won't be too long before we meet.'

'Aye, ta-ra, Flors, I'll look forward to that day, but hope it will be in happier times.'

\* \* \*

'What are you smiling at, darling? Have you some good news?' Cyrus asked, coming towards Flors along the corridor.

'I've just been reminded of Nanny Pru.'

'Oh, well, that memory would cheer anyone. What I wouldn't give to have her here helping you, my darling.'

'I'm all right, Cyrus. And do you know, I think we are soon to meet another Nanny Pru, in Betsy, Mags's friend. She's got what Nanny Pru would have called a "warm heart". It did me good to hear the lovely northern accent. But I do have hopeful news, darling.' She told Cyrus first about the bed move.

'I know. I've been turfed out of the way to make room for them to manoeuvre the beds. Well done, darling. Sibbie needs her rest, and yet to be with her Paulo. So what is the hopeful news?'

When Flors told him about the possible blood match, Cyrus didn't speak, but simply took hold of her hand.

Constantly going to the hospital entrance, Flors grew more agitated by the hour. It had been two hours now since she'd learned that neither she nor Cyrus was compatible. The sister's idea of testing the Polish pilots hadn't proved realistic. The time this would take, and the logistics involved, ruled it out; and this was also so of the French officers. Whoever could give the blood needed to be here, now.

At last she saw Ella, Susan and Mags running through the doors, just as she turned into the lobby. Ella stopped and stared at Flors. 'No . . .' Her head shook from side to side.

Flors ran to her and took Ella in her arms. 'There's a chance, Ella. But you and Lonia need to come with me. I have to take you straight to the path lab.'

'What? Why? Oh, Flors, I want to see my Paulo.'

'I'll explain as we go.' As she let go of Ella, Flors pulled Lonia to her. 'We have an important mission, darling – can you run?'

'I can run faster than anyone, Aunty Flors.'

'Good girl. We'll have a cuddle when we get there.' Turning to Mags, Flors smiled. 'No time to greet you, Mags, sorry. Take Susan along that corridor there. You need the fourth door on your right – it's quite a way. Sorry, Susan, I'll say hello later. Sibbie's all right.'

Flors grabbed Ella's hand then and ran with her and Lonia in the direction she'd already taken earlier. Though breathless, she told Ella what she knew as they went.

Once back in the ward, and with the hope she'd been given, Ella was able to control her emotions. Lonia climbed onto Paulo's bed. 'I'm here, Paulo. And I've had some blood taken for you. It's going to make you well.' She was gentle as she kissed his cheek, then placed her head on the pillow next to his and looked over at Sibbie. 'Are you going to be well, Sibbie? Will your pretty face come back?'

Sibbie gave a tired smile. 'Will you still love me, if it doesn't?'

'I will, Sibbie. I love you more, now you're poorly. Mama says that love can heal. So it is important that I am brave and show you my love.'

'That's true. Just having my mum with me, and feeling her love, is making me better.'

Susan smiled for the first time. Her eyes lit up with it and she leaned over the bed and held Sibbie. 'I never thought you would ever go through anything like this, Sibbie, but I'm so proud of you.'

'I had so many brave and strong women who guided me,

Mum. You and Aunt Betsy, and Aunt Mags; and, when I went to France, Aunt Flors and Aunt Ella. So how could I not be brave?'

Flors thought about this; and yes, they were all brave and strong. They'd all come through extreme adversity and had coped. Given time, they had coped. All she asked now was that Paulo was given that time because, with Sibbie by his side, she knew they would cope, too.

All the hushed chatter was a distraction. They talked of anything but the blood samples and the war. Even Ella, who must have been longing for news of Arnie.

At last Sister Baker opened the door. 'It's a match. Little Lonia is a match! Come on, little one, you're going to help to save your brother's life.' The sigh of relief that went around the room was the only sound. 'Now, all of you, out you go. Leave Paulo with some encouraging words. I've a wheelchair just outside the door for Sibbie. You can all go along to the day-room. My nurses need to get in here to prepare Paulo for surgery.'

'I'll go with Lonia; although she is a very brave girl, I need to be with her.'

Sister Baker nodded. 'Yes, that's fine, Mummy, come along.'

'She's Mama!'

'Oh, sorry, Lonia. Come along then, Mama, we've no time to lose.'


Paulo's recovery was slow, but each day saw some progress.

When at last Sibbie felt able to talk to him about the consequences, she asked, 'My darling, how do you really feel about having lost your leg?'

A tear seeped out of Paulo's eye. 'I am struggling to think how our future will be.'

'We'll find a way around everything. We're together, that's the main thing.'

'Yes, that is all I live for – the day that we can marry. But . . .'

'There are no "buts", my darling Paulo. I love you. Nothing can ever change that. I think we will need each other to help cope with our past, not our future. That is secure, with the knowledge of your love for me.'

At this, Paulo gave his lovely smile. It didn't matter to Sibbie that it was now lopsided, as his jaw hadn't yet mended; it was the hope in his smile that warmed her heart. And she knew that all the horror of the past lay behind them, and that they would find a way of tucking away what had happened and not letting it spoil what they had. Together, they would get through the difficulties of the future, too.

Paulo reached for her hand and, in taking it, these thoughts were sealed.

CHAPTER TWENTY-NINE

# London and Portpatrick

## Flors and Cyrus, Sibbie and Paulo

The joy felt at Paulo's slow but encouraging progress was shattered with the message that was received six weeks later. Monty had been shot by the communist Resistance group, after he was found to be a traitor to the cause.

Now a further two weeks had passed, and the front room of their apartment where Flors and Cyrus sat was silent, but for the ticking of the clock on the mantelpiece. The devastation caused by their youngest son's death, in disgraceful circumstances, had built a wall between them; an invisible and almost impenetrable wall. Their grief was like no other they'd previously experienced. It was knitted with shame and lack of knowledge, as no one seemed to know – or be willing to tell them – the extent of what Monty had done, and who had ordered his killing.

The clang of the doorbell made Flors jump.

'It's all right, I'll go.'

Flors watched Cyrus cross the room. Her emotions were shut down, leaving her just an empty shell. The usual reaction that she would have, to Cyrus showing such hurt, didn't come to her.

'It's Wills, Flors. Come on in, my boy. I hope you haven't come on official business. But if you have, please make it good news, as we are unable to take any further bad news.'

Flors looked at Wills, but didn't greet him.

'I came to tell you how sorry I am, and to give you some hope. There was a meeting this morning and it has been decided to bring Marjella home.'

'But that's wonderful. Thank you so much, as I know you will have had a hand in bringing about such an idea.' Flors at last felt some hope. 'When?'

'Well, there is a "but", I'm afraid. Randolph has now finished his training, and to an exceptional standard, and it is being proposed to exchange them.'

'Oh no. When will it ever end?'

'Darling, it won't until men like Randie and Freddy make it end. They are the right ones to fight this, not Marjella and Sibbie. I hate the idea of giving one of our children in exchange for the other, but Marjella has done so much. We need her home, to care for her.'

'Yes, I know you are right. But I just don't want any of our children in danger. I can't bear to lose any more of them.'

There was another silence. Flors wanted to scream that Monty was their child, no matter what he'd done, and how did they know that he hadn't been forced to become a traitor by the Germans? But she remained quiet, locked in a cocoon of grief that felt like a knife twisting in her heart. It was as if she wasn't allowed to grieve, and that she should be glad her son was dead.

'I can only say, Mrs Harpinham, that this is what is happening all over the world. Mothers and fathers are grieving over their sons and daughters, and children are grieving over lost parents. It sometimes feels as though the whole world is crying.'

'I know. I'm grateful to be getting Marjella home. Thank you.'

'I wasn't totally responsible. M was much more so. But I am very happy, as you know how much I love Marjie. It is agony to have her in danger.'

'Well, my boy, Marjella has made a wise choice in you. Both Mrs Harpinham and I are very happy at the prospect of one day welcoming you into the family.'

'Thank you.'

Flors caught the look that Wills gave her. She didn't want to confirm what Cyrus had said; she didn't want anyone to take her Marjella away from her ever again. Wills might do that. He was the son of a lord; he would be a lord one day. There was an estate to care for, and he would be responsible for that and for taking his place in the House of Lords. Marjella wouldn't be able to live in France with them – that's if it ever came about that they could live in their beautiful home again.

Cyrus coughed. 'Can we offer you some refreshment, Wills?'

'No, thank you.' Then, as if he knew her thoughts, he said, 'I – I, well, I want to reassure you that although Marjella and I will live at my home when we are married, we will travel to see you at least three times a year. I would never keep her away from you.'

Flors decided to fill the silence. Taking a deep breath, she nodded. 'Thank you, Wills. Forgive me, I'm not myself.'

'I understand.' He smiled. 'But it's good to see you in all lights, then I know what kind of mother-in-law I am getting.'

His laugh fell like a tin can on a stone floor. Wills reddened and went to apologize, but Cyrus stepped in. Smiling, he put his hand out to Wills. 'I'm still learning about my wife, so it will be an evolving process for you, but I can promise you it is all good.'

At that moment Flors felt the pain of the chasm between her and Cyrus and wanted so much to go to him. As if this had been conveyed, he turned and put out his arms to her.

Rising, she went to him and gladly allowed him to enfold her. The door clicked. Wills was gone. Guilt filled Flors, but Cyrus kissed it away. 'That's a very special young man, with the perception of someone much older than himself. We're so lucky to be getting him as a son-in-law.'

'I know, Cyrus. I'm sorry. I was very rude to him. Will you go after him?'

'No, that's not what's going to happen, or what he would expect. He made himself scarce as he saw that we just needed each other. I so need you, my darling.'

'Oh, Cyrus, love my pain away.'

They clung to each other. A mixture of emotions assailed Flors. Most of them were painful ones at their loss, while some represented fear for Freddy and Randie. But a little joy seeped into her, as she knew that no matter what happened in life, Cyrus would always be there for her and she shouldn't have shut him out – and also because her beloved Marjella was coming home.

It was almost Christmas by the time Marjie arrived. They'd said goodbye to Randie more than a month earlier, but it was thought he would need to work alongside Marjie for a time, in order to be able to take over the leadership of the Hérault Maquis.

Freddy had written often, and with much enthusiasm, about the advance of the Allied forces in North Africa, but of late his letters had been few and far between, as it was known that the Germans had the Allies pinned down, and they hadn't yet reached Tunisia.

Over the weeks and months since hearing of Monty's death, Flors had healed a little. She and Cyrus had been to the grave of their firstborn, Alice, in September and had put a heavy cast-iron vase on the side, to Monty's memory. It bore the inscription: 'We Live by the Decisions We Take. Remembering You Always as a Loving Son'; and underneath that, 'Montague Harpinham 1922–42, RIP'.

They had spent a long time there, hoping that, in God's eyes, Monty wasn't a traitor, but was fighting for the side he believed in; and that he was forgiven and resting with his lovely sister, Alice. A little peace had come to them at this. And Flors's splintered heart began to heal, with her acceptance.

And now they were waiting for Wills to bring their lovely Marjie home. She'd landed two weeks ago and, with debriefing and demobbing, was at last on her way. They could have seen her before now, but both were still on extended bereavement-leave and therefore weren't involved in anything at Baker Street HQ.

When the doorbell finally rang, both of them jumped from their chairs and rushed to open the door, almost colliding as they did, so that when they opened it, they were giggling like children.

'Mama, Papa. Oh, it's good to be home.'

All three fell into a hug. Tears, laughter and love filled the circle they made. 'My Marjella, my darling daughter.'

'And mine!' This indignant remark from Cyrus had them

laughing again, but this time it ended in sobs and they clung together, trying to heal all they had been through.

'There are things I have to tell you, Mama and Papa, and I don't know if you can forgive me.'

Flors felt shocked by this. *Did Marjella have anything to do with Monty's death? Please, no . . . No!*

Cyrus's voice, strong and meaningful, cut through these thoughts. 'Whatever decisions you made, or actions you took, were done as they should have been, I have no doubt about that, my darling. And so we have nothing to blame you for, or to forgive you for. We only have extreme pride in your ability to do the right thing, no matter what it cost you. You are truly our daughter, dearest Marjella. Don't let anything mar your peace of mind, or stop you going forward. Forget everything bad that has happened, and remember only the good that you have lived and the happy times. It is the only way.'

Flors knew in that moment that she had to release her daughter, just as she did her son. 'My darling, the wonderful, brave young woman who undertook her duty, and was called upon to make horrific decisions, didn't flinch in doing so, and neither should she have done. As Papa said, you did your duty, when it was asked of you. Put all of it behind you – everything. Nothing can erase the memory of your growing up, or the happiness we all shared in our beautiful home. So now look to what's in your future, and never let the past mar that.'

'Oh, Mama, Papa, I so needed you to say these things to me. To give me your understanding. A great burden has lifted from me, with you saying you don't have to forgive me.'

They huddled together again, but something in Flors had

died. That her children should have been through such horror, and that one of them, she was now certain, had to order the death of the other – how was she going to live with that? How was her darling Marjella going to?

But when they came out of the huddle and Marjella went into Wills's arms, Flors knew that he would help her. Wills would prove to be Marjie's salvation, and maybe their own, too.

Later, after they had eaten and the atmosphere had become more relaxed, Marjie approached the subject that was on her mind. 'Mama, Wills has some leave over Christmas and we were wondering: would it be possible to go to Scotland and be with Sibbie and Paulo and Aunt Ella, and everyone up there? They're all so lovely, and Portpatrick is a beautiful place.'

'That sounds wonderful. I know Aunt Mags and Uncle Jerome are going up there with Beth and Belinda, so it will be like . . .'

Marjie watched her mama draw in a deep breath.

'Not old times, Mama. Nothing can make those come back, but it will be a good start to new times. Something we can have in place for when Freddy and Randie come home. A get-together at Christmas time of all of those who can.'

'Yes, Marjella, that's right. After every stage – good or bad – there has to be a new beginning.'

With Cyrus saying this, Flors knew it to be so. She made herself smile and say, 'It sounds wonderful.'

When the car finally arrived in Portpatrick after a two-day journey, driven by Cyrus and Wills taking turns, Marjie could hardly contain herself. They were all there, waiting at the bottom of the road that led to Mags's and Betsy's shared house. The sea behind the little group looked dramatic, as it crashed waves onto the quayside and tossed the boats anchored in the port as if they were toys. Through the dark, tumbling clouds a weak sun glimmered a streak of light onto the angry water.

'Oh, it's beautiful – beautiful. No wonder you love it, Marjella.'

'I do, Mama. After just one visit, I have never forgotten it.'

'Aye, and us neither, I hope.'

'Never you, Betsy.' Marjie laughed, but then she caught sight of Sibbie. 'Oh, Sibbie! Sibbie! Paulo, oh, it's good to see you. I've missed you so much.'

Sibbie had a radiant, if tearful smile on her face as she let go of Paulo's wheelchair and rushed at Marjie. Tears wet their faces and their hair tangled together in the wind, as their bodies swayed in a hug of love, sorrow and, yes, hopefulness.

There were so many hugs after that, with Paulo, Aunt Ella and Lonia; Rosie, Aunt Mags and Uncle Jerome; and Beth, looking so grown-up, and Belinda, too. And, of course, Susan, Rory and Angus. When they reached Mags's house, their chatter went on and on.

Rosie was telling them of her new job, and how much she was loving it

'Aye, and she's done what I told her not to do, an' all – she's fallen in love with a doctor. By, how I'm going to live up to his family, I don't knaw.'

'Ma, you daft ha'p'orth! They're naw different from us. I told you, Walter surprised his parents by turning out to be a clever-clogs, and wouldn't be where he is but for a helping hand from the kindly lady who lived in the Grange in his village.' Rosie told them all then how Wally had been a gardener's boy at the Grange, and the lady of the house had taken him under her wing, educating him in so much that he hadn't learned at the village school. She had recognized his ability and helped him to university and paid for his medical training. 'His training was interrupted by war at first, but he copped a bullet or two at Dunkirk. He only has one leg, like Paulo,' Rosie told them. 'But Wally continued his training, once he could. He has a false leg. You will have one of those one day, Paulo.'

'Well, young lass, you never told me owt of this before!'

'Because you wouldn't listen, Ma. I did try.'

'Eeh, I'm sorry, our lass. I thought if I ignored it, it would go away. Now I don't want him to. Is Walter working over Christmas? If not, I'd be honoured if he'd join us.'

'Oh, Ma. Ma!' Rosie jumped up and hugged her mother, and for a moment it seemed that everything was going to come right for everyone.

'Well, I'm to get back to me duties or Cook'll be scalping me.' They all laughed at Betsy saying this. Aunt Mags had brought lovely Cook with her, now retired from full-time work at the Manor, but considered one of the family; and between them, Betsy and Cook were re-creating old times when they worked together.

When dinner was served, it was a wonderful meal of that day's catch, which had been proudly presented by Angus.

No one remarked on how tipsy Betsy and Cook appeared to be as they tripped around the table, their movements made in such a way as not to drop the food, but to stay upright. Afterwards they all sat around the blazing fire and chatted some more, to the noise of Betsy and Cook snoring gently.

'Och, I'm thinking I'm going to have to buy another bottle of sherry, as I ken those two have drunk most of the one I had ready for Christmas. But it's good to see me lassie so happy. It's something I couldn't ever see happening again. She's had her heart broken. But Lonia and our Rosie are helping it to mend. And all of you visiting has made Christmas less of an ordeal for Betsy.'

'And being with her is helping us all, too,' Flors said. 'Betsy's a tonic and I'm so glad to have met her at last – well, all of you: Angus, and you, Susan; and Rory and Rosie and Roderick. I feel as though I've known you forever.'

'And us you, Flors. Aunt Mags is allus going on about you. But it's lovely to be with you all at last.'

'Thank you, Rosie. I can see why you want to stay up here, Ella. Lonia is so happy and relaxed, and you say you're ready to start nursing again now, and that's wonderful.'

'Yes, I'm really looking forward to it. And it will help me. Remember, Flors, you always said that we find help in helping others.'

'I did. And I haven't done that.'

'Darling, although you can't talk about our work, it's very valuable to the war effort, and once we get back to it in the new year, that will help us, too, I'm sure of it,' Cyrus said.

With this from her papa, Marjie looked at her parents and knew their pain was healing a little. But, she wondered, would her own pain ever heal?

When she and Sibbie, and Wills and Paulo, found some time alone later that night, their laughter helped them all. Wills was so funny. His antics, as he told tales of his upbringing and some of the strange things their servants got up to, kept them from talking about the inevitable, although Marjie knew that one day they would have to.

That day came the very next day: Christmas Eve. The four of them went for a walk. It wasn't easy on the hilly terrain, with Paulo in a wheelchair, but Wills managed him well, and without making Paulo feel as though he was a burden. Sibbie took them to the churchyard to visit the grave of her step-father, Montel.

It was then that they had talked.

'Marjie, dear Marjie. How could it all have happened?' Sibbie held Marjie's hand and her eyes brimmed with tears. 'The lovely Monty. How could he have turned out as he did?'

'I don't know, Sibbie. I'm so sorry for what he caused you and Paulo. I'm so sorry.'

'No, none of this is your fault, Marjie.' Paulo took her other hand then. He was sitting in his wheelchair facing them, as the three of them sat on the bench. 'Monty always did anything to get what he wanted – you know that. We heard such horrendous tales of what was happening to those on forced labour, from those who escaped and joined us. Monty must have seen a way to save himself. He was so young. The consequences wouldn't have occurred to him.'

'And now that you know it was Monty who betrayed us, which led to all you went through, you can forgive him?'

'We're at war, Marjie. Things happen in war that none of us know how we will react to. I loved Monty like a brother. He was my shadow, as you know. If he'd known that this would have happened to me, as a result of his actions, he wouldn't have done it. I'm sure of that.'

Marjie couldn't take this in, but she was so grateful to Paulo for thinking like that. It helped, just a little, to ease her pain and guilt. But when she told them of how she'd ordered Monty's death, it all came rushing back and, no matter what they said, it didn't stop a shadow being cast over the next few days, which only Marjie could feel.

At night, she and Sibbie slept in the same bed. This was a comfort to them both. 'Will we ever forget, Sibbie?'

'No. And nor should we. But we will learn to live with it all, I'm sure. We'll help each other – the three of us. And Wills will help us. He's lovely, Marjie.'

'He is – I adore him. I'm finding it hard not to be with him, as we were before I left.'

'I know. Paulo and I have done it.'

'It?' They both giggled at this.

'Well, what can you call it? I don't even know the proper word, but I know it was wonderful.' Marjie didn't ask how Sibbie and Paulo managed to make love; she was just so happy for them both.

'Marjie, shall we go to them? Everyone will be asleep. No one will know. I'll creep along to the room they are in and send Wills to you. But we must make a pact to be back in our rooms by around three in the morning. Your father sometimes walks the landing then.'

'I know; poor love, he hasn't slept well for a long time.'

'He'll sleep even less if he finds out that his daughter is sleeping with her man before they're wed!'

Once more they giggled, as Marjie hit Sibbie with her pillow.

'No time for messing around, Marjie. I've more important things to do.' With this, Sibbie jumped off the bed and waved goodbye, before slowly opening the bedroom door and looking each way along the landing.

In no time Wills had slipped into her room and Marjie felt all her dreams come true, as he came to her and held her. 'Marjie, my Marjie.'

In his arms making silent love, she found her heaven. Her peace. Nothing intruded on the feelings Wills gave her when finally, after four weeks of wanting him so badly that she'd ached for him, he entered her. Marjie's world exploded, and her love for him overwhelmed her. She whispered, 'Wills. Oh, Wills, I love you.' It was for his ears only, just as his words of love were for hers.

By the time Easter came, Marjie knew that everything in her world was going to be all right. That the memories would stop haunting her and would be replaced with logic and understanding.

She'd visited her brother's memorial and, despite the ice clinging to the grass, had sat down and talked to him. 'I'm sorry, Monty. I so wished everything had been different. I miss you more than I can say.' The schism in her heart, which she'd not been able to heal, had opened up again.

Looking at Alice's inscription – 'A child loved dearly, now with Jesus and safe from pain' – she'd wished with all she had that she'd been able to know Alice. And thought how wonderful it would have been to have an older sister to talk to and turn to. But then she'd read the inscription on Monty's vase, and her heart and conscience slowly began to heal. Yes, Monty had lived by his own decisions, and it was those that had led to his death – not her. As Arnie had said, she had only saved lives with her decisions.

With this new way of looking at everything, Marjie turned away with a lighter heart. And now she knew that she could truly look to the future. A future not haunted by the things in her past that she couldn't change.

# EPILOGUE
# Britain, 1945

~

*Flowers to the Sea*

## CHAPTER THIRTY

# *London and Portpatrick*

## Ella and Flors

'Freddy's coming home. At last, my darling, our boy is coming home.'

Cyrus's joyful cry filled the apartment. Flors caught her breath in her lungs in a feeling of mixed emotions. *At last. To have two of my sons together again, thank God. If only . . .* Pulling herself up, she decided not to think like that. Monty was gone – well, from this earth, but never from her heart. She looked around at all the crates, packed ready to take back home. Soon a very changed group would be travelling back to their beloved France.

They knew, from what Randie had written and Arnie had told them, that both their own and Ella and Arnie's homes had been ransacked. Arnie had arranged for builders to come in, and Randie had been happy to stay on to oversee the work.

It had been sad to hear of all the destruction. But then they were only goods and chattels and were easily replaced, mainly by all that surrounded her at this moment – all pieces that Flors had come to love over the last few years; and although she hadn't made this apartment her home, these items would complete her home back in France.

The door burst open and Cyrus stood there, his face lit up as she'd not seen it for a long time. 'Can you believe it, darling? And there's another letter, too. It's from Randie. Everything is now ready, and he will be with us in the next couple of weeks. But he says he wants us to prepare ourselves for a big surprise – one that he knows will make us very happy, especially Marjie.'

Flors smiled at how easily she and Cyrus had taken to calling Marjella 'Marjie', but with everyone else doing so, using her formal name didn't sound right any more.

'Randie says he can't say any more, as he wants to save the moment for when he is with us.'

'Oh? What on earth can it be, Cyrus? I mean, the obvious thing would be that he has a young lady to introduce to us, but that wouldn't be a "big" surprise. A nice one, but why all the mystery?'

'Unless it's someone we know and wouldn't expect.'

They laughed together then, as Cyrus named all the unlikely women in the village – one widowed with five children, who had let herself go and, despite all the help offered to her, kept her children in a filthy house and did nothing but smoke and drink wine; and one a spinster whose fiancé had been killed in the last war. 'No, Cyrus, no – not Philomena! She's our age and a sourpuss, bless her. Stop it now, and think of someone more likely.'

'I can't. I didn't really know many of Randie's friends; well, the boys of the village, of course, as they were always around our house, playing football. No, it can't be one of them, can it?'

Flors laughed out loud. 'Randie? No, he's always had an eye for the girls. I bet it's one of Marjie's friends, and that is why he says it will make her happy. They were always around.'

'Yes, it could be any of those. Though, if I remember right, they had their eye on Freddy – especially that blonde girl. What was her name?'

'Felisa. A lovely girl. Yes, she only had eyes for Freddy. But he never showed any interest in her, always too busy studying his music. Like us, when we were younger . . . Darling, it's been a long time since we played.' As she said this, Flors looked wistfully at the grand piano that stood in the corner of the room. It hadn't been played since the news of Monty had come through.

'Well, there's no time like the present. I'll go and get that violin that I bought, tuned and then hardly played.'

'Cyrus, shall we practise a few tunes to play at the wedding? I bet Jerome will be playing a tune or two on his ukulele. We can get Mags to make sure there is a piano in the inn where the reception is to take place, so that I can play too. And you can bring your violin.'

'How will Mags manage to get a piano?'

'I don't know, but you know Mags: give her a task and she'll have it done in an instant. And now that she and Jerome have both retired, she relishes a challenge even more.'

'Lucky them, retiring when they are still both relatively young. We won't have that luxury, darling.'

'Partly we will. Surely the boys, and Paulo, will take on most of the setting up and running of the vineyard.'

'Oh, I think they should choose what they want to do. You have just mentioned Freddy's music studies and he may want to pursue a career in that. And Paulo always wanted to be a teacher, a profession that would surely suit his disability better than working in the vineyard?'

'Oh, I wasn't thinking. Of course you're right, darling.'

'Yes. Arnie and I will get the vineyard up and running

again with the help of Randolph – he always loved the work. Maybe he can take over one day. Anyway, I like your idea about playing music at the wedding, but we don't have long to practise.'

'I think it'll all still be there – our talent. We are talented, Cyrus; and yes, it would be so wonderful if Freddy pursued the career we were denied.'

'That is my thinking exactly. Anyway we all travel up to Scotland next week, so we'd better get started on re-awakening that talent. Oh, Flors, it's going to be so wonderful having the boys there as well. And seeing our darling Marjie and Sibbie and Rosie all get married together – a triple wedding. I can only imagine the frenzy of activity up in Portpatrick. It's a good job Mags and Jerome have been able to be up there for over six weeks. I don't think the others would have coped without them. Especially Ella and Arnie, as they have so much catching up to do.'

'Yes, three years apart. It . . . well, it takes some adjusting to. Life has been lived by each of them, but in a different way. With differing hopes and dreams, like two separate entities. Longing to be together but having to get on with the way things were.'

'Is that how it was for you, darling Flors?'

'Yes, up to a point. But it was a little different. You, poor darling, were in that awful prisoner-of-war camp, unable to live a life; and I had to make a life without you, and for you. There were a few adjustments that I had to make when we were reunited, but I was very happy to make them. For Ella and Arnie, they have both had to live in totally contrasting circumstances.'

They were quiet for a moment. *The past has a way of doing that*, Flors thought – *taking us back into its clutches for a time*. Marjie came to her mind. How she must suffer, with all that had happened to her. For though it had never been spoken of, Flors was certain that Marjie had had more to do with Monty's death than was really known.

Bringing the subject back round to Mags, she said, 'You know, Mags is still full of her girls, and having them back with her. When I spoke to her last night, she went on and on about how lovely it was, now that Beth and Belinda were home from the farm in Kent. She was so proud of them both for joining the Land Army.'

'Relieved, too, if the truth be known. I wish Marjie and Sibbie had done that.'

'Yes. They both went through so much. But they're happy now. How they've put off getting married until now, I don't know. But both they and Rosie wanted to wait until the world was stable again and everyone was home . . . those that could come home.'

'Poor Betsy, Rosie and Roderick. There are going to be some moving moments for them. And Angus too, of course.'

Once more they were quiet, as they thought of the two girls they'd never met, but felt as though they knew, through Betsy's and Rosie's tales of Daisy and Florrie's antics. 'And for us too, darling.' With a sigh, Flors brushed away the thought of how Monty was rarely included, when talking of those who had been lost 'Let's play for a while, darling; for some reason my fingers are itching to feel the ivory keys, and that hasn't happened in a long time.' Without asking which tune, Flors began to play.

After a moment Cyrus touched her arm. 'Strauss, darling?'

'Yes, we love this one – remember? "The Blue Danube" waltz.'

'I do I won't be a moment. I'll be back with my violin.'

393

When Cyrus joined her, the strains from his violin filled the room and Flors was once again transported back to a time in their home in Brixton, before their terrible secret was known even to them and they'd played this waltz together, and had dreamed of staging a concert. So much had happened since then. So many lives torn apart, but also twenty years of happiness as they'd built their vineyard together, with Ella and Arnie, and built their family, too. Sighing, she suddenly knew the waltz wasn't the right music for now and, without warning, changed it to 'My Old Man Said Follow the Van'.

'What? Flors?'

'Ha! Remember playing in that cockney pub for a few pennies?' Laughing, she mimicked the Londoners' way of singing the song: 'My old man said, "Foller the van, and don't dilly-dally on the way." Off went the van wiv me 'ome packed in it. I walked be'ind wiv me old cock linnet.'

She could go no further as they collapsed in laughter.

'Ella, darling, I love you. I love how you've helped everyone, and how that has helped you. You have filled my mind these last three years; no matter what I had to do, I did it with you in mind – and our future, and our family's. And to find you happy and coping means the world,' Arnie said.

'I know. Terrible things happened. Awful, disgusting things, and terrifying ones, too. I was broken when I first came home, but being here with Betsy and Susan, and knowing their pain and that of Rosie, I felt I was sent here to help them, not to dwell on my own troubles. It is them who got me through.'

'We're lucky. There's so many broken men, especially those coming back from Japanese prisoner-or-war camps, like Billy. How can we help him, Ella? It's breaking Betsy's heart to see her son as he is.'

'Can you and Paulo get Billy to talk? I know Angus and Roderick have tried, but they are too close to Billy and he can reject them, knowing they won't ever stop loving him.'

'We'll try, but I think you would be the best person. You have a way of helping people to get better – it is your vocation. Why don't we go for a walk up to the top of the cliff? I saw Billy go that way. He goes there most days.'

The September air still held a lot of warmth, though a slight breeze from the sea played with Ella's hair as they climbed the steps to the wooden bridge straddling the ravine that plunged to the sea below. Once over the bridge, they were able to hold hands again. When the ruins of Dunskey Castle came into view, they saw Billy sitting on a rock staring out to sea. Arnie called out to him.

Billy continued staring, as if he hadn't heard.

'Maybe this isn't a good idea, darling?'

'Let's try, Ella. For Billy's sake, and for the girls. They have waited so long to have a happy day. And Rosie wants Billy to give her away.'

'Oh, not Angus? When did you find that out? Won't Angus be hurt?'

'No. He was the one who told me. He said he thought it a wonderful idea. I think Roderick felt his nose pushed out of joint a little, but he is so enamoured with Belinda that his attention is taken up with wooing her!'

'Oh, Arnie. Betsy and Mags are thrilled at the prospect of one of each of their children getting together. But, you know, Mags is afraid, too. Belinda is so sophisticated, and Rod is a typical fisherman: steady, hard-working, not one for dances and such.'

'I think that is the problem he's having. Well, he'll have to learn to appreciate the finer things in life, if he is to win his fair lady.'

They both laughed. The sound seemed to disturb Billy, as he looked towards them and then stood up, in a manner that showed his impatience.

'Lovely day, Billy.'

'For some.'

'I would say for all of us who survived what we've been through.'

Billy shrugged.

Ella gave Arnie a sideways look. His face showed his bewilderment as he mouthed, 'What?'

Ignoring him, Ella walked nearer Billy. 'Billy, Arnie only wanted to walk this far, but I thought to cut across the field to School Brae and go down the lane and back around to the village. Would you walk with me?'

'I suppose.'

'See you later, Arnie.' His look of surprise made Ella smile, but he'd already shown how ham-fisted he was in handling the delicate Billy.

They walked across the field in silence. Ella waited, hoping Billy would break it, because even though it wasn't an uncomfortable silence, she didn't want to force him. At last he spoke. 'Ma tells me that you went through hell when you were imprisoned, Ella.'

'I – I did. I find it difficult to talk about, even though I want to, as I'm afraid no one will understand.'

Billy's 'I might' surprised Ella. She hadn't expected to get as far as this. Well, she wasn't going to miss this opportunity, even if it meant her opening up to him, something she'd only done with Arnie.

'Shall we sit on that stile over there, Billy? It's a long story, and I will need to sit down as I tell you some of it, as it makes me feel weak to remember it.'

'You don't have to tell me, Ella.'

'I know. But I somehow feel that you will understand, and I so want to unburden myself to someone. It isn't easy with someone you love, and who loves you. They are too hurt by it all.'

'Aye, I knaw about that. I want to talk, but I don't knaw how they'll all handle it. They won't understand.'

They'd reached the stile and Ella sat down. Billy stood for a while, which made this even more difficult for her. She didn't think she'd ever have to tell her story to a young man she'd only just met. But she took a deep breath and began to talk. Once she did so, she found she couldn't stop. Everything came out: the separation from Flors, the rape, her cruel treatment by the Germans and how she told them more than she should have done, in fear for her child's safety. At this point Ella couldn't stop the tears flowing down her face.

Billy sat on the grass in front of her and took her hands. This wasn't the Billy she'd been told of by Mags, who had always likened him to Harold. 'I'm sorry, Ella.' Tears seeped from his eyes as he said this.

Forcing herself to go on, she told him, 'I don't know why they didn't send me to an extermination camp straight away, once I admitted to having Jewish ancestors. It remains a mystery to me. I can only think they didn't have everything in place at that time – transport, and so on. As the Resistance had disrupted so much, they sent me to another camp for the time being. The camp I went to was run like a small community. The British had organized themselves well and gave no trouble, so it was largely a peaceful time. But then the Germans found out about the Jews in the camp who had hoodwinked them. They were rich, important people from Poland, really nice people, who had managed to buy their passage out and pass themselves off as British. They had false British papers.

'Then the terror came back, as the Germans began to flush the Jews out. They had these trains – well, cattle-transporting trucks. They rounded us all up and were transporting us. Oh, Billy, that train was awful, with so many packed in it that we could hardly breathe. We stood all the way, packed in so tightly that when a woman fainted, she couldn't fall to the ground. They . . . they taunted us, telling us they were sending us to extermination camps.'

The fear of it all revisited Ella and she was quiet for a moment, trying to compose herself. Billy held her hands the whole while and waited. He really did understand.

'Arnie had intelligence about this, and rescued me and got me back to England.'

'You're safe now, Ella.'

'Yes, but I still have fears. Nightmares.' She told him of her sister, and of how she learned that Calek had been sent to such a camp with her family. 'Arnie is taking me to Poland next year, when we hope travelling will be easier. I need to be there. To visit the street where my family lived. I think that will make it all real to me and I can truly grieve for my darling sister.'

Billy stood up then and sat beside her. His arm came round her, and Ella was glad of the comfort he gave to her. Sobs racked her body, as she felt she really was with someone who understood.

'Thank you, Billy. Thank you for listening. I feel a kindred spirit to you, as I know you understand what it was like to go through something you didn't think you couldn't bear, but had to. And . . . and, of course, the loss of your sisters, too.'

'I do.' His body shuddered. 'I want to talk about it, but it's hard to. And then, as you say, to come home and find that me si – sisters . . . I – I just don't want to live sometimes, Ella.'

'I know. And you mustn't talk until you are ready. But, Billy, you have so many who love you, and they went through hell, too. Imagine your Ma and Rosie, when they heard about Daisy and Florrie, and at the same time were worried sick they'd never see you again, either.'

'But they seem as though none of it affected them. I come home and they're all preparing for the wedding of the century. I left four half-sisters and find I only have two now, Rosie and Sibbie, and they just seem to think about getting hitched!'

Seeing it all through Billy's eyes, Ella understood why he'd been as he had. 'Oh, Billy. They've grieved, and still are grieving. And Rosie's grief was doubled by the man she loved dying from the effect of his wounds.'

'Rosie had a man afore Walter?'

'She did.' Ella left out the fact that he was German. 'An airman, who was shot down and she nursed him. She was in a bad way, with losing her sisters and not knowing if she was going to see you again.'

'Well, she ain't said owt to me.'

'You've been closed to them all, Billy. My impression of you was of someone suffering deeply, but unable to reach out. I understood, but to them you don't seem to love them any more.'

'What? Oh, Ella, they don't think that, do they? Don't they knaw as they were the only ones who kept me going through it all? Through the beatings, the starvation, the months in a dark, hot tin shed that I couldn't stand up in? Seeing me mates starve to death or die from dysentery. Being subjected to the cruel will of our Japanese captors? All I did was think of them . . . of – of Daisy, me lovely sister; Daisy, and how she'd clip me ear if I were naughty and cuddle me after.' A huge sob racked Billy. Tears ran down his face. 'And . . . and Florrie, allus soft with me and trying to reason me out of me moods. I – I want them h – h – here, Ella.'

Ella couldn't speak. Her throat tightened. She clung onto Billy, trying to help him with her love. He slouched on her and she rocked him as if he were a baby. Finding her voice, she said, 'They are here, Billy – you only have to talk to them. I do that with my first husband, Paulo, and my first baby, Christophe. I talk to them all the time, and they help me.'

Billy calmed. Then he began to talk again. 'Rosie . . . Rosie was in me mind all the time. We used to play together, and she'd boss me around. I had to be her baby boy, and she'd mother me and take me for walks. I was only three. I'd forgotten it, but it all came back to me. And how much I loved them all haunted my days and nights and willed me through. But nothing's the same. Even Roderick. Our Rod – a bloody kid who got on me nerves, but who I longed to be with and knew I loved so much – has changed. He's almost a man now and all he thinks of is getting a girl into bed.'

Ella laughed. 'Sorry, but I couldn't help that. Of course that's all he thinks about. Be glad for him, Billy. Thank God Roderick didn't have to go through what we went through.

But because of us, he's been allowed to mature into a normal young man . . . a horny one, I grant you.'

Billy looked shocked for a moment, but he wasn't anywhere near as shocked as Ella was at herself for saying such a thing. It had just come out! But then there was a sound that she never thought to hear: the sad, lost Billy laughing. He bent over double with it – an infectious laugh that tickled Ella and helped her overcome her embarrassment.

'Oh, Ella. Where did you learn such things? It sounded so funny, coming from you.'

'I'm a nurse, Billy. What I saw and heard in the First World War would curl your hair. Oh, it's already curly.' They were off again. Ella laughed so much that she had a sudden urge to pee. 'Excuse me, Billy – middle-age syndrome, I've got to go behind the hedge.'

At this, she thought Billy would have a seizure, he laughed so much.

When she emerged he had his arms open. Nothing about the gesture frightened or alarmed Ella. Billy was like a best friend, the little brother that she'd never had, and she went into his arms willingly. 'I just needed a hug, Ella. Ta, for today. I think this is another soldier whose life you've saved.'

She looked up at him. 'Oh, Billy, you weren't . . .'

'Aye, I was two minutes from jumping, when you and Arnie appeared. I was so angry at seeing you. But now I don't knaw if I'll ever be able to thank you.'

'You can thank me by agreeing to give Rosie away.'

'Me? Shouldn't that be Angus?'

'No. With no father to do the job, it should be the eldest brother – and that's you.'

'I'd be honoured. Aye, I would. Eeh, fancy that.'

'My demands aren't over yet, Billy. I want you to give

401

your ma a big hug and tell her how you missed her, and how thoughts of her got you through everything you went through. Don't let her have lost a son as well as two daughters, Billy.'

'Aye, I will. I've so wanted to, Ella. Now, any more demands? By, you're sounding like our Daisy – you're not a bit like I thought you were. I don't mind telling you, I wanted you all gone and to be left in peace, but now I can't bear you to go.'

Ella came out of his arms. 'That's a lovely thing to say, Billy, and I hope you'll visit us in France. We'd love that. And so would your Aunt Flors. She's lovely; you'll meet her soon. She's always wanted to meet you.'

'Aye, I don't knaw why, but all I heard were bad things about me da, so I didn't want to meet any of his kin.'

Ella thought this sad. And that maybe, if everyone hadn't been so keen to see his father in him and to judge him as such, Billy could have shone as the real person he was. 'Billy, I have an idea. We're going to need a lot of help to get up and running again. Why don't you come over to France for a while with us and give us a hand? You'll love it there.'

'Eeh, Ella. Ta. That sounds just what I'm needing. I heard from our Sibbie that the sun's allus shining and the sea is as blue as blue.'

'It is, and though it's a little way away from us, we often go on picnics. One more thing, though, Billy.'

'Ha, I thought there'd be a catch.'

'I want you to shake the hand of Angus and Roderick.'

'I can't wait to, Ella. I'm going to be a changed man. You've done that for me. You've made me see how everyone's suffered, and not only me.'

'I'm glad, Billy. Though I haven't worked any magic – I

haven't taken it all away. It's still there and will haunt you, but you have to find a way to cope. We all do. If we don't, then they've won, not us. What use is being the victors if we're broken and we hurt those around us, instead of going forward and making a good life for ourselves and enjoying our hard-won freedom?'

Billy stared at her, before saying, 'Ella, you won't get tired of helping me, will you? I mean, if I come with you and I have a bad moment, I can turn to you, can't I?'

'You can, Billy. And to Arnie and Cyrus. And Flors. All of them will understand, as will Paulo and Sibbie. When you hear their stories, you'll be amazed they survived, to go on to plan their future. A future of love.'

'I guessed as much, seeing as Paulo has lost a leg. And, well, I don't know what he and Sibbie and Marjie did in the war, or Arnie, but I've guessed they all suffered.'

'Come on. Let's get back. You've got a lot of hugging to do. I hope you're up to that! Your ma will smother you.'

Laughing, Billy said, 'Eeh, why didn't you leave me where I were?'

Ella pushed him playfully. She loved this new Billy who had emerged, and she held real hope for his future. To have him with them would be wonderful, as she knew they could help him even more as time went on. She just hoped that Betsy would agree, and be happy for him.

# CHAPTER THIRTY-ONE

# *Portpatrick*

## The Families – the Wedding

The sun shone brightly on three beautiful girls as they walked together into the church. Crowds stood outside, waving and wishing them well. Once inside, Rosie would lead them up the aisle, with Sibbie next and then Marjie. They'd laughingly drawn lots among the family, when it was realized they wouldn't be able to walk side-by-side.

All had long silk gowns on, the material having come from parachutes that were no longer in service. 'Make a change from relying on one to get you safely to ground, eh, Marjie?' Sibbie had said, with a sense of pride.

Sibbie had nudged Marjie as she'd teased her. And they'd laughed together, as they had never dreamed back then that they would ever be wearing a parachute. Sibbie glanced at Marjie and winked; her gown was so pretty and Marjie looked like a princess, as she'd chosen to have a flared skirt and the bodice was smothered in tiny pearl beads. They all wore long sleeves and short white gloves, and all carried red roses.

Rosie had chosen a straight skirt that had bands of lace around the bottom of it, and her bodice didn't have any decoration. 'Eeh, I don't want to draw attention to me bust.

It allus gets more looks than me,' she'd said, and they'd all laughed. Her neckline went into a collar that was like a polo neck and made her look very regal. Betsy had lifted Rosie's golden chestnut-curls on top of her head, and this added to the elegant effect.

Sibbie had chosen an empire-line that fitted under her bust, and she had a heart-shaped bodice that showed a tiny bit of her cleavage. Her gown was free of decoration too, but she wore her mother's pearl necklace, which had been her grandmother's, and to which she had attached a small pendant. It was a lovely oval shape, made of silver and painted by Montel for her – a likeness of her as a child. To Sibbie, it was the best thing about her outfit. She glanced up now at Rory, her stepfather, who looked magnificent in his kilt, and smiled at him, then turned to the other two and smiled. 'Ready, girls?'

They giggled, then Rosie moved forward on the arm of a very proud Angus, who looked wonderful in his highland kilt, too. Billy had graciously refused to take Rosie up the aisle. He and Rosie had gone for a walk and were away for a very long time. It was obvious, when they came back, that both had broken their hearts with grief, but they had been smiling when they returned. Rosie told them that Billy had been honoured by her request, but felt that it was rightfully Angus's job. 'He said as how Angus had allus brought us up and been a good and loyal da to us,' Rosie had said. 'And though Billy understood that it was traditional for the eldest brother to do the honours, in place of an absent father, in their case it was different, as he couldn't stand in for a man that wasn't his father – Angus could, and should, as he'd taken responsibility for Rosie on behalf of her father.'

They'd all been amazed at this from Billy, and at the

transformation in him. He was nothing like they remembered. Not now, after his walk with Ella. Now he was the brother they had always wanted, and although he was only a half-brother to them all, they loved and looked up to him.

Sibbie glanced at Billy and Roderick, looking wonderful in their suits – such handsome men, standing at the door greeting everyone.

'Let's do this, girls. Let's shout to the world how much we love our men.'

Marjie and Rosie didn't miss her meaning and both giggled again, as they had done out of earshot of Betsy, who was telling them they didn't know what they were in for, but they'd be very happy when they found out. They'd thought it the most hilarious teaching about the birds and the bees they'd ever heard, but were reassured that they had kept their secret trysts just that – secret.

'Aye, we'll do that. Follow me, girls.'

There the frivolity ended for a while as the organ struck up the wedding march, and the handsome men at the altar turned around to smile at them. Sibbie swallowed the lump in her throat to see Paulo standing there proudly. It had taken a long time to receive his false leg, but once it had arrived, he'd worked day and night to master it, sometimes making his stump bleed, until her mum had made him a soft, cushioned sock for it, which had stopped it chafing him. Next to him stood Freddy, Marjie's brother and her own cousin, whom Paulo had chosen to be his best man. Sibbie loved Freddy. He was a gentle person, who she remembered always had his head in a music book or sat playing the piano. It had been difficult to imagine him fighting in the army, but he'd become a hero and had received the George Cross. She was so proud of him.

Then there was William – Wills – handsome in a debonair way, every inch the aristocrat, but so very nice. His parents were here, under duress. It was unheard of that one of their family should be married anywhere but in a cathedral! For all that, they were a nice old couple.

And, finally, Walter. They all loved Walter. Another gentle soul, he coped so well with his false leg that you would never believe he had one, and his mother was a hoot. Sibbie didn't think she'd seen her without a cigarette dangling from her mouth. And the swearing – well! But she and Betsy had hit it off as though they'd been mates forever, which was lovely to see. Mrs Feller, the lady who had taken Walter under her wing, was here, too. She was much more at home with William's parents, and they with her, which relieved William from having to pander to them all the time. Walter had a friend as best man, another doctor, who had brought along his wife and two girls, aged seven and six. Lonia had taken them under her wing and now walked proudly with the girls, as all three were bridesmaids in lovely red velvet dresses that matched the roses.

The church was packed, and Sibbie hoped against hope that Randie had made it. After waiting for everyone for so long, and finally knowing they were all coming, it would be so disappointing for Marjie – well, for her, too – if Randie didn't make it. But she had no time to look around the church, as they were soon at the aisle and her Paulo had his hand out towards her. Taking it, she experienced a moment of extreme happiness as she looked into his eyes.

For Rosie, the moment Walter extended his hand and she touched his fingers was a moment when all past demons left her. She'd never forgotten Albie and had at times longed for him. Not that she had loved him more than Walter, but his memory burned within her and she couldn't erase it.

At that moment, something happened. Albie faded. He seemed to settle somewhere deep in her heart, but at the same time left the whole of it for Walter. As she looked into Walter's lovely soft grey eyes, Rosie gave to him all the love she could give. Walter's eyes filled with tears, and yet he was smiling – a lovely gentle smile full of love. Her last words to Albie's spirit were said in her mind: 'Goodbye, Albie. Rest easy. I will keep my promise to take your letter to your mother. I'll take my Walter with me. You'd love Walter. I do, with all my heart.'

For Marjie, the moment that Wills put out his hand to her was the most wonderful moment. Yes, they'd joined many times in a giving and receiving of love, but as she held his hand, she wasn't loving him with just her body. Everything that she was she gave to him. His lovely eyes glistened as they looked into hers. His whispered 'I love you' touched every part of her.

'Wills, my Wills.'

As they came out of the church, and the excitement of all the congratulations was over, a voice called out, 'Marjie!'

They all looked round. There was a silence that held anticipation. It was as if everyone was in on a secret. Marjie looked over to where the sound had come from, and then at Sibbie, who seemed mystified.

Marjie asked, 'Did you call, Papa?' As it was, he and Mama were standing where the sound had come from. Both had wide grins on their faces as they parted. Marjie stared, not believing what she was seeing, and then a scream of delight came from her and at the same time from Sibbie, and they both ran towards Randie . . . and, unbelievably, Gisele.

'Oh, Randie. Randie, it's so good to see you. And Gisele – how? I mean, are you all right? I can't believe it – it's so good to see you. Thank you, dear brother, for being here and for bringing Gisele to me.'

With this, Marjie enclosed them both in a big hug, laughing and crying tears of joy. At last they were back together. For a moment she felt a lump in her throat as memories threatened to overwhelm her, but she swallowed hard. Today was for happiness only.

As she came out of the hug, a little boy stepped forward and offered her his wooden toy soldier. 'Papa.'

Marjie knew immediately that he was Monty's son. The boy was so like him. She looked at the lovely Gisele. 'Oh, Gisele, what a beautiful gift on my wedding day.'

As she bent down, her little nephew put his arms up to her. Again, as she picked him up, he showed her his toy. 'Papa.'

'Yes. That is Papa – that is Monty.'

'No. Me Monty.'

Marjie looked at Gisele. Gisele spoke in French, her eyes pleading. 'Yes, he is called Monty. I – I told him about his father being a brave soldier.'

Marjie took a deep breath. This was so much to cope with, and she wondered at her mama and papa even thinking that she could. But then Wills was by her side. 'It's so lovely to meet you, Gisele. I know all about you and your very courageous work. And so this is Monty – how lovely to meet you, Monty. You are something really wonderful to come out of such pain.'

'Yes, yes, you are, little one.' Marjie had recovered. 'You're beautiful, Monty. I'm a very proud aunty.'

'Marjie – Gisele and I, we're in love, we're going to marry.'

Suddenly Marjie understood. There was nowhere better to have heard all this news, or to have met her little nephew, Monty's son. If she'd been told and had had it to look forward to, she would have suffered agonies of guilt. But now that the initial shock was over, all she felt was love for this little one, and for Gisele and her brother Randie.

'You've made my wedding day: seeing you, Gisele, holding little Monty, and having you with me, dear Randie. I'm so happy for you. But you will wait until we come back from our honeymoon, won't you? This is one wedding I'm not going to miss.'

Wills touched her arm. 'There's one more task for us, darling. Be brave, for Sibbie and Rosie.'

'I will.'

With this, the wedding party, led by Betsy, Rosie, Billy, Roderick and Angus marching proudly in front of them, walked towards the sea.

Once there, Betsy spoke. 'There's sommat as Rosie wanted to do. Now, this ain't to put a dampener on the wedding, but as we're all together, Rosie wanted to include her sisters, Daisy and Florrie. On the wall of our shop over there is a plaque dedicated to them, which Rosie had made for this day – her special day. She wanted to share the loveliness of today with them . . . Rosie, love.' Betsy gestured towards Rosie.

Rosie stepped forward and threw her bouquet into the sea. 'These are for the two flowers – my sisters – who the sea claimed. They go to them with my love. I miss you, Daisy and Florrie. I miss you.'

410

Through the silence that followed, Sibbie heard many sniffles. She went forward and held Rosie, then threw her roses, too. Marjie did the same. And the three girls stood together, watching the roses bob up and down on the waves, their hands joined, their job well done. Three girls who'd come through hell, saying goodbye to two of their number, whom they loved and missed so much.

As they turned, Rosie smiled through her tears. 'Thank you, everyone. We honour all those who lost their lives, and thank them for ours. Now we're to go forward, with their blessing.'

Someone said, 'Aye, aye.'

Then Betsy, lovely Betsy, lifted the mood and set the scene for a happy day. 'Right, I speak for our Daisy, and our Florrie, when I say it's time to celebrate our Rosie's and Sibbie's and Marjella's wedding. And for them as don't knaw, me old man's called Angus and he's a Scot; and they're known for looking after their pennies, and he's saved many of them for today and put his hand deep into his pockets. The first round of drinks is on him.'

A cheer went up and was followed by happy chatter. Walter had Rosie in his arms. Sibbie was held by Paulo. And Marjie snuggled into Wills.

As Marjie looked up, she saw her mama, Flors, with Mags and Ella, holding hands, and her heart swelled. These three courageous women had fought their war valiantly and had given their children the same courage to fight theirs. She ran to them, closely followed by Sibbie and Rosie, who took Betsy's hand and brought her into the group.

As they stood in a circle after hugging each other, it was Flors who spoke. 'Our brave daughters, we love you.'

# *Letter to Readers*

Dear Reader,

Thank you for choosing my book. I hope that I have been able to give you hours of enjoyment – and did not cost you too many tissues – as you read this final book in The Girls Who Went to War series.

I love to receive feedback from you, through the channels listed at the end of this letter, or, if you can, leave me a review on Amazon, Goodreads or Facebook and visit my website. Feedback and reviews are like hugging an author, as they help us to progress in our career, give us encouragement as we sit alone writing the next book, and are the biggest thank you in the world. And for me, they make me want to hug you back.

Researching my books takes me to many countries, which is a joy as I love to travel.

The Girls Who Went to War series took me to Poland and the South East of France.

In the UK I visited a working cotton mill in Uppermill and drove around Blackburn to find places that I wanted to feature – parks, churches and manor homes – including visiting Feniscowles, just outside Blackburn, where I found the perfect home for Mags's family.

I also visited the wonderful Portpatrick in Scotland and found where I wanted Mags, Betsy and Susan's retreat to be.

For Belgium and Singapore, I had to rely on the internet, although I would have loved to visit. But the internet is a great source of facts and inspiration – I always come across a story that inspires more books. For this series I was inspired by the story of Edith Cavell, a wonderful, brave soul who went to Belgium to nurse the injured and then helped them to escape. Sadly, Edith was executed by the Germans. May she and all brave souls rest in peace.

My research for *The Brave Daughters* also included reading *Heroes Among Us* by Jim Ryun and *They Fought Alone* by Maurice Buckmaster.

The Girls Who Went to War features four books, which follow the lives of three girls who met and formed a deep bond of friendship when they were sent by the Red Cross to Belgium in 1914. Each girl had volunteered to escape their lives at home and each has a story to tell.

The books are standalone reads so, if you missed the first three, don't worry. You can still enjoy reading Flora's story and learning about the beginning of the girls' friendship – what happened when they were trapped behind enemy lines, and what Flora faced when she returned home – in the first of the series, *The Forgotten Daughter*.

The second book, *The Abandoned Daughter*, follows Ella's story: how her search for her Polish roots left her stranded and heartbroken, and the courage she showed to fight back.

Mags's story is described in *The Wronged Daughter*. Tricked into marriage by Flora's hateful brother Harold, Mags's life spirals downwards, until she is rescued by her dear friend Betsy with the help of Susan – the very woman Mags should hate. With them by her side, can she become strong again and take her rightful place in life?

All of my past titles, as well as future ones, are available to order online or from all good bookshops and your local library – also look out for them in your local supermarket. And you can enjoy them in audio format, too.

And finally, I love to interact with my readers, and do so on a daily basis on my Facebook page and website – would you like to join me? If so, go to www.facebook.com/HistoricalNovels or search on Facebook for 'Books by Mary Wood and Maggie Mason'. Here you will be able to chat to me, enter my numerous competitions for giveaways of signed books and themed merchandise, and even have a chance to win a tea party with me and my lovely Roy.

On my website, www.authormarywood.com, you can receive all my news first-hand by subscribing to my regular newsletter, join in competitions and contact me via email on a one-to-one basis.

I am also available to book for events, meetings and library talks, and you can follow me on Twitter: @Authormary.

I look forward to hearing from you.

Much love to all,

Mary x

# Acknowledgements

Many people have a hand in bringing a book to publication and I want to express my heartfelt thanks to them all. My agent, Judith Murdoch, who stands firmly in my corner. My editor Wayne Brookes, who is always there for me, encourages me and makes me laugh – I love him to bits. Victoria Hughes-Williams, who does a wonderful, sensitive structural edit of my books, keeping my voice and tightening my work. Alex Saunders, Samantha Fletcher and Mandy Greenfield, who all do a wonderful job of editing my work and checking my research, till my words sing off the page. Ellis Keene, my publicist, who works towards getting exposure for my books and me, and meticulously organizes events to ensure I am taken care of on my travels. The sales team, for their efforts to get my books onto the shelves. The cover designer for my beautiful covers. And last but by no means least, a special thanks to my son, James Wood, who reads so many versions of each book, advising me what is working and what isn't as I write my draft manuscript, and then helps with the read-through of the final proofs when last-minute mistakes need to be spotted. All of you are much-appreciated and do an amazing job for me. Thank you.

My thanks, too, to my family – my husband Roy, who looks after me so well as I lose myself in writing my books, and is the love of my life. He's been by my side for almost sixty years and I couldn't do what I do without him or the love and generous support that he gives me. My children, Christine, Julie, Rachel and James, for your love, encouragement and just for having pride in me. My grandchildren and great-grandchildren, too numerous to name, but all loved so very dearly and who are all in my corner cheering me on. My Olley and Wood families, for all the support. Thank you to each and every one of you. You help me to climb my mountain.

And I want to thank my readers, especially those on my Facebook page, for the encouragement you give me, for making me laugh, for taking part in all my competitions, for pre-ordering all of my books, for taking the time to post lovely reviews and support my launch events, and for just being my special friends. You are second to none and keep me from flagging. Thank you.

If you enjoyed

## *The Brave Daughters*

then you'll love

## *The Forgotten Daughter*

by Mary Wood

### Book one in
### The Girls Who Went to War series

From a tender age, Flora felt unloved and unwanted by her parents, but she finds safety in the arms of caring Nanny Pru. But when Pru is cast out of the family home, under a shadow of secrets and with a baby boy of her own on the way, it shatters little Flora.

Over the years, however, Flora and Pru meet in secret – unbeknown to Flora's parents. Pru becomes the mother she never had, and Flora grows into a fine young woman. When she signs up as a volunteer with St John Ambulance, she begins to shape her life. But the drum of war beats loudly and her world is turned upside down when she receives a letter asking her to join the Red Cross in Belgium.

With the fate of the country in the balance, it is a time for bravery. Flora's determined to be the strong woman she was destined to be. But with horror, loss and heartache on her horizon, there's a lot for young Flora to learn . . .

*Available now*

# The Abandoned Daughter

by Mary Wood

## Book two in
## The Girls Who Went to War series

Voluntary nurse Ella is haunted by the soldiers' cries she hears on the battlefields of Dieppe. But that's not the only thing that haunts her. When her dear friend Jim breaks her trust, Ella is left bruised and heartbroken. Over the years, her friendships have been pulled apart at the seams by the effects of war. Now, more than ever, she feels so alone.

At a military hospital in Belgium, Ella befriends Connie and Paddy. Slowly she begins to heal, and finds comfort in the arms of a French officer called Paulo – could he be her salvation?

With the end of the war on the horizon, surely things have to get better? Ella grew up not knowing her real family but a clue leads her in their direction. What did happen to Ella's parents, and why is she so desperate to find out?

*Available now*

# The Wronged Daughter

## by Mary Wood

### Book three in
### The Girls Who Went to War series

*Can she heal the wounds of her past?*

Mags has never forgotten the friendship she forged with Flora and Ella, two fellow nurses she served with at the beginning of World War One. Haunted by what she experienced during that time, she fears a reunion with her friends would bring back the horror she's tried so desperately to suppress.

Now, with her wedding on the horizon, this should be a joyful time for Mags. But the sudden loss of her mother and the constant doubt she harbours surrounding her fiancé, Harold, are marring her happiness.

Mags throws herself into running the family mill, but she's dealt another aching blow by a betrayal that leaves her reeling. Finding the strength the war had taken from her, she fights back, not realizing the consequences and devastating outcome awaiting her.

Can she pick up the pieces of her life and begin anew?

*Available now*

# The Street Orphans

by Mary Wood

## Outcast and alone –
## can they ever reunite their family?

Born with a club foot in a remote village in the Pennines, Ruth is feared and ridiculed by the superstitious neighbours who see her affliction as a sign of witchcraft. When her father is killed in an accident and her family evicted from their cottage, she hopes to leave her old life behind, to start afresh in the Blackburn cotton mills. But tragedy strikes once again, setting in motion a chain of events that will unravel her family's lives.

Their fate is in the hands of the Earl of Harrogate, and his betrothed, Lady Katrina. But more sinister is the scheming Marcia, Lady Katrina's jealous sister. Impossible dreams beset Ruth from the moment she meets the Earl. Dreams that lead her to hope that he will save her from the terrible fate that awaits those accused of witchcraft. Dreams that one day her destiny and the Earl's will be entwined . . .

'Wood is a born storyteller'
*Lancashire Evening Post*

*Available now*

# Brighter Days Ahead

## by Mary Wood

### War pulled them apart, but can it bring them back together?

Molly lives with her repugnant father, who has betrayed her many times. From a young age, living on the streets of London's East End, she has seen the harsh realities of life. When she's kidnapped by a gang and forced into their underworld, her future seems bleak.

Flo spent her early years in an orphanage and is about to turn her hand to teacher training. When a kindly teacher at her school approaches her about a job at Bletchley Park, it could turn out to be everything she never realized she wanted.

Will the girls' friendship be enough to weather the hard times ahead?

*Available now*

## Tomorrow Brings Sorrow

### by Mary Wood

### You can't choose your family

Megan and her husband Jack have finally found stability in their lives. But the threat of Megan's troubled son Billy is never far from their minds. Billy's release from the local asylum is imminent and it should be a time for celebration. Sadly, Megan and Jack know all too well what Billy is capable of . . .

### Can you choose who you love?

Sarah and Billy were inseparable as children, before Billy committed a devastating crime. While Billy has been shut away from the world, he has fixated on one thing: Sarah. Sarah knows there's only one way she can keep her family safe and it means forsaking true love.

### Sometimes love is dangerous

Twins Theresa and Terence Crompton are used to getting their own way. But with the threat of war looming, the tides of fortune are turning. Forces are at work to unearth a secret that will shake the very roots of the tight-knit community . . .

*Available now*

# All I Have to Give

## by Mary Wood

### When all is lost, can she find the strength to start again?

It is 1916 and Edith Mellor is one of the few female surgeons in Britain. Compelled to use her skills for the war effort, she travels to the Somme, where she is confronted with the horrors at the Front. Yet amongst the bloodshed on the battlefield, there is a ray of light in the form of the working-class Albert, a corporal from the East End of London. Despite being worlds apart, Edith and Albert can't deny their attraction to each other. But as the brutality of war reveals itself to Albert, he makes a drastic decision that will change both Edith and Albert's lives forever.

In the north of England, strong-minded Ada is left heartbroken when her only remaining son Jimmy heads off to fight in the war. Desperate to rebuild her shattered life, Ada takes up a position in the munitions factory. But life deals her a further blow when she discovers that her mentally unstable sister Beryl is pregnant with her husband Paddy's child. Soon, even the love of the gentle Joe, a supervisor at the factory, can't erase Ada's pain. An encounter with Edith's cousin, Lady Eloise, brings Edith into her life. Together, they realize, they may be able to turn their lives around . . .

*Available now*